UNTETHERED

The Illumination of the Siann Dha
Book 2

by Lisa Pelissier

www.SneakerBlossom.com

ISBN 978-1-965521-01-4

With gratitude to my beta readers:

Ned Brause

Debe Herdtner

Tesla Mathews

Thanks to my amazing cover illustrator:

Helen Holmes

And a nod of appreciation to:

C.S. Lewis's *Discarded Image*

the inspiration behind Gannoir and its inhabitants

And a note for my readers:

See the ***Appendices*** at the back of the book

for pronunciations and definitions of

non-earthly words.

Check Out:

The Skies Below

Book 1 of the Illumination of the Siann Dha

__Trigger warning__: While no rape occurs in this book, it comes up as a fact in the history of several characters.

Chapter 1: Tass

Tass pushed her body through the water, stretching against the pain in her shoulders—the pain that never left her. The pain felt good. It meant she was alive, something she couldn't always discern from the state of her soul. She thought of the blood she had lost in the fight against Gelu and Kleibald a month earlier. It had been a part of herself. She had watched it encounter the darkness, the evil blotches that were seeping into Gannoir through its icy exterior. Her blood had overcome the darkness—a small part of it, at least.

It had been Igracio's blood that had done something big. *Blood . . . blood in the water makes light,* she thought to herself, looking at the twinkling blue illumination of the sea around her. Blood makes light, and light is life. And without blood, Igracio had died. His blood had brought life to everyone else, all those who would have been lost if Kleibald's plan had succeeded. Instead of inverting Gannoir, pushing the fiery core to the exterior and relegating the icy crust of their world to the center, Igracio's blood, together with a power that had shot down from the Ghalon, had healed the rift in the shell of Gannoir. Her world was whole.

Her world was a shambles.

Igracio was gone. Not only that, he hadn't died to save Gannoir. He'd entered the water to save her. He'd died for her. The thought of his sacrifice was as excruciating to Tass as the thought of his death.

Now she was alone.

She had always been alone.

Tass drew a deep breath through her gills and let the cool liquid soothe her anguish. Reaching forward, plying her webbed hands against the waters of the sea, she propelled herself downward.

Someone collided with her, bumped her back toward the surface. Tass turned quickly and looked toward her assailant in surprise. She'd disobeyed the master by diving deep, by reaching for the gradually yellowing layers of the sea. They were running distance sprints, not diving today. No one was supposed to be this far from the surface.

She frowned as she saw Bizu next to her. He was gesturing toward the surface with his freakishly long fingers. His tala, the webbing between his fingers, extended to the tips of each digit. He was the best depth diver at the Calix.

"Master wants you," Bizu called, practicing his still-clumsy underwater speech.

Tass glared at him through her transparent eyelids.

Bizu collected his limbs around his body and then shot off toward the surface.

Tass hesitated. She didn't want to go back to class. She wanted . . . she wanted . . . She wasn't sure what she wanted, but going back to class wasn't it. She had already proven herself. The scars on her shoulders were a visible indicator that she had won, that she was important. She had given her blood for Gannoir. She had been in battle, of a sort. There was nothing left for her to prove.

Closing her outer eyelids, Tass let herself drift in the water.

Why go back?

Despair washed over her as inevitably as the blood rushed through her veins.

Why not go back?

She let herself float toward the surface, only making an effort to push herself through the water once she saw the red glow of the Ghalon, the light source of their world, through the thin layer of liquid above her head. Emerging from the sea, she shook her head, flinging the water out of her eyes and ears. She drew a sharp breath of air into her lungs and looked around.

"Glad to see you've decided to rejoin the class, Ms. Galan," the Master said bitingly.

Tass didn't respond. She could feel the air around her head, swirling with the Master's words, not just the ones he had just said, but with every negative thing he had ever said to her since she had been brought to the Calix at four years old. Ducking her head back under the water to avoid the mental noise, she pushed herself toward the dock where the other students were waiting.

They shuffled aside to make room for Tass. Not one of them echoed the Master in his sarcasm. Tass had won their respect—won it by the scars on her shoulders and the battle she had fought.

"We are working on distance swimming, Ms. Galan. You were supposed to swim to the Zafir clatry."

Tass looked at the Master defiantly. His perfect body, his waxen, yellowed form, his huge gill slits, had always irritated her. He was the image of an ideal Mayim—a water person. She had spent her first seven years at the Calix trying to impress him, trying to be the best. And she had been, or at least she'd been one of them. Bizu was the best deep-diver, and sixteen-year-old Sarhi was the fastest, but

Tass, younger than either of her rivals, was the best all-around swimmer. Or she had been before her injuries.

She stared at the Zafir clatry, one of the many islands of floating, latticework rock, hundreds of yards across the sea. The floating island was made of a lattice of diamond-hard rock. A few skyscrapers rose from the bluish base, shining red in the light of the Ghalon. It wasn't far. Not for her. She looked at the Master and waited.

"All of you," the Master said, after breaking eye-contact with Tass, "are going to swim to Zafir and back when I give the signal. The first three back will get an extra day added to your weekend pass."

Tass felt nothing. Nothing at all. She tried to muster the old competitive spirit, the desire to be the best, but she didn't care anymore. She could be one of the winners. Despite her maimed shoulders, she was still among the fastest. But why? What would be the point of an extra day of leave? Where would she go? She may as well stay at the Calix. Most of the other students had families to visit, or friends to adventure with. She had nothing.

And yet . . . and yet . . . The condemning voices swirled around her head, and she longed to be back in the water, where the voices couldn't—or wouldn't—torment her. Winning would mean her time was her own. It was something.

When the Master gave the signal, she threw herself into the sea like a bullet, zooming ahead of her peers. The voices faded and she was alone in her head again. Blissfully alone.

Chapter 2: Xylo

Xylo smiled as his son and daughter-in-law entered the room. A breeze swirled around them, ruffling their clothing and hair despite the fact that they were deep inside the labyrinthine tunnels of the Dynroc's dwelling.

"What did you bring?" he asked.

Ceres let go of Case's hand and pulled the woven bag from her shoulder. "We didn't have to go all the way into Obumbro this time," she told her father-in-law. "There was a peddler much closer selling fish cakes and salt oranges." She pulled the seaweed-wrapped packages from the bag. "The oranges are pre-soaked, ready to eat," she grinned.

"We saved so much time that we went berry-picking on the way home," Case said. He opened his knapsack and dumped a horde of berries onto the stone table.

Xylo's eyes lit up. Rucloce berries were one of his favorite foods. Each of the large, waxy white berries had a different flavor and color at the center, and each was more delectable than the last. "Beautiful!" he exclaimed.

The breeze rearranged the berries on the table, organizing them into three rows.

"Thanks, Gaoth," Xylo whistled.

The breeze whistled through Xylo's fire gills, communicating its care and its fussiness effectively, but without words. Sometimes Gaoth used words, but the effort exhausted him and most of the time words weren't necessary for him to make his point.

"Shall we eat?" Xylo said, lifting a loaf of bread from a stony shelf and bringing it to the table.

The three of them sat down to eat. The caves of the Dynroc were not ideal for any of them. Ceres was Mayim. She spent hours every day in the water. The humidity in the caves was not enough to keep her skin healthy. Case and Xylo, however, were Esh—fire people. Most of the Esh, the sect called the Esh-qadar, worked in the heights of the Orbokth, the rocky mountains that surrounded the sea. Their fire-gills helped them breathe the superheated air near the Ghalon, the fiery core of Gannoir, while their full-length body tala let them glide down from the heights effortlessly. The caves of the Dynroc were too damp and too cold to be ideal for the Esh, even for the Esh-maor, the leadership caste among the Siann Dha. Xylo put up with the discomfort, but Case spent a lot of time in the heights, on the opposite extremity of the world from his bride.

"Have you heard from Tass?" Ceres asked as she bit into a rucloce berry.

Xylo shook his head. "Not since she went back. Gaoth visited the Calix, her school, and he said she's there and seems to be prospering, but he didn't talk to her."

Case shrugged. "He can't talk to her anyhow," he pointed out. "She's Mayim."

Xylo smiled wryly. "Only the Esh can understand the wind."

"And only the Mayim can understand the water," Ceres added.

No one said what they were all thinking.

There had been one person who was different.

Igracio could hear both.

Igracio had been different. Special.

And now he was gone.

They had looked for him right after it was over. Igracio had thrown himself into the blood-filled water in an attempt to save Tass from bleeding to death. Case and Ceres, safe on the shore, had seen him go. And then everything had gone crazy. The water and the wind turned into a vortex, channeling energy from the heights of the Ghalon down to the bottom of the sea—to the edge of Gannoir itself. When it was over, the mansion-sized boulder, the safe haven where the evil ones in charge had hidden, was gone, sucked out into the chaos outside their world. The hole in the exterior of Gannoir was closed and sealed.

They had won and Kleibald had lost.

And Igracio was gone.

Ceres and Tass had both looked for him in vain afterward, but they had known it was impossible. The amount of blood that had been needed to cause the cataclysm meant only one thing—it wasn't just blood, but life-blood. Igracio had given everything he had, and in doing so had saved Tass—and had saved Gannoir and all who were in it. But there was nothing left of Igracio to be found. It had taken everything he had and everything he was.

"I hope she's okay," Case worried. "After losing Igracio and her mother at the same time . . ."

"She lost Afa long before the battle," Xylo frowned.

"Death is a lot more final, though," Ceres noted quietly. "She'll never be reconciled with Afa now."

"It's better this way," Xylo insisted. "At least this way she can imagine her mother may have wanted to be a mother to her again someday. The continual rejection has ended. It was the will of Tel-Maor."

At this, Case and Ceres both grew silent. Xylo's heart wrenched within him. Everything that had happened to Afa had been his fault. From the day they had fallen into Garradh Gannoir on the other side of the Orbokth, calamity had been their constant companion. He should never have sought out Afa for his mission. Had he gone alone, Afa would still be alive, living her meager existence in the lowlands of the Orbokth. But because of him . . . because of him . . .

"Try this berry," Ceres said, handing Xylo half of a rucloce berry. "It's sweet and salty at the same time."

Xylo took the berry from her and popped it into his mouth. It was delicious, the caramelly center oozing around the crisp white exterior. It was more than he deserved, but he was grateful.

No one ever had to know the whole truth about what had happened.

No one ever had to know that he had heard the name of Bracha Elisus—Afa—long before it turned up in connection with his missing son.

Chapter 3: Talag

Talag woke with a start and tried to sit up.

His head crashed into the metal shelf over his head. Dizzily he lay back down on his bunk and wished he were back at home. He and the others were living a strange existence inside of a windowless stone house. His parents hadn't explained anything to him other than that they were going on a trip with his grandparents.

He'd known something was wrong. He'd heard them talking, crazy talk, impossible talk, words about the end of the world. Only those who escaped from Gannoir inside their skyboulder would be saved. He'd thought he was dreaming, that he'd heard their words in a nightmare or a hallucination. It couldn't be real.

Yet here they were, forty people, imprisoned in a miniature world with an artificial Ghalon at the center, a glass orb filled with phosphorescent turquoise light that illumined every open space in the roughly spherical skyboulder. The chaos outside the boulder pulled them toward the outside, making the floor of any room the side against the outside and the glass orb at the center like a beacon above their heads. They slept ten to a room, in metal bunks stacked five high. Four rooms for sleeping, out of the eight total rooms in the skyboulder. He shared a room with his extended family—eight people—and two grumpy citizens of Garradh Gannoir, a man named Lefty and his wife. During the day there was nothing to do, and nights were worse. Food was scanty and there was a general sense of panic running through the skyboulder.

Whatever was supposed to have happened—the implosion of Gannoir—hadn't happened. They were supposed to be safe, and now they were the ones who were in danger. Even yet no one had addressed him directly. All he knew he'd learned by listening diligently for snatches of conversation.

Back to Gannoir. That was where they needed to go. But the passageway through which they had left Gannoir had closed, and they were now trapped on the outside of their world.

He had put most of the pieces together in his head, because no one was interested in involving a thirteen-year-old boy in their plans.

Talag rolled over carefully and rubbed his eyes. His bunk was the highest of the five stacked bunks on his side of the room. Trying not to wake the four men sleeping on shelves beneath him, Talag leapt into the air, catching the wind on his Esh-tala so that he could glide soundlessly to the floor. It didn't work. The room wasn't large enough, and he landed with a thud.

"Sorry," he whispered.

Lefty, the grumpy uncasted man, glared down at him. "Aren't things bad enough without you kids making tons of noise and waking us up?" His voice descended into a discontented grumble. "Why they brought children with us . . . children . . . useless . . ."

It was weird to him that Lefty and his wife, not to mention some of the others, were uncasted. His mother had tried to explain that part to him and to his sister. There were others, his mother had told him. People who lived on the other side of the Orbokth. While everyone who lived in Luca was casted—Mayim, Esh, or Gulot—those from the other side of the Orbokth were born of plain blood. They just . . . were. They were nothing, his mother had explained feebly. They weren't even worthy of being Mayim, the lowest caste.

"Not nothing," his mother, Milis, winced after realizing how bad her statement sounded. "They're people. They're valuable in the eyes of Tel-Maor."

Donamys, his sister, had rolled her eyes at that. She understood just as well as he did what his mother was really saying. These others were less than they were, significant only because, presumably, Tel-Maor allowed them to live for some unknown reason.

What his mother hadn't been able to explain was why his grandfather, the Esh-Maor of Luca and the force behind their departure, had opted to include fourteen of these underlings on their voyage. Forty people, meant to be the only survivors of the implosion of Gannoir, and fourteen of them were uncasted and lowly.

Talag slid open the metal door that separated the sleeping compartment from the area he occupied in what passed for daytime in his new world of endless blue light. Carefully he slid it shut behind him, hoping he hadn't disturbed anyone except Lefty. Lefty was one of "them" and his grumbles wouldn't amount to much. His father and his grandfather, however, had the power to make his life miserable.

The day chamber was empty except for one other occupant, a wrinkled gnome of a man, who grinned at him as he crawled through the opening. The skyboulder may have had the same dynamics as Gannoir as a whole, with the light at the center and the gravitational pull sucking them toward the exterior, but its much smaller size made it hard to navigate. He raised a hand in greeting at the smiling old man and settled himself onto the stone wall. It was bumpy, in a way that was meant to approximate seats, if only one could orient oneself correctly and comfortably.

"What's your name?" the little man asked him.

"Talag. What's yours?"

"Dynny," was the reply.

"Are you . . . Gulot?" Talag guessed politely, all the while wondering why he hadn't met this tiny old man before. By his calculations they had been in the skyboulder for a month now.

The man shook his head. "Only the Old Ones are like that. I'm the Dynroc, 59th of that name. It's an important job." He beamed at Talag.

This gnomish old man was not right in the head. That much was apparent. But somehow, Talag liked him. "I'm sure it is," Talag replied, grinning back at the Dynroc, 59th of that name. "I'm Eshmaor," he told him. He hoped knowing his superior status wouldn't upset the little guy.

But Dynny's eyes lit up. "Like Xylo! Xylo is my friend."

This was odd. "You have a friend from Luca?" Talag asked.

Dynny nodded enthusiastically. "Xylo is my friend from Luca. And Case and Ceres and Igracio and Tass and Afa . . . but she was sleeping. But she would be my friend if she knew how good I took care of her."

None of the names were familiar to Talag. "Are they all Eshmaor?" he asked interestedly.

Dynny frowned, and the expression on his face seemed to convey that he was thinking hard. Finally, he shook his head. "No. All castes. Water, land, and fire. We had all three. We had to stop Gelu from digging. Stop the digging. Water, land, and fire. They needed me because I'm the Dynroc."

Gelu was a name Talag knew. Gelu was his grandfather's associate from the other side of the Orbokth and was on the skyboulder with the rest of them. If this little man had been working against Gelu, then he had been working against his grandfather. For a minute, Talag wondered if he was going to be in trouble for liking the little man, for listening to him. But, he quickly realized, Dynny was on the skyboulder. He wouldn't be on the skyboulder if he was some sort of enemy. His grandfather had hand-picked the occupants of the skyboulder, so if Dynny, the Dynroc, 59th of that name, was here, there could be no harm in befriending him.

"Well, I'm glad to meet you, Dynny," Talag grinned. "Want to come with me and find some breakfast?"

Dynny smiled back with his ignorant, simple smile. "Yup."

Chapter 4: Tass

It felt like banishment, not a reward. For the weekend, Tass had no home. She could have chosen to stay at the Calix. There was nowhere she wanted to go. The other students would have badgered her, though, about not using the extra day's pass that she had won. Sarhi and Amathys had won the other two passes to freedom, and they were planning a shopping expedition together. Sarhi was the fastest swimmer, but the fact that Amathys had finished the race close on Tass's heels had been a surprise. Amathys had never been one of the top students. She wasn't fast, skilled, or smart. She was known as a troublemaker—someone who continually sneaked out of the Calix when she ought to have been asleep. Most of the other students had learned that association with Amathys would get them in trouble as well. Amathys had few friends. That she was now a protégé of the talented Sarhi seemed absurd.

It wasn't like Tass wanted Sarhi to pay attention to her instead of to Amathys. She respected Sarhi, but she didn't need any friends. She'd had one—Igracio—and look how that had turned out.

She had left the Calix in the only way that made sense to her.

She'd swum. She wondered why there were no underwater cities in Luca. It would have made sense since a third of the inhabitants could have comfortably lived there. But even in the early days of Gannoir, the people had lived on land, first on the Orbokth, and later in the shining metal buildings balanced on the clatry, floating on the water.

That was a problem. She could spend all weekend in the sea, but it wasn't a destination. Tass pushed the water aside with her webbed fingers and reached for the depths. The brilliant blue of the water turned green and then paled to a yellow lime. She could feel the chemical composition of the water changing as she dove deeper. Only the top layer of the sea was made of water, and even then, it was only water during the first part of the day, before the intense heat of the Ghalon had a chance to suck it back into the sky. When the Ghalon turned its darkened third toward Luca in the night, the heat abated and thick rains returned the water to the sea, where it shimmered on the surface deceptively. The caustic nature of the other sea liquids permitted only the Mayim to swim in it safely. The Gulot and the Esh were effectively banned.

That was something. If she had to be a member of the despised lowest caste, at least the lowest caste had something it could call its own, a realm in which they were the masters.

Tass strained downward, letting the lemon-yellow liquid of the sea swish against her face like a breeze. The sea, even at this depth, was teeming with life. Little creatures swam around her, pursued by larger creatures. Floating plants rode the currents and added mystery to the depths. Every once in a while, she saw the metallic gleam of a dga, a tiny insect-like fish covered in vicious spikes. She had seen a giant dga once, but these were small enough that to Tass, the sharp appendages were not threatening.

Suddenly a current caught Tass and tossed her. She

somersaulted more than once before regaining control of her body. Her first thought was that she had been found by a lumalaua, an enormous fish festively arrayed with phosphorescent floating appendages. But when she looked, she could see nothing large enough to have caused her to tumble.

"Dwoyra?" Tass called using her water voice.

An inrush of liquid in her gills told her she was right. Tass hadn't felt the presence of her watery acquaintance since she had come back to the Calix.

"What, Dwoyra?" Tass communicated. Her gill-speech had improved, but she was by no means fluent, nor was Dwoyra, but for different reasons.

"Help," Dwoyra ooshed.

Tass reached her hand out in front of her, and Dwoyra formed the water into grasping fingers. "What help?" she asked.

"Darkness. Darkness. Bad."

"The black blobs?" Tass asked.

Dwoyra's essence swished through Tass's gills affirmatively.

Tass frowned. She knew how she'd fought the darkness before. With her blood. She shook her head and felt Dwoyra's dizziness as her liquid essence shot out of her gills. "No, Dwoyra. No more blood. I'm spent."

"Need."

"No."

"Fight darkness."

"Find someone else," Tass requested firmly. A twinge in her shoulder reminded her of the cost of bloodletting. "Find someone else."

Tass felt the water churn around her as Dwoyra made a

dramatic exit. She sighed, forgetting for a second to use her gills instead of her air-lungs. She coughed. Not even the water was safe. She rotated her body and shot toward the surface. She knew what she was going to do. There was one place she could go where no one would ask anything of her.

Chapter 5: Xylo

Xylo surveyed the crowd. He had been conducting educational meetings daily in the short weeks since he had decided to stay in Garradh Gannoir instead of returning to his home in Luca, bringing the ancient teachings to the deadbloods—the uncasted.

Now the people were clamoring for him to be named the 60th Dynroc. Xylo was willing. He saw their need for a leader, and he felt he was equal to the task. But there was more to being the Dynroc than just possessing the name. There was a supernatural power that the Dynroc, the true Dynroc, owned. Nothing of any import could happen without him. And Xylo wasn't the Dynroc. It was Dynny, the mentally challenged old man who had spent his years as a servant, who had been named the 59th. And there was a chance that Dynny was still alive, which would render any attempts by Xylo to have himself named 60th not only invalid, but a grievous crime against Tel-Maor, the Creator. Despite the wishes of the people, he couldn't declare himself Dynroc unless he knew for sure that Dynny was dead.

And he was by no means sure.

Justice demanded that Kleibald and Gelu be brought back to Gannoir to be tried for their crimes. They had attempted an act that would have resulted in tens of thousands of deaths. Igracio and Afa had died as a direct result of their actions, not to mention Afa's daughter, Mailu, who had died at the hands of Gelu and his people months earlier. Xylo had seen them cart Mailu's airtight coffin down into the skyboulder. He had heard Gelu speaking about reanimation of the dead girl. He wondered why Gelu cared. He could have no use for Mailu now. She was just molecules. Her soul had flown.

Justice.

Xylo mentally pushed down his own soul's cry for justice. Seeing Kleibald escorting his ex-wife, Ardanach, and his own two children, Gryf and Aythylla, onto the skyboulder had bruised his soul. He hadn't even known he had two grandchildren until he'd seen them following his son into the spaceship. A boy and a girl. Esh, from the looks of them. He wished . . . he wished . . .

But he couldn't wish. He wasn't his own anymore and his vengeance couldn't be a personal one.

He wondered if the leaders of the two civilizations of Gannoir had a backup plan. Kleibald was smart—he had to admit that. It seemed unlikely that Kleibald would have counted solely on the impending implosion of Gannoir to recreate the world in the image he preferred. Kleibald's goal, he knew, had been commerce with other worlds.

His heart turned icy at the thought. Although Xylo wasn't religious, he knew the ancient myths. The reason Tel-Maor had turned the world inside-out had been to prevent the forces of evil in the chaos outside Gannoir from corrupting his world and his people. If Kleibald initiated contact with these evil forces outside Gannoir, if he was able to ally with them against Gannoir, then anything was possible.

He couldn't let that happen.

The gaping hole in the ice-layer surrounding Gannoir had closed for the first time since the gogyvehr, the inversion of the world, only weeks before. Finally, they were isolated in a cocoon of safety.

But he had no choice. He was going to have to find a way to crack open Gannoir long enough to retrieve the skyboulder.

Impossible.

Dangerous.

The list of things that could go wrong was so voluminous he couldn't begin to think about any one scenario.

Xylo closed his eyes.

He had to try.

Somehow, he had to try.

He rested his face in his hands, trying to prevent the headache he felt pressing against the edges of his mind.

A ripple of laughter shivered around his head. *You're no better than Kleibald . . .* the voices accused him. *Risking all Gannoir to bring your grandchildren home again . . . Selfish . . . Megalomaniac . . .*

Xylo winced. Grandchildren. The voice of his accuser was correct. He had to be careful. He had to be a leader, to belong to the people and not to himself.

Justice.

It had to be about justice.

Chapter 6: Talag

Talag followed Dynny into another chamber of the skyboulder, the one in which the provisions were kept. Uncle Nadim was in charge of distributing the food, making sure it would last as long as they needed it to last, but he had been sleeping in one of the bunks in Talag's tower when he'd left. He wondered who would be handing out food at this hour. He wondered what hour it was. The everlasting blue glow had not grown less at any time in the month they had been in the skyboulder. As far as he knew, there was no way to assess daytime and nighttime save for the pangs of hunger in his own stomach.

When they came to the room reserved for eating, Talag found several others whose stomachs were apparently on the same schedule as his. He had talked to them all at least briefly, but without finding a companionable one among them. There was something wrong with him. His parents had been saying it for ages. His grandparents had been saying it for ages. His sister had picked up on it and had used it as a point of torment. She was more Esh-maor than he was, she taunted him regularly. It hurt because it was true. He wasn't a leader. He wasn't ambitious like the rest of his family. His father was a governor. His uncle would probably become Esh-Maor after his grandfather died or retired. He was the only grandson. He should have been something. He should have been worthy.

But he wasn't. He enjoyed studying, but he loved the knowledge for its own sake, not because it could advance his career. He didn't care if he scored well on tests. He didn't care that he wasn't leading his class. His sister Donamys did. She was always first in everything. Talag frowned. He didn't want to be like Donamys. She was rude. But he hated to be a disappointment. He knew his parents still had high hopes for him, hopes that he would change as he grew older.

Talag greeted each of the people in the dining room by name as he passed them. It was the stocky, dark woman, Minnidair, who was distributing the food this morning. She smiled solicitously at him when he approached and held out a packet of food and a ration of water in a cup. He looked curiously at the bangles on her arms and the rings on her fingers. They were made of wood, he knew, but wood was a substance he had never seen until he had come to Garradh Gannoir. Trees were the stuff of myth and legend in Luca, but in Garradh Gannoir they were plentiful. Minnidair's husband was a wood trader and carver. The woman's jewelry was intricately carved with patterns and images. Talag could have looked at the carvings for a long time, but already Minnidair was looking past him to the next person approaching her for food.

He followed Dynny to a quiet corner and they opened the food packets. Dynny ate quietly, smiling up at Talag at intervals, but without saying anything. Talag strained his ears to catch pieces of the conversations going on around him. The important people, the ones from whom he could have gleaned information, were still asleep in his own bunkroom. What he was hearing was just speculation. Would Gannoir implode soon? Maybe it just hadn't happened yet. Would they land on the icy exterior of Gannoir and make their home there? Maybe that was what Gelu had intended from the beginning. Maybe, if their plans for Gannoir had failed, they would colonize another world. It would be exciting. They would be the first settlers on an unknown world. Hadn't anyone noticed that they had been chosen for this mission in pairs?

Talag shuddered at that thought. Only one Esh-girl other than his sister was on board the skyboulder, and she wasn't his type. If his father forced him to marry her . . . He shook his head. It wouldn't happen. It wouldn't come to that. Once enough time had passed, they would go back to Gannoir, and life would go on has it had before. He would go back to school among many others, his friends included. He had no thoughts of selecting a wife yet. He was only thirteen. He knew his sister, a year younger than he, had her eye on a boy a few years older than herself. It was ambition, not admiration, that had caught Donamys's attention, though. The boy was at the top of his class and was strong and muscular as well. If anyone at school was pegged to be Esh-Maor after Uncle Nadim, it would be that boy.

With a sigh, Talag turned to Dynny. "Is your bunk comfortable?" he asked.

Dynny shook his head. "No bunk. Just blankets on the floor."

Talag cocked his head. "No bunk? The sleeping quarters have ten bunks each. My father told me so."

"No bunk," Dynny repeated. "I have a special job. I'm the Dynroc, 59th of that name. I sleep in a room by myself. With Mailu. Because she's dead. I have to stay with her to take care of her."

"You take care of someone who is dead?" Talag asked, perplexed.

"She's in a box," Dynny said, nodding vigorously. "We can't take her out. She'll die."

"I thought she was dead already."

"She's dead in a box," Dynny agreed, not seeming to notice any inconsistency in his statements.

"If she's dead in a box, how could she die if you took her out?" Talag asked. This conversation was getting very weird. Why would his grandfather have brought along a dead girl in a box?

"I have to take care of her," Dynny said, the glow of his important responsibility filling his expression with pride.

"Did she die after we left Gannoir?" Talag wondered. He hadn't heard anything like that, but he supposed it was possible. Maybe Grandfather was trying to preserve her so she could have a proper ceremony back on Gannoir.

"No . . . no . . ." Dynny said sadly. "She died months ago. She's Gulot, but Xylo said they put her in water and that's why she has so many blisters. That's why she's dead."

None of this made sense. "Could you take me to see her?" Talag requested.

Dynny pondered this. Then, "Gelu won't like it."

"I won't tell Gelu," Talag promised. "I want to meet her."

Dynny squinted as if he were thinking hard. "Okay," he finally agreed. "After Gelu wakes up. Once everyone is awake, we can try. I'll take you to see her. Don't let Gelu know."

"Don't let Gelu know," Talag repeated. "I won't."

Dynny smiled back at him and then gnawed at his dried fish until a chunk broke off in his ancient mouth.

Chapter 7: Tass

"Tass!" the woman exclaimed, her eyes softening with love and pain.

"Can I stay here this weekend?" Tass blurted. She winced. She hadn't meant to be so abrupt. Maybe because of that, Igracio's mom would turn her down.

But she didn't. "Of course, sweetie!" Rahela Barat said, reaching out to embrace the girl.

Tass stiffened. She wasn't a hugger.

"You have a whole weekend to do whatever you want? To go anywhere?" Rahela asked.

Inwardly Tass squirmed. She knew what Rahela was really asking. She wanted to know why the Master had let twelve-year-old Tass free on her own for an entire weekend. She wanted to know why no one was taking care of such a small child. She was wondering what Tass had done to get in trouble.

Tass lifted her chin. "I won a weekend pass. I swam the fastest." It was almost the truth. Her second-place finish wasn't an important part of the story.

"And they let you go? Just like that?"

"I won," Tass pointed out.

"But you're so young to be running around on your own," Rahela protested. Her big dark eyes were full of motherly worry.

At some level Tass knew that Rahela's concern was meant kindly. But she had been alone for a long time—since she was four. She didn't need anyone to look after her. She was beginning to regret her decision to go to Igracio's home for the weekend. Why had she come?

"I've always been alone," she snapped. She was angry. This woman, Igracio's mother, who had loved him fiercely even after he had been identified as Mayim, was ignorant and soft. She saw the hurt in Rahela's eyes as she snapped at her. She had meant to hurt her, but she felt a twinge of regret.

Rahela backed away and gestured toward the living room. "Make yourself at home. I'll just be getting lunch now." Her long dark hair swung in its ponytail as she walked into the kitchen. Tass moved toward the living room. Bleached rattan chairs circled a small table. A boy was sitting in one of them. Even though he was only a year older than Tass, he looked so much like Igracio that Tass felt startled every time they met.

"Hey Tass," he greeted her, seeming unsurprised by her presence.

"Hey Peodar," she smirked back at him.

"Want to play a game?" he asked, pointing to a board with movable pieces sitting on the table.

Tass shook her head. "I don't know how to play."

"I could teach you," he offered kindly.

He wouldn't be so kind if he knew the whole truth, if he knew that Igracio died while trying to save Tass in particular. She'd been there when Xylo had reported Igracio's death to his family. "Died to save Gannoir. A hero," Xylo had told them. He had explained the effects of Igracio's death, how he had bravely risked and lost his life to save others, all Gannoir, in fact, from a violent death due to the implosion of their world.

They'd been devastated, of course. Tass had watched Rahela's face as it crumpled into a wrinkled mass of grief. She's seen Igracio's father, Laso, clench his fists so tightly that his fingernails drew blood from his palms. And she'd witnessed Peodar's little-boy tears at the death of his beloved brother.

Beloved.

Something she would never be.

Igracio had everything that she had never had.

Now she didn't even have him.

But somehow, she had them.

And Igracio, who had always been a scaredy-cat, was the hero. He'd made a split-second decision that had cost him his life. And now the coward was a hero. Was that all a hero was? Nothing innate in a person, but only a split-second decision that cost everything?

It should have been her.

She came back to herself with a snap.

"Tass! Tass Galan!" Peodar was nearly shouting.

She looked at him and flinched again at how much he resembled his older brother. "What?" she crabbed.

"The game. I could teach you. Can I? Will you play?"

Tass sighed. "All right. If you think you can teach one of the stupid Mayim to play your game . . ."

Peodar wrinkled his nose. "Why're you so grouchy? Igracio was Mayim and he really liked this game."

"Igracio was different." It was a vast understatement.

"C'mon, Tass. Just until lunch," Peodar pleaded.

"Why?"

"For fun."

She frowned.

"To learn something new?"

Tass rolled her eyes.

"'Cuz there's nothing better to do?"

She sighed. "Okay." And she finally gave in. She was there at the Barat's apartment. The least she could do was play Peodar's stupid game. He was right. It would pass the time. She had nothing better to do.

Nothing mattered anyway.

Chapter 8: Xylo

"The people here love you," Ceres noted over dinner that night.

"They follow a leader pretty easily," Xylo noted with a twinkle in his eye.

"Don't sell yourself short," Ceres admonished him. "It's the will of Tel-Maor. You're supposed to lead. Kleibald is gone. Dynny and the Dynroc before him are gone. Gelu is gone. There's no one left."

"A fine endorsement," Xylo replied good-humoredly.

"She's right though," Case agreed, reaching for another slice of halas bread. "You're the logical choice to take over Garradh Gannoir. You're educated. You're smart. You're old. You're . . ."

Xylo laughed out loud, but then grew thoughtful. "As dubious a qualification as 'old' is, I do truly agree with you. It hurts my soul to see how the people here have blindly followed Gelu. I would like to bring them up to think more clearly, more independently. I want to lead and bring justice to them."

"Not much to need protection from now that Kleibald and Gelu are gone," Case quipped. "Maybe a yovod here and there . . . a giant scolopendra . . ."

"No one's ever seen a giant scolopendra," Ceres criticized her husband. "Who could believe in colossal eels that fly through the air!"

Case sighed. "They're technically not eels. And I didn't literally mean Dad would be protecting the people from scolopendrae," he explained. "I just meant that the only dangers left are things like wild animals. Nothing really evil."

Xylo gave Case a weary glance. "You think Kleibald and Gelu took all the evil in the world away with them? You're wrong. You're very wrong." He was thinking painful thoughts about justice, blame, and guilt—his own guilt. The two leaders of Gannoir had not taken evil with them. Evil was there inside his own soul.

"Your dad's right," Ceres agreed. "I was going to wait to tell you until I was sure, but . . . I think I saw something in the water today. Maybe I'm just seeing things. Or making things up because of everything that's happened in the last few weeks. In fact, I probably am . . . but . . ."

"What did you see?" Case pressed.

"In the sea. The blobs of darkness. Tiny bits of disembodied evil floating or hitching rides on different creatures. A dark patch on the side of a vauzigk. Speckles of darkness on the sides of a dga. Beakfish leaping through the green light zone and ingesting . . . darkness. Just darkness." She shook her head. "Tell me I'm not crazy."

"You're not crazy," Case said reflexively.

"You're not crazy," Xylo agreed. "Evil is with us. It always has been."

Ceres shook her head. "I spend a lot of time in the sea, you know. It's never been like this. Never."

Silence filled the cavern as the three Siann Dha pondered the meaning of a new influx of darkness.

Finally, Xylo spoke. "It's possible that when the skyboulder broke free, some of the darkness from the chaos outside Gannoir slipped in. When the gap in the Bec closed, the darkness was trapped on the inside of our world. More evil than we've ever experienced in the past." His heart ached.

"What do we do?" Ceres asked.

"Fight it," Case answered.

"How?" Ceres asked.

With a sigh, Xylo set down the dried fish he was eating. "I'll look into it. There are scores of books here. One of them must have some answers."

Case and Ceres exchanged a glance.

Xylo saw it and understood what it meant. "You're thinking you know the answer already. You're thinking the fight isn't over. The completion of the gogyvehr wasn't the last time the blood of the Siann Dha would be required."

Their faces told him it was, indeed, the conclusion they had silently reached.

"You may be right," he agreed solemnly. "But then again, there may be another way. I'll figure it out."

Later that night, Xylo lay in his bed in his room, formerly the room that had belonged to Arros, the 58th Dynroc. He pondered what Ceres had told him. Darkness, a new darkness in the seawater, clinging to the animals. She could have been mistaken, but Xylo didn't think so. It would account for the voices he heard almost continually now, accusers buzzing around his head that no one else could hear. The darkness that manifested as black blobs in the seawater was also in the air, floating like an invisible black cloud of evil.

There was some relief in this. Xylo knew he had done wrong over the course of his life, but he had never felt the kind of despair he had been experiencing since Afa's death.

Afa.

Even her name was like a knife to his soul. She was dead and it was his fault. It wouldn't have weighed so heavily on him if all that had happened was her inadvertent death in the course of their mission. The fault there was Kleibald's, not his. But that wasn't why he had recruited Afa. The electric shock he'd felt throughout his body upon finding out that the mother of his son's companion was Bracha Elisus . . . he had felt a sense of destiny there. Bracha Elisus. It was a name he'd heard before—long before he found out her daughter and his son were on a mission together. Long before he'd recruited her to search for them. He should have tried to find her years earlier, when the man had first died. But he hadn't. He had thought it better to let it go. But he'd never stopped thinking about her—and about the dying man's confession.

When he'd discovered that Bracha Elisus was Mailu's mother, he had been gripped by a feeling of destiny. He should have gone to her years earlier, but he hadn't. Now he was being forced to. He knew he should have spoken to her about the man, but even then, he hadn't. She'd died without hearing his last words, his repentance, his sorrow. He should have said something. Now it was too late.

Like a blinding light, the memory impressed itself on his mind—the water-man, his skin dry and peeling, burned red from the heat of the Ghalon on the heights. And his fingertips had been glowing, un-Mayim-like. Only the Esh had glowing fingers. The man was more than just a Mayim. He was something else. Something new. Or else something very old.

Xylo shoved the thoughts aside. He tried not to remember the one other place he'd seen a Mayim with glowing fingertips. There was no connection between the man and Igracio. None at all. It was Afa, Afa who had been Bracha Elisus, who was tied to that man, that dead man. He had chosen not to tell her—chosen deliberately and based on his own self-interest.

He cringed as he thought of it.

You're worthless . . . You're as evil as Kleibald . . . the voices hissed through his fire-gills. *Anyone who would make you their leader is ignorant . . . asinine . . . foolish . . .*

Xylo could see the grayish aura of the voices as they expertly serenaded him, just like they tortured Afa, and just like they're tortured the man.

"Stop it," he told himself aloud. "Don't listen."

He had to make it stop somehow. Ceres' words had brought him hope. They would fight the evil together. Fight for the man . . . for Afa . . . for Igracio . . .

He just had to figure out how.

Chapter 9: Talag

Talag followed Dynny into a section of the skyboulder he had thought was another storage room. Unlike the other chambers, this room's ceiling was low—Talag's hair scraped on it as he walked toward the tiny corner of the room from which the skyboulder's central blue light emanated. The ceiling was higher there. A long rectangular stone box stood along one of the two straight sides of the room. A pile of blankets was heaped along the other wall.

"See!" Dynny chortled. "There she is." He ran a loving finger along the smooth stone of the girl's coffin.

"Who is she?"

"Mailu!"

"I know. You told me her name before," Talag agreed. "But, I mean, why? Why is she in a box? Who is she?"

"She's Siann Dha. Gulot," Dynny told him. "From Luca."

"A lot of people are from Luca," Talag told the little man. "I'm from Luca. My family is from Luca. More than half of the people in this skyboulder are from Luca. What's so special about a dead Gulot girl that they made a whole separate chamber on the skyboulder for her?"

Dynny pressed his fingers to the bridge of his nose and wrinkled up his gnomish face. After some effort, which clearly cost him, he replied to Talag's question. "Gelu thought she would come back to life. When Gannoir imploded."

"But Gannoir didn't implode," Talag noted.

"It didn't?" Dynny looked surprised.

"I heard my grandfather and my uncle talking. Gannoir is whole. It sort of spat us out into the chaos, but when the skyboulder left, whatever was supposed to make Gannoir implode didn't happen. It just sat there."

"Can you see it?"

Talag shook his head. "There are no windows. I don't know how grandfather and Uncle Nadim know it didn't happen. They couldn't have seen it either."

"So she's going to stay dead?"

Dynny looked so disappointed that Talag didn't have the heart to confirm his fears. "Maybe not. Maybe something else will happen to make her come alive again."

Dynny brightened. "That's what Gelu said!" he announced, as if he just remembered. "He said Mailu was a better Siann Dha. A three-in-one. What do you think he meant?" He looked at Talag hopefully.

Talag leaned over the glass-topped coffin and peered at the dead girl. He was getting over the initial creepiness of the whole thing. The girl was young and beautiful. She was also covered with blisters that looked as raw and painful as they would have the day she had gotten them. She really didn't look dead. There was a pink glow to her skin that seemed to indicate otherwise.

He tapped on the glass.

Nothing happened.

"She's really dead?" he asked. "Are you sure?"

Dynny nodded. "Gelu said so. And Kleibald said he was stupid to think she would come alive again. The Siann Dha can die. And this one did. But Gelu said she's different. Three-in-one. Three-in-one!"

"I don't understand," Talag frowned.

"I have to guard her. Let no one but Gelu come in here. Gelu told me he wouldn't do any more bad things. No more trying to kill Gannoir. Only life. Life for us in the skyboulder. And life for Mailu."

"Was Gelu doing bad things before?" This was hard for Talag to digest. Gelu was in league with his grandfather, Kleibald. It was because of their alliance that he was on the skyboulder. He wondered if he should tell his grandfather if Gelu was doing something really bad.

Dynny nodded. "Digging. Digging a hole through Gannoir. Through to the chaos. Stop the digging. I went with Xylo to stop the digging. I got lost. Now I'm here. But Gelu told me he's going to do good now. He told me I had to guard Mailu. Because I'm the Dynroc, 59th of that name."

Talag heard the whoosh of air as the door to the chamber slid open.

"What's going on in here?" Gelu's voice was loud, and his face was red. He looked from Dynny to Talag and back again, his thin blue-gray braid of hair swinging on his back as he did so.

"My friend wanted to see the dead girl," Dynny explained calmly. "So I brought him here to meet her. Beautiful Mailu."

Talag watched Gelu's face as Dynny spoke. He could see the seething anger there. Dynny was not supposed to bring visitors to see "beautiful Mailu." He wondered what the taller man would do. He was surprised when Gelu's face became thoughtful.

"Ah," he said shortly. He turned to Talag. "And what do you think of Mailu?"

Talag blinked. "She's beautiful," he admitted. "Is she really dead?"

An uncomfortable silence filled the space between Talag and Gelu.

Finally Gelu asked, "What do you think?"

Sigh. "I don't know. She's in a box. Dynny said it's airtight. She must be dead. But she looks as though she just died a moment ago, not months earlier like Dynny said."

Another long silence ensued. Then, "I'm going to trust you, boy. You're old enough to understand these things. But you mustn't tell your grandfather or anyone else. Kleibald disapproves of my fascination with the girl. Since she was dead, he gave me leave to dispose of the body as I saw fit, and I shall, once my experiments are done."

Talag felt sick. "Experiments?" Was Dynny sure Gelu's evil-doing days were over?

Gelu smiled softly. "Nothing bad. Mailu has one final task to complete before she can be returned to the gods. One last gift to give the world."

"What is it?" Talag asked. He still felt sick.

"You can't tell anyone you've been in here," Gelu cautioned him. "Swear it to me."

Talag didn't want to promise anything to Gelu. Anyone who would experiment on a dead girl had to be crazy at best, possibly evil. But one look at Gelu's expression suggested that disagreeing with him would be a bad idea. "I promise," Talag agreed.

Gelu exhaled heavily, almost triumphantly. "She's going to bear a child. My child. It will be the first of a new race of people. She will be the mother of the new world, of the new Gannoir."

Crazy, then, Talag thought. He smiled, trying to humor the madman in front of him.

Dynny was excitedly shifting his weight from one foot to the other. "He told you the secret! It's the big secret!" His eyes shone.

Gelu looked at the little man. "Life and new birth, not death and destruction, right, Dynny?"

Dynny nodded. "I have to make it happen. Only the Dynroc can make the magic, right, Gelu?"

"That's right," Gelu told him. "We need you. You're important to the continuation of Gannoir. Gannoir must have a Dynroc."

"It's me!" Dynny grinned. "I'm the 59th of that name."

"How is a dead girl going to have a baby?" Talag asked logically.

"Kleibald doesn't know everything," Gelu retorted.

Talag digested this non-sequitur. "My grandfather . . . doesn't think dead girls can have babies?" he asked. That sounded like good sense to him.

Gelu waved a hand as if to shoo away an irritating intruder. "Kleibald knows she's special. His people investigated the matter. This Mailu is powerful beyond all belief. She can do things no one has ever done before. Who knows what great feats she may perform."

"Even though she's dead," Talag quipped humorlessly.

"You sound like your grandfather," Gelu growled.

"I just don't think . . ."

"That's the problem. None of you are thinking," Gelu shot back.

"But . . ."

"If you tell anyone about my work with this girl, you will have the blood of thousands on your head," Gelu threatened.

Talag winced. Gelu was crazy. "I won't tell anyone," he promised. He wasn't worried about having the blood of thousands on his head, but he was worried about the revenge Gelu would thrust upon him if he disobeyed. "Can I go now?" he asked.

"Go," Gelu motioned toward the open door.

Dynny started to follow Talag, but Gelu grabbed his collar. "Stay here. Your job is to be with Mailu . . ."

Chapter 10: Tass

Tass squirmed uncomfortably as Laso Barat began to pray over their supper. Belief that gods inhabited the Ghalon was an ancient myth on Gannoir, but it was one that Igracio had firmly believed to be true. Tass tried to imagine the kind of being who could live inside the fiery core of her world. She failed. Nothing could live there. It just wasn't possible.

Laso kept on at length, addressing his petitions to Tel-Maor, the god who created Gannoir and who, presumably, lived in fire and could, at the same time, hear the prayers of all the nutcases who were talking to him all over Luca.

"We lift up to you the souls of our departed loved ones, Igracio,"—Rahela gave a little whimper—"Papa and Mama Barat, and cousin Hamell, and the others, like sweet Tass's mother and sister. May their souls inhabit the Ghalon and walk amongst the stars. Please give us your protection and keep evil far from us. Thank you for your constant provision, for our home and our family and . . ."

The Barat's sure did have a lot of provisions, Tass reflected as she waited impatiently for the prayer to end. And as for walking among the stars . . . she frowned. Her mother's body had never been found. Sucked directly up the tornado of wind and water and into the Ghalon, said people who had seen it happen. Her sister, Mailu, the sweet older sister she could barely remember, was trapped in a box, stolen by Gelu and his cronies. She sure wasn't walking among the stars. Then Tass began to laugh aloud. She couldn't help it. Mailu's body had been aboard the skyboulder. Possibly her sister was out there among the faraway and mythical stars that existed somewhere in the chaos.

Peodar kicked her under the table but that only made her laughing worse. She sucked her breath through her nose and plugged her ears, trying to stop the hysterical laughter that had overtaken her.

Igracio's father finished his prayer abruptly and then turned to Tass. "Praying is something new to you, isn't it?" he asked kindly.

"Don't hassle her," Rahela admonished him. "She's lost her family, poor girl. It's not surprising that she would react when you mention them."

"It was fitting to pray for their souls," Laso reminded his wife gently.

Peodar kicked Tass again. She took her fingers out of her ears and shifted uneasily on her seat, trying to neither laugh nor hiccup.

"Tel-Maor is real," Laso said. "He created Gannoir. And when the evil forces from the chaos attacked Gannoir, he's the one who made the gogyvehr."

"The gogyvehr destroyed a lot of Gannoir," Tass observed unkindly.

"It was necessary," Laso said staunchly and unemotionally. "The people of Gannoir were consorting with the evil ones. The destruction began with them. By inverting the order of the world, pulling the fire of the Ghalon to the center and pushing the ice to the edges, Tel-Maor created a barrier between Gannoir and the chaos. Because of Tel-Maor, we are safe inside Gannoir."

"Safe . . ." Tass echoed, irony twisting her mouth into a bitter curve. "Igracio's dead. You call that safe?"

Rahela winced as though the news of Igracio's death had pierced her anew.

Laso looked at Tass, stared into her eyes and would not look away, like he was trying to see into her soul. Finally he spoke. "Igracio is dead, yes. He died to save Gannoir. But he died as a member of Tel-Maor's army. His spirit walks among the stars now. He is free. He is safe. Death holds no fear for the righteous."

"I would have died for Gannoir," Tass retorted. "I was in the water. I was nearly dead. But it was Igracio whose blood completed the gogyvehr. I wish it had been mine." She pressed her lips tightly together. Igracio'd had everything to live for. He had people who loved him. He was smart and educated. He was gentle and kind. He was whole. It should have been her. She had no one and nothing. Her soul was a shredded mass of agony. Being a hero would have been the one thing she could have done to redeem herself. But instead, it had been Igracio who had been given that too.

Rahela's face filled with compassion. "Tass, don't say such things. We are so glad you are alive. You're young. You have your whole future in front of you."

And my past behind me, Tass reflected bitterly. Her mother had rejected her. Her sister had been torn from her. She didn't even know who her father was. She was completely alone. Nothing would change that.

Peodar kicked her under the table again.

"What?" Tass turned on him angrily.

Peodar stuck out his tongue at her.

Tass's eyes narrowed with rage. Was he going to make a mockery of his brother's death? She looked down and saw a faint glow surrounding her fingertips. Quickly she pulled her hands off the table and sat on them.

"Have some bread," Laso said, passing a sea-reed basket to Tass.

"Vegetables," Rahela noted, passing a beautiful green corundum bowl to Peodar.

They were silent while they dished up the food. Laso and Rahela discussed news of the city while they ate.

Tass listed with half an ear. She didn't care which of the Esh-maor became *the* Esh-Maor. As long as Kleibald was gone, it was enough for her.

"He's coming back, you know."

Tass looked up sharply, not sure who had spoken. "Who's coming back?" she asked.

Laso, Rahela, and Peodar looked at her curiously.

"No one said anything about coming back," Peodar noted.

"Someone . . ." Tass began. Then she realized what had happened. It was the voices. Again. Whenever she left the water, she was vulnerable to their voices. They never said anything good. Only horrible things she didn't want to hear.

"Are you feeling all right?" Rahela asked. "You look a little sick."

Tass set her spoon down and pushed her chair away from the table. "I'm just . . . I guess I'm not feeling well. I'm sorry." Her eyes filled with tears, stupid tears of rage, not sadness. She whirled around and strode toward the door.

"Tass! Wait!" Rahela called after her.

"I have to go," Tass hollered back, trying to sound as sick of body as she felt in her soul. She had to get to the water. She had to get away from the voices. She had to get away from Igracio's happy, weirdly religious family. She should never have come.

She grabbed her knapsack and then opened the sliding door that led to the corridor in the apartment building that would take her away, out of the structure, down to the clatry, and into the sea.

When the water washed over her toes, it brought her the feeling of relief she sought. With her knapsack tightly bound around her body, Tass dived into the sea.

Chapter 11: Xylo

Xylo set the book on the table with a heavy thud. His soul too, felt heavy, but it was different. He could feel the edges of his soul as though an electrical current ran through him. He felt alive. He would get justice for Gannoir and at the same time, revenge for the personal wrongs Kleibald had committed against him. Rage coursed through him like power.

"Dad? Where are you, Dad?"

Xylo snapped back to reality. "Case? I'm in the library."

A second later his son entered the room. "Did you find out how we can fight this new evil?" he asked.

Xylo didn't want to tell his son how much rage was in his own soul. How was he going to fight an abstract evil represented by smudges of blackness in the water and the air if he couldn't even quell his own evil impulses?

Xylo snorted lightly. "That's the question of the universe," he remarked.

Case looked at him knowingly. "It's blood, isn't it? Our blood?"

"Where's Ceres?" Xylo asked abruptly. "She should hear this too."

Xylo looked at his son and daughter-in-law. "There are two ways to fight the evil on Gannoir," he began. "You were right. One of them is by the blood of the Siann Dha. By our blood. When applied directly to the soul of the evil being, it will kill."

"How do you put blood on a soul?" Ceres asked wonderingly.

"A better question is, 'How do you have enough blood to cover all the evil?'" Xylo commented. "The answer is—you don't. Not without great sacrifice of life."

"What's the other way?" Case asked.

"The other way is to destroy the matter that the evil is indwelling."

Ceres looked confused. "Like the dark spots in the sea? We ought to destroy the liquid of the sea?"

"I don't get it," Case confessed.

Xylo looked from one to the other. "I'm thinking about Kleibald. Kleibald and Gelu."

"You think we should destroy Kleibald and Gelu?" Case asked.

"Does that sound wrong?" Xylo asked.

Case bit his lip. "No. They should be punished for what they did to Mailu, and to me, and to all the others. They tried to destroy the world. Their intention was to make Gannoir implode and kill all life. Destruction would be too good for them."

"It's murder, though," Ceres said softly. "We can't just kill everyone who wrongs us, everyone who does something evil. It's murder."

"That's right," Xylo replied. "An individual killing another individual is murder. But when the killing is an execution sponsored by the people and affirmed by their leaders, then it's not murder. It's justice."

"Justice . . ." Ceres still looked puzzled.

"You want Kleibald and Gelu to stand trial?" Case asked.

Xylo nodded. "We must bring them back. We must hold them accountable for what they tried to do to Gannoir, for what they did to Afa, Mailu, and Igracio, for what they did to my son, my little Dochym." He swallowed the last word, his dead son's name, with a little noise that might readily have evolved into a sob.

"Is it possible?" Case asked.

"Anything right is possible," Xylo declared heavily.

Ceres shook her head. "But how? Do we turn back time and open the boundaries of the world? They closed for good when Igracio died. Our world is finally completely protected. Safe. There's no way we can bring them back, even if it's the right thing to do."

"I've been thinking about that too," Xylo replied. "And I have an idea."

Chapter 12: Talag

Talag's eyes popped open.

He was pretty sure it was still nighttime. He could hear the rustling of the slow breaths of those in the bunks beneath him and beside him. He glanced across the little room at his sister, asleep on the top of the women's quintuple bunk. An occasional snore from underneath him meant that Lefty, at least, was sound asleep.

"Psst!" A voice was beckoning to someone.

Talag wondered if it was Dynny, coming to find him and take him to see "pretty Mailu" again. He wanted to lift his head and check who the interloper was, but he didn't want to get in trouble for encouraging the little man.

Straining his eyeballs to the right, he tried to see the doorway without moving his head. It wasn't working.

"Psst!"

A bunk below him creaked. "Shh! I'm coming."

Not Dynny coming for him, then.

Talag waited until he heard someone shuffle out of bed and

through the sliding door. Then he sat up. Something was afoot and he wanted to know what it was.

Carefully he climbed down from the fifth bunk, taking note of who was in the room and who wasn't. First, he passed Lefty, who snorted and rolled over, then his father, who was sleeping flat on his back, his posture strict even in sleep. Uncle Nadim was curled in a ball like a small child. His grandfather's bunk was empty.

Talag tiptoed to the door and put his ear against it.

The voices echoed off the metal door, producing a reverberating, tinny sound that was nonetheless distinct. Talag held his breath in order to hear better.

"... didn't go as we planned. It's time to think again," Kleibald was saying.

"Are we going back? Can we penetrate the Bec layer? It's like a shield around Gannoir," the other voice—not his grandfather's— said.

Talag heard the echo of a snort. "Gannoir was supposed to die," his grandfather said with a relish. Something cold washed over Talag's heart. Gannoir was supposed to die? Supposed to? He had known that they were escaping from their ultimate destruction—his parents wouldn't have left their world behind unless it was really, really important that they do so—a matter of life and death. But his grandfather's tone told him something he hadn't known before. His grandfather had wanted Gannoir to die.

Talag felt sick.

"So?" the other voice said.

"You know the resources we have at our disposal," Kleibald retorted. "You know their powers."

"What are you saying?"

"Gannoir must die."

Silence.

"We have to go back. We have no choice."

"We can't go back. There's nothing left for us there."

"But Mailu . . ."

"You're a fool!" Kleibald interrupted sharply. "She's dead. She's dead now and she'll always be dead. And I was a fool to let you bring her."

"She's carrying my child."

Talag knew, now, to whom the second voice belonged. Gelu.

"Your dead child," Kleibald snorted again.

"No. You know as well as I do that this girl is special. You brought me the information. That's why she was the one I chose to be the mother. You and I made the plan together. To unite the Siann Dha and the people of Garradh Gannoir. You sent her to me. I'm not just going to let go because she's temporarily dead."

"Mailu will stay dead if we go back to Gannoir," Kleibald drawled.

"It was the reversal of the gogyvehr that was supposed to infuse her with life again. The power of the blood and the power of the Ghalon, coming together to invert the world and make things right. This isn't just about me. You hand-picked the girl because of what she was—because she was something different, something new. She is supposed to be the mother. There's no one else who can take her place. She's the one."

"She's dead. And the reversal of the gogyvehr didn't happen."

"That's why we have to go back. The blood and the Ghalon contain the necessary powers to bring her back to life—the girl and the child."

"It's too late."

"We can't destroy Gannoir. We have to find a way to go back."

"There are other worlds. If we destroy Gannoir, we can inhabit one of those. The spirits have told me so. They've offered us a place there. But only when Gannoir is gone. That is their price."

"But the child . . . my child . . ."

"There will be other children. We brought members of each caste with us as well as deadbloods from your side of the Orbokth."

"But this child was special . . . blood of the triad and the blood of death. This child is the one who was supposed to create a new race of Siann Dha. This child is meant to bring new life to the blood of my people!"

Gelu was nearly shouting now, Talag discerned.

"Be quiet!" Kleibald admonished his co-conspirator. "We don't need the whole skyboulder knowing about our plans."

"Your plans . . ." Gelu snorted.

"Our plans," Kleibald corrected him firmly. "Together with the spirits, we will destroy Gannoir. They can't do it without us, without physical creatures from Gannoir. Once it's gone, we will be given a new world to populate with people born on Gannoir but destined for a new life of commerce with the skies."

"The others won't agree to this," Gelu protested.

"That's why we're not going to tell them," Kleibald explained condescendingly. "There will be an 'accident.' Something we will seem to try to prevent. Gannoir will be destroyed. We will escape with our lives. It will all be very sad, but sometimes things like that happen. Do you understand?"

"You're not paying attention. Mailu needs the power from the Ghalon to infuse her with the life necessary for my child to be born. We have to go back. We have to try again."

"You're a fool," Kleibald retorted. "You will do as I say, or you'll have no part in the new world. An unfortunate accident will happen . . . to you."

Talag quietly climbed up to the top bunk and pulled the blankets over his head. He was terrified. He was overwhelmed. He didn't understand what he'd just heard, if he'd really heard it at all. Maybe it was a nightmare. Maybe he'd never slipped out of his bunk at all, never heard the heated conversation between his grandfather and the leader of Garradh Gannoir.

The door to the bedroom slid open and Talag heard his grandfather climb back into his bunk.

It was real.

Talag tried his hardest to sound like he was asleep. He wanted to cry. He wanted someone to tell him everything was going to be all right. But now he knew something else too. He was alone. His grandfather was a bad man. And if his grandfather was a bad man, what about his father and mother? What about his uncle? He couldn't trust anyone. Everyone had lied to him. Everyone.

Chapter 13: Tass

The water shut out the noise of the voices. Tass felt like herself in the water in a way she could never be on land. She was Mayim through and through. Peering through her inner eyelids, she pushed herself through the chemical sea, through the surface layers where the ymolenegth was a rich, glimmering blue, down into the teal and then the green and lime layers. She felt her skin reacting to the icy water, her pores closing, her body pushing heat to the edges of her skin to keep her warm.

Tiny creatures swirled around her, most of them too small for her to see any details. The water was yellowish and nearly opaque. Tass looked at her own limbs and saw that they were nearly invisible.

"Dwoyra," she said hesitantly. "Dwoyra, are you here?"

Large fish and sea creatures swirled around her in a hectic array of color. But it wasn't color she was looking for. It was invisibility.

"Dwoyra?"

A gentle nudge on her left caused Tass to collide with a bonefish. She could feel its crusty exoskeleton as it scraped against her skin. She turned away from it to see what had bumped her, but nothing was there.

Her spirits rose. "Dwoyra?"

"Come," the word rushed through her gills.

Tass waited for further instructions.

She felt the water take shape beside her. Watery fingers reached out for her own, tugging her deeper into the sea. Tass kicked her feet and let the invisible being guide her. The light changed from yellow to orange, then to a gentle salmon color.

"Where are we going?" Tass asked, using her gills and water-speech instead of her mouth and lungs to talk.

"Down."

The sea creatures accompanied them as though they were all in a parade. Bonefish, bouncing round globus, silvery schools of beakfish, and even a blubbery vauzigk. The vauzigk was so large that the water heaved with every blow of his flippers, creating waves that rocked Tass and Dwoyra and the other animals out of any chance of a purely linear journey.

Tass could see the edges of the Orbokth forming the ceiling above her. The Orbokth, the rocky parts of her world, descended deeply into the sea, but not all the way to the ice layer that formed the exterior of Gannoir. The land floated. They were diving under the deepest part of the Orbokth. The light, finding its source in miniscule molecules of blood in the water, did not diminish as they went deeper, but it did change color.

They were close to the edge of the world now. Tass was freezing, her body starting to slow down to match the motion of the molecules that could produce such extreme coldness. Dwoyra let go of Tass's hand, and a moment later Tass found herself wrapped in the arms of the vauzigk. Igracio had taught her about the sea creatures. Because the vauzigk lived in the magenta depths of the sea, Igracio had said, Tel-Maor had given him loads of fat to protect him from the cold. His body was thoroughly unlike the sleek bodies of the other sea animals. It was rotund, amorphous, fleshy. And warm. Tass leaned back against the creature, confident that Dwoyra had sent it to protect her.

Tass couldn't feel Dwoyra anymore, but she thought her watery friend was leading the vauzigk to whatever it was she wanted her to see. Tass turned her head to the side so she could rub her achingly cold face in the warm flesh of the creature that cradled her so gently.

Moments later, she felt the watery fingers prying her head away from the vauzigk. She turned to look. A school of tiny black fish swarmed frantically in the glowing fuchsia water. She didn't know what they were. She'd never seen their kind before.

Tass reached out a hand to touch them, to let them flow through her fingers as they traveled together through the sea, but Dwoyra knocked her backward. The vauzigk, startled, released her. The shock of the cold water stunned her into immobility. Dwoyra grabbed her head again and forced her to look up.

Tass quickly drew in water through her gills, gasping at what she saw.

The entire underside of the Orbokth gleamed silver and black. Thousands, millions of tiny dga, with their metallic silver exoskeletons and needle-sharp legs, clung to the rocks above her head. And each of them was bearing on its back a droplet of darkness, of blackness, of evil.

She knew what Dwoyra wanted.

Blood.

Her blood.

The blood of one of the Siann Dha.

It had worked before. Each drop of blood could annihilate one spot of darkness. She'd seen it. She'd done it.

But this . . . She looked around as though she were expecting to see Dwoyra waiting patiently and expectantly for her to bleed. There were millions of dga, and therefore, millions of splotches of darkness.

No one would have enough blood for this.

No one.

Chapter 14: Xylo

"Can you bring back samples of the darkness?" Xylo asked.

Ceres scrunched up her face. "Maybe. They're mostly free-floating, but many of them have attached themselves to plants and animals. Maybe I could bring one of the animals or some plants up. It'll only work if the darkness doesn't fall off on the way. It's not a solid. It's more like . . . more like . . ." She shook her head. "I don't know what it's like. It's not like anything I've seen before. It's just . . . bad."

"Try," Xylo urged her. "We have to find out what's going on—whether the darkness is growing. Do what you can."

Ceres left for the water, passing Case in the corridor, and giving him a quick kiss.

Case strode into the room bringing his report. "We can't fight this. It would be like fighting the wind. It's in the air."

"You're sure? You've seen it?" Xylo asked.

Nodding, Case continued. "It seems like a shadow or a darkness filling the air, one moment contracting and the next expanding. One minute it's huge, and the next minute it's in a million tiny pieces. It's not just in the water like we thought before. It's on the heights too. The light of the Ghalon seems dimmer, like the darkness is blocking its ability to glow."

"The gogyvehr is complete," Xylo sighed grimly. "Nothing new can get into Gannoir from the outside."

Case frowned. "Not from the place where the opening was before, maybe. But what about other locations? Gannoir is enormous. Could there be another hole far from Garradh Gannoir and Luca both?"

"There's nothing in the legends about holes," Xylo hedged.

"Do they say there isn't anything like holes?"

"We're playing word games now, son. Of course, it's possible that there is another hole, another way that the darkness is seeping in from the chaos outside Gannoir. But how do we find it?"

"Ceres can look. She can swim to the edges and look. She can find the places where the dark things are the most abundant."

"Ceres can't swim to the outskirts of the world," Xylo said. "No one could. It's too cold. Too dead."

"What about Tass?" Case asked.

Xylo frowned. "What about Tass?"

"Tass could help. She's swum deeper than anyone else. She told us so. She can endure the great depths better than any other Mayim. If anyone can figure out where the tear in Gannoir's Bec layer is, it's Tass."

"We'd need a million Tasses."

"There's only one," Case grinned, knowing he'd made his point.

Xylo sighed. "I need to make a trip to Luca anyhow. I'll talk to her while I'm there."

Xylo was waiting outside the cave system when Ceres got back. She'd taken bottles with her to collect samples. Her cross-body sack bulged with them. Still, that didn't mean anything. They could be empty. "What did you get?" Xylo asked.

Ceres lifted her yellowish hands in a helpless gesture. "I got everything. Sea bramble, sea reeds, cincinny fish, crabs, ribbon snails . . . I picked up everything I saw the darkness clinging to. But after I put the lids on, when I looked inside, there was nothing there. No blackness. No blobs. Nothing."

She followed Xylo into the tunnel. Once inside, she set her sack on the table and started pulling out her samples. She'd told the truth. There were many.

Xylo picked up a large jar and peered inside. A coiled ribbon snail floated inexpertly in the seawater Ceres had collected. Its long tentacles waved with the motion of his hand. "I don't see black spots," he noted.

"That's what I mean," Ceres said miserably. "They were there, clinging to its shell and curled around the base of its tentacles. But by the time I got it in the jar they were gone. It was like they never were."

The snail cautiously poked its eyestalks out of its shell and stared at Xylo solemnly.

"He doesn't look too sad about it," Xylo quipped. "You've probably done him a favor."

"Yes, but I wasn't trying to do him a favor. I was trying to collect evil."

"Case and I were talking," Xylo began hesitantly. "We are thinking about persuading Tass to come help us . . . help you . . . with the search. With two of you looking, we will be able to find out how the black things are getting in much more easily." He was careful not to say that Tass's abilities far outweighed Ceres'.

"That's a good idea," Ceres said absently. She ran a hand through her short, damp hair. "Maybe she'll see something I haven't seen."

"You think she'll come?" Xylo asked.

"No," Ceres answered honestly. "She turned you down before when you asked her to stay here with us. She won't have changed her mind. I don't know Tass that well, but I do know that much."

Xylo gave an appreciative snort. "You're probably right. But still, we need to try. I'm going to go to Luca. I have to meet with the Esh-maor. While I'm there, I'll talk to Tass. See if I can get her to listen to reason."

Ceres made a wry face. "Good luck."

"I'm going to need it."

Chapter 15: Talag

Talag stayed in his bunk as long as he could the next morning. He heard the others get up and start moving about. He heard them go into the next room to find their breakfast.

He didn't want to talk to them. He didn't want to talk to anyone. His mind was so agitated he felt like his skin was on fire. Everything he'd believed about everything was a lie.

He'd realized that at some point during his sleepless night in his bunk. It wasn't just about their current situation on the skyboulder. If his grandfather was a bad man, then he'd been a bad man before he'd made the decision attempt the destruction of Gannoir. He'd always been a bad man.

What followed from that was the bone-chilling knowledge that he couldn't trust anyone. His grandfather had always treated him well. But behind the Kleibald that he knew was another Kleibald, the real Kleibald, who wasn't anything like the nice guy Talag had thought him to be. What about his parents? What about his grandmother? Were they all in on it? Were all the adults in the skyboulder in on it? Had they all agreed to the destruction of their world, the murder of thousands upon thousands of people? Or were they like himself, innocent victims who just happened to have been chosen to survive?

Talag understood that the only reason he was chosen as one of those who would live through the ruin of the world was because he was his grandfather's grandson. Donamys might have been chosen based on her intelligence or her ambition even if she hadn't been Kleibald's granddaughter. The other young people, three boys and three girls of each caste plus four deadbloods, had probably been chosen for the same sorts of reasons. Maybe even the young people were guilty of the attempt to destroy Gannoir. There was no way to know. He could ask them, but they would lie.

And Dynny . . . Dynny had also been chosen. That was a bigger mystery, Talag reflected. Dynny was not the sort of person his parents or his grandparents would have chosen to associate with. He was simple-minded. He was old. He wasn't likely to assist with the population of a new world. According to Dynny, he had some sort of official position among the deadbloods, but it seemed more likely that his grandfather would have gotten rid of someone like Dynny than he would have been to preserve his life.

Hunger conquered Talag's desire to stay in his bunk. He climbed down the long ladder and moved toward the door, reluctant to show his face among those he now suspected. Would they be able to see his agitation? Would they perceive that he was afraid?

He would have to pretend.

Just like they did.

He organized his face into what he hoped was a casual smile and went into the next room. The young people were eating, talking, flirting. He tried not to look cynical as he reflected that his grandfather and Gelu's plan of peopling a new world seemed to be well on its way to working.

Of his family, only his Aunt Aythylla was present. She was married to Uncle Nadim. Talag had never liked her, but he'd never understood why. Now he thought he knew. She was the sort of person who would go along with a plan to destroy the world and everything in it. She just was. She didn't converse with anyone unless she thought that doing so would be to her benefit. Consequently, she and Talag had never been close. Talag looked at her with new eyes after hearing his grandfather's conversation. Aunt Aythylla knew. He was sure of it. She knew and she approved of the plan.

Talag nodded a greeting to her and then walked into the next room to get food. His mother was the distributor this morning. Her pale face lit up with gladness on seeing her son. She leaned toward him and hugged him. Talag let her, but he felt stiff and wary.

"What's wrong?" she asked.

Talag shrugged. "I didn't sleep well."

It wasn't a lie.

Milis put a hand to her son's head, looking concerned. "No fever," she noted. "You feel just as warm as an Esh-boy should feel. Do you want to lie down? Go get some sleep?"

"No," Talag answered. "I just want to eat."

His mother handed him the rations for the meal. "I hope you feel better," she said kindly.

Talag sighed as he went back to the living space. His mother couldn't be in on it, could she? Unlike Aunt Aythylla, his mother was sweet and caring, always ready to help others. There was no way she would have agreed to killing the entire population of Gannoir, minus forty. There was just no way.

But, he reflected, she wouldn't be any help either. His mother was kind, but she wasn't smart. She always believed everything his father said. And whatever lies his father had told to get her onto the skyboulder were, for her, the absolute truth. He would never be able to make her understand the evil plans he'd heard. And even if he could make her understand, he wouldn't want to. It would hurt her, maybe even break her.

Talag, gnawing on the coarse jerky that was his breakfast, climbed through the hallway that separated the two small bathrooms, and entered the second living space. Everyone in the room looked up. Kleibald and Ardanach, his grandparents, were sitting with Gelu and his wife Ceci. A couple of the deadbloods were there too, a young man named Benet and his wife Glenna. Benet and Glenna had been friendly to him over the course of his stay in the skyboulder, but that was before. Now that he saw them consorting with the grandfather, he thought that trusting them would be a mistake. The other person in the room was his sister, Donamys. She narrowed her eyes to slits and looked at him arrogantly.

"Sorry," he said, backing up. "I was looking for . . . Uncle Nadim. But he's not here so I'll go look somewhere else." Before he'd taken two steps into the corridor, he bumped into someone coming out of the bathroom.

It was Dynny. A broad grin split his face.

"Come," Dynny said, taking his hand.

Talag let himself be led away.

Chapter 16: Tass

"Healing," Dwoyra managed to communicate through Tass's gills.

Tass wrenched herself away from the watery fingers. "I can't. I did it before and now look at what's happened. There's more darkness than ever."

She looked up at the silvery dga lining the underside of the Orbokth. The metallic exoskeletons were usually hard to see, as they reflected their surroundings perfectly. But with the black spots clinging to their sides, they took on an ominous visibility.

"Where did it all come from?" she asked.

Dwoyra didn't answer, from which Tass deduced that she didn't know. Tass swam closer, pushing her face upward until she was inches away from the vicious-looking creepy-crawlies. The darkness seemed to waver before her eyes, more like a dark fog than an actual substance clinging to the dga. She reached out a hand experimentally.

A sudden wall of water knocked her back.

"Why, Dwoyra?" she panted with her gill-breath.

"Bad . . . Danger . . ." The water rushed through her head at a frantic and slightly painful pace.

"I know," Tass complained. "That's why I wanted to see what they were made of."

"Hurt you . . ." Dwoyra predicted.

"Tiny," Tass argued. "I'm big."

"Foolish," Dwoyra argued.

Tass was frustrated. First Dwoyra brought her to the brink of the world and asked for her help. Now she wouldn't let her do anything.

Anything but bleed, that is.

Tass was exhausted. She felt like the next drops of blood she gave for Gannoir would empty her of life altogether. She had nothing left to give. Nothing.

She rubbed her stiff shoulders with icy hands and looked around for the vauzigk. She spied him hovering at least three body lengths away from her. Pushing the water out of the way, Tass swam toward him, aching all over. She nestled into his bloated warmth and let it minister to her frozen, stiff body.

Dwoyra hovered anxiously. Couldn't anyone just be her friend? Everyone wanted her blood. It wasn't fair. It wasn't nice. *There was Igracio,* a little voice inside reminded her. Tass slapped the voice back into her subconscious. Her world was much simpler without that renegade thought.

She wasn't going to offer her blood anymore. She was done with that. Maybe she could help Dwoyra with her problem and maybe she couldn't. But she wasn't going to do it with her blood. She waited until Dwoyra's hovering seemed to recede behind the vauzigk and then, propping her feet against the creature's solid hips, she propelled her body upward, stretching glowing fingers in front of her.

Her hands slammed painfully into the Orbokth, scattering the dga to either side. The blackness that surrounded them remained on the rock. She couldn't see the blackness against the dark surface of the Orbokth, but she could feel it. Tiny bits of darkness, of evil, slid over her fingers, down her arms, and onto her neck. She writhed in the water, trying to shake them off, but it was no use. They were everywhere, crawling over her fitted clothing, oozing between her fingers and toes, sending shivery jolts of sensation along her scalp, and washing in and out of her gills.

And that wasn't all.

Her one refuge, the one place where she'd been safe from the voices that had plagued her since Igracio's death, had been taken from her.

You're worthless, the darkness whispered in her ear. *No one loves you. No one ever has.*

Tass steeled herself against the words of the evil. They were words she had said to herself all her life. But they were also words she'd successfully managed to ignore, to shove down inside her somewhere she couldn't access. The thought of being plagued with darkness all the time, even in the water, with no hope of escape, was revolting. She couldn't take it. She couldn't. She would rather die.

"Dwoyra!" she hollered in the loudest gill-speech she had ever managed. Desperately, "Dwoyra!"

There was no reply.

Chapter 17: Xylo

"That's why we need your help. Your cooperation," Xylo finished. He looked from one face to another. Some of the Esh-maor looked nervous. Others seemed skeptical. Still others looked back at him, stone-faced. He wondered what they were thinking.

"You don't think Kleibald is able to come back on his own?" a man named Arth asked.

Xylo recognized Arth and some of the others, but as far as he could tell, no one knew who he was. They had known him as Adam Xalantaka, not Xylo. Xylo had known Arth in his younger years. Arth was several years older than he was, and Xylo had liked him as far as he'd known him. Arth had never been a strong student, just a genial one. Xylo wondered how he'd come to follow Kleibald in his destructive plans.

Xylo looked into Arth's watery green eyes. "Kleibald's plan failed. You know that as well as I do. He was trying to reverse the gogyvehr. To turn Gannoir what he thought of as right-side-out. As you can see, Gannoir is the same as it's always been. We're all still here and Kleibald is trapped outside the world in the chaos."

A woman who had introduced herself as Tsakali Oeloor spoke next. "Is he trapped, though? He's Kleibald. He would not have left himself without a plan." She shook her head. "He will be back when he's ready." She folded her arms across her chest and the diaphanous red fabric of her tunic floated around her body.

Xylo shook his head. "That's just what we don't want. While I'm sure Kleibald is capable of coming back on his own, justice must be our first priority. Kleibald tried to destroy Gannoir. Because of his actions, people died. We can't let him return whenever he wants. We must draw him in and hold him accountable for his crimes."

"Surely the deaths were accidental," and elderly Esh-woman said gently, giving her name as Dallasha Budach. She hadn't been to school with him. Xylo guessed she was probably a generation older than himself. He hadn't known her during his days as an elder, which seemed odd. She must have joined the council later.

Xylo shook his head. "You knew he was trying to reverse the gogyvehr. That means inverting the structure of Gannoir. The icy exterior would collapse into the core and the Ghalon would explode and revert to its prehistoric state as the part of Gannoir that faces the chaos. No one on Gannoir could survive that. No one."

Arth sighed. "Kleibald explained that. Some would die, of course. A few. But the clatry would retain its form throughout the transition. We would be safe in the cities, in the high-rise buildings Kleibald spent the last thirty years building. That was why he built on the clatry—so that everyone would be able to take shelter when the gogyvehr was reversed."

"We were all hoping Kleibald's plan would work. Imagine! We would be able to see the cosmos! To trade with other worlds. To be part of the universe at large again!" This was from a middle-aged Esh-man named Frigo who was the son of one of Xylo's classmates. The classmate had died young, but not before marrying and producing three offspring to carry on his work with the council of the Esh-maor. He and Xylo had been friends, or friendly, at least. Xylo wondered if his old friend would have looked like his son, had he lived to have gray hair.

Xylo faced the council, a theater filled with a hundred men and women who made the decisions for all Luca. Some of them were Xylo's age and had supported Kleibald in his bid to be Esh-Maor many years earlier. He wondered how many of them knew how Kleibald had driven him out, killed his son, and stolen his wife and two other children.

He tried to focus. He had come to Luca to see the Esh-maor in order to bring about justice for Gannoir, not justice for his own losses. Not that Dochym's life didn't matter. It did. But it wasn't going to convince any of Kleibald's cronies to put him on trial. He had to make them understand the ramifications of Kleibald's plan to reverse the gogyvehr. Were they all so blinded by their devotion to Kleibald that they had lost their ability to reason? Anyone with half a brain would know that the clatry, as solid as it was, wouldn't protect anyone from the blinding, burning fire of the Ghalon. He had worked on the heights. He knew that powerful heat of their world's energy source. It had been near the extent of his endurance, even as an Esh and biologically equipped to bear the heat. Maybe they didn't understand. They'd lived their lives indoors, away from the heat and filth of the lives of the soil miners. He closed his eyes and tried to think charitable thoughts.

"Please," he said slowly. "Please investigate this matter. Kleibald conspired to kill all of you. All of us. All of Luca and all of Gannoir. The clatry wouldn't have protected you from the fire in the Ghalon. Neither would the buildings. They're metal. They conduct heat. Do some research. Do some experiments. Decide for yourself, based on facts and evidence, if what Kleibald told you was true. If it was, fine. I'll go back to Garradh Gannoir and continue in my role as interim Dynroc. But if you decide, as I have, that Kleibald made a deliberate attempt to annihilate all life on Gannoir, then we can work together to hold him accountable. That's all I ask."

He looked around at the resistant faces of the Esh-maor. "I'll be back in three days for your answer."

And without looking to see whether his words had been well received, he turned around, swinging his arms so his tala caught the air, and strode from the room.

Chapter 18: Talag

Dynny shuffled slowly through the short, narrow corridors of the skyboulder. Talag didn't have to wonder where they were going. They were going to Mailu. He wondered why the strange little man was so obsessed with the dead girl.

No one tried to stop them as they passed through the living quarters and the bunk room in front of the door to Mailu and Dynny's tiny chamber. Dynny pushed the button that opened the door and then shut it quickly once they were inside. When he turned to look at Talag his expression was enigmatic.

"What is it, Dynny?" Talag asked.

"Is she dead?" Dynny asked. "Really dead?"

Talag shrugged. "I guess so."

"Then dead people can be alive again?"

"Gelu thinks so," Talag hedged.

"Others?" Dynny asked hopefully.

"You mean others besides Mailu? Can other dead people besides Mailu be brought back to life?"

Dynny beamed and nodded. "Like Mama and Papa. And Arros."

Talag thought it was unlikely. Gelu had a reason for enclosing Mailu in an airtight box at the instant of her death. The reason probably had something to do with his plans to reanimate her. Probably whatever Gelu had in mind required the body to be fresh. Still, it pained him to grieve his friend. He wrinkled his nose and bit his lip. "I don't think so," he said hesitantly. "I think maybe Mailu is special. Different."

Dynny's face fell. Talag felt a surge of what he had to admit to himself was jealousy. Dynny'd had parents he could trust. And someone else as well, this Arros, whoever he was. His imagination conjured up righteous people who would never lie, would never kill anyone, people who would never try to destroy the world. Was it so much to ask?

"Dynny," Talag said, deliberately changing the subject. "Have seen any evidence that Mailu is going to have a baby?"

"A baby!" Dynny chortled. "Gelu said Mailu will have a baby. That's why they brought me. I'm excellent with babies!"

"What I meant was, have you seen her belly growing? Or any signs of life in there?"

"Gelu's bad, but he's smart. He knows about the baby." Dynny replied.

"So you haven't seen anything?" Talag pressed.

"A baby. A baby." Dynny grinned happily.

Something in Talag relaxed. He could trust Dynny. Even if the old man wasn't very smart, he wasn't evil either. He wasn't completely alone. Dynny wouldn't be much help. He couldn't help him come up with a plan for saving Gannoir from whatever destruction Kleibald had planned for it. But he wasn't Aunt Aythylla.

He wasn't going to desert a friend just because he wasn't useful. Dynny would help him, once he knew what was going on. Once Talag made him understand.

He wasn't alone. It was a comfort.

Chapter 19: Tass

"Dwoyra!" Tass projected the sound as far as she could through the water. Gill-speech was not as loud as lung-speech, but she was doing the best she could.

The voices in her head continued to haunt her, echoing the words she said to herself when she was at her worst. Worthless. Unlovable. Inferior.

Tass shivered. The water was ice cold, but her horror of the black things subsumed any physical discomfort.

"Dwoyra!"

Even the vauzigk was gone. The water was murky, but glancing upward, Tass could see that the black specks had settled on the dga again—fewer of them now. Tass's hand was bleeding from a cut she supposed she had received when she'd slammed into the Orbokth. She couldn't see the blood, only the faint glow in the water that told her that ymolenegth had been activated. She held her hand in front of her face, but she couldn't see well enough to discern more than that she wasn't bleeding profusely.

She reached forward and propelled her body through the

water, away from the army of dga and from Dwoyra's expectation that Tass would bleed and make everything all better.

The voices followed her.

Tass didn't know what to do. She felt like she was losing her mind. The voices weren't strictly audible in the sound-waves-and-eardrums sense. They went deeper than that. It was like they were plucking the cords that held her very soul together. Thrum! *Worthless.* Thrum! *Unlovable.* Thrum! *Daughter of evil.* She swam faster, trying to get away from everything. She had to go somewhere else. Anywhere else.

But there was nowhere to go.

Snap out of it, Tass, she ordered herself. *This is an attack. Go back to the Calix.*

Tass swam as fast as she could toward the Calix. She didn't care anymore that people would judge her for wasting her long weekend by staying at school. Everyone there was Mayim. They were water. Someone must have encountered these dark sludges before. Someone must know what to do about them. Not the students. The Master. She'd go to the Master. He was strict and remote, but he was also steadfast and knowledgeable.

Push through the water. Kick. Breathe.

Worthless. Unlovable. Evil.

No!

Faster. Swim. Kick. Breathe.

Inferior. Friendless.

The water became the royal blue of the surface. She was almost there.

When her head broke the surface, the voices grew dim. She could still hear them, but only as faint echoes in the distance. She sighed with relief. But it didn't do any good. Almost as soon as the water-voices faded, the airish voices took over, singing the same song in a different key.

Tass turned to the only weapon she had—the one she'd used since she'd been abandoned at the Calix by her mother when she was four. She closed her heart and most of her mind. She would not feel the pain. It was too much to bear, so she wouldn't do it. She felt her soul hardening within her, felt her grief for the loss of Igracio grow cold and smooth until it didn't hurt anymore. She was not nothing. She was extra. She had a power that most people didn't have. She was strong. Pain couldn't touch her.

With measured strokes, Tass swam back to the Calix and effortlessly tossed her body onto the clatry. Her hand was bleeding more now, but it didn't hurt. Even her shoulders, which had pained her constantly since her ordeal in the mine, were like nothing. She couldn't feel. She could only do.

Shaking the water out of her short hair, Tass wandered to the dormitory, went in, and collapsed on her bed.

She didn't know how much time had passed before someone knocked on the door. Without waiting for an answer, another girl entered.

Tass rolled over and sat up. "Ana? What are you doing in here?" She scowled.

"Master wants you," the younger girl reported. "There's someone here to see you. Your grandfather or something." Ana looked at her expectantly, pleased to have brought this news.

Tass shook her head. "I don't have a grandfather."

"I didn't say he was your grandfather. I just said he looked like he could be," Ana protested.

Tass smoothed her hair, which had dried in spikes, and stood.

"He's outside by the water," Ana told her. "Want me to show you?"

Tass was irritated. "I think I know where the water is."

Ana gave her a frightened, hurt look and fled. Tass walked slowly out the door of her tiny room and went down to the clatry. She could see the waxy, perfect body of the Master as he stood at the edge of the training pool talking to an old man wearing a voluminous tunic.

Xylo.

She should have known.

"Galan!" the Master barked.

Tass frowned. The Master's tone was no kinder than that of the voices that spun around her head in an endless din. She approached.

"Your friend has come," the Master informed her. Then he left.

Xylo reached out to Tass with both hands. "Tass!" he said.

Tass thought he seemed glad to see her.

"Hi, Xylo," she answered. "What's up?"

"I was in town meeting with the elders and thought I'd like to visit you while I was here," Xylo began.

"Did you want something?" Tass asked. It had been the voices who had suggested it, but she thought it was probably true.

Xylo sighed and then looked into her eyes searchingly. "Come back with me," he requested. "Come back to Garradh Gannoir."

"There's nothing for me in Garradh Gannoir," Tass retorted.

"I'd like you to come. I feel as though you're a daughter," Xylo told her.

"And we'd be a big happy family? You and me and Case and Ceres?"

"Yes."

Tass shook her head. "Why?"

"I told you why. You're like a daughter to me. And we have work for you there. We need someone of your particular skill set."

He's using you, the voices pressed in around her.

Tass's head was starting to ache. Maybe the voices weren't evil. Maybe they were just bent on relaying painful truths. "I'm not coming, Xylo. It wouldn't work."

"We need you, Tass. Please."

"The whole 'daughter' thing is just a manipulation," Tass snorted.

"No!"

"I'm not going to come to Garradh Gannoir and donate blood again. It was bad the first time. I'm never going to heal from these wounds." She gestured toward her scarred shoulders. "You think I want to come and risk my life again? It didn't do any good the first time. It won't do any good now. And this time, there won't be any Igracio to come to the rescue. You don't know what you're asking of me." Her eyes narrowed. "Or maybe you do." She felt a tingling in her fingertips, a sensation that meant they were beginning to glow. She balled her hands into fists to hide her un-Mayim-like disorder.

"There's darkness in the water, Tass. A strange new evil. Ceres has brought reports from the sea under the mine. Something slipped into Gannoir when the boulder shot out of it. The door slammed shut behind the boulder. The evil is trapped in Gannoir. Trapped in the water. Or maybe it's still coming in. Maybe there's still a hole in the Bec."

The din of voices buzzing around Tass vibrated with laughter. She pressed her lips together in exasperation. It wasn't just in the water. She could have told Xylo that much.

"And what am I supposed to do about it?" she asked.

"Just swim. That's all we want. No more blood. We're looking for another opening in the Bec layer. Some place that's still open to the chaos. A way for the dark evil to get in," Xylo told her.

"You have Ceres. You don't need me." Tass felt weary, aged.

"You're better than Ceres." Xylo laid the words before her like an offering, like a temptation.

"I am," Tass agreed.

"Please, Tass. Come."

She shook her head. "I'm done playing savior of the world." Her anger was dying away. She was purposely stuffing it down inside her where she put everything she didn't want to feel, everything she didn't want to master her. Her fingers started to feel normal, and she relaxed her hands.

Xylo's eyes strayed to her hands as she clenched and unclenched her fists. His gasp told her that he'd seen what she'd been able to hide from everyone until that moment. He looked from her fading, glowing fingertips up to her face. "Tass," he whispered. "Your fingers . . ."

"Just a birth defect," Tass snorted. "And it was so sweet of you to mention it."

"I'm sorry." Xylo stumbled over the words. "I didn't mean . . ."

"It's nothing," Tass insisted. She knew what Xylo was thinking. Igracio also had been a Mayim with glowing fingers. And it had been his blood, his abnormal, multi-casted blood that had given life to the molecules in the Bec layer and forced the Bilik, the hole that led to the chaos outside Gannoir, to close.

"But . . ."

Tass shook her head. "No, Xylo."

She turned, and with a quick sprint, ran to the edge of the clatry and dove into the sea.

Chapter 20: Xylo

The three days passed. Xylo stood before the council once again, waiting on their decision. Either they would believe him, or they would believe Kleibald. It was his youth repeating itself. He tried to read the answer in their expressions, but there was no clear consensus. Some of the faces were sad. Others looked angry. At him? At Kleibald? There was only one way to find out.

Arth was leading the meeting. He stood up, his smooth white hair giving him the look of a seasoned sage. He strode toward Xylo as the others watched from their seats in the tiered room.

"Xylo. I'm glad you returned."

"The three days have passed. What have you learned?" Xylo asked.

Arth sighed. "There is much we don't understand. There are aspects of this that are complicated and indicate something much more grave than the bald-faced 'destruction of the world' that you came here bellowing about."

Xylo waited.

"Frigo?" Arth called on the middle-aged elder.

Frigo stood, looking young and vigorous despite his gray hair. "Kleibald has done much for Luca," he began. "In the decades since Kleibald began to oversee our land, progress has been exponential. The clatries were barren latticeworks of stone floating on the water before Kleibald took over. It was through projects Kleibald spearheaded that the great cities rose, including the capital, Lucedth. The gleaming buildings, hospitals, feats of engineering, the enhancement of the ymolenegth, and the seawater purification plants that have allowed us to have pure water all day long . . . they are all due to Kleibald's vision. We do not believe that Kleibald would have knowingly set out to destroy all he had accomplished."

Xylo's expression hardened, but before he could speak, Frigo continued.

"Nonetheless, there are aspects of this thing that we do not understand. The inversion of the gogyvehr, according to every scientist we consulted, would surely have resulted in the demise of all life on Gannoir. There is no escaping that fact. Kleibald must have known the risk he was taking. And knowing this risk, we believe that Kleibald would have taken steps to protect Luca from destruction."

"But . . ." Xylo began.

Frigo held up a hand to silence Xylo. "We have uncovered what we think may have been part of this plan. May I introduce Ieska Thayl?"

A woman walked up from the wings of the council room. Not an elder, then. Xylo looked at her. She was about his age, with straight gray hair that extended as far as her body-length tala did. Her hair was tied with seaweed ribbons at six-inch intervals all the way down her back. Her eyes were black and intelligent. He knew her. She had been in school with him. She'd been one of the popular girls, with a stake in everything that happened. He hadn't liked her then, and he was prepared to dislike her now.

Recognition lit her face when she saw Xylo and he realized that finally someone in Luca knew who he was. As her hand flew involuntarily to smooth her hair, Xylo tried to hold back a knowing smile. Ieska always had to look pretty in front of the boys, he remembered. With an embarrassed twist of her lips, Ieska started to speak. "I was part of the research team in the early days of Kleibald's rule. Some of those who participated have since passed away, and other were unwilling to testify. But I thought it was important to bring the truth to light."

Xylo was interested. This was not the arrogant Ieska of his schooldays. This woman sounded old, wise, and humble.

"For a long time, Kleibald was obsessed with the idea of creating a person who wasn't either an Esh, a Gulot, or a Mayim, but all three. Someone who had gills and could endure the harsh chemicals of the sea like the Mayim. Someone who at the same time could bear the heat of the heights and had the tala to coast on the wind. Someone whose blood would be more powerful that the blood of anyone who had come before him. Kleibald isn't one for religion, but he's very knowledgeable about the ancient myths. He knew that the ancients believed there was a mystical power in their blood. He wanted to find out the truth behind the myth. Like our blood has the power to cause the ymolenegth to glow, the blood of the three-in-one, the blood of the triad would have powers that would seem almost supernatural to us. A man was selected. A Mayim. One of the . . ."

Xylo interrupted her. "You mean Kleibald actually sanctioned experiments on a living person? That's unconscionable!"

"The man—the subject of the experiments—was a thief and a liar. He had already bastardized his own soul. Kleibald figured it wouldn't make much difference if the scientists"—her face grew mottled with shame—"if we did the same to his body." She paused, overcome with emotion.

The murmuring among the elders of the council rose in a self-righteous, horrified din. Even though he couldn't hear any of their words distinctly, Xylo could feel the waves of disapproval washing toward Ieska, and his heart swelled with pity. She had been a victim of Kleibald as much as he had.

"Please continue," Arth encouraged her, motioning for the elders to still their voices.

"Kleibald thought that once we finished the genetic modifications and the transplant surgeries, that this man would have the power to . . . well, he said it would be the power to beget a new race of people for Gannoir. Supermen and superwomen. They would have powers far beyond those of the Mayim, the Gulot, and the Esh. His blood—their blood—would be able to produce ymolenegth light. He would be able to swim more swiftly than the fastest of the Mayim, and dive deeper. He would be able to endure missions to the Ghalon itself, to explore regions of Gannoir about which we have only been able to speculate. Maybe, he said, the man would even be able to fly. The tala would become more than just a means to glide down from the heights. It would become wings like those of a scolopendra."

Something of the excitement of Kleibald's vision shone from Ieska's black eyes. Xylo could see how much she wanted to know, to discover, to learn, and to create. What she and the others had done was wrong, but he understood it. Often he'd wondered why the Esh were not born with the ability to fly, only to drift downward, when his soul longed to reach for the heights.

"What happened?" Xylo asked.

Arth shot a glance at Xylo to remind him that he was not the one directing the council meeting. Xylo pressed his lips together and sighed.

Ieska shook her head. "We did our best. We worked with the man, making incremental adjustments to his blood, to his genetic code, and to his body. We also worked on his moral sense. As I said before he was a thief and a liar. The same qualities that had left him fit to be the object of our experiments also made him unfit to be the father of a new race. We wanted to install goodness in him along with the Esh and Gulot genes."

She paused to look around the room, receiving a few barely perceptible nods of approval and absorbing them as a balm for her guilt. Then she sighed. "It didn't work. He couldn't fly. His Esh-tala was never functional, not even for gliding. And the genetic modifications made it hard for him to breathe underwater. Instead of being the three-in-one, the triad, the superman, he became nothing. His blood did cause the ymolenegth to glow more brightly than the blood of an average person of Luca, but it was too small a compensation for all that we had put into the experiment. Just a tiny gleam of brighter blue light."

"And what of his moral sensibilities?" Arth asked, pressing her.

Ieska's face grew more sorrowful, and, Xylo thought, more beautiful in her grief. "I thought he understood. I thought he was growing and changing. Becoming a person with integrity. But he betrayed me. He betrayed us all." Her face seemed to crumble like the gritty, volcanic rock where the miners chipped away at the cliffs of the Orbokth. Xylo wondered what had happened to make her look like that. Surely not just a failure to turn a thief and a liar into something she could be proud of. It had to be more than that.

"Where is this man now," Art asked.

Ieska shook her head. "It's been over twenty years since I've seen him. Once Kleibald saw that the experiment had failed to make a Superman, he ordered him released. I . . . I never saw him again."

Xylo frowned. "What does this have to do with Kleibald trying to reverse the gogyvehr? Why bring this up now?"

Arth motioned for Ieska to sit down, and then he beckoned to a young blond man wearing a rich navy-blue tunic and cloak that billowed luxuriously around his Esh-tala. The man came to the front.

"Aradamas Aonta, you have something to tell us?"

The blond man grinned, and Xylo felt offended. What was there to look happy about?

"I do. A few years ago, Kleibald ordered a new scientific study to be done—one in conjunction with a thorough search of ancient literature in order to complete our knowledge of the triad. What we found in the literature and through the study was intriguing. It seemed possible that because of the genetic modifications, the object of the experiments might have been weakened, but his offspring, any children that he fathered, would be the beneficiaries of the changes that had been made by the first scientific study. This second generation would be the Supermen—or Superwomen—the ones Kleibald had hoped to create. Their blood would be able to perform miracles, as it were. Or so Kleibald came to believe. Although Kleibald never mentioned reversing the gogyvehr, he did drop hints— significant hints—that their blood would bring protection to the people of Luca. Supernatural protection. Looking back, knowing what we now know, it seems that this must have been what Kleibald had in mind. After the studies were complete, he commissioned me to head a committee of elders dedicated to discovering any offspring the man—this thief and liar—may have had."

Ieska leapt to her feet. "You found the man?" Her eyes were wide with some emotion Xylo couldn't interpret.

Aradamas shook his head. "No. As you know, the man was given a new identity when he was released. His new papers identified him as a Gulot named Methiant Migas. He was given an apartment in a high-rise on the Nepell clatry. Records show that he lived on Nepell for about a year. Then he disappeared."

Xylo was frustrated. "What does this have to do with anything? Kleibald must be brought to justice. By his actions he attempted the destruction of Gannoir and all who live on it. Now you've told us that he perpetrated further evils, upon this poor soul, this Methiant Migas, and you're asking me to believe that this mitigates the evil Kleibald sought to accomplish? Kleibald must be brought back! He must be . . ."

Arth stayed Xylo's tirade with a glare and an upraised palm. "Let him finish."

Aradamas wasn't grinning anymore. He shuffled his feet anxiously, glancing at Xylo as though the older man might attack him at any moment. "I'm sorry," he said, looking at Xylo. "I'm getting to the point, I promise." He turned to address the assembly at large. "Methiant Migas disappeared, but in the laboratory records we had genetic information. Theoretically, if he had children, we knew we should be able to find them, even if it required testing the blood of everyone on Luca."

Ieska inhaled heavily and deeply, and then exhaled. "Which you have the power to do because of Kleibald's program of blood collection." All the citizens of Luca were required to donate blood yearly in order to keep the light of the ymolenegth shining.

Aradamas nodded. "It would have been possible to search that way, but we didn't have to. During our search, we interviewed a doctor at the hospital on the Nepell clatry. Knowing how the experiments had rendered the would-be triad very unhealthy, we thought it likely that he had sought medical care near his new home. The doctor didn't remember treating anyone of Methiant Migas's description, but he had something else to tell us." The young blond man looked around the room nervously. "A woman had come to him for help—a colleague, a nurse who worked at the hospital with him. She had been"—Aradamas gulped uneasily—"raped. By a man who fit the description of Methiant Migas. She came to her friend, this doctor, to be treated a chronic condition caused by the assault, but she insisted she didn't want to file a report with the police. She just wanted to get relief from her pain and then forget the whole thing happened. The doctor, wanting to protect his friend from further grief, did as she asked. The rape was never reported. The nurse soon transferred to another hospital on another clatry, and he never saw her again. He never looked for her. He didn't want to increase her pain. He said he thought it was best to let her have the fresh start she was obviously seeking. We were the first people he ever told."

Xylo felt his blood rushing through his veins. His fingers began to glow. The pieces of the story began to come together in his mind. What he'd known before . . . what he'd just been told . . . He knew how the story ended. He hid his fingertips in the folds of his tunic, not wanting the others to see his agitation. Kleibald. This was another person who had been destroyed by Kleibald. He knew this woman. He'd known of her before he met her. He had sought her out. He had taken her with him. He had unwittingly brought about her destruction.

He forced himself to turn his attention back to Aradamas. ". . . and we traced the woman. Her name was Bracha Elisus."

Chapter 21: Talag

Talag had been thinking. He'd been desperately trying to find a way to make things right again, to make his grandfather stop planning to destroy Gannoir. Dynny would be on his side, he knew that, but Dynny didn't have the brainpower to think of a plan. Neither do I, Talag thought ruefully.

After he went to bed that night, he had lain awake until the others in his room were asleep, the other nine people in the quintuple bunks on either side of the tiny bedroom. There was one part about his grandfather's plans that scared him more than anything, more than the notion that his grandfather, and possibly his entire family, was evil. It was the thing about spirits. What was it his grandfather had said? The spirits wanted to destroy Gannoir, but they couldn't do it alone. They needed . . . whom? His grandfather? Everyone in the skyboulder? Or just someone from Gannoir? And that after the destruction was complete, the spirits would give them a new world to populate.

Spirits.

Who were the spirits? Talag had been schooled as an Esh. He'd heard about spirits in the ancient mythology, but he'd been taught that the spirits were fictions, beings created to explain natural phenomena like the rotation of the Ghalon and the glowing of the ymolenegth. Things like that. They weren't real. There wasn't any god in the Ghalon, some mysterious being called Tel-Maor who created Gannoir and lived in the fire above them. So what was his grandfather talking about? Kleibald clearly believed the spirits were real.

Maybe his teachers and his grandfather were right. Maybe the ancients had stories about made-up gods and spirits, but his grandfather had found real ones. It didn't scare him any less that way, but it made the whole idea easier to stomach. Even if his grandfather was a bad man, his teachers hadn't knowingly taught him untruths. They couldn't all be liars. It wasn't possible.

Something, though, was in the chaos outside the skyboulder. And somehow that something was communicating with his grandfather, and with his grandfather alone. Why? How? Why weren't they talking to Gelu too? It seemed that Gelu had almost as much authority as his grandfather. Kleibald ruled Luca. Gelu was the leader of Garradh Gannoir on the other side of the Orbokth. Gelu, it seemed, believed there was something magical about the dead girl. What had he called her? Talag shook his head. He couldn't remember. Only that Gelu expected her children to have some sort of powers that ordinary people didn't have.

A gentle nudge from a corner of his brain turned Talag's thoughts to a different aspect of the issue. Gelu and his grandfather had fought. His grandfather had threatened Gelu in order to force him to go along with his plans for the destruction of Gannoir. Could that be a weak point in their alliance? He certainly wouldn't continue being friends with someone who threatened to kill him if he didn't do what he wanted. Maybe he could talk to Gelu . . . could convince him to . . .

Instantly he rejected the thought. Gelu was a bad man, just like his grandfather. Dynny had said as much, and he trusted Dynny. And if he made an alliance with a bad man, then he would be bad too, right? He could try to trick Gelu into turning on Kleibald. That might work. But what if Gelu told his grandfather what he was doing? Mightn't his grandfather's unholy wrath land on his head instead of on Gelu's? After what he'd heard, Talag didn't believe his grandfather would shirk at the notion of destroying him just because they were related.

Talag shuddered. He didn't know what to do. Quietly, he climbed down from the top bunk, trying not to disturb any of the others in the room. Uncle Nadim rolled over and snorted as Talag passed his bed. Talag paused, but continued his climb once he heard his uncle's snoring resume. He tiptoed out of the room.

Chapter 22: Tass

Tass pushed her body through the water, trying to outrun the voices that whistled around her ears. *Your only value is in your blood . . . You're like a vauzigk—useful for meat and that's all . . . No one loves you . . . Everyone wants to use you . . .*

She felt the truth of it. Even Xylo, one of the better people she'd ever known, wanted to use her. She strove against the water more energetically, as if she could push away her thoughts along with the liquids of the acrid sea.

The voices were undeterred. Their murmurings turned into shriekings that reverberated through Tass's entire being. There was no way to escape. She felt her soul giving in. The voices were telling the truth. She was worthless and unlovable. She was just a container for her blood. Dwoyra wanted her blood. Xylo wanted her diving skills— and probably her blood too. At the Calix, the Master wanted the glory that would come from training a talented Mayim.

At least they want you, the voices taunted her. *Your mother . . .*

"Shut up!" Tass screamed through her gills.

She propelled herself down as far as she could dive. She wasn't sure where she was going—just "away." The underside of the Orbokth passed over her head, and she looked up to see silvery dga lining the rock, their sides still mottled with the blotches of darkness. The voices around her resounded like bells, laughing at her, laughing with the black blotches and the voices. Tass felt her soul crumbling within herself, shattering into pieces too small to be worthy of a name. She was nothing, just like they said.

Watery arms embraced her and tugged her into the depths, far below the ceiling of glittering dga.

"Stop it, Dwoyra," Tass moaned. "I just want to be left alone."

"Come," Dwoyra's voice rushed through Tass's gills. "Come."

The voices were dimmer now, as though Dwoyra cushioned the water around her and muffled the sounds. Tass drew in her breath slowly and tried to gain a foothold in her mind. What was true? Was she really everything the voices said? Was there nothing to look forward to in life? Success, glory, winning . . . they had always been important to her. The hunt for them defined her.

Safe in Dwoyra's arms, Tass knew the truth. Success was a fleeting thing. She would own it for a second and then be forced to cede it to someone else. Glory was the same way. She knew what had changed her way of seeing. It wasn't just her near-death experience at the mine. It wasn't her loss of prowess due to her injuries. It wasn't the death of her mother.

It was Igracio.

He'd been her friend.

Her only friend, ever.

With his friendship she'd had something far superior to success, glory, and winning. She could never look at those things as ultimate again.

And now Igracio was gone.

She had nothing.

The bitter water of the sea seemed to seep into her soul, shriveling it up until all that was left was a crusted, wrinkled nut of matter, worthless and dry.

"Tass . . ." Dwoyra squeezed around her.

Tass was exhausted. "I can't do it. I can't bleed anymore. I'm done, Dwoyra. I'm done." She wasn't sure how much of what she'd said Dwoyra was able to understand. Gill-speech wasn't something she was particularly adept at.

The watery arms released her sadly. Dwoyra was gone.

Tass let herself float in the yellowish water of the depths, unsure what direction to take. She could go back to Igracio's house. Or to the Calix. She rejected both ideas. Being with Igracio's parents was too painful, too confusing. And the Calix held no fascination for her now. Besides, if she went to the Calix, Xylo would come back, asking again and again that she come to Garradh Gannoir and help him . . . help him and Case and Ceres . . .

Your mother hated you . . . the voices poured into her gills. *You're nothing. You're no one. You don't even have a name . . .*

Tass could feel her skin contracting in the icy water, striving to protect her from the cold.

No one loves you. Your mother didn't love you. Your father didn't love you. All they want is your blood . . . just your blood . . .

Tass, with a monumental effort, hardened her mind to the voices. "Igracio loved me," she said, spitting the last word out through her lips instead of her gills. A cluster of bubbles rose from her mouth and seemed to be laughing with the same flickering light as the dga she could no longer see.

Igracio's dead. You have no one. He's the only one who ever loved you and he's dead . . .

Tass curled her body into a ball, partly as a defense against the cold, and partly to try to block out the voices. It wasn't working.

No one loves you . . . The voices were nearly singing now.

An image popped into Tass's head. Someone cuddling her and telling her stories, brushing her long hair.

Someone had loved her once upon a time. It wasn't her mother. She had no warm, fuzzy memories of Afa. She knew who it had been . . . Sister. Her older sister. She had taken care of Tass from the time she'd been born. She hadn't seen her sister since her mother had abandoned her to her training at the Calix. Upon finding she had a Mayim child, Afa had changed Tass's name from Talassa, the blue sea, to Katurima, one who has wet herself.

Sister.

Mailu.

Tass suddenly knew what she had to do.

Chapter 23: Xylo

Aradamas continued speaking. "The committee decided to find out if Bracha Elisus became a mother at any point in her life. If children of the triad existed, we intended to find them." He paused to look around the room.

Xylo looked too, gauging the reactions of the elders. Most of the faces were stony and blank, not giving anything away. Some of the elders had to know what had happened. Some of them must have been privy to the "scientific mission" that had taken Case, Mailu, and Ceres to Garradh Gannoir. He couldn't see it in their eyes. Maybe Kleibald had chosen to take his conspirators with him into the skyboulder. Maybe all those in the council room were innocent of the plot to murder the three innocent young people. Or maybe some were corrupt enough to hide the truth behind a mask of ignorance. Xylo pressed his lips together and waited to see what Aradamas would say next.

"Records show that Bracha Elisus became a mother only one time—and no marriage registration could be found for either Bracha Elisus or Afa Elisus, which is the name she legally assumed eight years ago. This child, Mailu Elisus Harreg, was born twenty-three years ago. No trace of her has been seen in Luca in the past three years. But we were able to find some details about her life before that time. Her friends from school remember her fondly but were unable to confirm that she was anything other than a Gulot. But the absence of a father in her birth listing as well as the lack of any marriage records for her mother would seem to confirm that she is the one. She is the daughter of the triad."

The elders were silent for a moment, and then noise erupted throughout the room. Xylo listened, trying to pick any distinct comments out of the din. He heard words like "superwoman" and "protect Gannoir" and "genius." He felt sick. The information Aradamas had provided was making Kleibald into a hero instead of a villain. Was it possible it was true? Was his own perspective skewed because of what had happened to Dochym . . . and because of his bitterness over the loss of his wife and children to Kleibald? Was it possible that Kleibald had changed? Had he misinterpreted everything that had happened?

He came to his senses quickly. Kleibald and Gelu had ordered a blood sacrifice—the lives of his son Case and the others. If Kleibald had been counting on Mailu to save Gannoir, he would have been forced to come up with a new plan when she had died. Instead, he and Gelu had simply loaded the girl's coffin into the skyboulder. Mailu was dead. She wasn't going to save Gannoir.

Xylo stood up, raising both arms above his head. His wrinkled tala flapped against the sleeves of his tunic. No one was paying attention. He tapped Arth on the shoulder and whispered something in his ear. Arth passed the message to Aradamas, and together, the three quieted the crowd.

Arth and Aradamas sat, ceding the floor to Xylo.

Xylo surveyed the room. There were no blank faces now. He saw anger—directed toward himself—as well as indignation on behalf of the reputation of Kleibald. He would have to be careful. Reason wasn't going to sway the elders to his cause. Their faith in Kleibald was too strong. They were still too much under his power. He was going to have to use his wits.

"Friends," he began slowly, trying to gauge the level of hostility around him, "I have seen this Mailu. Recently." He waited until the whispering died down again. "It may be as you say, that Kleibald intended her to be a protection for Luca, for all Gannoir even. It may be that she is the daughter of the triad. It may be that she will be the mother of a new and better Gannoir."

He could feel the tide of emotion turning in his favor. He was saying what they wanted to hear, and they were warming to his tale.

"I have seen this Mailu," he repeated. "And I know where she is now." He let the words hang in the air and watched their impact on the elders. Hope was born anew in many. Disgust roiled through him as he forced himself to keep playing the game that would eventually bring justice to Kleibald. He knew he couldn't tell the elders that Mailu was dead. They would find that out as soon as they brought the skyboulder back inside Gannoir. By then it would be too late. They would have to question Kleibald about his intentions, about his plans for Gannoir.

"She is with Kleibald on the skyboulder!" he proclaimed.

Voices rang out immediately.

"Mailu! The triad!"

"On the skyboulder!"

"Bring them home!"

"Kleibald the Reformer . . . now Kleibald the Magnificent!" an awed voice added to the din.

Xylo cringed. The important thing was that they commit the resources to bring the skyboulder back. Somehow before it reentered Gannoir he would make them understand what had really happened.

He sat down and waited while Aradamas and Arth addressed the crowd. Money and resources were quickly allotted toward bringing the skyboulder back. Scientists were given new assignments—emergency assignments—to discern the best way for Gannoir to redeem the chunk of itself that had broken free without causing the implosion of their world. A supply of blood was allotted to be taken to Garradh Gannoir to light the depths of the mine so they could examine the icy Bec layer in detail. Metal, fibers, boats, soil, food—all of it apportioned with the priority of bringing the skyboulder back.

And all it had taken was lies, Xylo thought ruefully.

Lies.

Xylo was old enough to know that even though he hadn't said anything untrue, he had nonetheless set out with the intention to deceive. And he had succeeded. He had gotten what he wanted.

Kleibald would be coming back. Gelu too. Eventual justice was not a certainty, but he would work on that.

Mailu would be coming back. He owed Afa that much, at least.

And his son, his daughter, and the two grandchildren he hadn't known existed would be coming back as well. He hadn't wanted to admit to himself how much he longed to know them. It was likely that they, too, would reject him in favor of Kleibald, just as his ex-wife Ardanach and his children had done. But at least they would live.

As he went back to his daughter Yasamina's apartment in Lucedth after the meeting, Xylo reflected on everything he had learned. The triad. The child of Afa and the rapist. He sighed. It was possible that Mailu was not the daughter of Methiant Migas. Just because Afa had been raped didn't mean that a child had been born of the illicit union. She could have been born of an affair or of an unregistered marriage. After all, she had a last name, Harreg, that didn't come from her mother.

Then Xylo thought about the thing he hadn't mentioned to the elders. He knew something they did not. Afa Elisus had not one child, but two. Mailu and Tass. Who was Tass's father? She called herself Talassa Galan, but no birth record existed, and no marriage records to anyone, much less a man with the last name Galan, were found for Afa. Kleibald had staked the success of his mission to reverse the gogyvehr on the notion that Mailu was the superwomen, the second-generation triad being. He didn't know about Tass.

An image of Tass, her fingers glowing dimly as she clutched them in her fists, rose up in Xylo's mind. He gasped as the realization dawned on him.

Mayim don't glow.

But Tass did.

An ache of fear passed through him like a shudder. If Kleibald found out… if the elders found out that Tass glowed . . .

He clenched his teeth. He wouldn't tell them. He would protect Tass. After all, it was possible that she wasn't the daughter of Methiant Migas. It was possible that some random genetic quirk had left the child with the rare trait of glowing fingers. But he didn't think so. It was one coincidence too many.

Tass was the one.

Tass was the triad.

He was sure.

Chapter 24: Talag

"Dynny!" Talag whispered urgently, his hand on the shoulder of his snoring friend. "Dynny! It's me!"

Dynny smiled in his sleep and pulled his single blanket closer around him.

Talag shook the elderly man. "Dynny! Please wake up. I want to talk to you."

Dynny rolled over and opened his eyes. After a gasp of surprise, he grinned at Talag. "Hi, friend."

"Hi, Dynny," Talag said. His fondness for the elderly disabled man had grown exponentially since he had decided that Dynny was the only person he could trust on the skyboulder. He felt a rush of relief at seeing Dynny's pleasure in his presence.

Dynny sat up. "What's going on?"

Talag sat down on the floor of the chamber and leaned his back against Mailu's stone coffin. "What are spirits?" he asked.

Dynny looked confused.

"My grandfather was talking about spirits. He said if Gannoir is destroyed, the spirits will give us a new world to inhabit. What are spirits?"

A knowing look came into Dynny's face, accompanied by a childlike pride. "I know this one!" he chortled. "Arros taught me." He began to recite his knowledge in a singsong voice. "Tel-Maor is a knowing spirit, body has he not. The Orbokth is all body with no spirit and no love. People have knowing inside the bodies theirs. Animals have spirit but their body reigns supreme. Sleeping spirits light the vegetable ones."

Talag tried to digest this. Was it a nursery rhyme? A piece of ancient wisdom? It seemed obvious that he wasn't just a body. He was alive inside his body, doing un-body-ish things like thinking and feeling. Plants were alive just like he was, but their souls didn't know . . . didn't think and love. Animals were somewhere in-between. And the Orbokth . . . the Orbokth wasn't alive. It was all body. Tel-Maor, who the ancients believed created Gannoir, was all spirit and no body. It would explain their belief that he could live in the fiery Ghalon, he reflected.

But none of it answered his question.

"I don't think that's what grandfather means," he hedged. "He's talking about spirits who can destroy Gannoir and give us a new world. Spirits out there in the chaos. Not Tel-Maor. Others."

Dynny's face took on a wary look. "Bad ones out in the chaos. Tel-Maor wouldn't like it. That's why he made Gannoir the way he did."

"What way?"

"The gogyvehr," Dynny explained carefully. "He made a wall so the bad ones couldn't get inside Gannoir."

"That's an old myth," Talag said. "No one knows exactly why the gogyvehr happened, but they think maybe there was some sort of explosion or maybe a collision with an object nearly as large as Gannoir. That's why a third of the Ghalon is dark. It either used up all its energy in the explosion or it was damaged in the collision. We learned about it at school."

Dynny shook his head. "That's not what Arros taught me. Arros said Tel-Maor didn't want the bad ones to get us, so he turned Gannoir inside-out. He was protecting us."

"No one believes that anymore," Talag said shakily, very afraid that what Dynny was saying might be literally true.

"Everyone believes that." Dynny gazed at him, perplexed.

"Evil spirits are floating around in the chaos around Gannoir?" Talag tried the theory on experimentally.

Dynny nodded. "The spirits in the chaos are bad. Everybody knows that."

"Not in Luca," Talag noted.

"Kleibald believes it," Dynny pointed out, astute for once.

Talag pondered for a moment. "Yeah," he admitted. "I guess he does. And he's talking to them. Or he thinks he is."

"What should we do?" Dynny asked, looking at Talag trustfully.

Talag bit his lip. "I don't know. Stop them somehow. I heard them. They want to destroy Gannoir. We could never go home again. And everybody in Luca would die."

"And in Obumbro," Dynny added, naming his hometown within the larger area of Garradh Gannoir.

Talag banged his head against Mailu's stone coffin as though he hoped the action would knock some ideas into his brain.

Dynny patted him on the shoulder.

"We need to know more," Talag said finally. "How are they going to destroy Gannoir? How is grandfather talking to the evil spirits, if they really exist? And how, how, how can we get back home?"

Chapter 25: Tass

Tass needed help. She knew that. Wherever the passageway between Luca and Garradh Gannoir was, she knew it had to be in the deepest part of the sea, closest to the icy Bec layer. She would need protection from the cold as well as guidance if she was going to find the route. There was only one being she could ask. The person who had brought her to Garradh Gannoir the first time.

"Dwoyra!" she called, making the farthest-reaching sound she possibly could with her yet-untrained gill-voice. "Dwoyra!"

Fish swirled around her, drawn to the unusual sound. Tass pushed herself slowly through the lemon-yellow sea. The chemicals at that layer were caustic. Anyone but a Mayim would have been burned beyond saving. But the waxy coating of the skin of the Mayim made such a dive a pleasure. It felt good, like scratching an itch that covered her entire body.

The current pulled her along as she swam. She didn't often take note of the currents of the sea, mostly because she was so accustomed to them. It was one of the reasons Gannoir could continue to exist with fire at its core and ice on the exterior. The continual rotation of both the Ghalon and the Bec created a current in the water—not just of wave-like motion but of electromagnetic power—that generated a sort of force field that kept the ice from crashing into the Ghalon and extinguishing its light. Igracio had tried to explain it to her, but his own feeble grasp of the concepts involved had made it difficult for him to make clear and for her to understand. But she knew the current was more than just "the way the sea was." It was important.

A school of tiny silver fish took refuge beside her. She was, in a sense, blocking the wind and creating an artificial harbor for them. She wondered if the current was blowing into Luca from Garradh Gannoir or the other way around. If it flowed toward Garradh Gannoir then all she had to do was let it carry her away. On the other hand, if it was flowing from Garradh Gannoir into Luca, then she ought to be swimming upstream. She tried to orient herself, to remember how they had come back to Luca after everything that had happened on the other side of the Orbokth, but a journey over land is not the same as one under the water. Everything was so different, so incredibly different.

A lumalaua circled her. It was longer than she, and she marveled at its beauty. Its head was magenta and its tail end, yellow. The gradient between the two colors was resplendent with color. Phosphorescent appendages swirled around the creature, each ending in an air bladder that glowed in the water. The only part of lumalauae that Tass didn't like was their faces. A ring of orb-like, beady eyes surrounded an "X" of a mouth. It was not like a face at all. It was creepy.

Warmth settled on Tass as the lumalaua swam in circles around her. The lumalauae had done this for her before—protected her from the icy cold in the depths of the sea. If the creature stayed with her, she would be able to take her time looking for the passageway to the other side of the Orbokth.

She had something to strive for now. Mailu, her sister, her sister who had loved her, was on the skyboulder. Dead, to be sure, but someone had said something about Gelu wanting to bring her back to life. About Gelu thinking such a thing was possible. Maybe it had already happened. No one knew anything about the repercussions of leaving Gannoir, of entering the chaos. Maybe they were all dead. Maybe Gelu's faulty plan had been a fatal one. But maybe it had been the opposite.

She had to find out.

If there was any chance of bringing her sister back, she had to fight for it.

Fighting felt good.

She'd always fought, ever since she'd been abandoned to the care of the Master and the other teachers at the Calix. She'd fought to be the best. She'd fought to have a name she didn't have to hate. She'd fought with everyone.

But this was worth fighting for.

She had Igracio to thank for the fact that she knew that now.

The voices were silent now, and Tass was grateful. She wasn't sure if Dwoyra had driven them away or if they couldn't swim this close to the Bec—the water was orange now—or if they were strategically biding their time for another attack.

She swam lower.

When she was low enough that the water was a bright fuchsia, Tass paused to look around. There were no walls here. No passageways. She thought of the Orbokth high above her head, covered on its underside with tiny menacing dga.

Maybe there was no passageway. No tunnel.

Maybe it was all tunnel.

A big open sea with the Orbokth floating on top. All she had to do to get to Garradh Gannoir was swim in liquid so cold it was almost gelatinous. All she had to do was keep the lumalaua with her for warmth. All she had to do was swim there.

In the right direction.

Drawing a large amount of purple liquid through her gills, Tass hollered with all her might. "Dwoyra!"

It hadn't hurt as badly as she'd thought it would. The water wasn't as cold as it should have been. She was grateful for the warming presence of the feathery sea creature, but she wondered if her shouts had gone outside of the perimeter established by the lumalaua's circles.

"Dwoyra," she breathed softly.

A minute later she had her answer. A warm liquid rushed into the bubble created by the lumalaua and held Tass so close it was like she was wearing it.

"Dwoyra!" she exclaimed. "Please . . . I need to get to Garradh Gannoir."

A rush of questioning goo rushed through Tass's gills.

"I'm not going to bleed," Tass reminded the watery creature. "But I'm going to go look. I'm going to see."

She did not tell Dwoyra that she was going to see about opening the Bilik, reversing the healing that Igracio's death had bought.

Dwoyra would not have approved.

Chapter 26: Xylo

Xylo was exhausted. He had spent the morning consulting with the elders and a few of the top scientists of Luca, trying to figure out exactly how to open a portal large enough to admit the skyboulder without causing catastrophic damage to Gannoir.

The skyboulder had left Gannoir, the elders had pointed out. Bringing it back should be no more destructive than its expulsion had been. Xylo disagreed. The skyboulder had left under unusual circumstances. There had been other factors involved. Supernatural factors. The cyclone of wind and water that had risen to the Ghalon . . . the power of electricity flowing through the eye of the storm from the Ghalon, down into the depths of the sea. It was not something he thought they could replicate. It was not something he ever wanted to see again.

"Kleibald must have had a plan for coming back," Arth pointed out logically. "He built a ship to carry him outside Gannoir. He had to have thought about the best way to return."

"We could just wait for them to come back," Aradamas suggested. "There's no use sending all these resources to make something happen that's going to happen anyhow if we can only be patient."

Dallasha shook her gray head slowly. "If they could get back, they would have been back by now. You heard the scientists' evaluation—size of the skyboulder, the number of people estimated to be onboard. They won't make it much longer. We need to intervene to save them. Otherwise, they'll die."

Xylo didn't want to say what he was thinking. Kleibald had no plan to return. Kleibald had expected Gannoir to implode. He'd expected to reverse the gogyvehr. If he'd thought of returning to Gannoir at all it would have been to a very different Gannoir—an uninhabited one. Reversing the gogyvehr would have killed all life, including plants, algae, and fish. There would be no food. Not for generations. Kleibald's plan could not have been focused on continuing his life on Gannoir. He must have had some other destination in mind. But what? It was impossible. No one knew anything of Gannoir beyond its outer limit—beyond the Bec. Maybe, he thought, Kleibald had found something in the writings of the ancients . . . some knowledge that had lived through the gogyvehr and had been passed down for generations . . . knowledge about other worlds . . . inhabitable worlds . . .

But to say so would be to infer that Kleibald had intended evil. The elders weren't ready to accept that yet. He would have to keep playing along.

"I agree with Dallasha," he said heavily, sadly. "We have to rescue them."

Tsakali tossed his dark head and snorted. "I thought we were supposed to punish them." He looked at Xylo with a challenge in his eyes.

"Punish . . . reward . . . These things are secondary when lives are at stake," Xylo said sternly. "And there are more people than just Kleibald on the skyboulder. Some of them, it is likely, are innocent."

"But how do we do it?" Frigo chimed in looking worried. "Is it even possible?"

Xylo didn't have an answer for that. It seemed no one did.

"We'll call all the scientists to a consortium to be held in the morning two days from now," Arth decided. "That will give the ones who live in the farthest reaches of Luca time to cross the sea in the night. We need all the minds of Luca to come together to figure out what to do."

***

Xylo leaned against the metal wall of the restaurant. It felt cool and soothing to his fuddled mind. He wasn't sure what he'd expected. Utter ignorance of how to proceed wasn't it. These were the elders, the leaders of Luca. If Kleibald had figured out how to leave Gannoir, then surely those who had been trained at the same schools as Kleibald could figure out how to bring the skyboulder back. He'd been away for too long. He'd forgotten how the Esh-maor were regular people just like he was.

He closed his eyes, trying to decide whether to put his energies toward profound thought, or toward blocking out the same.

The sound of someone sliding into the booth across from him pulled him out of his reverie. He opened his eyes.

Ieska smiled at him. "Someone told me you were here, Adam."

Xylo smiled back. "No one has called me Adam in years. Not since I left the council of elders."

"You'd rather I called you Xylo?" Ieska asked.

Xylo nodded. "I'd rather not remind any of the others of my identity. You're the only one who recognized me."

"The only one willing to admit it," Ieska retorted lightly. She brushed a strand of hair out of her face and motioned for a waiter. After she'd ordered tea, she turned back to Xylo. "What happened at the meeting?"

Xylo hesitated before answering, wondering whether he should give Ieska the sanitized version of the council meeting, or if he ought to tell her his true thoughts. She wasn't an elder . . . she had that much going for her. But she was Esh-maor and had been working actively with the elders.

"They've agreed to attempt a rescue," he told her. "You probably know most of it already. You were part of the experiments. You know what they think Mailu is. Since I was able to confirm that she was on the skyboulder, they're doubly anxious to bring it back."

Ieska smiled wryly. "The triad. The three-in-one. It didn't happen for Methiant Migas, but that doesn't mean it won't happen for one of his children." She winced as she said it, as though the idea wounded her.

"Are you sorry you were part of that?" Xylo asked.

Conflicting emotions played across Ieska's face. Xylo wondered that she could have any gladness about such an immoral experiment. He fought to keep his expression neutral.

"It should never have happened," Ieska said finally. "Even if the experiment had been a success, it was wrong to experiment on a criminal without his permission. Even if it had produced great good for Gannoir. We can't progress at the expense of our collective soul." She looked at Xylo as if daring him to object.

She was beautiful. Xylo nodded. "I agree. Kleibald had done much in the name of progress that was morally dubious." It was a mild statement coming from him and considering all that had happened. "To destroy a man, body and soul . . ."

Ieska looked at him sharply. "The man was a criminal. His soul was already filthy dirty."

Xylo flinched from the bitterness in her voice. "You're angry?" he guessed.

The waiter brought the cup of tea and set it before Ieska. She curled her hands around it and looked down at the pale liquid. "I wonder how much I can trust you," she said, lifting her eyes on the last word to look directly at Xylo.

"You know something."

Ieska bit her lip.

"I didn't come here to hurt you, Ieska," Xylo reassured her. "I came here for justice. I want Kleibald to pay for the things he's done. Any help you can give me . . ."

Brushing a tear out of the corner of her eye, Ieska tried to smile. "When the time is right, I'll tell you. For now"—she tried to smile—"let's talk of other things."

Xylo sighed but tried to make it sound like he wasn't frustrated. "What things?"

"How have you been since you left the elders?" Ieska asked. "What has life brought to you?"

Xylo longed to tell her about Dochym's murder, about Case and Mailu and the blood sacrifice, about Igracio's death, but he, like Ieska, was low on trust. "You probably know Ardanach and I split up," he said, trying not to sound bitter. "The kids stayed with her, and I was . . . free. I found a job mining soil on the heights of the Orbokth. My second wife was Esh-qadar. I worked for her father, and after he died, I ran the family mining business."

"Did you have children?" Ieska asked with genuine interest.

Xylo nodded. "Two, a boy and a girl."

"What are they doing now?"

"Yasamina's married and works at the university in Lucedth. Case is living with me in Garradh Gannoir and is engaged to a lovely Mayim girl."

"They're both Esh?" Ieska asked.

"No. Case is Esh-maor, but Yasamina is Gulot. Her husband, Dano, is Esh-maor. He's not on the council though. Not yet."

Ieska's eyes lit up. "Yasamina Sapor Xalantaka? With her being in research and me being a scientist, our paths have crossed. I don't know her well, but she seems like a lovely person. I should have connected the last name to you."

Xylo shrugged. "No reason you would have. She wasn't born the last time you saw me. And there are other families with the same last name."

"Do you have grandchildren?" Ieska asked.

A wrenching pain shot through Xylo's heart. His grandchildren, whose existence he had just discovered, were on the skyboulder. It wasn't information he was ready to share. "Case and Yasamina have no children yet."

"You and Ardanach had children . . ." Ieska pressed.

"We're estranged," Xylo said softly but abruptly.

"I'm sorry."

"Me too."

They sat in silence for some moments, drinking their tea. Finally, Xylo spoke. "What about you?" he asked. "Did you marry? Any children?"

Again, Xylo could see the conflict in her face. It was a straightforward question. He laughed ruefully to himself. He hadn't exactly been forthright with Ieska. Maybe she'd seen the same range of emotion enter his expression that he was now seeing on her face. He wondered what her secrets were.

Ieska stroked her long ponytail with one hand, twining her fingers in her hair. "I never married. I'm devoted to science."

She was telling the truth, Xylo was sure. "Children?" he asked.

Ieska swatted at him playfully. "I just told you I never married." Her black eyes were as hard and cold as marbles.

Xylo let it go. She had at least one child. He felt sure of that much. But pressing the issue would not result in knowledge, only in a broken relationship. If he wanted to keep seeing her . . .

His mind exploded with surprise. Keep seeing her? What was he thinking? He was in Luca for a brief time for a specific purpose. There was no room in his life for an Esh-woman who had a vibrant career in the city. He was going back to Garradh Gannoir, going back to serving as the temporary Dynroc.

"What are you thinking about?" Ieska asked.

"You want to go for a walk?" Xylo blurted. "We could go up to one of the rooftop viewing points. I haven't done that in a long time . . ." He let his words trail off, flushing.

Ieska smiled. "Yeah. I'd like that," she returned shyly.

Xylo felt an uncomfortable smattering of glee burst in his mind. "Let's go then."

Chapter 27: Talag

Talag and Dynny had settled themselves against a wall of the skyboulder with their breakfasts. They sat as near to Kleibald as they could without appearing to be eavesdropping.

Kleibald was sitting with Ardanach and Aythylla. They had finished eating and were conversing softly. Kleibald was perched uncomfortably on a stump of rock jutting from the side of the rocky boulder. Ardanach leaned against the curved wall. Aythylla sat cross-legged on the floor, her arms wrapped around her knees so that her tala enveloped the whole of her. She looked tired.

Talag held a finger to his lips to remind Dynny to be quiet.

Dynny winked back.

"... can't believe this," Aunt Aythylla was saying. "You brought us here to die. We'll starve. We'll asphyxiate. We'll ... we'll ..."

"We'll end up killing each other if we don't get somewhere sometime soon," Ardanach finished dryly. "What on earth were you thinking?" she growled at her husband.

Kleibald gave her a stony stare. "I was thinking about leaving a dying world. I didn't bring us here to die. I brought us here to live. To start a new world."

"What was wrong with the old one?" Aythylla complained.

"Gannoir is dying," Kleibald began.

"Not fast enough," Ardanach snapped. "You miscalculated. We probably could have lived out our lives in comfort on Gannoir. It may not die for thousands of years. What are we doing up here in the sky?"

"The spirits . . ." Kleibald stuttered.

"I don't care about your invisible friends," Ardanach shrieked. "What are you doing to get us back home?"

Kleibald pushed himself to his feet with the agility of a much younger man. "I don't owe you an explanation."

"You owe me a world to live on!" Ardanach groused to his retreating form.

Talag nudged Dynny. They exchanged a glance. It seemed that Kleibald was the only member of the family who could talk to the spirits, whatever they were.

"Should we follow him?" Dynny whispered loudly.

Talag shook his head. "Eat your food," he hissed in reply. "It'll look suspicious if we follow right on his heels. Once we're done eating, we'll find him again."

Dynny nodded and took a bite of the dried meat and pellig-flour cracker he held in his hands. Talag glanced at his grandmother and aunt, who had shifted their complaints from grousing directed toward Kleibald to a quiet and disgruntled conversation of which Talag could not hear a word. *At least they aren't looking at us,* he thought with relief. He put the last bit of cracker into his mouth and washed it down with the rest of the water in his cup. Then he pushed himself to his feet and stretched. Dynny brushed the crumbs off his tunic and rose also.

In the next room, Kleibald and Gelu were talking. They both looked up as Talag and Dynny entered the room.

"Hi, Grandfather," Talag said cheerfully. "How's it going?"

"Can you boys please go somewhere else," Kleibald requested. "Mr. Pagos and I are having a private discussion."

"Okay," Talag replied.

He backed out of the room, bumping Dynny along behind him. After the door slid shut, Dynny looked up at him sorrowfully. "Why didn't we stay to listen?"

"They wouldn't let us," Talag told him.

"Why not?"

"They're probably going to argue," Talag answered hopefully. "We'll listen through the door."

Sure enough, the voices of Kleibald and Gelu soared in anger, and Dynny and Talag were able to hear snippets of the conversation through the door.

". . . having my child."

"She's dead, you fool!"

"Not all the way," Gelu protested.

There was a pause. Talag imagined his grandfather rolling his eyes at his accomplice. The voices came back more softly.

". . . bring her back to life."

". . . reversal of the gogyvehr . . . didn't happen . . ."

". . . spirits . . . motive power . . ."

Gelu's voice then exploded so that Talag was able to hear every word distinctly. "You mean you didn't have any other plan? The spirits told you they would take care of you, and you believed them?"

Kleibald's voice came through loudly. "They haven't led me wrong so far."

"Oh really?" Gelu's pitch had risen to an ear-shattering scream. "What about the gogyvehr? What about the fact that Gannoir is still whole, and we're out here trapped in the chaos? What about the fact that we're going to die? What about those?"

"The spirits will place us on another world," Kleibald said. "All we have to do is . . ."

"Destroy Gannoir? How are we going to do that?" Gelu was still shouting.

Kleibald's reply was too quiet for Talag to hear anything other than the fact that he replied. He ached to know what his grandfather's answer had been. He planned to destroy Gannoir, but without knowing how he planned to do it, there was nothing Talag could do to stop him.

"They're grumpy," Dynny observed.

Talag snorted a tiny laugh. "Yeah," he replied. "They sure are."

"Do you really think they can destroy Gannoir?" Dynny looked worried.

Talag thought about his grandfather, about how he had successfully convinced forty people to come with him into the unknown. About how he'd attempted to invert Gannoir through the reversal of the gogyvehr. His grandfather was powerful. When he gave orders, people obeyed. "Yeah," he answered. "Yeah, I think they can. And it's up to us to stop them."

Dynny nodded. "We need to go home. The people will be waiting for me. I'm the Dynroc, 59th of that name. They need me." The little man's wizened face was filled with duty and pride.

"You're right, Dynny. You're right."

Chapter 28: Tass

Tass pushed through the water. Dwoyra had led her back to the yellow layer of the sea where it was easier to swim. They wouldn't need to descend until they got close to the passageway into Garradh Gannoir. The Orbokth projected down into the water with the same complexion that it had above it. Upside-down mountains poked their tops toward the icy Bec, creating a complex and beautiful undersea world. Tass, who was used to the open seas of Luca, was intrigued despite herself.

Dwoyra led Tass with an occasional verbal command, but more often, she led with a swish of the liquids to indicate the direction Tass ought to take. A few times Tass got the instructions wrong, and Dwoyra was quick to aggressively bump her back on track.

The sea here was full of creatures. The lemon-yellow color hid the tails of the lumalauae, making them look truncated and ridiculous. Schools of tiny silvery fish wove their paths around Tass as she swam. Globus puffed and sucked, inflating their comical round bodies and then shooting the water out behind them to propel themselves forward. Their green and blue colors were easier to see in the yellow sea than they were nearer the surface, and the glowing dots of color shone from their sides, contracting and expanding in an impressive display. Other kinds of fish passed them too—or were passed by them—as they swam. Tass didn't recognize all of the types, but she was aware of the burning brightness of the sea around her.

Blood. It glowed because of blood.

Not her blood this time, thankfully. Probably the blood of whatever sea creatures died that day or the day before. Whatever it was, whatever its source, it was enough to render the sea more illuminated that the brightest day above water. The orange mist of midday under the Ghalon could not compete with this shining, golden luminescence. Tass wasn't sure she liked it. It hurt her eyes. It revealed too much. There were few secrets that could be kept under the kind of light with which she was surrounded.

All the way, throughout the entire journey, every time Tass looked up at the underside of the Orbokth, she saw them—tiny dga, waving their metallic silver limbs. And the smudges of blackness obscured the glow. So much darkness. Tass wondered how Dwoyra could ever hope to overcome such a plenitude of evil.

For Tass never doubted that the black spots were bad. They had come from outside Gannoir. Igracio had taught her that everything in the chaos outside Gannoir was evil, but she would have believed it of the black spots even without Igracio's tutelage. There was something about them . . . something frightening.

Dwoyra shot ahead. Tass felt the backdraft, and she flicked her feet and arms to try to keep up. She wished Dwoyra would stay near. The voices . . . the wretched voices that spoke to her mind as she swam . . . they were almost inaudible when Dwoyra was near. Whenever she broke away, the voices would press in on her again. Unlovable. Ugly. Lowly. Despised. Alone.

And all of it was true. That was the part that grated on her the worst. If the voices had been spewing lies, she could have stood against them. As it was, all she could do was agree and let her soul sink lower and lower and her despair grow.

She felt the voices recede as watery arms dragged her down, down, down into a tangerine-colored world, still as bright as the yellow layer, but replete with different chemicals and different animals swimming alongside them. Tass was glad Igracio had taught her to read and write. If she ever had the chance, she felt she'd like to write about the zones of the sea, what lived in them, what chemicals were present in each and how the animals made use of the chemicals. The study of the elements was not something Igracio had taught her. He'd only made her aware that such a field of study existed. Her imagination did the rest.

A new thought occurred to Tass.

I'm smart, she said to herself. *I'm not like the other Mayim. I'm not only the fastest and the best student at the Calix, I'm also the most intelligent.* Tass had never lacked pride, but the idea of her own intellect puffed her up even more. *I may be unlovable,* she thought. *I may have been rejected by everyone who ever met me, but I'm not worthless. I'm not.*

Dwoyra circled around her, drawing her still deeper into the sea. The colors changed from pale orange to the dark ruddy shade of the salt oranges that grew in Luca. Dwoyra pushed her lower still, embracing her in arms that kept the frigid sea at bay.

Tass closed her outer eyelids and let her watery friend lead her. She felt her blood turn cold, congeal, almost turn to ice. She opened her eyes. They were in a magenta region of the sea. The Orbokth descended almost to the Bec here—for she could see the undulating colors of the ice layer enclosing Gannoir. She slowly sucked the cold water into her gills. The Bec was alive. Once more she was sure of it. It wasn't just ice, but something more like Dwoyra, the living water, or Gaoth, the living wind. The Bec wasn't just something—it was someone. She reached toward it, longing to know its secrets.

Dwoyra quickly snatched at her reaching arms, drawing them close around Tass's body.

"Let me go!" Tass insisted. "I'm . . . I want to . . ."

But she had noticed something. The fiery waves of the Bec layer were out of sync in a single spot, marred by a syncopated rhythm that Tass quickly realized must be the scar from the healing of Gannoir—the completion of the gogyvehr. She was seeing the end of the creation of her world. It was as though it had happened centuries ago, but Tass knew it had only been months.

Something large floated into Tass's field of vision. Flashes of purple light reflected off the silver arms of a giant dga. The creature, many times larger than Tass herself, stood like a sentry in front of the scarred Bec layer. Blotches of darkness proportional to its size clung to it like mucus. A thrill of fear shot through Tass's body, and she felt her fingers begin to tingle. When she looked down at her hands, she saw that the tips of her fingers were glowing again. She didn't understand it. Her fingers had never glowed before. Not until Igracio . . . not until Igracio . . .

Igracio's fingers had glowed.

She slapped the thought away angrily. This wasn't the time to think about Igracio.

Dwoyra pulled her gently up through the ragged sides of the Orbokth. She was careful not to touch the rock, however. The water began to cycle through the spectrum of colors again. Red. Orange. Tangerine. Yellow.

Tass felt Dwoyra's arms relax. She pushed herself through the water, up and up and up, watching the colors change. The voices, like her own personal dark parasites, once again returned to torment her mind. Unlovable. Unlikeable. Unworthy.

Tass pushed her body through the green layers of the sea. The liquids here were strangely empty after the long journey she had made surrounded by life. Nothing lived here. The sea was empty and much darker than Tass was used to.

She knew where she was.

There was only one place in all Gannoir where she'd felt such emptiness.

She was in Gelu's mine.

Chapter 29: Xylo

"That's the box fish," Xylo said, pointing at a particular arrangement of glowing red fissures in the Ghalon over their heads. It was always one of my favorite convenalations."

Ieska smiled. "I always liked the winged man the best. I used to imagine my tala was wings . . . that I could use it to fly." She swung her arms wide and let her tala catch the air.

It was the middle of the night, and the rain had slowed to a drizzle. Xylo and Ieska had been alternately standing and sitting on a roof deck of one of Lucedth's public buildings for hours fervently talking about nothing.

"I always felt that way too. Like we were supposed to fly, but something went wrong and all we got was tala and the ability to glide."

Ieska grinned at him mischievously. In the dim light of the Ghalon and with that look on her face, she could have been a girl of twenty instead of an old woman.

"What?" Xylo asked suspiciously . . . delightedly . . .

"What if we flew now? It's late and I need to get home. We could glide down from here."

"Glide? In the city?" Xylo asked, bewildered. No one used their tala in the city. Not like that. Gliding was something soil miners did on the heights. A safety measure. Not a fun diversion.

Ieska nodded. "I do it all the time."

"What if we don't land on the street? What if we land in the sea?"

"It's the middle of the night. The top layers of the sea are mostly water. It would be okay even if we landed in the sea. But we won't."

"You do this all the time?" Xylo wasn't sure what to think. He knew Kleibald and the elders would disapprove. But then, Ieska wasn't an elder. And he was by no means opposed to offending Kleibald or his elders.

"Come on," Ieska teased him. "No one will notice. Everyone's asleep."

"This isn't the Orbokth," Xylo retorted dryly. "The city of Lucedth never sleeps."

"Getting too old to glide?" She grinned at him saucily.

"You're the same age I am, Ieska Thayl," Xylo snorted.

"So you'll do it?"

"On one condition," Xylo replied, a serious note catching in his voice. "Tell me about your child."

The playful grin left Ieska's face. "You've no right to ask me that."

Xylo knew she was right. He'd known it as soon as he heard himself say it. He wanted to know, but this wasn't the right way or the right time. He'd let his curiosity take over and very possibly had spoiled whatever it was that he and Ieska had begun. He sighed. "You're right." He looked steadily into her eyes. "I'm sorry. I shouldn't have asked."

"It's okay," Ieska replied without looking at him.

"I'll make it up to you," Xylo said desperately.

Ieska looked up.

"Let's glide."

Ieska smiled, filling Xylo with hope. Maybe he hadn't ruined everything. "Okay."

Xylo reached out his hand and grabbed hers.

Shaking her head, Ieska pulled away. "You weren't paying attention in science class," she twitted him. "Holding hands will ruin the aerodynamics. We'll crash-land."

She stopped walking near the edge of the building. "Are you ready?"

Xylo nodded.

Together they spread their wings and coasted onto the main boulevard of Lucedth hundreds of feet below. It was a perfect landing. A few passersby cast startled stares in their direction, but Xylo and Ieska just laughed. This time when Xylo reached for Ieska's hand, she didn't pull away.

The next morning Xylo returned to the Calix. The weekend was over, and Tass should have returned from her extended leave.

"Is there a reason you need this particular Mayim?" the Master asked coldly.

"Tass is a friend," Xylo replied. "We've been through a lot together. She's a fantastic swimmer and diver, and she's already familiar with the waters of Garradh Gannoir. She would be an asset to the work."

"I've been assembling a crew for you," the Master said, ignoring Xylo's request to see Tass. "I have twenty of our best students ready to help in whatever ways are needed in order to bring the skyboulder back.

This was good news. Xylo knew the retrieval efforts would require much work to take place in the water. Twenty might be too few. It was a good start. But he wanted Tass. He needed Tass.

"Will Tass be on the team?" he asked.

The Master's steady yellow face grew even more still. His lips were a thin slit in his waxen countenance.

"What's wrong?" Xylo pressed.

The Master looked away. "She didn't return from leave after the weekend," he told Xylo through gritted teeth. "I don't know where she is. But you can bet she'll be disciplined. And it won't involve being chosen to be part of a special project, I can promise you that much."

Xylo thought about Tass, about her uncertain parentage, her glowing fingers, her personal angst . . . If what he thought was true, if Tass was the daughter of Methiant Migas, then she had to be found before someone else discovered her glowing fingers and decided to use her for their own purposes. If she was the triad, the three-in-one . . .

It was stupid to assume she was in danger. Kleibald, and probably Gelu, were the only ones with any power who knew about the triad, and they thought their search ended with Mailu. Mailu was with them, and they couldn't get back into Gannoir if they tried. He was the only one who suspected that Tass was the triad.

"What are you planning to do about finding her?" Xylo asked sharply.

The Master shrugged. "She broke the rules. If she comes back and endures the discipline I mete out for her actions, then she'll be allowed to continue her education. If not"—he shrugged again—"she's on her own."

"She's twelve," Xylo answered. "And she has no family."

"That's not my problem," the Master barked.

Xylo closed his eyes. He thought of Afa—Bracha Elisus—whose name he had first heard so many years ago. He thought of the man from whom he'd heard it. The man whose death he had witnessed. The man whose death he should have stopped. His heart stung with guilt. It was his fault that Methiant Migas was dead. It was his fault that Afa was dead. If he'd acted sooner . . . if he'd found Afa as soon as Methiant's death had been confirmed, he could have prevented everything—Mailu's treacherous kidnapping, Afa's death, Igracio's death . . .

Igracio . . .

Now his mind attacked him with a storm of new ideas. Igracio had glowing fingers. Glowing fingers was an Esh trait, not a Mayim trait. But Igracio'd had functional gills. He was Mayim. By some twist of destiny, Igracio had been triple-casted. Just like the triad. What if . . . what if . . . but the thought was too ridiculous to be entertained. Igracio was not the son of Methiant Migas. He was the son of Laso and Rahela Barat, whom he had met, with whom he had mourned after the death of their son.

Methiant Migas . . . Xylo had known him by another name.

". . . will be available at your call," the Master was saying. "You may come for them then."

Xylo's mind snapped back to the situation at hand. The twenty Mayim. "Thank you," he replied vaguely. "Once we are ready, I will send word. And if you hear from Tass, if she comes back, please let me know. I'm staying with my daughter, Yasamina Sapor Xalantaka." He gave the Master his daughter's address.

Chapter 30: Talag

Talag was huddled in the corner at one side of Mailu's stone coffin, trying to be invisible. Gelu had come to talk to Dynny. For some reason, he hadn't seen Talag crouch down.

"It's very important that you keep watch, Dynny," Gelu ordered. "No one should be near Mailu's box. No one. If the glass breaks or if any air gets in at all, then Mailu will die. Do you understand?"

A frightened Dynny nodded. "I'll take good care of Mailu. Caring is what I do best."

"She's important," Gelu barked. "She's going to play a huge part in our homecoming. Nothing must stop that. Mailu must live."

"Oh, yes!" Dynny agreed. "Mailu's going to have a baby."

"That's even more reason to keep Mailu as healthy as possible, isn't it?" Gelu said.

"I'll take good care of her," Dynny said. He glanced at Talag.

Talag shooed him away and pointed at Gelu, hoping Dynny would turn his gaze back to the large blue-haired man towering over him.

"I also heard you and Kleibald were going to destroy Gannoir," Dynny commented. It was evident from his expression that he was struggling to do a heroic thing. Dynny was terrified of Gelu. Gelu's attack had killed his former master, Arros, the 58th Dynroc. Dynny couldn't feel safe with Gelu.

Talag winced. Gelu was never going to answer direct questions about the destruction of Gannoir.

Gelu frowned. "You're a good listener," he told Dynny. "But I don't want you to worry. You're safe here with us. Gannoir died when we left. All dead, down to the last person. We can't go back."

"Are you going to blow it up?" Dynny asked with his singularity of focus.

Talag was stuck on the notion of "all dead." Could Gelu be telling the truth? Had the explosion that propelled the boulder into space have also killed all life on Gannoir? He wanted to go home, but what if there wasn't a home to go back to? He shook his head. If that were the case, it wouldn't be necessary to destroy Gannoir. If what Gelu was saying were true, Gannoir was already destroyed. It would be redundant of Kleibald to destroy it again. He had to be wrong. He just had to be.

"Not me," Gelu said. "I wouldn't even know how to begin." He smiled.

That was probably true, Talag reflected. He didn't know of anyone who would know how to blow up the world. Gelu wasn't anything special.

Gelu wasn't talking to spirits in the chaos.

"Just keep Mailu safe." Gelu's eyes narrowed. "There's not enough food on the skyboulder. You'll be the first one we eat if you neglect your duties."

Dynny looked frightened. He ran a hand through his thin, gray hair. "I'll take good care of her. You can't eat me."

Talag wanted to punch Gelu. Why was he scaring Dynny? But he kept his mouth shut. If Gelu found out he was in the room, Dynny was toast. Literally.

Gelu strode from the room, sliding the door shut behind him. Talag relaxed and crawled out from his hiding place.

"Are you okay?" he asked the trembling little gnome of a man.

Dynny shivered as Talag put an arm around his shoulders. "He said they were going to eat me," he wailed.

"They're not going to eat you," Talag told him with certainty.

Dynny blinked. "Why not?"

"First, because you'd always take care of Mailu. Caring is what you're good at, right?"

Dynny nodded and became calmer.

"Second . . ." Talag hesitated.

"What's second?" Dynny asked hopefully.

"Well . . . why did they bring you on the skyboulder?" Talag asked. "Was it just to take care of Mailu?"

"I'm a good carer," Dynny reminded Talag.

Talag sighed. "I know you're a good carer. But it's not a very hard job to take care of a dead girl. They could have brought someone with way less ability than you have," he told Dynny diplomatically. "Why'd they bring you? What else can you do?"

Dynny puffed up his chest. "I'm the Dynroc, 59th of that name. Even Gelu knows it. He knows it's not him, even though he told Kleibald he was it. They made me do a magic spell before we left. Gelu and Kleibald both know I'm the one. I'm the Dynroc."

"So they need you? Need your powers?"

Dynny nodded happily. "I'm probably the most powerful person on the skyboulder."

"But what can you do?" Talag pressed uncertainly.

Dynny scrunched up his face, thinking hard. "I don't know," he answered finally. "But they need me. None of the magic can happen without the Dynroc."

"What magic?" Talag asked, breathless with expectation.

"Any magic," Dynny said. "The Dynroc has to be there. They couldn't have healed Gannoir without the Dynroc being there at the time. That's what I do. I be there."

The lack of grammar didn't bother Talag. It had a marvelous clarity that he realized he'd never experienced in talking with his family. "If you weren't on the skyboulder, we would never have left Gannoir," Talag speculated.

Dynny nodded. "We got out by magic. My magic." He seemed proud.

"And the new magic that they're planning . . ." Talag mused, "It can't happen without you either, right?"

"What new magic?" Dynny asked.

"The destruction of Gannoir," Talag reminded him. "It has to be magic."

"You think I'll magic away Gannoir?" Dynny was scandalized.

"Not on purpose," Talag reassured him. "But what if they can't do it without you?"

"They can't do anything without the Dynroc," Dynny reverted to his earlier theme.

"And you're the Dynroc. And you're here. So their magic will work."

"How can I stop them? I can't leave the skyboulder," Dynny frowned. Then his face grew sad. "Maybe it would be best if they did eat me."

"Don't be silly," Talag retorted. "No one's going to eat you. Can you turn the magic off? Or abdicate or something? So you're not the Dynroc?"

Tears filled the little man's eyes. "I am the Dynroc. Arros said so."

"Please, Dynny. We have to save Garradh Gannoir. We have to figure something out. We have to stop them."

"Keep thinking," Dynny replied. "We have to keep thinking. I'm the Dynroc, 59th of that name."

Chapter 31: Tass

Most of the mine basin was surrounded by vertical cliffs, ajumble after the earthquakes of a few months back, skewed, but upright. At one place, the Orbokth came down to meet the sea. Tass pulled herself out of the water onto the shore and looked around to get her bearings. It was early in the day. Tass could tell by the chemical composition of the liquid around her. It was mostly water, as it should be after a night's rain. The Ghalon above her was a sliver of red and the mists, palely golden. She sat on the rocky shore, watching and waiting, trying to ignore the voices that spoke to her out of the mist.

Their song had subtly changed with the change of scenery. In Luca, the voices seemed intent on smashing her soul flat—telling her she was worthless and unlovable. But in Garradh Gannoir the voices had an urgency about them, as though they were pushing her, goading her, manipulating her into doing something specific.

Tass tried to close her mind to them. She didn't want to know what they wanted her to do. Whatever it was, it didn't matter. She knew what she planned to do. Bring back her sister. Bring back Mailu. She just didn't know how she was going to do it. And she was hungry.

She'd snacked on some water plants, but she was used to eating cooked food while in the air, not raw plants while under the sea. Her stomach was queasy, and she wondered whether it had more to do with the difficulty preventing fluid from getting into her air lungs while she ate, or if it were from the food itself.

Without money, she had few choices when it came to getting food. She could hike into the city, into Obumbro, and steal from a street vendor. Or she could find someone who would give it to her. Reluctantly she decided the second option was preferable. All Obumbro already thought she was some sort of a primitive, mythological goddess because she could swim in the tainted water of the sea. All Obumbro knew what had happened when the cleft in the Bec had been healed. They knew that she was Siann Dha. They knew she'd lost both her mother and her best friend in the incident. She couldn't pretend to be a random thief, sneaking food when no one was looking.

She sighed. In Luca her yellow skin and webbed fingers were normal for someone of the Mayim caste. In Obumbro, the only Mayim were Ceres and herself. Inconspicuous was something she couldn't hope to be.

So she'd use it. They'd feed a starving mythical goddess, wouldn't they? Any of them would. She only hoped they wouldn't carry the tale of their Siann Dha sighting back to Xylo. She'd swum to Garradh Gannoir alone because she had wanted to explore things for herself. Not for Xylo. Not for justice for Gannoir. Not to help Ceres.

Hurry. Must hurry, the voices whooshed around her head.

"Hurry for food?" Tass wondered aloud.

You could finally do something important . . . with us you could be more than the little nothing you are . . .

That was more like it. As wretched as the voices' words were, Tass felt relieved that they were falling back into their derogatory patterns.

She stood up and began hiking up the rocky shore toward the grassy areas between the mine and the city. It wasn't far. She could see the whitewashed dwellings rising on the cliffside in the distance. Someone would be there. Someone who would be glad to feed her.

As she walked, she applied her mind to the problem of bringing Mailu home. Much as she hated to admit it, she knew she would have to start where Xylo wanted her to start—by finding if there were any more holes, even small ones, in Gannoir's protective Bec layer. The enormous gap through which the skyboulder had escaped had completely closed. But that didn't mean that there weren't smaller gaps. Maybe dangerous fissures marred the Bec. Maybe holes existed naturally for unknown, unexpected reasons.

There were two problems she would encounter even if she found holes in the Bec. The first was Dwoyra. Dwoyra didn't want anything to happen that would open Gannoir to more of the dark chaos from outside their world. If Tass tried to create a gap, even one too small to admit the skyboulder, she'd be fighting against Dwoyra. She'd had enough tussles with Dwoyra to know that she couldn't win. Dwoyra's ability to change her shape and the consistency of her physical essence made fighting impossible.

The second problem was the Bec itself. She thought about her fleeting encounters with the cold, purple fire of the Bec. She hadn't stayed long enough to know with any empirical sureness, but she believed with all that she was that the Bec was more than just a thick layer of ice. The Bec wasn't just body. The Bec had a soul. It had reached toward her, wanting something from her. And if the Bec had a soul, and that soul was bent on completely enclosing Gannoir with its protective arms, then would she even have a chance to break a hole in it large enough for the skyboulder's return?

As she pondered, she could almost feel the chemicals of the sea on her skin, so immersed was she in the world of her mind. She didn't see the stranger approach until her hand reached out to touch her shoulder.

Tass jumped away in surprise.

"You're the one, aren't you?" the girl said, awed.

Tass blinked.

"You're the one who almost died a couple months ago, right?" The girl nervously pushed her long, light-brown hair out of her face.

"I'm Tass Galan."

"You're the one, then," the girl sighed with delight. "My name's Rio. Wait until I tell my mom that I met you!"

"Could I come and meet her?" Tass asked boldly. "I'm hungry after such a long time traveling under the water. Do you think she would feed me?"

"What do the Siann Dha eat?" Rio asked, her eyes wide with her good fortune.

An unaccustomed burst of humor twittered through Tass's mind. She could ask for anything, any delicacy, and this girl and her mother would try to prepare it for her. What did she want?

"Anything will do," she said at last.

"Then come! Come with me!" Rio chortled.

Chapter 32: Xylo

Xylo had managed to get Ieska a spot on the team going to Garradh Gannoir. It hadn't been hard, given her status among the Eshmaor. He'd simply asked, and they'd agreed. She was coming. Xylo fiddled with the tala hanging below his wrist in a nervous gesture that he hadn't used since he was a boy. He needed to tell her. He wanted to have someone on his side—someone who understood.

Then he laughed at himself ruefully. That wasn't the truth. Not all of it. He already had Case and Ceres who understood and believed his stories. He didn't need another person to believe him. He needed—he wanted—Ieska. He wanted her on his side because he couldn't stand to have her not know the truth about Kleibald. She already knew Kleibald was flawed. But he would take the time to tell her all of it before they left.

Ieska looked at him curiously. "So all the talk about Kleibald and his crimes against Gannoir being the reason for bringing him to justice . . . that was all just a front for your personal vendetta against him and an excuse to bring your grandchildren back to Gannoir?"

Xylo's skin felt hotter than usual. "Of course not. With everything I am, I believe that Kleibald deserves to be brought home and punished for the things he's done. But I wanted you to know the rest. Not for the sake of Kleibald, but for my sake. I just . . . wanted you to know."

"I'm sorry about your son," Ieska said softly, taking his hand. "I wish there was something I could do to help, but I know there is nothing. But I am sorry for your loss."

"There's more," Xylo said heavily.

"More about Kleibald?" Ieska asked.

"More about me," Xylo replied.

"What?" Ieska said, trying to tease him out of his dark mood. "Are you a robber? A murderer? What?" She grinned at him.

"Please don't joke about it," Xylo requested. "If there's going to be anything between us then you must know what I am, what I'm like. I have to tell someone. I mean, I want to tell you. Do you . . . can you bear to hear?"

Ieska led him over to one of the benches in the empty rooftop courtyard of the skyscraper that floated on the clatry over the sea below. The mist was so thick she could only see his face if they sat quite close together. She pulled him down beside her and leaned against his side. "I can bear it, Xylo. Whatever it is."

Xylo took a deep breath. "I've never told this story to anyone," he began. "It was years ago now. I don't know how many. Five? Ten? I should have done something about it at the time, but I didn't know how important it would be, how important it would become. I didn't realize . . ." His voice caught in his throat.

"What did you do?" Ieska asked, sitting up and looking toward him through the fog.

A sigh. "Remember how I told you I worked as a soil miner on the heights?" Xylo said. "One day while I was working, a man approached me. It was odd because he clearly wasn't Esh. No tala," he remarked, tugging at the wrinkled flesh hanging below his arm. "No one but the Esh-qadar go up that high on the Orbokth. It's simply too hot for a Gulot or a Mayim to endure."

"Who was he?" Ieska prompted after Xylo paused for too long.

Xylo pressed his lips together. "He gave his name as Mantais Nayro. He was of medium height and build. No Esh-tala, like I said, but he did have some scarred tala between his fingers. Probably a Mayim, I figured. I asked him why he'd come to the heights. It couldn't have been comfortable. The skin of a Mayim would dry up in a second that close to the Ghalon. He had to have been miserable. He said he had come to the heights because he wanted to get as close to Tel-Maor as he could. He had a debt to pay, and he wanted to pay it."

"A debt to Tel-Maor?"

Xylo rubbed a hand across his forehead. Then he squinted through the mist, making sure they were still alone. Satisfied, he continued. "This Mantais Nayro told me that he'd committed crimes. Horrific crimes. He had a compulsion, he told me. He couldn't help it. He spoke of others . . . people who had changed him, destroyed his mind and his will. He lived his life in a cycle of soul-shattering guilt on the one side and an insatiable hunger for evil on the other. He was stuck. He could never be free. He'd come to the heights to return his soul to Tel-Maor—if there was anything left of him still fit to be given to the One who ruled from the Ghalon.

"In my mind, I scoffed at his primitive religious ideas. If Tel-Maor exists at all, the Ghalon cannot be his physical dwelling place. It's a ball of fire. Nothing could live in it. He was no closer to the gods on the heights than he would have been in the water. I tried to tell him so . . . tried to explain . . . but he was in no fit state for philosophy. He had come for action . . ."

Ieska pulled her feet up onto the bench and hugged her knees, wrapping her tala around herself. "What kind of action?"

Xylo looked at the old woman beside him in surprise. "Are you cold?"

Ieska shook her head. "No. Just trying to be more . . . comfortable. Keep talking."

"He told me he wanted to confess to someone. If it wasn't going to be Tel-Maor, then he'd confess to whomever he found on the heights. And the person he found was me." Xylo stopped talking and shut his eyes, a pained expression on his face.

Ieska shook her head slowly. "What did he say? What had he done? Was it so bad that it's causing you so much pain now, so many years later?"

Xylo's voice grew harsh. "It's not his deeds that are causing my pain. It's my own. It's the evil I could have prevented but didn't . . . But let me finish. Just let me finish."

Ieska reached out a hand and laid it on Xylo's shoulder, all the winsome mockery missing from her usually exuberant expression. She was serious now. "I'll still be your friend, Xylo. I promise."

"Maybe you will and maybe you won't," Xylo retorted flatly. "But I need to talk to you about what he said . . . and what I did."

Ieska looked at him, her eyes damp with either emotion or the thick mists of midday.

"This man, Mantais, had been the subject of scientific experimentation. Horrors. They had trimmed his tala. They had chemically treated his skin, trying to change his caste. He'd been drugged. He hadn't been a good man before it had all happened, he told me, but afterward he was never the same. He had compulsions to . . . rape." Xylo said the word with all the horror and respect it deserves. "He confessed these things to me, incident after incident after incident until I couldn't bear to hear it any longer. I asked him why he was telling me, a plain old soil miner, when he could have gone to the elders with his troubles, or to a family member, or to a doctor. I didn't want to hear anymore. I couldn't stand it. So much pain. So much destruction. So many ruined hearts. There was nothing I could do about it. Nothing at all. The man's grief was so great, so overwhelming, that I couldn't help but feel pity toward him. I wanted to help him in some way, but there was nothing I could do. After a long time during which he stared out across the horizon, looking at nothing, it seemed, he spoke again. 'You asked why I was telling you,' he said. 'Someone has to know. Someone has to help them.' 'Help the women?' I asked. And he told me what he meant. One woman, one of his victims, had a child—his child, he was sure. 'Help her,' he requested. 'Someone has to help her . . . and the child.' He looked into my eyes, and the look on his face was so full of anguish, so full of pleading . . . I had never seen anyone look like that before, not in all my life."

"And did you?" Ieska asked.

"Did I what?"

"Help the woman?"

Xylo scrunched up his face and continued without answering. "After he explained what he wanted, he stood up—we had been sitting on a rocky outcropping—and walked to the edge of the cliff. Looking back, I understand that I knew what he was going to do. I knew and I didn't stop him. He . . . he . . . he threw himself over the edge. Off the cliffside into the sea. His body bounced on the cliffs as he descended. He was dead before he hit the water."

"And the woman?" Some of the horror of the story had seeped into Ieska's voice. It was thick with emotion.

"He told me her name," Xylo said, wincing and closing his eyes. "It was Bracha Elisus. The man was your Methiant Migas."

Ieska looked shocked. Xylo was surprised. He thought she would have understood far earlier that the story was about Methiant Migas. He had expected that she would be horrified by the tale of what the man had done. And she knew about Bracha—about Afa—already. The tale of numerous rapes instead of just the one for which they had confirmation was horrifying, but not shocking. He hadn't even gotten to his own transgressions yet—not contacting Afa until her name came up when he was looking for Case. He'd ignored the dying man's last request, refused assistance to a woman who, he found out too late, could have used help. He'd recruited Afa without telling her what he knew about her and her child and had led her to her death. That was the part that should have been shocking to her. Not this. He wondered what was going on in her mind.

"What is it?" he asked gently.

Ieska hugged her arms around herself more tightly. "I thought you were going to say something else."

Xylo shook his head. "I don't understand."

Ieska slid off the bench and took his hand. "Come. Come with me."

Chapter 33: Talag

The whispered conversations boded ill. The food supply was dwindling. If it ran out, the skyboulder would become their coffin.

There was nothing he could do about the food. The matter of greater urgency was Kleibald's need for his plans to come to fruition. Talag knew that he and Dynny had to figure out what to do quickly, before Kleibald and Gelu destroyed Gannoir. Not knowing how his grandfather planned to destroy Gannoir was a significant obstacle to thwarting him.

The answer, therefore, at least for the moment, would be found in figuring that out.

Talag pondered the matter and had decided that the only way he was going to obtain the knowledge he needed was if either his grandfather or Gelu told him what their plans were. And the only way either of the leaders was going to confide in a fourteen-year-old boy was if he had something they needed.

He didn't have anything they needed.

But Dynny did.

He didn't want to use Dynny. Dynny was faithful, caring, brave, and steadfast, but not smart enough to outwit his grandfather or even Gelu. He would have to do it himself. If the only thing that was useful to them was the Dynroc, he would become the Dynroc.

Dynny objected. "I'm the Dynroc, 59th of that name," he protested. "Arros said so. He told me to take care of the books and the people. It's my job."

"You'd still be the Dynroc," Talag comforted his friend. "We'd just make-believe that you were abdicating and giving the job to me. To trick Gelu and my grandfather."

Dynny shook his head. "I'm the Dynroc. A fake Dynroc won't be able to do the magic."

"That's what I'm counting on," Talag explained. "If they think I'm the Dynroc, then they'll try to use me and my powers to destroy Gannoir. But I won't have any."

"You're not the Dynroc," Dynny agreed.

"If they think I'm the Dynroc, they won't try to use your powers. They'll try to use mine."

"But you don't have any powers."

"Exactly. So whatever they're planning won't work and Gannoir will be safe."

Dynny blinked at him uncomprehendingly.

"I'm going to pretend to be the Dynroc," Talag said slowly. "And you're going to help me. Like being in a play. Pretend. After that, I'm going to pretend I want to destroy Gannoir. I'll pretend to help them. I'll find out what their plans are. We can't stop them if we don't know what they're planning to do."

"You'll find out and stop them!" Dynny finally understood.

Talag nodded vigorously. "I'll find out and stop them. But I need you to play along with me. Pretend to be abdicating and making me the 60th Dynroc. Pretend you're angry with me when I start taking my grandfather's side about the destruction of Gannoir. I'll find out what we need to do. Then we'll figure out how to stop them."

"But you won't be the Dynroc," Dynny pressed worriedly.

"That's right. You'll still be the Dynroc. We'll just be pretending."

Dynny nodded. "Okay. Right now?"

Talag grinned with relief. "Let's practice first."

In the dinner line that evening, Talag and Dynny began their charade.

"I'm too old and tired," Dynny complained. "I can't do it anymore."

"But I'm just a kid," Talag protested. "I can't possibly do your job. There's no way. Maybe in a few years. If you train me after we get home. I can learn what to do and then I can be the Dynroc. But not now!" He spoke loudly so that he could be heard even in the adjacent compartments. He winked at Dynny to remind them that they were pretending.

"No," Dynny said sadly, winking back at Talag. "I'm too tired now, not later. You have to help me. I need someone to take over for me."

"But I . . ."

"Talag Dineaweth Xalantaka, I deem that you are the Dynroc of Garradh Gannoir, 60th of that name," Dynny pronounced is as regal a voice as he could muster. "You are now the guardian of the old knowledge, keeper of secrets, successor to the Dynrocs of the past. You are the wisdom of Garradh Gannoir and the advisor of the people. In the name of Tel-Maor, I pronounce that you . . ."

"What's going on here?" Gryf interrupted as he strode into the room.

Talag looked at his father, trying to convey the fear he was supposed to be feeling as the unwilling recipient of the office of the Dynroc, all the while wondering why it couldn't have been his grandfather who had wandered into the room. "Father!" he cried. "Oh, Father! Dynny's trying to make me take over his job! I don't know if I can do it. I'm too young for something like that."

Gryf looked at the wizened little man. "Is this true?"

After a quick glance at Talag for reassurance, Dynny nodded. "He's the Dynroc, 60th of that name, successor to . . ."

"He's a child!" Gryf objected. "He's my child. And he's a resident of Luca, not of Garradh Gannoir. How dare you!"

Dynny trembled. "I can't take it back. I made the proclamation in the name of Tel-Maor. He's the Dynroc now. He has to be. I'm old. I'm tired."

"Don't make me do it, Dad! Don't make me!" Talag begged.

"Of course you don't have to do it," Gryf sputtered. "This is ridiculous."

Gryf continued to lambaste Dynny with both logical and illogical reasons why Talag could not assume the role of Dynroc, but, to Talag's relief, Dynny did not back down. After some minutes of the tirade, Kleibald and Gelu entered the room to see what was going on.

With an accusing finger pointed at Dynny, Gryf explained.

Talag saw a shrewd light fill his grandfather's eyes. It was working. He could almost hear his grandfather thinking how much easier it would be to manipulate a fourteen-year-old child, and his grandson as well, than it would be to force Dynny to endorse his plans. He saw Kleibald tilt his head as though he were listening to a faraway sound. His expression grew satisfied. It was all Talag could do to conceal his revulsion.

"Gelu," Kleibald barked. "We need to talk."

The two men quickly exited. Talag's father followed them closely, complaining about Talag's incompetence, Dynny's presumptuousness, and the fact that no one had consulted him before accosting his son. Dynny and Talag grinned at each other. It had worked.

"I'm still the Dynroc, right?" Dynny whispered to Talag.

Talag gestured to Dynny to be quiet and then reached for the food that his mother held out to him. Her worried eyes almost made him regret the subterfuge. He wished he still trusted her. But for all he knew she was in on it too. "Thanks, Mom," he said. "Come on, Dynny. Get your food and then you can come tell me all about being the Dynroc."

Dynny started to object, but Talag cocked his chin toward his mother and gave the old man a knowing look. Dynny took the food from Milis without further comment.

Chapter 34: Tass

The meal had been good. Tass knew that Rio's mother had given her the best food she had—not only the basics like halas bread with gwynant, fried fish, and berries, but savory zigk moak, the fried fatty meat of the marine animal, the vauzigk, and methyglyn, an alcoholic beverage that was as rare as it was expensive. Tass had clumsily pronounced a blessing over Rio and her family before she'd left, delighting them utterly. They would, she knew, tell the story of their visitation by one of the Siann Dha for the rest of their lives. She was a legend. She was a myth. She was one of the Old Ones.

She was a twelve-year-old girl who just wanted her sister back.

Pushing down through the liquids filling the mine, Tass reflected on the irony that anyone would think she was some sort of celebrity. In Luca, she was just one of the Mayim, the lowest, least-respected caste. Even her mother didn't love her. Yet in Garradh Gannoir, she was a somebody, and Igracio was a hero. Had been a hero.

Igracio had never been a hero.

But he'd been hers.

And all Gannoir's.

The color of the water changed from turquoise to the varied greens of the lower level. The water was still warm, but, as always, the mine was empty of life. It was only when she got below the level of the digging, below the place where Gelu's miners had punched through the rocky Orbokth to the sea beneath it, that the creatures surrounded her in any great numbers. She ran the tips of her fingers through a school of tiny silvery fish. They tickled as they slid over her tala, frenetically trying to follow their mates on their endless trek through the sea.

Kicking her feet behind her, she pushed through the colors of the sea, through the yellow waters, then the gleaming tangerine. It was colder now. Tass wondered how she was going to explore the outermost layers of the world without bringing Dwoyra or a sea creature with her for warmth. Close to the Bec, it was too cold for her to do much more than survive. Her blood would congeal in her veins. Her mind would slow. Time itself ran more slowly near the Bec. Hadn't she seen that before? The gogyvehr, the cataclysmic event that had occurred at the beginning of time itself hadn't even been finished until a burst of energy from the Ghalon had streamed into the mine, buoyed by the rational wind, Gaoth, and Dwoyra, and fueled by Igracio's potent blood.

She had no such help now. No Igracio. No magical three-in-one blood. No force behind her striving to destroy the world. Dwoyra would not be in favor of Tass's plan to widen an existing hole in the Bec, or to break through it, if need be. She could depend only on herself.

The voices swirling through her gills were quiet for once, and she nervously wondered why. Nothing spoke to her of her insufficiency, her unworthiness. Nothing drove her to immediate action. She was alone. Completely alone. Pausing in the tangerine level of the sea, she looked around for the any of the creatures who had been her warmth on her previous forays to the depths. She saw hundreds, thousands, even, of smaller creatures—globus, bonefish, dga, both with and without the little dark blotches—but the larger creatures that she needed were not there.

She knew better than to dive past the salmon-colored sea into the reds and pinks of the lower levels without a companion. *A vauzigk,* she thought with a sigh. That was what she needed. She thought back to the meal she'd eaten in Obumbro. The vauzigk meat, zigk-moak, had been delicious, but the creature would have been more useful to her alive. The blubbery flesh was the perfect protection against the cold, and her previous experience with the vauzigk had told her that the irrational beasts did not care where she went like the lumalauae and Dwoyra did.

But no vauzigk were in sight.

Another solution presented itself to her mind. It was a quiet voice, a whisper trickling through her gills and into her mind. She resisted it at first, wondering if it were coming from the voices. But they'd never sounded like this. This was more like a thought, something born in her own mind and of her own will.

Trick Dwoyra.

She could do it. She could pretend she was looking for gaps in the Bec in order to find a way to close the gaps. She didn't have to tell Dwoyra she was looking for a way to readmit the skyboulder. She could . . . pretend.

The more she thought about it the more appealing the idea was. Dwoyra would think Tass was working with her. Tass could keep trying to find a way to bring Mailu back. And with Dwoyra's protection, she could explore the very brink of the world. Nothing would be impossible.

Yes . . . Yes . . . a thin wisp of thought whistled through her mind. It was nothing like the voices. Nothing at all. She would do what she needed to do. And once Mailu was back, once Mailu was alive again . . . She felt a stab a despair shoot though her body and her fingertips began to glow again. She wished they would stop doing that. What had she inadvertently inherited from Igracio? How had he managed to bequeath his miscasted trait to her? She tucked her fingers inside her fists and hollered with her gill-voice.

"Dwoyra!"

Chapter 35: Xylo

"Where are we going?" Xylo asked.

Ieska had led him to the opposite side of Lucedth, the capital city of Luca, to the harbor on the far side. She shook her head in response to his question. "There's something I need to show you," she told him. "But I can't talk about it."

The answer had been the same all afternoon. She wouldn't tell him where she was taking him or why. Protests that he had work to do in preparation for their trip to Garradh Gannoir went unheeded. But he knew that whatever it was, it was important. Ieska's manner had changed. He was seeing another side of her—not a truer side, but a side of her that was equally as real as the Ieska he had come to know over the past days. If he and Ieska were going to continue their relationship, then he had to see what she wanted him to see.

As the Ghalon turned its face away from Luca and the darkness began to rule the land, they got in line for the ferry. Boats could only travel after the rains had filled the top layer of the sea with water. Earlier in the day, when the water in the sea was mist in the air, the caustic liquids of the sea prohibited travel. Xylo made a mental note to find out what materials were used for boats on the other side of the Orbokth in Garradh Gannoir. Their boats were resistant to the acids in the sea. They could travel whenever they wanted.

Ieska and Xylo watched hand in hand as the boats were launched from their dry docks into the sea. The time had not yet come—it had only been raining for a short time, but when the sea was ready, the boats would leave for the far shores immediately. They purchased tickets for the farthest clatry from Lucedth.

Xylo tried to remember what he knew about the far clatries. The latticework of rock that formed the floating clatries there was of a pink color, he knew. Corundum, most likely. In the early years, it had a reputation of being holier than the white and off-white clatries nearer to Lucedth. There were buildings on the Rhosen clatries, but nothing like the gleaming metallic skyscrapers of Lucedth and the surrounding area. It was a rural area, inhabited by people who ranched and farmed the sea. Most of the people who lived there were religious, he remembered. They believed the old myths—about Tel-Maor inhabiting the Ghalon, about the evil spirits in the chaos outside Gannoir, about Tel-Maor being satisfied by the sacrifices of blood that kept the waters of the sea glowing with the blue ymolenegth that lit their world in the nighttime.

Try as he might, he couldn't imagine what Ieska might be taking him to see on the Rhosen clatries. What had he said that had prompted her sudden desire for revelation? Something about Methiant Migas . . . about Afa . . . about the child . . . The child . . . That had to be it. Ieska had a child. He knew that, although she hadn't admitted as much. But why would Ieska's child have anything to do with the farthest reaches of Luca? Any child of Ieska would have likely been Esh-maor—the ruling class—and would have been raised in the schools of Lucedth and then Nozoffi where the university was, but never on the Rhosen.

Ieska looked up at him as they boarded the ferry, a fifteen-passenger barge with safety railings on all sides. Her expression conveyed worry. Xylo wondered what terrible secret Ieska was hiding. He remembered that he hadn't yet told her the worst of his own secrets—how he had failed Afa, never helping her with her illegitimate child, her despair, her anger . . . how his interactions with her had been wholly centered on his own selfish interests—bringing his son home. And how his actions had eventually led to her death. Whatever Ieska was hiding, it couldn't be as bad as that.

Xylo reached for Ieska's hand and gave it a comforting squeeze. "Whatever it is," he said, "it's okay. I'll still care."

"I know," Ieska replied. "That's why I'm taking you with me. If I didn't trust you, I would have left you back in Lucedth."

"I'm not a good person . . ." Xylo began.

Ieska shushed him. "No one is. Not in this fallen, inside-out world. But because of what you've been through, because of . . . everything . . . you may be the one who can help me. Who can help us."

"Us?"

Ieska shook her head. "Later," she said.

The rain beat down on them as the ferry slid over the sea. Mayim were playing in the sea, splashing and ducking each other with a carefree abandon that Xylo envied. "It must be wonderful to be able to swim," he remarked.

"A little like flying," Ieska smiled.

They stood at the front of the boat looking out across the sea. When the boat arrived at its farthest stop, Rhosen Faide, Ieska and Xylo disembarked. A few huts occupied the shoreline, with larger dwellings further inland. Nets extended from the clatry on three sides, havens for the fish and mellila shrimp that were raised there. Sea plants grew in abundance over the nets. Xylo saw a floating bush heavily laden with salt oranges. The memory of their sharp tangy flavor rushed through his mind.

"Is this what you wanted me to see?" he asked.

Ieska looked up at the Ghalon. The ceiling of their world was completely black save for the glowing red convenalations that crisscrossed the cracked orb that hovered overhead. "Come," she said.

As the barge slipped back through the sea in the direction of Lucedth, she led him through the narrow streets between the houses and farms toward the other side of the clatry. He looked around with interest. Xylo had spent his early life in the city and the second half on the heights of the Orbokth. The low-lying farms were something new to him, although he had visited briefly as part of his education many years earlier. The smells were something he remembered vividly. Salt oranges, blood, spices . . . it all combined to make the Rhosen a completely different world than either the city or the Orbokth.

Xylo and Ieska emerged from the streets onto the opposite shore. A tiny house with a boat strapped to its side was the last building on Rhosen Faide. Ieska rattled the dried-seaweed curtain that served as the house's door.

An elderly man opened the door. He was Esh, but Xylo didn't recognize him. He wondered what an old Esh-qadar was doing living so close to the sea, but he didn't ask. The man's wrinkled face folded into a smile as he saw Ieska. He waved them inside. Pushing through the seaweed curtain, Xylo beheld a small, plain room. Like most of the dwellings on the clatry, the structure was made of metal, but its dull sheen and lumpish texture gave it a different atmosphere. The floor was covered with seagrass mats and a low sofa occupied one wall. A cookstove and pump-operated sink occupied the other.

"Sit down, sit down. Welcome," the man said. He looked at Ieska. "Who is your friend?"

Xylo shot Ieska a warning glance, telling her not to reveal the name he'd gone by in his youth. She looked back at him, understanding his request, but asking something in return. Xylo couldn't tell what it was she wanted.

"His name is Xylo," Ieska answered. "I want to take him to Cudth Deorth." Her words hung in the air, suspended on the sudden rush of electricity that seemed to shoot through the air as she named the place.

Xylo held his breath, wondering what was going on. Ieska was looking into the pale blue eyes of the old man as though she were trying to hypnotize him. As Xylo watched, the old man's body seemed to grow frailer, his skin to hang from his gaunt bones as though it were a precursor to death, as though his soul within him had grown too powerful to occupy the wasted body any longer. He wondered who this man was and how he could look so shriveled and yet so alive at the same time.

Finally, the man spoke. "Why?" He didn't look at Xylo.

Ieska pressed her lips together. "He may be the one who can help us."

The old man shook his head. "No one can help us. We have to help ourselves."

"He won't betray us," Ieska promised. "He's not like the others."

"You're in love with him," the man observed, his mouth twisting in wry mockery.

Ieska flushed, and Xylo's heart beat faster.

"You know I wouldn't bring someone here for nothing," she protested. "How I feel about him is of no importance. I have a brain as well as a heart. And you know where my loyalties lie. You've known me for twenty years."

"Nineteen," the man corrected her.

"We need you to take us across," Ieska pressed.

"I don't know this man. You—all of you—have trusted me for protection. You're asking me to break faith with the others—to take you at your word that his man is somehow different. I need more than that."

"He's in a hurry," Ieska argued.

"I'm not," the man shot back.

Ieska sighed, and Xylo knew that the old man had won the first round.

"Sit," the man ordered.

Ieska and Xylo sat.

"I'll make tea." The stranger shuffled toward the cookstove and sink as though hospitality had been his intention all along, as though he hadn't just expressed his outright distrust of Xylo, as though they were welcome and cherished guests.

After handing the mugs to Ieska and Xylo, the old man drew up a stool and watched them. "Who are you really?" he asked.

Xylo returned his gaze, wary. "Who are you?"

The old man drew up his legs onto the stool and wrapped his loose tala around his body—a cocoon of a man who suddenly seemed younger because of the smooth surface of the stretched tala. "My name is Torcalon," he said. "I'm a guardian."

"A guardian of what?" Xylo asked.

"If I told you, I wouldn't be very good at my job," Torcalon noted.

That was probably true, Xylo reflected, impressed by the vitality of the broken man before him.

"What do you want from him?" Ieska interrupted. "Whatever it is, he'll tell you the truth. There is a need for haste."

"I'll decide whether haste is in order," Torcalon replied. He looked back at Xylo. "Tell me who you really are."

Ieska nodded at Xylo, urging him to comply. Xylo sighed. It wasn't likely that this old man would tell anyone his story. And it wasn't even imperative that he keep his story a secret, really, not with someone who wasn't part of the inner circle of the Esh-maor. He sighed again. "My name is Adam Xalantaka. I knew Ieska tangentially while I was in school at Lachar."

Torcalon's white eyebrows shot up when Xylo mentioned Lachar, the training college for the Esh-maor. He shot a disturbed glance toward Ieska.

"Not everything that comes out of Lachar is bad," she reminded the old man.

He sniffed derisively but turned back to Xylo to hear more.

Xylo told the man what had happened, how Kleibald, through nefarious schemes, had won the election to the position of Esh-Maor. How he'd thwarted all Xylo's attempts to serve in his administration, finally driving Xylo into exile, stealing his wife and children, and killing Xylo's youngest son, four-year-old Dochym. Then he related the more current events—how Kleibald, in an effort to reverse the gogyvehr, had escaped from their world with a handful of others.

Torcalon looked at him at him quizzically. "What does this have to do with me? And with Cudth Deorth?"

"Afa's real name was Bracha Elisus," Ieska interjected. "This man was there when she died. And there's more." She looked at Xylo encouragingly.

Reluctantly Xylo related the story of Methiant Migas, his confession, and his death by suicide on the heights of Gannoir. "And so," he finished, "if there is anything I can do to atone for ignoring the pleas of a despondent man, I'd like to do it. I can't help Afa now. I can't help Mailu, her daughter whose body is in the skyboulder with Kleibald. I don't even know why we're here." He looked at Ieska.

Torcalon looked pensive. "This Mailu . . . she was . . . another?" He directed the question toward Ieska.

Ieska shrugged. "Kleibald thought so."

"Another what?" Xylo asked.

Torcalon pressed his lips together. "You've told him nothing?"

"Nothing," Ieska promised.

The old man unwound his tala from around himself and slowly placed his feet back on the floor. "All right," he said, nodding. "Let's go."

He lifted a fur coat from a hook by the doorway and placed it around his shoulders. Xylo wondered if the fur was goat hair or something more exotic. Not many wore fur in Luca. It was too warm, and mammals were too scarce to be killed in any numbers. Only the mhowis goats abounded in the hills of the Orbokth. But the fur did not look like any goat he'd seen. Torcalon pushed the hanging seaweed curtain aside and walked through the rain to the shore. The sea was watery, but it was still early. Rain pelted them as they walked, and Xylo noted how much colder it was in Rhosen than it was nearer Lucedth. For the emaciated old man, it was probably freezing.

He wondered about Torcalon. The old man, though had demanded Xylo's story, had still not told him any of his own. He led Ieska and Xylo to a shed by the shore. Opening a hatch, he cranked a lever that lowered a small boat into the sea. The boat was scarred and looked as though it were as old as Torcalon. They got into the boat and cast off into the night.

Chapter 36: Talag

Talag nervously followed the boy his grandfather had sent to fetch him from his bed. He wondered why his grandfather hadn't come himself. The skyboulder was not large—only ten rooms. It's not like he would have had to walk far. He'd been aware from the time he was small that Kleibald was a powerful man, but he had always acted the part of the proud and doting grandfather with Talag and Donamys. That he should suddenly resort to formality was an ominous sign. He wondered if someone had heard his discussions with Dynny. If someone had told his grandfather that Talag and Dynny were trying to keep him from destroying Gannoir, there was going to be trouble.

The boy nodded at him sleepily as he left Talag by the door to the living room. He'd talked with the boy before, of course. He seemed like a nice person. He wondered who had woken the boy up so that he could fetch Talag. His grandfather? Hardly. Talag giggled a little as he pictured an endless chain of servants, each waking the next so his grandfather wouldn't have to do the job. He took a deep breath before opening the door, trying to settle his nerves. His whole body felt electrified with fear, excitement, anticipation, and the fervent desire to save his world.

"Ah. Talag," Kleibald said as he entered. "Come here and sit down."

Talag obeyed. The room was empty except for his grandfather and himself. He wondered if Gelu had chosen not to participate in the interview or if his grandfather had purposely excluded him. He yawned deliberately and looked at his grandfather with sleepy eyes. "What's up?"

Kleibald examined him. Talag returned his gaze, blinking and sighing occasionally to make his grandfather think he was still half-asleep. Finally he spoke. "You're the Dynroc, I understand." His gaze seemed to burn into Talag's soul. He wondered how his grandfather could look at him like that without seeing the truth.

"I am," he said in a quavering voice. "I didn't want to be. But Dynny's my friend and he's so tired and old—I had to tell him I'd help him." He put on an anxious look.

"So you don't really know anything about what the Dynroc does?" Kleibald asked, his tone indicating grandfatherly concern.

Talag shook his head. "I know it's something about being wise, living in a cave, and looking after the old books of the people on the other side of the Orbokth." He shrugged. "But . . . there's probably more to it than that. Maybe . . . helping people?" he ventured, wrinkling his nose convincingly.

Kleibald smiled. "Just a bit more, young man. It will be a lot of work for you. But I'm confident you can do the job."

Talag was surprised, but he tried not to let it show. "Can you tell me about it?" he asked. "They haven't taught us anything about the other side of the Orbokth in school yet."

"Until a few months ago, few people of Luca even knew about Garradh Gannoir, the opening on the other side of the Orbokth. Now it's common knowledge. But Gannoir is dying."

"Dying?" Talag asked, confused.

Kleibald nodded solemnly. "The old prophecies said that when the two parts of Gannoir began to merge into one, the end would be near. And we were seeing signs of it. The shrinking of the seas. Heightened temperatures on the heights. Electrical storms. Gannoir is going to . . ."

"Going to what?"

"There's no easy way to tell you this," Kleibald said heavily. "Not when there were so many people left behind . . . perhaps people you care about."

"What? What's going to happen?" Talag asked.

"It's going to implode. The balance between the heat of the Ghalon and the supreme cold of the Bec layer is fragile. A slight bobble in the rate of the rotation of either and the world will cave in on itself. The water will burn up. The ice will melt. Gannoir will be restored to the glory it had before the gogyvehr."

"Glory . . ." Tass repeated. "But everyone on Gannoir will die."

"Yes."

"Can we do anything? Can we stop it?"

"You know nothing of the powers of the Dynroc?" Kleibald asked again.

Talag cocked his head. "Powers?"

Kleibald leaned toward Talag, his gray hair sweeping his shoulders. "You can stop Gannoir from dying. Only you have the power."

Talag shut his eyes. He wasn't the Dynroc. Dynny was the Dynroc. Which meant that if his grandfather was telling the truth, only Dynny could stop the death of Gannoir. His head felt muddled. He wished he'd had a good night's sleep before this conversation. Nothing made sense. He'd heard his grandfather and Gelu talking about working with the spirits to destroy Gannoir. Now he seemed to want to save it. Had he heard wrong before? Maybe his grandfather wasn't evil after all. Maybe he had misinterpreted what he'd heard. Maybe saving Gannoir had been the plan all along. When he looked at the situation from that angle, all the uneasiness of the past few days seemed to disappear. His family hadn't betrayed their world. None of them were evil. Everything was just as it had always been.

Or Kleibald was lying to him.

"We need you, Talag," Kleibald urged him.

They needed Dynny, Talag thought. But he said, "What should I do?"

"The spirits of the chaos will tell you what to do," his grandfather said. "They've been guiding me from the beginning. It's because of them that we were able to catapult ourselves out of Gannoir before the end. We're safe here. And if we do what they say, we'll stay that way."

Talag looked around. "Where are they?" he asked.

Kleibald smiled indulgently. "You can't see spirits. You'll hear them when the time is right. In your fire gills. You'll hear them talking to you. Listen and do what they say."

"They brought us out of Gannoir? But that would mean they were there inside Gannoir, not just in the chaos out here. The ancient stories say that all the spirits of the chaos were trapped outside Gannoir at the time of the gogyvehr," Talag protested.

"You know the ancient stories are just myths," Kleibald replied. "Although they got some things right, there was much they did not understand. Some of the spirits of the chaos were trapped on the inside of Gannoir when Tel-Maor damned our world to isolation. They've been trying to get out for centuries."

"You believe in Tel-Maor?" Talag was surprised. The belief in a god who created the world and then inverted its structure was considered laughable by everyone in the academic community of the Esh-maor. Tel-Maor was an invention of the ancients, something they created to explain scientific phenomena they didn't understand.

"I didn't at first," Kleibald said. "But when the spirits came to me it was apparent that they believed. They are fighting against the unjust punishment inflicted on our world by Tel-Maor. There's a big universe out there. Other worlds we could communicate and trade with. We could expand our knowledge and our technology. We could travel to other worlds. We could experience things we could never dream of. If only Tel-Maor hadn't chosen to close Gannoir in on itself."

"So Tel-Maor is real." Talag digested this. He'd heard Dynny talk about the ruler of their world, the god who lived in the fiery Ghalon. He'd excused it in the little man. He had a childlike mind. It seemed natural that he should also have childish beliefs. Yet here was his grandfather telling him that Dynny's primitive take on life was actually true.

"He's real. And he's evil," Kleibald asserted. "That's why we have to work with the spirits of the chaos. They're trying to set us free from the oppression imposed on us. You can understand that, can't you, boy?"

"They want to reverse the gogyvehr," Talag realized.

"Of course!"

Talag closed his eyes, wincing. "But that can't be right. Turning Gannoir inside out would kill everyone in the world. It wouldn't save Gannoir. It would destroy Gannoir."

"Gannoir isn't water and fire and rock," his grandfather said gently. "It's people. The people of Gannoir. The Esh and the Gulot and the Mayim. And the others. They're what needs saving. The world of Gannoir is dying. We need your help to save the heart of Gannoir. The people." His grandfather looked at him with sincere, imploring eyes.

"I'll do it!" Talag exclaimed sincerely, forgetting for a moment that he was not, in fact, the Dynroc. None of this was what he had expected. He had thought his grandfather was evil. But he was really trying to save his people. His grandfather was a hero.

Kleibald placed a hand on Talag's shoulder. "I knew you would agree once you understood. Go back to bed. And keep your gills open to listen for the voices. Now that you're the Dynroc you'll be able to hear them. Do what they say, for our sake and for the sake of the people of Gannoir."

Chapter 37: Tass

A cord of water knocked against Tass and then swirled around her.

"Dwoyra!" she exclaimed in her gill-speech.

"Tass . . . help . . . help . . ." Dwoyra pleaded.

"What?" Tass asked, wishing she were more adept at speaking with the watery being. She wondered if Dwoyra would repeat her request for blood. Was that what it was going to take to convince Dwoyra she was on her side? She exhaled in the gill-lung version of a sigh.

Dwoyra shoved Tass through the water, guiding her . . . somewhere. Tass let herself be taken along. Under the shelf of the Orbokth she again saw the thick coating of dga, their shimmering metallic exoskeletons blurred and obliterated by the spots of darkness. The sight of them was oppressive, evil.

Tass shuddered. "Dwoyra, I can't. I can't possibly bleed that much. It would take the blood of thousands of the Siann Dha to counteract that much darkness."

"Light is life," Dwoyra spoke inside her head.

And blood makes light. Tass knew it was true. Darkness wasn't a thing. It couldn't be. Darkness was what happened when light didn't exist. It wasn't a thing in itself. Yet here it was, blotches not of a substance that was the color black, but blotches of darkness, casting darkness instead of light. Waves of darkness. An immaterial evil that could only be conquered by . . . what?

She shook he head. "I don't think it's going to work, Dwoyra," she garbled. "Won't work. Too much darkness."

"Light is life . . . blood . . ." Dwoyra insisted.

"How?" Tass asked, trying to figure out how with her limited ability to speak in her gill voice she could communicate what she needed to say. "Where did they come from?"

Dwoyra swirled around her in agitation.

"How?" Tass repeated. "Too much darkness."

Dwoyra's shape changed from a roughly cylindrical thick column of water to a globe encircling Tass. "Holes," she asserted. "Fissures." The globe of water that was Dwoyra began to spin around Tass. Tass closed her eyes as the creatures in the water around her grew blurred by Dwoyra's obstructing presence. Dwoyra continued. "Cracks. Holes. Gaps. Hurry."

Tass started to understand. It was what Xylo had sent her to find. What Ceres had tried to find but couldn't. Holes in the Bec layer. Holes that threatened the existence of Gannoir. Holes through which the darkness was seeping into her world. She seethed, unwilling to do Xylo's bidding. Or Dwoyra's. She didn't want to obliterate the holes. She wanted to crack one of them wide open. To make a hole big enough for the skyboulder to come back. For Mailu to come back. She wanted her sister.

Now was the time for deception. "Show me," she requested.

The sphere of water around her shattered into a million droplets and then reformed as a column of water again. "Too deep," Dwoyra protested.

Tass bit her lip in frustration. "What do you want?" she managed to ask. What she wanted to ask was how she was supposed to solve the problem. Dwoyra wouldn't take her to the frigid purple layers of the sea to see the holes in the Bec. The watery creature seemed to expect her to swim around bleeding for all eternity, gradually annihilating the darkness by the power of her blood. The blood of the Siann Dha.

What did Igracio's death matter now, if the Bec was springing holes in it? The water would leak out first, out into the chaos. The seas would be gone. Eventually Gannoir would implode, and everyone would die. She couldn't stop it. Even if she and all the people of Luca bled continually for the rest of their lives it wouldn't be enough to negate all the darkness.

She didn't have to do what Xylo told her to do. She didn't have to obey Dwoyra. She had to do what she had to do. Save Mailu first. Bring the skyboulder home. And then worry about the holes in the Bec later. *Maybe,* she thought, *one of the holes is big enough already.*

"Go down?" Tass asked Dwoyra.

The column of water swirled around Tass anxiously. "Cold."

"Lumalauae," Tass protested. The lumalauae had kept her . . . not exactly warm, but alive in the depths before. They could do it again. She tensed as she thought of the icy depths, of how her mind and body slowed near the Bec layer to almost complete inactivity. Time itself seemed to hold still at the fringes of their world.

She could tell Dwoyra was still fretting.

"Show me," she begged. Tass pushed through the water, passing from the glowing yellow of the chemical sea into the orange layer. She felt the change in the water's composition as she drew nearer to the bottom. Cold. Stinging. Acidic, even more so than the yellow layer had been. The lumalauae followed her, as did Dwoyra. A blubbery vauzigk swished past her in the distance, and then another.

"Vauzigk!" Tass said as loud as she could through her gills. If she had the protection of both a vauzigk and the lumalauae, she might be able to keep her mind alive at the depths. She might be able to figure out a plan, both to open a gap wide enough for the skyboulder and to close the other holes in the Bec. She had to be able to think.

She felt Dwoyra rush away from her. Dwoyra would fetch one of the warm, furry creatures to embrace her in the cold. She kicked her legs above her, letting the water catch against the tala between her fingers and toes as she pushed into a salmon-colored layer of the sea.

Chapter 38: Xylo

The mist was thick as they arrived on the distant shore of the Orbokth. Xylo shivered, wishing he had a coat like Torcalon's furry one. He looked at Ieska. She didn't seem to mind the cold. Xylo wondered how that was possible since she, like himself, was Esh and built for the heat of the heights.

The mist was golden with the feeble strands of firstlight. Although looking up he couldn't see the ceiling of their world, Xylo knew that a sliver of the fiery side of the Ghalon must have slid into view. The rain had turned to mist during their journey. In Lucedth, the mornings were clear and the temperatures, moderate. The water in the air had fallen as rain during the night, and at the break of day, before the heat overwhelmed Luca, the evaporation that caused the mists would not yet have begun. He wondered how the rains had failed to dissolve the mists here. It lent an eerie atmosphere to the shore.

Torcalon docked the little boat in a cove behind a rocky outcropping of the Orbokth. They climbed ashore onto the rich brown boulders. Xylo wrapped his wrinkled tala around his body, trying to stay warm. Torcalon's eyes twinkled at him. "Cold?"

"I'm Esh," Xylo grumbled.

"He's not used to it here," Ieska said mildly. She took Xylo's hand. Her skin was warm.

"What kind of fur is that?" Xylo asked, looking at Torcalon's coat. "I'd guess it was mhowis goat, but it doesn't look like it."

Torcalon snorted. "You'll see soon enough," he said.

The cliffs of the Orbokth rose high before them on all sides save for the narrow inlet through which they had rowed into the cove. If anyone lived there, Xylo saw no signs of it. He knew asking questions would be useless. Torcalon was eminently tight-lipped, and Ieska was just as reticent. Whatever her secret was, she was determined to keep it until the last minute.

Torcalon began to climb the cliffside. Ieska followed, nimbly for an old woman who had spent her life as an academic in Lucedth, Xylo thought. Having spent years as a soil miner on the heights, Xylo was used to climbing. Over many years he had perfected the talent of using his tala to catch the breeze to improve his balance and propel him along on his way. Torcalon and Ieska, he was surprised to note, had the same ability. He wondered if Torcalon had spent years as a soil miner just as he had. Ieska, however . . . he couldn't fathom how her skills had come to her.

The air warmed as they climbed. Xylo wondered if there was a community of Esh mining soil at the top of the Orbokth. He hadn't heard of a mine on this side of Lucedth, but then it was possible that it had not existed during the years he had been in the leadership of Luca. He didn't know everything. Not anymore.

While the cliffs were still high overhead, however, Torcalon turned aside, neatly slipping behind a jagged tor of rock into a crevice. Ieska and Xylo followed him. It was dark inside and it took some time for Xylo's eyes to adjust to the change in light. He felt his way with hands and feet, anxious lest the rocky ground descend or ascend in front of him. Eventually he noted that it wasn't completely dark. The tunnel was lit by bits of phosphorescent algae, the same kind he had noticed on his first foray into the other side of the Orbokth on his journey with Afa. He sighed. Thoughts of Afa were always saturated with his gut-wrenching guilt. His thoughts wandered darkly until he suddenly realized he couldn't see the shadowy forms of Ieska and Torcalon in front of him anymore.

"Ieska?" he called in a low voice.

"Over here," her voice echoed back to him.

Xylo followed her voice, carefully picking his way through the uneven, rocky tunnel. The tunnel had forked while he was lost in thought, and he had kept on going straight where Ieska and Torcalon had turned. He entered the new tunnel, which was lit by a strange light from a greenish variety of glowing algae and by a faint red glow from above. Mixed, they lit the tunnel with a sickly, brownish haze. They descended on a steep, damp path. Here, however, and much to Xylo's relief, the ground was smooth and had a strange spongy quality.

Gradually the light increased, although whether it was due to the gradual adjustments in his vision, to the dawning day, or to the coming end of the tunnel, he couldn't tell. He could see the dark silhouettes of his companions ahead of him as he walked. Their footsteps were even and unhurried.

After some time, the ceiling of the tunnel grew farther from them. They were descending on an ever-widening path. Plant-life tickled Xylo's ankles above his shoes as he walked. He wished it were light enough to see what the plants were. As a soil miner, he'd seen plants on the heights, plants with dry, papery leaves and slim, reddish stalks. There had been fuuegn too, as well as other types of fungus. But there had been nothing like what he felt at his feet now. It was soft and damp. When he bent to touch it, he found that the leaves were thin, fragile, and fragrant. He felt himself slowing, beginning to enjoy Ieska and Torcalon's easy pace. It gave him time to think. Time to wonder.

The greenish light of the phosphorescent algae dimmed as the red-orange light from ahead grew brighter. As they emerged from the broad tunnel into an open space, Xylo put a hand against the wall of the cliff behind him and was surprised to find it streaming with water. Plants grew on either side of the rivulets running down the face of the rock. He stood gazing for some time, astonished by what he saw. It was like nothing he had ever seen. Accustomed to a world of reds and oranges, lit by the fire of the Ghalon, Xylo found the pervasive blues and greens of the foliage jarring. The space was not large compared to Luca or Garradh Gannoir. Still, it was big enough. The brilliant turquoise water occupied most of the low-lying places, and he could see people splashing and leaping as they swam. The smoke from a cooking fire rose and mingled with the golden mists in the air.

Now that he could see more clearly, Xylo bent again to examine the plants at his feet. They were a bright green with feathery leaves and flowers of blue and purple, delicate, fragile, with tall, slender, green stems. He had never seen plants such as these, not even in Garradh Gannoir where plant life was more abundant. The space was surrounded on all sides by cliffs covered in a variety of green, blooming plants. Dark blotches occupied the crevices everywhere he looked. He gasped with amazement when he realized what the dark blotches were. Ugaz. They were ugaz. The unusual life-forms were thought to be nearly extinct the world over. With mammalian bodies and plant souls, the headless beings had been hunted by the ancients for their fur and meat until they were all but gone. But here . . . here in this hidden pocket of life, they lived on.

Xylo's sense of urgency faded. If there were places like this still, places where the cross-over life-forms still existed, what else might he find? He reached out a hand to touch the fragile ugaz nearest him. The creature shuddered as he stroked it, and he wondered at the existence of mind that was so sensitive, and yet immobile and irrational. The mind of a plant in the body of a beast. He looked over at Torcalon, whose eyes were twinkling at him again.

"It's ugaz, isn't it?" he asked. "The fur of your coat?"

Torcalon nodded. "As you can see, they are plentiful here. Even so, we are careful with them. Careful with their lives. We harvest only the largest ugaz, and make sure that the offspring recolonize the empty part of the cliff. This may be the last pocket of ugaz on Gannoir, but I don't think so." His eyes grew dreamy. "I don't think so at all."

"I can see why you brought me here," Xylo replied, awe in his voice.

Ieska took his hand and looked into his eyes. "I would have brought you just for this," she told him. "But . . . that's not why we're here."

He looked at her, remembering his earlier expectations. "Yes?"

"There's someone I want you to meet," she told him.

Xylo couldn't read her expression. Too many emotions flickered across her features at the same time. Pride. Humility. Terror. Hope.

He took a deep breath. "Your child?" he asked.

She bit her lip. "My daughter." She hesitated and looked at Torcalon.

He nodded encouragingly.

"My daughter . . . and the daughter of Methiant Migas." She looked at Xylo as though expecting him to . . . to . . . what?

Xylo tried not to let his shock show on his face. Methiant Migas was the father of Ieska's child? Methiant Migas . . . the criminal who had been the subject of the scientific research Ieska and others had been ordered to conduct. Methiant Migas . . . whose soul had been destroyed by Kleibald's illicit experimentation. Methiant Migas . . . who had raped Afa and, according to his own words, had fathered a child with her. Methiant Migas . . . who had killed himself after confessing his sins to Xylo.

As he looked into Ieska's eyes, he felt as though his soul were imploding within him. Her pain became his pain. He understood something that had been puzzling him since he had told Ieska about his encounter with Methiant Migas. She had thought he was telling her story, the story of her own rape and impregnation, not Afa's.

Guilt closed over Xylo's heart like a flood. Here was another woman whom he had failed. He couldn't have known. Methiant Migas had only mentioned Afa by name. He had known there were others, but he hadn't bothered to try to find them, to try to bring Kleibald to justice for the pain he had caused to so many. Yowling agony flowed through his body as he thought of his own failure to act. He should have done something. He should have tried. He should have . . .

He turned away from Ieska, closing his eyes. "He raped you," he said in a low voice.

"He did," Ieska replied.

"I'm sorry."

Torcalon stepped into the conversation. "Not as sorry as I am."

Xylo opened his eyes and looked at the old man, marveling again at the intensity of his spirit within his shriveled, broken body. He shook his head. "What do you mean?"

Torcalon's eyes bored into Xylo's soul. "The man you call Methiant Migas . . . He was my son."

Chapter 39: Talag

Once he heard his grandfather climb into his bunk in the chamber they shared with eight others, Talag waited for his breathing to quiet to the even, regular pace that indicated he was asleep. Then he crept out of his bunk and slipped out of the room.

He went into the hallway and made his way to the room where Dynny slept, keeping guard over Mailu. He waited until the door had slid shut behind him and then shook the little man by the shoulder.

"Dynny!" he whispered. "Dynny! Wake up!"

Dynny sat up, blinking rapidly. "I'm the Dynroc," he muttered sleepily.

Talag grinned. "You're the Dynroc," he affirmed. "Wake up, Dynny. You're dreaming."

Dynny looked at Talag and his eyes slowly focused. "Is it still night?"

"Yes. But I had to come tell you before anyone else was up. My grandfather just talked to me. He's not doing anything bad after all!" Relief and joy were in Talag's voice. "He's not trying to destroy

Gannoir. Gannoir is dying. He's trying to save the people so they won't die with the world."

Dynny frowned, his wrinkles meeting over his eyebrows in comical consternation. "Gelu's bad. Gelu killed the Dynroc, 58th of that name. And Kleibald is his friend."

"I don't know about Gelu," Talag admitted. "But my grandfather's not doing anything wrong. He just wants to help people. They'll die unless he helps them."

Dynny blinked. He seemed to be struggling to understand. "I thought they were trying to destroy the world."

"I must have heard wrong," Talag replied. "Grandfather said that Gannoir is going to implode. No matter what any of us do, Gannoir is dying. He's trying to reverse the gogyvehr, to turn Gannoir right-side-out again so our world can be the way it was made to be. But he needs you, the Dynroc, to help him so that the people don't die when it happens."

"Tel-Maor made the gogyvehr," Dynny protested. "Tel-Maor doesn't want the bad spirits to get us."

"Grandfather says that the spirits aren't bad. They're trying to help us."

"The spirits are bad. They're fighting with Tel-Maor," Dynny stubbornly argued.

This was going badly, Talag reflected. His elderly friend was thoroughly entrenched in the religion of the ancients. He hadn't bothered about it before. It had seemed like a harmless illusion. But now . . . now he had to convince Dynny to go along with the plan if they were going to save the people of Gannoir. Dynny was the Dynroc, and Kleibald said the powers of the Dynroc were needed. If he couldn't convince Dynny to listen to the spirits and obey them, then everyone was going to die when Gannoir imploded and turned itself right-side-out.

"Maybe . . ." Talag said hesitantly, "Maybe not all of the spirits are bad. Maybe some are bad, like you said, but maybe there are a couple good ones out there. Ones that are trying to help us. Trying to help Gannoir."

Dynny looked at Talag suspiciously.

"Grandfather said the spirits are talking to him. Good spirits that want to save the people of Gannoir."

"Gelu killed Arros," Dynny noted, his voice full of sorrow and anxiety.

"Gelu wasn't there," Talag told him. "Just Kleibald. Maybe they're not on the same side. Maybe Kleibald is just tricking Gelu so he can save more people." He wasn't sure he believed this, but if it served to persuade Dynny to donate his powers to the cause, the potential lie was worth it.

"The spirits aren't talking to Gelu?" Dynny asked.

Talag shook his head emphatically, reflecting briefly that he wasn't altogether sure it was true. "Nope. Just Kleibald. They're good spirits. Trying to save the people of Gannoir."

"I won't help Gelu," Dynny pouted.

"You won't have to," Talag told him. "Just listen to the voice of the spirits. Grandfather said they'd talk to me now that I'm the Dynroc. But I couldn't tell him that I wasn't the Dynroc, that you were. So it will have to be you. The voices will come and tell you what to do. Okay?"

Dynny looked at Talag with frightened, anxious eyes. "I don't want to talk to spirits."

"Good spirits," Talag promised. "Just like Tel-Maor."

"Tel-Maor is good," Dynny agreed.

"And Tel-Maor is a spirit, right?" Talag pressed, hoping his assumption was correct. He wasn't sure he believed in Tel-Maor, or even if he believed in good and bad spirits, but if his grandfather was right and the only chance to save the people of Gannoir was to listen to voices from the chaos, he wanted to make sure that listening happened.

Dynny looked perplexed. "Tel-Maor isn't a spirit. He's Tel-Maor. He lives in the Ghalon."

"Only a spirit could live in the Ghalon," Talag pointed out. He watched Dynny's face for any sign of understanding or agreement.

"Tel-Maor is good. Are you sure he's a spirit?" Dynny finally asked.

Talag smiled encouragingly. "Of course he is. He couldn't live in the Ghalon otherwise. So that means sometimes spirits are good, right?"

Dynny's wrinkles of concentration smoothed out. "I think you must be right."

"So you'll listen to the voices and do what they say?" Talag asked.

"Yes," Dynny replied. "Tel-Maor is good and Tel-Maor must be a spirit. So it must be all right."

"Thanks," Talag whispered. He didn't tell Dynny what his grandfather had said about Tel-Maor. Kleibald believed Tel-Maor was evil. Kleibald believed that Tel-Maor was holding them captive in an isolated and dangerous world.

He brushed off the prickings of conscience as he made his way back to his bunk. He'd done what was necessary to save his people. Did it matter if he lied to one mentally challenged old man?

Chapter 40: Tass

Dwoyra swam ahead. Tass balled her body up and nestled into the warm, blubbery flesh of the vauzigk. Three lumalauae swirled around the pair, making a nest of warmth. The sea around Tass turned pink and then magenta as they descended.

Without Dwoyra, Tass found that her tormentors, the voices that spoke anguish into her gills and into her mind, once more resumed their torment.

You're nothing . . . your mind is inferior . . . you're Mayim . . . you don't know who to trust or who to follow . . . they're all against you . . . you're the only one who wants to rescue Mailu . . .

Tass fought against the voices, but at the same time, she found herself believing their message. She was Mayim. She was of the uneducated water caste. She didn't know much. She wasn't as smart as the Gulot or the Esh. She thought she understood the motives of those around her—Dwoyra, Xylo, the Master at the Calix—but it was possible that there was more going on in them than she perceived. She would have to be careful. Trust was inappropriate. They were right.

And as far as rescuing Mailu went, the voices were again correct. Dwoyra had no thoughts of rescuing Mailu. All Dwoyra wanted was a continuous flow of Tass's blood to expel the darkness from Gannoir. Xylo wanted to use her as a scout to find out where the cracks in the Bec layer were, to find out how the darkness was getting in. She wasn't sure if his motives were just to protect Gannoir or if there was more going on that she didn't know about. No, she surely couldn't trust Xylo. And the Master wanted her to obey.

She snorted, drawing the acidic seawater in through her nose accidentally. She coughed and spat, trying to force the seawater out of her air-lungs while continuing to breathe with her gills. The caustic liquid burned her sinuses. The Master . . . she had never been obedient to the Master. Not really. She'd done what he said when it seemed to be in her best interests. But all the Master wanted was glory for himself and for the Calix.

She was the only one who had any thought of bringing Mailu back, of trying to infuse her with new life. Her sister needed her. The voices continued to hiss truths into her gills, coaxing her, goading her into action. She would follow Dwoyra. She would see where the cracks in the Bec were. But she wasn't going to give her life for Gannoir like Igracio had done. Noble Igracio. Foolish Igracio. She squashed her pain as she thought of him, her first and only friend, the one person who had treated her kindly since she had been expelled from her home and from the loving arms of her sister. The fleeting memories of an older sister who had loved her had ballooned to an all-encompassing passion in Tass's soul. She had to do what she had to do, no matter what Dwoyra or Xylo wanted and no matter what the Master said she had to do.

The seawater around Tass grew darker, and she felt her blood slow in her veins. Her thoughts dimmed and became sludgy. She was close to the edge now. In the distance she could see the giant dga guarding the scar over what had been the Bilik, the hole in the Bec layer that the power of Igracio's unique blood had healed. She wasn't close enough to see it, but she knew the blotches of darkness still obscured its metallic sheen.

Suddenly Dwoyra was swirling around her, adding warmth to that provided by the vauzigk and the lumalauae and driving away the voices that had plagued Tass since they had separated. Dwoyra created a current that drew them further from the Bilik. Tass could see the dancing fire of the Bec layer, not a solid and frigid layer of ice, but a cold fire, atoms moving in a vast symphony and creating an impossible harmony that was more solid that ice and colder as well. It was nothing and it was everything.

The Bec was inhabited by a soul, or souls. It was rational. It was a being, a person, someone she could know. Someone she ought to know. But there was no way to communicate with it. No way to draw near enough to let that ultimate flame push into her gills and tell her about itself. She wondered if trying such a thing would result in her death. Could she live through an infusion of something so cold it wasn't a liquid or a solid, but something beyond both? Or maybe the spirit itself could speak to her mind like the voices did, without being embodied in the burning coldness of the Bec.

Dwoyra circled the vauzigk again and turned it so Tass could see the section of the Bec directly below her. A slash of darkness barely bigger than her finger interrupted the purple flames. Darkness. Was it the darkness merely standing between her and the Bec so that she couldn't see through it? Or was it a hole, a gap in the cold fire itself? She suspected she knew the answer.

"Hole?" she asked Dwoyra slowly. Her thoughts were racing, which she attributed to the warming presence of the creatures surrounding her, but her body was still moving much more slowly than usual.

"More," Dwoyra spoke back to her inside her head. Tass could feel the watery creature's sorrow. "More holes . . ."

Dwoyra led Tass and her entourage forward, zigzagging back and forth over large swaths of the Bec. It was riddled with tiny holes, little rips in the fabric of their world. Tiny dga swum through the waters carrying lumps of darkness on their backs. There were no other sea creatures at this level, and Tass wondered if it were because of the darkness that had invaded the sea or if it were just due to the temperatures. She suspected it was the former.

Even Tass, determined as she was not to join Dwoyra in her crusade against the darkness, was disturbed to see the gashes in the Bec and the sheer quantity of darkness, of evil, that was riding the dga into the world of Gannoir. She wondered idly what vehicle the darkness would choose should it come out of the sea onto the clatries or the Orbokth. The life forms of Gannoir largely inhabited the sea. There were few animals on land except in the highest heights of the Orbokth where things like mhowis goats and yovod, the enormous wildcats, lived. She'd heard rumors about giant scolopendra, the elongated flying creatures with thousands of disgusting legs, and vervol, the flying worms, but she had never met anyone who had actually seen them. Would the dark blotches choose one of those to ride just as they rode the dga? Or would they choose a person—a Mayim, a Gulot, or an Esh? Which caste would be most hospitable to a dark visitor, she wondered.

Tass put out a hand, reaching toward the tiny rents in the fabric of her world. They were small enough that they seemed like they would be inconsequential, but she knew they were important. If she could touch one of the holes, if she could put her hand into the cold fire, immerse it in the dancing flames, maybe she could figure out a way to bring Mailu home.

Tass nestled back within the blubbery body of the vauzigk, withdrawing her outstretched hand. Feelings of hopelessness left her colder than the icy water did. She had no idea what she could do to bring her sister back. She couldn't reach out into the chaos beyond Gannoir to grab the skyboulder and pull it home. Dwoyra circled around her anxiously, muttering about darkness, evil, and holes. Tass pressed her lips together. She could no more solve the problem of the tiny gaps in the Bec than she could solve the problem of how to create a larger one.

Suddenly Tass's shoulders began to ache with the cold. The lumalauae still circled, but she felt dull and listless. She wanted to go home. She wanted to rest. She wanted . . . she wanted . . .

Kicking her legs, she broke free of the embrace of the vauzigk and propelled her body upward through the water. The lumalauae followed her, creating a cyclone of the acidic water that stung her skin with a life-giving intensity.

She wanted to go home.

Chapter 41: Xylo

For the second time in just a few moments, Xylo was taken aback. "Your son? Methiant Migas was your son?"

Torcalon's face was grave. "He wasn't a good man. But they destroyed him. They took his soul and ripped it to shreds."

"I ripped it to shreds," Ieska said softly.

Xylo closed his eyes as he felt the seething pain of his companions like a force hovering in the air around them. Ieska had been one of the scientists who had conducted the experiments on the man who came to be known as Methiant Migas. She had done it in good faith, trying to create something extraordinary. She had done it because she'd been ordered to do so by the elders. But she, better than anyone else, knew the evil that had come of her actions.

"This wasn't your fault," Xylo said softly. "You didn't mean . . . you couldn't have known . . ."

"I don't blame Ieska," Torcalon said. "She's a victim too. Like my son. Like your Afa. Like the others. All of them." He gestured toward the people walking on the rocky paths, swimming in the water, climbing on the vine-covered walls of the Orbokth.

Xylo followed his moving hand. "All of these, then . . . all of them . . ." He took a deep, slow breath.

"They're my grandchildren," Torcalon told him. "The biological children of my son—and their families. They couldn't stay in Lucedth. They didn't fit in there. They don't belong anywhere." His face was sad.

"Anywhere but here," Ieska said, smiling at the old man. "They have this place. And they have each other."

Xylo watched as a young man gripping a vine far above his head suddenly spread out his tala and glided quickly into the water. He gasped. "It happened then? The children of Methiant Migas . . . they're tri-casted? Three-in-one . . . All of them . . ." He thought sadly of Igracio and his impossible sacrifice, and of Tass with her newly glowing fingers.

"I'd like it if you could call my son by his original name," Torcalon requested. "It was Methiant Migas who committed the crimes that created this tribe of misfits, but they bear the blood of my son and possess some of his finer qualities." His eyes were full of love for his son and for his grandchildren. "He was called Mantais. Mantais Nayro."

Xylo repeated the name after the old man.

The gravity of the moment was interrupted as a small furry creature sprang from the abundant foliage and raced across Xylo's foot. He yelped in surprise. "What was that?"

Ieska grinned and Xylo saw her exuberant personality for the first time since they'd come to the mysterious land. "It's a feollyr," she told him. "There are many here."

Xylo stared at the creature, which had paused on an outcropping of rock near the streaming wall. Its caramel-colored fur was thick and plush. Flexible translucent violet ears were large compared to the size of its head and they came to a delicate point at the top. A tail longer than its body was coiled around a thick stalk of one of the climbing plants. He shook his head in wonder. "Many? I've never even heard of them. Feollyr, did you say?"

Ieska nodded. "They're everywhere. A pest, really, stealing food and small items and making off with them."

"Are they mixed souls like the ugaz?" he asked, looking askance at the little creature as though it might suddenly speak to him.

"Animal soul and animal body," Ieska said with a laugh. "Like teeny tiny mhowis goats. Only cuter."

"You'll find there are many undiscovered creatures here," Torcalon told him. "When we found this hollow, we knew it was the right place for our children. A place for beings who are different and who want to remain unknown to the elders of Luca. It's perfect."

"How many are there? Three-in-ones, I mean, not undiscovered creatures. How many grandchildren do you have?" Xylo asked.

"There are seven that I've found," Torcalon told him. "Anywhere from twelve years old to twenty-five."

"And they all came here with their families?"

"Not all," Torcalon replied. "Some were abandoned at birth. Their existence caused too much pain to their mothers. Others were left once it was discovered that they were not able to be casted. With finger tala as well as body tala, their differences were apparent early on in their lives. Four came with at least some family. The other three were adopted into the families that were willing to abandon Lucedth for the sake of their offspring."

Xylo looked at the settlement. Dwellings had been carved into the walls of the Orbokth, he now saw. He hadn't noticed at first because of the abundant green foliage that overhung the doorways. He counted four openings in the rock and assumed there were others that he had not been able to discern with his untrained eyes.

A young woman glided down from the heights and threw her arms around Ieska. Her eyes were a bright shade of blue but otherwise she looked almost exactly as Xylo remembered Ieska from their younger days at Lachar. As she let go of Ieska, Xylo saw her glowing fingertips.

"Your daughter?" Xylo asked, knowing what the answer would be.

Ieska stroked the girl's long black hair. "This is my daughter, Saoradi Thayl Nayro. Sadi, this is Adam Xalantaka. Xylo."

"What is he doing here?" Sadi asked bluntly, looking at Xylo with a mix of curiosity and suspicion.

"Many things are happening in Gannoir," Ieska replied. "Kleibald is gone, expelled from the world. Xylo is trying to bring him back. To bring him to justice."

Sadi made a face. "Expelled from the world wasn't enough?" She turned to greet her grandfather, an individual whom she obviously adored. She hugged the gaunt old man and kissed his wrinkled cheek.

"There are other things to consider," Ieska told her daughter. "If it were just about Kleibald and others like him, I would agree with you. A slow death of starvation while floating aimlessly in the chaos would be something akin to justice for a man like Kleibald. But more needs to change in Lucedth. Not just Kleibald. The elders need to know what he has done, how he has hurt all of us and all Gannoir. For his actions to be brought to light, he must be brought back."

Sadi frowned. "Expelled from the world . . . I want to hear more about it. How it happened. I want to understand."

"We will gather everyone," Ieska said. "They should all hear the story." She looked at Xylo expectantly. "You'll talk to them?"

He nodded, knowing that he wouldn't be able to present only Kleibald's public crimes to these people who had been so deeply scarred because of what Kleibald had done. He would have to give them his heart if he expected them to understand. And, he thought, they all deserved to hear about their father's suicide in sorrow over the wretched state of his soul.

He looked at this young woman, trying to see in her something of the desperate man whose last moments he had witnessed. He could barely remember the man himself. The image that had been burned into his mind was the sight of him falling from the heights his body prone in the air, going to his death. He tried to remember if Methiant Migas . . . Mantais Nayro, that is . . . had his daughter's electric blue eyes.

He sighed. "Of course. Let's gather your family and I will tell you all what I know."

Chapter 42: Talag

Talag overslept the next morning. Sleep hadn't come easily to him the night before. His thoughts had been full of all that he had learned. Almost he had become accustomed to the idea that he could trust no one, that his grandfather was the instigator of an evil plot to destroy the world and that the rest of his family—the adults at least—were in on it. He still felt dazed by the reality. His grandfather wasn't doing anything wrong. His family wasn't plotting against Gannoir. They were on a mission—all of them—to save their world. His heart swelled with pride and anticipation. And fear. Despite his new solidarity with his grandfather, there was still work to be done. Dangerous work. Frightening work.

Talag heard giggles as his sister, Donamys, and two of the other girls came into the sleeping chamber. Even though they were whispering, he could hear every word. They probably didn't realize anyone was still in bed. Their secrets were stupid, he realized, and with a groan he rolled over and covered his head with his blanket, hoping to shut out their irritating voices and go back to sleep.

Sleep did not come.

The girls finished exchanging confidences—asinine secrets about the crushes they had on boys on the skyboulder and their plans for who would marry whom. Like they would have had a choice. Even if his grandfather's original plan had succeeded and they had lit on another world, Kleibald would have been the one doing the matchmaking, not the giggly girls. Talag knew, however, that his condescending attitude was not just born of disdain. His sister had made friends during their months on the skyboulder. He had not—at least not friends his own age. Just Dynny. It had always been like that, and it always would be, even though Donamys was shallow and bratty, and he (he reasoned carefully) tried to always be kind to others.

A stab of guilt shot through him as he remembered his lies the night before. He shouldn't have lied to Dynny. He was relatively sure that his grandfather and Gelu were working together. Nothing had suggested otherwise. Nothing except his own words to Dynny, his only real friend in the skyboulder. Ashamed, he resolved to tell Dynny the truth as soon as he was able, as soon as they were alone where no one could hear him.

Talag bit his lip. What if Dynny wouldn't help save Gannoir? What if his determination not to have anything to do with Gelu and his plans resulted in the destruction of everyone in their world? He didn't much like Gelu himself, but he would work with him if it meant saving the people of Gannoir from destruction. He would have to make Dynny understand. When the voices came, Dynny would have to do what they said. He would have to. Everything depended on it.

Something inside Talag relaxed as his guilt about his lies abated. He felt himself drifting off to sleep again, and he was grateful.

It seemed that no time had passed at all when he heard someone calling him. Groggily he scrunched up his face and tried to determine whose voice he was hearing. Was it worth it to wake up all the way? Or should he pretend he hadn't heard? He strained his ears to hear the intermittent calls, finally opening one eye to increase the power of his hearing. It wasn't Donamys and her friends. The voice was too low. Grandfather? No. Maybe his father or his uncle Nadim? He rejected those ideas as well. And it wasn't Dynny. Dynny wouldn't have stood at a distance occasionally calling his name. Dynny would have climbed up on the bunk and forced him to wake. He sighed and laughed a little at the thought, wishing it were Dynny who had come for him. Then he could get it over with—he could make his confession and relax.

The voice continued to call him. "Talag . . . Talag . . . Talag . . ." The frequency was increasing, but it had a mechanical regularity to it that surprised him. It sounded like whoever was calling him was timing the words, adjusting the intervals by seconds with each time he spoke. It was . . . wrong.

Talag sat up and looked down at the sleeping chamber. The bunks of the five-berth-high women's tower opposite the men's bunks were empty. He couldn't see below his own bunk to learn whether any of the men were present.

"Uncle Nadim?" he said tentatively.

There was no answer.

"Grandfather? Father?"

All he heard was "Talag . . . Talag . . . Talag . . ."

Talag frowned and tried the name of his final bunkmate. "Mr . . . ah . . . Lefty?"

No one was there. Talag was alone.

A sudden chill enveloped him.

Voices.

Voices calling him.

Voices speaking to the Dynroc, bringing instructions for the salvation of Gannoir . . .

His breath caught in his throat. He felt his heart jump. Why were the voices talking to him? They were supposed to talk to the Dynroc, to Dynny. Dynny was the Dynroc still. Their mock ceremony had done nothing to change that. A spirit would know the difference. A spirit would be able to see the presence of the powers—whatever they were—that his grandfather believed the Dynroc possessed.

It couldn't be spirits.

Someone was playing a trick on him.

His old doubts returned as he wondered if the prankster could be his grandfather, or Gelu, or one of the other men in the skyboulder. Maybe his grandfather didn't believe in spirits after all. Maybe he just said that so Talag would obey his commands. And now he was pretending to bring spirit messages to Talag, to make him . . . to make him . . . to make him do what? He wasn't sure. But the thing of which he was certain was that he was not the Dynroc. Dynny was. And only he and Dynny knew it. Whoever was trying to make him believe he was hearing spirit voices was ignorant. A spirit wouldn't be ignorant. So it couldn't be a spirit. It had to be a trick.

He lay back down on his bunk and pulled the blanket over his shoulders. He would wait—wait and listen. He was no longer sure whether to believe his grandfather. If his grandfather had been telling the truth, the spirits would have been speaking to Dynny, not to him. But if his grandfather was trying to trick him, then could he believe anything he said?

He scrunched up his face in frustration. It didn't make sense. If his grandfather didn't believe in the powers of the Dynroc, then his grandfather wouldn't be trying to rally Talag to his side with fake voices. And if his grandfather did believe in spirits and powers, then the voices were no trick. And if the voice was no trick, if it was a spirit voice who could see the power of the Dynroc like an aura, then that meant . . . that meant . . .

Talag covered his ears as though it would stop his thoughts from continuing.

Was it possible?

Could it have happened?

What if . . . what if . . .

What if their fake ceremony had actually transferred the powers of the Dynroc from Dynny to Talag? What if he really was the Dynroc?

The thought sat like a boulder on his brain, crushing out all thought.

It couldn't be.

There was no way.

And yet . . .

Chapter 43: Tass

Rain fell on her face when Tass pushed her head through the ceiling of the sea into the air above. The evening was young, and the rain was light, falling gently but steadily into the water of Gelu's mine.

Home.

She wanted to go home.

She didn't even know what she meant by that.

A pale blue ymolenegth lit the sea and cast eerie shadows onto Tass's face. She saw some of the people of Garradh Gannoir pointing toward her, gesturing excitedly. She shuddered. The non-casted people of Obumbro would feed her, would give her shelter, would treat her like royalty, but it wasn't what she wanted. Not now. She didn't want to be one of the exalted creatures of legend just then.

Ducking her head, she dove back into the lifeless water of the mine. She couldn't stay there. It was Gelu's folly, his attempt to pierce Gannoir to arrive on the outside of the world. Swimming downward, she pushed herself into the depths, beyond the rock of the Orbokth that had been perforated by Gelu's miners. Some sarxworms had pushed their way out of their holes in the underside of the Orbokth. They weren't Tass's first choice for dinner, but they would do. With meaty bodies and plant-like souls, the worms were nourishing and had a rich, intoxicating flavor that only the Mayim could stomach. A few of them would suffice for a meal.

She swam forward and grabbed the largest of the flailing creatures, trying to ignore its gaping mouth. She never liked eating their heads—not while they were still alive. With a tug, Tass ripped the sarxworm from its anchor deep inside the rock. It bled from wounds at the base, illuminating the seawater with a gentle, turquoise glow. Once it stopped wiggling, she snapped the head off and began to eat.

Once she was satisfied, in body at least, Tass thought about her problem. She wanted to bring Mailu home, but she couldn't do it alone. She needed help. Dwoyra, who might have the power to help her, would never agree to any plan that opened holes in the Bec. Their goals were opposite. It would be the same with Gaoth, the rational wind who, with Dwoyra and by means of the power of Igracio's three-in-one blood, had effected the closure of the Bilik. She needed to find someone powerful enough to crack open the shell of the world and draw the skyboulder back in, either by supernatural means or physical force.

Pushing through the water, she examined the underside of the Orbokth, looking for a place she could stop and rest for the night. Despite being a native of the sea, Tass had never slept in it. She didn't know any of the Mayim who had, although she'd sometimes fantasized about an underwater world inhabited only by the Mayim, one where they could rule and live without the Gulot telling them they were inferior or the Esh lording over them. In her dreams the Mayim would construct a city of caves in the Orbokth, like those people had in the world above before Kleibald built the cities on the clatries. She pondered this and then decided she would sleep in a cave or a crevice—if she could find one.

As she searched, her mind returned to her dilemma—physical force or supernatural strength. She sighed and little bubbles rose from her gills. Whoever was going to help her, it couldn't be a person. Even the strongest of the people of Luca couldn't tear a hole in the Bec. The best anyone could do was to tunnel through the Orbokth. But all they would find there was the sea. The Bec was something different. Something other.

Something alive.

The thought reverberated through her mind and then her body. Her fingers began to glow, and she instinctively balled her hands into fists, even though no one was nearby to see.

The Bec had a soul.

If she could find a way to talk to it, to befriend it, to convince it that it needed to create an opening big enough to readmit the skyboulder, then she would have her sister back. She would be home.

Mailu is dead, a voice whispered as it swirled around her head. *Dead, dead, dead.*

Tass swatted at the water, as though she could push the voice away.

Befriend the Bec. Convince the Bec.

Mailu.

She would do it.

Is.

Somehow.

Dead.

Tomorrow.

Chapter 44: Xylo

The people gathered in a natural amphitheater on the Orbokth next to the brilliant turquoise water that characterized the blue and green world of Cudth Deorth, the hollow where the children of Methiant Migas lived. A visitor was a novelty—an alarming one—and they were all curious to meet the stranger.

Ieska introduced him to her daughter's half-siblings and their families. "Bridima is our matriarch," she said next, gesturing toward a smiling white-haired old woman who must have been at least as old as Xylo. She was tall and solidly built, and Xylo could see the Eshtala hidden in the folds of her tunic. "She and I were the founders of Cudth Deorth. We met by chance and soon realized our children shared their unusual characteristics. We knew we had to find a place for them where they would be safe, where no one could exploit them. She stayed in here to raise the children, and I worked in the city, earning money to support us."

"It was just the two of you, each with a child, at the beginning?" Xylo clarified.

"Bridima was widowed when Unaleah was small," Ieska said, pointing to a tall young woman with Sadi's dark hair and amazing blue eyes. "She had adopted Gudall before I met her." Ieska pointed to a young man who could have been Unaleah's twin. "His parents abandoned him at birth due to his unusual tala." Gudall unsmilingly lifted a hand to greet Xylo. "She took care of the children—Sadi, Unaleah, and Gudall—and I came out as often as I could.

"This is Kari and her father Widman," she said, pointing to a round-faced blond man and a girl of about sixteen who shared his blond hair but not his dark eyes. Her eyes were the same shade of blue as Sadi's. "Ninach lives with them," she noted, pointing to a young lady with mousy brown hair and green eyes. "Widman and Kari have been here for sixteen years, and Ninach came to us a year later."

Ieska turned to the other side of the curving shoreline. "The Efteri family came to us twelve years ago, and they've been a great blessing to us. Rhyder built all our shelters. Before he came, we had been living in caves in the cliffs." Ieska smiled at a middle-aged man with short dark hair and extensive finger tala. "Finnan, his wife, is a weaver and is adept at gathering and preparing food from the sea. We've been eating delicacies on a continual basis since she came to us." Finnan was clearly Mayim—Xylo could tell by her finger tala, but she wore her red hair long and loose, something the Mayim never did.

Finnan grinned at Xylo cheerily. "I'm hoping you'll join us for a meal while you're here. There's nothing better in all Luca."

Xylo grinned back. "I'd love that."

Ieska continued. "Their son, Laetu, is triad,"—she gestured toward an awkward-looking red-haired boy—"and Camilly is learning to help her mother with the diving and cooking."

Camilly looked to be about the same age as Kari—middle teens—and had her mother's long red hair and cheerful face. She waved at Xylo.

"Pax and Byid came to us a year after the Efteris." Ieska told Xylo, pointing to the final two people at the gathering, young adolescent boys. "Torcalon had known about Pax—he's one of his grandsons—since shortly after his birth, but his life seemed stable at first despite his dual tala. He had a loving family who lived on the Orbokth, not in the city, so it seemed unlikely they would encounter any sort of difficulties, or that their existence would come to the attention of the elders. Their mother, Caedi, passed away then Pax was three and Byid was only a year old. Their father soon became unstable and fled, leaving them in the care of neighbors who didn't have the means to care for them. Torcalon stepped in and brought them here."

The boys nodded solemnly at Xylo. They were alike in their dark brown hair, the same shade as the rock of the Orbokth, and blue-green eyes. But Pax had a gleam in his eye and the body and finger tala of a three-in-one, whereas Byid had no tala at all.

Xylo took a deep breath and looked around the circle, his eyes coming to rest on Torcalon. "You have beautiful grandchildren," he said sincerely.

Torcalon's eyes grew soft. "That I do. And I would do anything to protect them."

Xylo wondered if he was imagining the hint of a threat in the old man's voice. "I won't betray your family," he said. "Kleibald is an evil man, and he has perpetrated great evil on Luca with what he did to your son and with the crimes he has committed against others as well. You have my great respect for what you've done in building something beautiful amid so much pain."

A stillness fell over the group as the people listened to Xylo's words.

"Tell them the story," Ieska urged. "Tell them about Mantais. Tell them what happened."

Xylo nodded. "They deserve to hear it." He proceeded to tell them about the man, Methiant Migas—Mantais Nayro—and how he had come to the heights to make a final confession before his death. He recounted the painful story of Mantais Nayro's suicide, how he had killed himself rather than continue to live the destructive life that had been forced upon him by a mind ruined by the experiments Kleibald had authorized.

Torcalon wept openly during the telling of the tale, despite having heard it from Xylo earlier. They were cleansing tears, however, rather than bitter ones. Xylo noticed that many of the group had tears flowing down their faces during his story. He read compassion there.

"Mantais Nayro was a victim, just like you all have been," Xylo told them. "Kleibald's attempts to create a tri-casted person ruined his mind and soul. My greatest regret is that I never reached out to the one woman, the only victim whose name he knew. I should have helped her, helped her child. And I should have looked for the rest of you. Even at the time, ten years ago, I knew that there must be more children. According to the man, his crimes took place continually over many years."

At the mention of Bracha Elisus and another child, a hum ran through the group.

It was Kari who spoke first. "You know of another child? Who is he? Or she? Where are the child and its mother now?"

Xylo pressed his lips together. He knew that his confession had been incomplete. He took a deep breath and, looking at Ieska for encouragement, continued to speak. "Bracha Elisus is dead. I never told her about Mantais Nayro's confession or his death. May Tel-Maor be gracious to me, I should have told her. I could have brought some peace to her. Instead, I took her with me on a mission to find our children, who had been sent on a mission by the elders and went missing."

The people grew still and their expressions grim at the mention of the elders.

Ninach frowned "Did the elders pick the woman's child on purpose for the mission? Did they know she was tri-casted?" There was a ferocity in her look, a desire to protect the sibling she had never met.

Xylo glanced at Ieska. He hadn't told her about Tass yet. He had let her believe that Mailu was triad, just as the elders believed. To reveal Tass's existence to these, likely her siblings, was the right thing to do. There was no danger for her here. Still, he hesitated. A look at Torcalon's broken gaze urged him forward. "Bracha's daughter, Mailu, was sent by the elders because they believed she was triad," he told them. "She died under the care of the uncasted people living on the other side of the Orbokth.

He paused to let this sink in before continuing. "I have reason to believe that it was not Mailu Elisus Harreg who was the child of Mantais Nayro." He glanced at Ieska to see how she was reacting to this revelation. Everyone seemed to be on edge, anticipating his next words. "Bracha Elisus—Afa—had another child, a daughter.

He shook his head, looking around at the seven offspring of Methiant Migas, at their dual finger and body tala. Tass had only finger tala, but her fingers glowed as though she were Esh. Mailu had no tala at all. Doubt began to creep into his mind. And yet Methiant Migas himself had said so, had told him that Afa had borne his child.

It had to be either Tass or Mailu. And if it was one of them, it had to be Tass.

Xylo sighed. "Tass is twelve," he told the group. "She's a student at the Calix. She was casted Mayim at the age of four and given up to the care of the Master there. She has no body tala, but in the last few months her fingers have begun to glow . . ."

An excited murmur rang through the group. To have another sibling meant they were less alone.

"Can you bring her here?" Camilly asked, clasping her hands in front of her in glee. "Another sister! A little sister!" She made a face, half mocking and half teasing toward her little brother Laetu and the other boys younger than herself. "I'd take a little sister any day!"

Sunshine broke over Torcalon's face. Camilly wasn't his biological granddaughter like her brother was, but he loved her as though she were all his. "That's my girl," he said with tears in his eyes. "Bring this Tass home!"

Chapter 45: Talag

As Talag stumbled through the morning, the voices continued to plague him, but only with his name. He deliberately ignored the steady call of *Talag, Talag, Talag . . .* and avoided Dynny. If he was the Dynroc, then Dynny wasn't. The idea burned his heart like fire. Dynny was his only friend on the skyboulder, and he'd betrayed him—inadvertently, but still betrayed him, stolen his identity. He didn't know how he was going to tell him.

It was difficult to avoid anyone on the skyboulder. Ten small chambers were all that were available to the forty occupants. Talag spent as much of the day as he could in the bathroom, but even that was not foolproof. With only two bathrooms for forty people, someone was always knocking at the door asking him why it was taking him so long.

He would have to face Dynny. He would have to tell him what had happened. He couldn't fix it, and Dynny needed to know. After lunch he made his way to the chamber where Mailu slept. That was where Dynny spent most of his time. His grandfather gave him a conspiratorial wink as they passed each other, and even Gelu looked at him with greedy hope.

"They just want to save Gannoir," he recited to himself. "The people of Gannoir deserve to be rescued. The spirits of the chaos are going to find a way to use the power of the Dynroc to save everyone and get them from Gannoir to another world." It sounded impossible even as he said it to himself.

He slid the door open and went into the tiny crypt where his elderly friend kept guard. Dynny was sitting on an outcropping of rock with his chin resting on his hands and his elbows on his knees. His eyes lit up when he saw Talag.

"I didn't see you at breakfast!" he said. "You were tired, right?"

Talag nodded. "I was up half the night. I slept late."

Dynny nodded enthusiastically.

"How's Mailu today?" Talag asked in a conversational tone.

Peering through the glass at the beautiful, scarred body, Dynny's eyes grew soft. "She's the same. How can her baby grow if she doesn't eat?" he fretted.

Talag had no idea what to tell his anxious friend. He was certain Mailu was dead and that no baby would be forthcoming, but it seemed cruel to take away Dynny's sense of heartfelt obligation, especially after he had inadvertently usurped the role of the Dynroc. He made himself smile. "Maybe that's why you were chosen to guard her," he suggested, feeling guilty as he said it. "Maybe her baby grows by the power of the Dynroc."

Dynny stroked the glass on the top of the stone coffin. "I'm helping," he said solemnly.

"Of course you are. That's one of the reasons they chose you," Talag said, aware that his condescension was out of line. Smart or dumb, Dynny was his friend. He was treating him like he was inferior—the way his grandfather and Gelu treated him. Guilt rose in his belly and pushed tears to the corners of his eyes. "I can't . . ." he muttered. "Dynny, I'm not being honest with you. I don't think Mailu is going to come back to life. And I don't think she's going to have a baby either. And . . ."—he squeezed his eyes shut as he prepared himself to break Dynny's heart—"I've been hearing the spirit voices all morning."

Dynny looked at him uncomprehendingly. "You've been hearing the spirit voices?"

Talag nodded miserably. "They've been calling my name. I can hear them."

Dynny blinked. "What are they saying?"

"Just my name so far. Talag. Over and over again." He watched the old man's face for any sign that he was beginning to understand the implications of the voices, but nothing happened.

"I'm worried, Dynny. I'm really worried. The voices were supposed to talk to you, not me. You're the Dynroc."

"Maybe Kleibald told them to talk to you," Dynny suggested calmly. "We tricked him. Now he's tricking the spirits."

The answer was so simple that Talag was taken aback. And yet it could be the truth. Maybe the spirits didn't have an inherent awareness of the aura of the Dynroc. Maybe it really was as simple as Kleibald pointing him out to them. He felt his whole body relax. "I never thought of that," he answered truthfully.

Dynny bit his lip. "Do you really think Mailu is not going to get un-dead?"

Talag frowned. He had prepared himself to answer Dynny's questions about the transference of the office of the Dynroc. He hadn't thought up any answers about Mailu. He sighed. "I don't know, Dynny. She doesn't look any different than she did when were first left Gannoir. She hasn't moved. She hasn't changed. She hasn't done anything that would make me think she's still alive."

"Gelu said she was going to have a baby," Dynny reminded him.

Talag nodded. "I know."

"Gelu's evil, but he is pretty smart," Dynny reasoned.

With a half-smile, Talag replied. "You think he might be right?"

"Gannoir is dying. We have to save the people. And Mailu is one of the people, right?"

Talag agreed silently.

"So we can save her," Dynny triumphantly finished.

Talag wasn't so sure. Dynny's reasoning sounded logical, but he didn't think the little man was right. But it didn't matter. If they couldn't figure out how to save Gannoir, they would have nowhere to go and they would all die.

"You're right," he agreed, just to end the argument. He sat down on the floor with his back leaning against Mailu's sarcophagus. He could hear the faint but steady drone of the voices calling his name. Turning his mind toward the spirits, he listened. He would make a conscious decision to hear what they said. Saving Gannoir was the important thing. And Dynny was right. He wasn't the Dynroc. They hadn't transferred the role to him when they acted out their mock ceremony. And he and Dynny would work together, with Dynny doing whatever the spirits told the Dynroc to do, so that the people of Gannoir could be saved.

Chapter 46: Tass

Tass awoke from her night's sleep feeling refreshed. Her gills felt strange to her, like they were too relaxed, taking in too much water. She peeked out of the crevice in which she had spent the night. Pushing her feet against the rock above her, she shot down into the depths. Yellow. Orange. Then orange faded to red.

It was cold. Too cold.

Tass felt her blood slow in her veins, and the thoughts in her mind oozed thick and slow. Maybe if she stayed in the red layer, her body would adjust. She was made for the sea. That ought to include all the parts of it, even the cold ones. Too cold to shiver, Tass made herself keep swimming as vigorously as she could. She ached all over, especially in her injured shoulders.

Kick, stroke, turn. Kick, stroke, turn. Tass kept a regular rhythm to her swimming, making sure to activate as many of her muscles as she could, just like she'd been taught in the survival classes at the Calix. Maybe the Mayim weren't meant to dive so deep, she thought with a wince. If it were safe, then they wouldn't have had class on survival techniques.

The rotund form of a vauzigk appeared in the distance. Tass saw it through the glowing red haze.

"Come here!" she hollered in her gill voice.

Then she stopped, stunned. She had never been able to speak loudly in her gill voice. What had happened to her? Worry crept over her. Was there something wrong with her gills? Was there something right with her gills? Her fingertips began to glow yellow-orange against the backdrop of the red chemical sea. She took a deep breath and tried again. "Vauzigk! Help me!"

It hadn't been a fluke. Her gill-speech was loud and clear now. She wondered if it had been sleeping underwater than had caused the change. She grabbed hold of that idea as though it were her last hope. If it had been caused by sleeping underwater, then it wasn't happening because of whatever it was that was making her fingers glow. One of her teachers at the Calix had noticed her glowing fingers and had told her not to worry, that it was probably just that she was growing up and her body was changing. But Tass knew the woman was lying. She'd lived at the Calix for eight years. She'd never seen a Mayim with glowing fingers, not one of any age, boy or girl—except Igracio.

She pushed the thoughts away as the murky outline of the vauzigk grew smaller. Kicking her legs behind her, she sped toward the bulky creature. It didn't stop, didn't answer her call. It dove deeper, down into the magenta part of the sea where Tass knew she couldn't go alone. She sighed and spun her limbs around her body until she was little but a ball of anger.

At least the anger kept her warm, she reflected. She stayed that way for a long time, curled into a heap of Tass, pondering what she needed to do. Despair crept over her mind like a gray fog of nothingness. There was no hope. She couldn't bring Mailu back. Not if she tried for a thousand years. Not if she gave every drop of her blood to the effort. There was nothing she could do. She may as well go back to the Calix like a dutiful Mayim. Uncoiling herself, she let her body drift upward.

The voices seemed to come at her from every side. *Not impossible. It's up to you. Open the Bilik. Crack the seams of the world. You can. You can.*

The voices were being uncharacteristically encouraging. They were wrong, she was sure. "I can't," she replied aloud. "There's no way I can break open Gannoir by myself. And there's no one who would want to help me."

Water . . . helper . . .

Tass couldn't believe she was talking back to her tormentors. She'd heard them before but hadn't tried to converse. "Dwoyra wants to close the gaps in the Bec, not open them wider. She won't help me."

The voices made metallic sparkling sounds. *Lie,* was their simple recommendation.

Then they were gone, leaving Tass to wonder why they hadn't tried harder to convince her.

Lie.

Lie to Dwoyra.

She could do that.

She could tell Dwoyra that she was on her side. That she wanted to heal the fissures in the Bec. She could pretend she was willing to donate blood to the cause and to rally others of the Siann Dha to donate as well. Saving Gannoir was a noble cause, she'd say. She'd be more than happy to participate in the efforts. So elaborate did her thoughts become that Tass almost began to believe her lies herself. It was another path to glory. Glory wasn't painful like family was. Mailu had loved her, but Mailu had left. Glory couldn't die. She would do it. She would do what it took to save Gannoir.

Mocking laughter rang in her gills.

What had she been thinking? Glory could die, and it would likely die quickly. Already the respect she had won after being a participant in the completion of the gogyvehr had begun to fade. It wouldn't be long before everyone forgot it altogether. She'd sampled glory and it had left a bitter taste in her mouth.

She would rather have Igracio.

She would rather have her mother, even if Afa had hated her.

She would rather have . . . she would rather have . . .

Mailu.

Chapter 47: Xylo

After the introductions, the young people gave Xylo a tour of Cudth Deorth. Their homes were simple, primitive buildings, the back halves cut out of the rocky Orbokth, and the fronts being constructed of woven vines and dried sea plants. The weave was so tight that Xylo could tell that the nightly rains couldn't get through. Moss coated the structures, thicker on some, so that he could tell which were the oldest. Only thirteen people lived in Cudth Deorth, so their needs for shelter were minimal. All the huts had their back sides built into the wall of rock that was the Orbokth.

"We made use of the natural caves," Laetu explained proudly. "There was less to build that way, and it's warmer."

"It's warmer here anyhow," Sadi said. "Much colder than on the clatries or on the Orbokth across the sea."

"That's how come the ugaz live here," Byid added, pointing to a cluster of the furry plants in a crevice near one of the huts.

Xylo peered into the first hut they came to. A comfortable living room greeted him. Furniture, obviously imported from the city, gave the room a homey feeling. There was even a bookcase in one corner. A dark staircase was barely visible at the rear of the room.

"Who reads?" Xylo asked.

Sadi glared at him. "Who doesn't read?"

"You all read?"

"Of course," Camilly grinned. "Even Finnan and Rhyder, who couldn't read when they came here."

"I couldn't read when I came here either," Byid noted.

Camilly laughed. "You were a baby when you came here."

"Like I said . . ."

Camilly shoved him playfully.

"Whose house is this?" Xylo asked.

"It's ours," Kari told him. "Me and Dad and Ninach. The stairs in the back lead up to the bedrooms. Dad has his own small room and me and Ninach share the other one."

"The bedrooms were the first dwelling in Cudth Deorth," Ninach said softly. "Bridima lived there. She had one room for a bedroom and the other for a living room."

"They all lived in caves until we came," Byid related. "My dad built the bigger huts, and my mom helped with the weaving."

"We all helped with the weaving," Kari objected.

"It was a big job," Byid agreed without taking offense.

"You didn't weave," Camilly pointed out. " 'Cause you were a . . ."

"I know. A baby," Byid smiled at her cheerfully.

They moved to the next hut. It was large than the last, and included an abutment annexed to the house on the outside.

"Who lives here?" Xylo asked.

"That's where Bridima lives. It's the biggest because six people live in it," Camilly told him.

"I live there," Byid added.

"Don't forget me," Pax said, with a twisted smile.

Xylo got the impression that Pax wasn't happy, and he wondered why. The others seemed content and relaxed.

"It has four bedrooms," Byid said proudly. "Me and Pax share the biggest bedroom, and Unaleah, Gudall, and Sadi have the other three. Bridima lives in the grass part."

"Another of the original caves," Kari explained. "At the beginning it had only two rooms and was used for storing food and supplies. My dad helped excavate the other two bedrooms."

Xylo pointed to a third hut a short distance down the shore. "And this one belongs to the Efteri family?" he guessed.

Laetu nodded. "Dad just built the extra grass room for Camilly. She told him she was getting too old to share a room with me."

"I am too old to share a room with you," Camilly said, tossing her long red hair.

Many dozens of yards down the shore, a half-built edifice was in progress.

"That's for Gudall," Byid confided. "He's going to get married and live there when he grows up."

"Gudall is grown up," Ninach noted with flushed cheeks.

"Who is he going to marry?" Xylo asked.

Byid shrugged. "One of the girls, I guess. They're the only girls he knows."

Xylo looked at the two teenage girls who had come along for

the tour. The young people were siblings—half siblings—but maybe because of their circumstances and because of the genetic manipulation that had created Methiant Migas, it didn't matter so much. From Ninach's blush he suspected he knew which girl Gudall preferred, but it may have been only that Ninach was hopeful, not certain. Love or a crush—it was hard to tell which. And there were also the two older girls to consider.

"There are other rooms," Byid continued, unaffected by the romance in the air. "We have three storage rooms in the caves. One for food and the others are for stuff."

"Stuff?" Xylo asked.

Byid shrugged. "Yeah. Just stuff."

"Supplies. Tools. You know," Laetu added.

The group passed Gudall's future home and continued along the shore. It was easy to see why they had chosen to build where they had. The ground was flat there. Here, the Orbokth dropped vertically into the sea with only a very narrow ledge upon which they could stand. Xylo's eyes were still dazzled by the pervasive greenery that covered every inch of the rocks. It was a lush, gorgeous paradise. Even the sea seemed bluer in Cudth Deorth than it did anywhere else in Luca. An illusion, perhaps, caused by the reflection of the foliage in the water.

Xylo bent down to the sea for a closer look. He could see the plants growing under the clear turquoise water. Little silver fish swam unconcernedly in and out of the plants as though they were playing hide-and-seek in a miniature forest. He focused on the liquid, trying to let his eyes adjust, to see the shade of blue he was used to seeing from the glowing ymolenegth. He cupped his hands around his eyes, shading the seawater from the rest of the world of Cudth Deorth.

The color didn't change. It wasn't just the reflection of the greenery. The seawater was glowing more brightly than he'd ever seen before. Light is life, he reflected. And light comes from blood.

He shivered a little, wondering whose blood produced such a vibrant glow. The triad children? Some unknown sea creature? He tried to remember if Igracio's blood had made the sea glow with this eerily luminescent shade of blue, but he didn't think he'd ever seen Igracio's blood—not until those last minutes when everything had gone wild—the water, the wind, the Ghalon . . . there was no way to tell what was the result of Igracio's blood and what was the result of the strange magic that had closed the Bilik.

He didn't ask who was bleeding in the water. He wasn't sure he wanted to know.

***

"There's more to the story," Xylo said over dinner that night. He was seated with Ieska, Torcalon, Bridima, and Widman, the blond widower. "It's about the boy who gave his life to save Gannoir when Kleibald tried to destroy it. Igracio." He shook his head. "Igracio was . . . different. Special. It's almost as if . . ."

"As if what?" Bridima pressed.

"As if he was tri-casted. Glowing fingertips, tala between his fingers, although it was slight. And he was intelligent. He'd been raised Gulot until he just before he died."

"Doesn't mean he was tri-casted," Widman interrupted gruffly. "There are always a few intelligent ones among the lower castes. And the tala and glowing fingers could have been vestigial traits." He held up his own hand to demonstrate. About a centimeter of tala connected each of his fingers. "I'm Gulot. Lots of us have a little tala."

"It wasn't just the tala and his smarts," Xylo disagreed. "It was what happened. His blood made it happen. His blood was unique, different from the blood of the rest of us."

"It is possible," Ieska said softly. "Have you talked to his mother? Asked her about the circumstances surrounding his birth?"

Widman snorted. "It's not his birth he needs to ask about."

Bridima rolled her eyes. "We all know what she means. And have you asked?"

Ieska looked at Xylo expectantly.

"It just doesn't seem possible," he answered. "I've met Igracio's parents. I've seen his brother. He and his brother are so alike they could have been twins. Genetically, they were a match."

"Looked at his genes, did you?" Widman snorted again.

"You should ask," Bridima advised Xylo mildly.

"What would be the point? Igracio's dead," Xylo replied.

Torcalon looked at him with pain in his eyes. "I'd like to know," he answered softly. "If this boy was my grandson, I would want to know that. And his mother . . . well, knowing how my son died might mean something to her. The fact that he was sorry. That he was so incredibly sorry." Torcalon set down his spoon and wiped a tear from his eye.

"I'm sorry too," Xylo replied.

"You should talk to her," Ieska urged him. "It's important."

Xylo gazed at Ieska, this woman he had quickly come to care for, trying to read her soul in her eyes. He mustn't forget what Ieska had suffered. Her whole life had changed because of one incident, because of one man's crime. "Hearing about him helped you?" he asked her.

She looked back at him, her wide eyes drawing him in, inviting him to walk in her sorrow with her. "More than you can understand."

"All right," he agreed with a sigh. "I'll talk to Rahela. May Tel-Maor have mercy."

Chapter 48: Talag

Talag didn't want to hear the voices anymore. They had stopped saying his name and had started giving him instructions. That was why he was upset.

They wanted his blood.

Well, not his blood, really. The blood of the Dynroc. Dynny's blood.

Dynny was old. Dynny was frail. Sort of. And he wasn't Siann Dha. Talag had been told that the blood of the people of Luca, the Siann Dha, was different from the blood of the others. The blood of the Siann Dha made the waters glow. That was the kind of blood he would have thought the spirits wanted. Dynny was one of the others, one of those with plain blood.

Maybe being the Dynroc changed his blood. Maybe it could do other things that his own blood couldn't do. The idea sounded irrational. How could being declared the Dynroc change the type of blood a person had? It didn't make sense.

At any rate, he didn't want to injure Dynny, not even a little bit.

But, his mind nagged him, all the people of Gannoir will die if you don't do this thing. Dynny would gladly give up some of his blood and endure a little pain if many could be saved. Talag knew that was true.

Finally, egged on by the voices, by his grandfather's repeated questions about how he was getting on with the spirits, and by his own conscience, Talag ventured to talk to his elderly friend about the issue.

"It doesn't have to be a lot of blood," he explained quickly. "They never said it had to be a lot. Just a little cut. We'll collect some blood in a cup and then it will be over."

Dynny agreed to this, although he looked worried. "Can you do it on my foot?" he requested. "My foot hurts sometimes, so I can pretend it's doing the thing it always does."

Talag agreed to this and proceeded to make a tiny cut in the old man's foot. He collected a thimbleful of blood and then pressed on the wound to stop the bleeding.

The voices howled at him in response. *Blood of the Dynroc, you coward!* Their calls were clear and violent now. *You would cut an old man and try to substitute his blood for your own? What kind of a Dynroc are you?*

Talag winced and cringed. Even though the voices weren't audible to anyone except himself, they hurt his ears.

"What's wrong?" Dynny asked, his face full of compassion.

Talag shook his head. "The voices. You were right. They think I'm the Dynroc. They want my blood, not yours."

"I'm the Dynroc," Dynny protested.

"I know," Talag replied. "But they don't know that. Remember? My grandfather told them it was me."

He slumped down and leaned against Mailu's ever-present, never-changing coffin. "What do we do now?" He had to shout to hear his own voice over the screaming of the angry spirits.

"Can we explain that it's me?" Dynny whispered.

Talag shook his head. "They might tell Grandfather."

"We can pretend," Dynny hissed with a gleam in his eye.

"Pretend?"

"Cut yourself. Let them see you doing it. Then give them my blood," Dynny replied with a surreptitious glance around the room as though someone might be listening.

It was an ingenious plan. Talag couldn't believe his mentally challenged friend had come up with it. "Okay," he whispered.

"Okay!" he yelled, focusing his energies toward the spirit voices in his head. "I'll give you my blood!" He slashed at his foot, being careful to keep up the charade that he was angry with the voices for calling him a coward. When his blood started to flow, the screams in his head abated. Inwardly, he relaxed. It was working.

"I don't have another cup," he whispered to Dynny.

Dynny held up the seaweed wrapper from the dried salt orange he'd eaten earlier. Talag let the blood drip from his foot into the curving piece of dry plantstuff. He held it up as though the spirits were going to inspect it. They probably were.

Throw the trash away, he heard a voice instruct calmly inside his head.

Talag frowned, confused.

"What did it say?" Dynny asked.

"It said to throw the trash away," Talag reported. "Do you think they mean the seaweed?"

"If you throw the seaweed away, you'll throw your blood away with it," Dynny replied logically.

The voice spoke again in Talag's head and gave him the same instructions it had a moment earlier. It became more and more insistent, despite Talag's obvious bewilderment. He held up the blood in the makeshift cup, trying to demonstrate that he couldn't throw away the seaweed wrapper without disposing of the blood as well.

"Don't you need my blood?" he asked in thought and aloud.

Dry. Scabs. Later, the voices hissed in his mind.

Scabs? The blood they wanted was scabs? Light was life and life was blood . . . but what were scabs?

"What?" Dynny asked anxiously. "What are they saying?"

Talag wrinkled his nose. "They don't want blood. They want scabs."

"Scabs?"

Talag nodded. "Weird, right?"

"We should have scabs by tomorrow," Dynny guessed.

"Then this will be over," Talag noted gratefully.

"I'm the Dynroc," Dynny reminded him.

"We'll use your scab," Talag whispered in his friend's ear.

Dynny smiled. "Because I'm the Dynroc."

"And that's what it's going to take to save the people of our world," Talag added.

Chapter 49: Tass

"Dwoyra!" Tass hollered. The reverberations of her shout echoed in her ears and gills.

In an instant, the watery creature was by her side, pushing at Tass with eager fingers, letting her know she was there. Tass wondered if she hadn't been following her all along.

She steeled her nerves. "I want to help you," she said aloud. "I want to make sure Gannoir is safe."

Dwoyra circled around her and then gave Tass a powerful shove downward. Was Dwoyra angry? Tass wasn't sure.

"Show me the fissures," Tass requested. "The little holes in the Bec. I want to understand more."

"Blood," Dwoyra requested, and Tass detected sorrow in her tone.

Her heart raced. Had something happened? Had things become worse? "You know I can't bleed enough to blot out all the darkness," she hedged. She didn't want to give blood at all. She'd bled enough in these waters. Her gill-speech came easily, and she was able to articulate all her words more clearly than she'd ever done before.

"Dark things . . . more and more and more and more and more . . ." The water made a thousand tiny whirlpools around Tass.

"Take me to the Bec," Tass requested. "I want to see. I want to understand."

"Blood," Dwoyra urged.

"After I talk to the Bec," Tass promised. "He's the one with the wounds. I need to talk to him."

"Talk won't help." Dwoyra was frustrated.

Tass knew she had to push the idea. She had what Dwoyra wanted. Blood. And Dwoyra had the power to take her to the Bec safely. She had to talk to the Bec. Convincing the Bec to deliberately readmit the skyboulder was her only hope of getting her sister back. *Sister. Love. Home.* She could feel the voices in her head, not verbalizing, but hissing their support. Go to the Bec. Talk to the Bec. Convince the Bec to crack open the Bilik just long enough to let the skyboulder come back. Do it. Do it.

"I won't give you blood until you take me to the Bec," Tass insisted.

A whistling noise fizzled through the water. In a moment a vauzigk appeared and enveloped Tass in its arms. Lumalauae circled Tass and the vauzigk, making a sphere of protection. The water warmed quickly, and Tass relaxed. She was winning.

She swam downward, wondering if Dwoyra would follow, would listen to her conversation with the Bec. She watched the miniature phosphorescent air bladders of the lumalauae. The seawater around her sparkled with fairy lights. The furry, blubbery vauzigk gave her warmth. The liquid around her changed from red to magenta and at last Tass could see the waving purple flames of the Bec beneath her. She wondered how she would converse with the cold fire. It wasn't a liquid, nor was it a solid or a gas. Even had she the fire-gills of the Esh, it wouldn't help. Should she speak with her lung-speech? Her gill-speech? Or just think the words at it? It was all she had. She wondered if Dwoyra could talk to the Bec. Dwoyra had never given her any indication that she believed the Bec to be a soulish sort of thing. Maybe she didn't know.

Tass swam lower. Even with the protection of the vauzigk and the lumalauae she was cold. She could see the tiny fissures now, tiny blacknesses among the icy purple flames. There were thousands of cracks. Thousands. Dark blotches streamed from the purple fire, making it look like the holes were larger than they were. She shuddered despite herself. Dwoyra was right. This had to stop. But later. After she brought Mailu home.

She pushed herself toward the Bec. It was the coldest water she had ever had to bear. Tucking her fingers and toes into the loose, furry flesh of the vauzigk, she called out. "Bec! Oh Bec, protector of Gannoir! Answer me!" She'd used her gill-speech.

There was no reply.

She tried her lung-speech, but still nothing happened.

Dragging herself downward, she held her breaths until she felt she was going to pop. Her fingers glowed with a fiery orange light, a color she'd never seen them display before. With every ounce of strength she had, she let the words burst forth from her mouth, from her gills, from her mind. Something seemed to pop in her head and a warmth tickled her gills. Had she hurt herself? But it didn't hurt.

This time there was an answer. It wasn't in words, but in a feeling that someone was listening, a knowledge that her words had been received. Holding her breath beforehand, she again cried with all her might and power, "Bec! Oh Bec!"

Little one. The voice filled up her entire head with its depth of tone and resounding, overwhelming noise. She could barely discern the meaning of the words.

She took a deep breath and then belted with all her might, "I need you! Skyboulder. Home." It was all she could manage.

Tass thought she saw the purple flames flinch, pause in their endless dance for a fraction of a second.

I must protect Gannoir, the gargantuan voice exploded in her mind.

Breathe. Talk. It got easier every time. "Skyboulder. Home," she repeated.

Impossible. Wrong. Backwards.

"Needful! Skyboulder. Open Bilik."

A sound akin to thunder slammed against her mind. She reeled, unable to think for a few seconds. *A thousand years and the Bilik is closed. The gogyvehr is complete.*

"Needful," Tass repeated. "Good. Skyboulder. Home." She gasped, breathless at the effort it cost her to speak.

Impossible. Wrong.

"Necessary!"

Why?

Tass felt the mind of the Bec probing her own mind with a stinging intensity. She wondered if it could read her thoughts. She hoped not. If she was going to bring her sister home, she would need to trick the Bec into believing she wanted something that was good for Gannoir. Opening the Bilik was by no means good for Gannoir. She knew that.

"Justice," she finally answered, trying to provide a plausible reason that would be acceptable to the Bec, whom she instinctively knew was good.

Danger. Unjust, the Bec replied.

She was getting nowhere.

"Stop the darkness," she told it, lying with all her might. Opening the Bilik would only admit more of the dark blotches.

Again, the probing pain rattled her mind. Did the Bec know she was lying? Did it know she didn't care about the darkness? Could it see that all she wanted was Mailu? Mailu was all she had. If bringing her back wasn't justice, she didn't know what was.

The darkness is inside you, the Bec replied, its tone deeper and quieter than its other words. Tass could barely understand it.

It wasn't true. The darkness wasn't inside her. It was clinging to the dga. It was floating in the sea. It was possessing the voices that spoke to her in her mind. But it didn't belong to her. It wasn't part of her. It wasn't clinging to her like it was clinging to the dga. It was impossible. She would have known. She would have seen.

"Skyboulder. Home!" Her voice was a shriek.

We are not fighting on the same side of the war, the Bec replied, not angrily, not confrontationally, but with a sad wisdom that frustrated and dismayed Tass.

"Justice. Rightness." Then, "Help . . ."

A warmth flowed through Tass's thoughts and trickled into her gut and then into her limbs. Love. The Bec was giving her love. She relaxed inadvertently and then stiffened her body. She hadn't gone to the Bec for love. She'd gone to the Bec for help in bringing her sister home. The Bec had the power to unclasp its hands, to open the Bilik and let the skyboulder come home. Instead of giving her what she'd asked for it was giving her love and warmth and . . . pity.

Angrily, Tass pushed herself upward, away from the icy purple flames. It was no use. She'd never convince a being like that to do what she wanted. It was too holy. Too good. To self-righteous to help a little girl when it meant taking a risk. The voices were wrong. She couldn't bring the skyboulder back. She couldn't crack open the Bec layer. She'd never see Mailu again. She'd never find home.

The seawater around her glowed magenta, then red, and then orange. The lumalauae spun their sphere larger and larger until they were far from her, and then they swam away. Tass untucked herself from the warm flesh of the vauzigk, and it floated away into the distance. The chemical sea caressed her skin in the way characteristic of the orange layer. Most Mayim never came deeper than yellow, she encouraged herself. She'd done the impossible. She'd gone to the Bec. She'd talked to the Bec.

But all was still lost.

A voice interrupted her self-torment.

Dwoyra.

"Blood?"

Chapter 50: Xylo

Xylo, Ieska, and Torcalon sat on the shore. The others had gone to bed, and the rain was falling gently, rewetting the land after the evaporation of the day. The convenalations glowed red above their heads, diffused in the mist. The insane turquoise glow of the sea became even more brilliant in the darkness of night.

"The ymolenegth is a different color here," Xylo ventured, wanting to ask why but avoiding the question.

"The sea is small here," Ieska replied. "It's only an hour's journey by boat form one side of the sea to the other. It stands to reason."

"Is it . . ." Xylo hesitated, "Is it their blood? The triad blood? Is that what makes the color so bright, so vibrant?"

Torcalon nodded. "You can see why we felt it was necessary to hide the children here. If Kleibald learned the power that was in their blood . . ."

Xylo had known that would be the answer. It necessitated his next question. "We need their power in Garradh Gannoir," he stated quietly.

Torcalon and Ieska both looked at him gravely.

Xylo continued. "My daughter-in-law, Ceres, is Mayim. She's reported oddities in the water. Splotches of darkness. They're growing more and more abundant. We believe they're tiny blotches of evil seeping into Gannoir from the chaos outside our world. Only the blood of the Siann Dha can counteract them, can obliterate the darkness."

"I thought the rift in the Bec was healed with Igracio's death," Ieska said.

"We believe it was," Xylo said. "Maybe the darkness seeped into Gannoir when the skyboulder exploded to the exterior. It's possible that the increase in dark blotches only represents their diffusion over time. But it's also possible that there are other holes in the Bec layer through which they are entering. If that is the case, then something must be done to stop them before they destroy Gannoir."

"The tales of the ancients mention that some darkness was sealed inside Gannoir at the time of the gogyvehr," Ieska remembered. "Is it possible that this is just part of that darkness? That it was released from wherever it had been trapped by the catastrophic events surrounding the completion of the gogyvehr? Maybe it's not a new darkness at all."

"It's possible," Xylo admitted. "And if that is the case, a concentrated effort by the people of Luca, through continual blood donations, can fight the darkness and can at least keep it at bay. Or at best, eliminate the darkness altogether. If that is the case, then there's no reason these tri-casted children can't stay here in hiding."

"You don't think that's the case," Torcalon observed.

"I don't," Xylo agreed. "Ceres has been seeing a continual increase in the darkness in the sea. The ymolenegth still glows in the water, but it's dimming. Light is life. And life is blood."

"You want the blood of my grandchildren." Torcalon stood and looked ready to fight.

"I want what's best for Gannoir," Xylo argued.

"You also want to bring Kleibald and the skyboulder back into the world," Ieska said. "That would involve creating a hole in the Bec layer and drawing them back in."

This was the truth. He did want the bring Kleibald back, to enact justice for the deaths of Igracio, of Afa, of Mailu, of Dochym, and many others, including Mantais Nayro and for his children. It wasn't too much to ask. He understood, however, how much he was asking from Ieska, Torcalon, and the others. He owed them his honesty. He owed them his heart.

"Kleibald tortured and killed my four-year-old son," Xylo said heavily. "My desire for justice is tainted by my own desire for revenge." He bowed his head, his heart heavy with grief, angry, guilt, and lust for Kleibald's blood.

"I'm sorry for your loss," Torcalon said sincerely. "May Tel-Maor bring you comfort."

"I don't need comfort. I need justice. And so do you," Xylo replied.

"We want to help," Ieska said after a quick glance at Torcalon.

Xylo's heart ached with gladness. They were on his side. They loved him despite his guilt over Afa and Mailu, over his desire for revenge, over . . .

"My grandchildren and children are on the skyboulder," he blurted out, revealing the last of his secrets. He told them about his marriage to Ardanach, how she had left him for Kleibald, taking his older two children with her. How he hadn't known that Gryf had children until he'd seen them entering the skyboulder as a family. "A boy and a girl," he said, his eyes full of pain. "Already past the first part of childhood. I never knew they existed."

Ieska looked at him with her clear, dark eyes. "It's natural that you want to bring them back. You don't have to feel guilty."

"I'm the acting Dynroc of Garradh Gannoir," Xylo protested stoically. "I must serve justice, not self."

"Bringing the skyboulder home is a just cause," Ieska answered him. "Kleibald must be brought to account for his crimes, not just against you and your family, but against Torcalon, against me, against all the women who were victimized due to his vicious experiments. And it is just to bring back the others on the skyboulder. They shouldn't have to die for Kleibald's guilt."

"I'll talk to the others in the morning," Torcalon offered. "We're with you in this."

"You're putting your family in danger," Xylo reminded him.

"Maybe. Maybe not. We may never be able to return to our hidden life. But then, we may. Or we may not need to."

Xylo looked around at the lush paradise surrounding him on all sides. "This place ought to be preserved."

Torcalon smiled. "That's a separate issue."

Xylo saw that he was right. Taking the offspring of Methiant Migas to Garradh Gannoir would in no way necessitate the exposure of the settlement at Cudth Deorth. All they had to do was refuse to reveal the location of their home. Still . . . "What I'm asking them to do could be dangerous," Xylo said.

Ieska bowed her head. "We knew danger would come someday. Better that it come for the sake of good than at the hands of people who intend harm."

"They'll each have to decide for themselves whether they will participate," Torcalon noted. "I won't force any of my grandchildren to risk their lives."

"I understand," Xylo agreed.

The next morning, Torcalon took Ieska and Xylo back across the sea to Rhosen Faide where his home was. From there they took the ferry back to Lucedth.

"Do you want me to come with you when you meet with Igracio's mother?" Ieska asked, resting her head on Xylo's shoulder as they embraced.

Xylo sighed. "It's a horrible question to have to ask. If Igracio was the son of Methiant Migas, then I'll be asking Rahela to re-live something horrifically traumatic. She may be unwilling to talk about it."

Ieska leaned back and looked into Xylo's eyes. "I've been there," she reminded him. "And you're right. It will be asking a lot of Rahela. But it is better that she know what happened. She should know about Kleibald's experiments and about Mantais's suicide. She should know he was sorry . . . sorry unto death."

"Come with me," Xylo requested.

Ieska nodded.

"I don't just mean to visit Rahela."

"What are you talking about?

Xylo took a deep breath. "I mean . . . marry me." He waited, hopeful and afraid.

"All right," Ieska smiled up at him.

"Once this is over . . ." Xylo began.

"Now," Ieska repeated. "There may not be an afterward."

Xylo stroked her cheek. "I'd marry you yesterday if I could."

Chapter 51: Talag

The atmosphere inside the skyboulder was tense. At first Talag thought he was experiencing his own anxiety about the voices, the blood, and the mission, but he finally realized that he wasn't the problem. Everyone on the skyboulder was on edge.

The food supply was running out. Water too. They couldn't survive much longer—not without restocking. And the only way to replenish the food and water was to come to rest on a world that had those things to give them, either Gannoir or another place.

Two days had passed and the scab on his leg itched. He wanted to pick at the scab, but he knew it wasn't time yet. He had to wait for Dynny. Dynny's injury had not healed as quickly as Talag's. The blood over his cut had dried some, but the skin around the site was still pink with irritation and the wound was still oozing. Talag knew it was too soon to ask the old man for the scab.

The spirits had been urging him to pick the scab off, to give it to his grandfather. Together with the physical discomfort of the itchy, crusted place, it made the agony almost unbearable. But he had to wait. If he and Dynny were going to save the lives of the people of Gannoir, it had to be Dynny's scab that they gave to Kleibald, not his.

"Grandfather's looking for you," Donamys told him with a scathing tone and through clenched teeth. She had noticed her grandfather's new preference for Talag and had been angling to win back the prime place in his affections. The girls with her giggled. Talag wondered what she'd said to them, what had made them look at him as though he were a joke. Donamys was only twelve, but controlled every situation masterfully, in a way that fourteen-year-old Talag had never been able to manage.

"Did he say why?" Talag asked, trying to sound casual.

Donamys narrowed her eyes. "There's something going on, isn't there?"

Talag sighed. "What could be going on?"

"We're all going to die pretty quickly after the food runs out. Grandfather is worried. Everyone's worried. But it's you he wants to talk to. Why you?"

A stroke of humor stabbed through Talag. "Maybe he just wants to say goodbye," he suggested. "He'll probably want to talk to you next."

Donamys tossed her brown curls, turned around, and flounced out of the room, letting her Esh-tala catch the air as she did. She always knew how to make an exit.

Talag stood up and straightened his clothes. Then he began to look for Kleibald. It wasn't a long search. Kleibald was in the food-distribution room, deep in conversation with Gelu.

"Grandfather? Donamys said you wanted to see me."

Kleibald looked up. "Come closer, boy."

Talag obeyed.

"You have something for me?" Kleibald asked, holding out his hand.

"No."

Kleibald glanced at Gelu. Gelu's eyes flickered, but he said nothing.

"The spirits have told me that you have something for me. Now you say you don't. I'm disinclined to doubt the spirits, you know." Kleibald gave him a hard look.

"It's . . . it's . . . not ready yet," Talag hedged.

"Perhaps if you tell us what it is, we can help you speed things up," Gelu suggested.

They didn't know! This thought heartened Talag until it occurred to him that eventually he would have to tell them the truth. But at least this way they couldn't attack him and pick the scab off his foot. Inside his head, Talag flinched. He trusted his grandfather. His grandfather wanted to save the people of Gannoir. That was what this whole thing was about. Why had his mind conjured up a picture of an attack? Shaking his head quickly, as though to dispel the unwelcome thought, Talag searched his mind for an answer.

"The food supply is running short," Kleibald reminded him. "We have three days left. Three days of reduced rations. After that we play a waiting game to see who dies first. The more quickly you give us whatever it is that the spirits have told you to give us, the better it will be for everyone. You wouldn't want your parents to die, would you? Or your sister? Your aging grandmother who dotes on you? Or your half-wit friend?"

Talag's heart ached. He didn't want anyone to die. But he couldn't make Dynny's foot heal any more quickly than it could heal. There was nothing he could do.

"I'll give it to you as soon as I can," he promised. "You know I want to save Gannoir. I do." He looked at his grandfather and Gelu with a pleading look.

Then he left.

"Maybe by tomorrow?" he asked, looking at Dynny's oozing foot.

Dynny smiled and nodded encouragingly. "By tomorrow."

"Grandfather says we only have three days until the food runs out. This has to work." Talag felt close to tears.

"Tel-Maor won't let everyone die," Dynny answered confidently. "He made Gannoir. He'll take care of the people."

Talag wished he could believe like Dynny did. But it was all just myth. Comforting myth, but still, just a myth. There was no Tel-Maor living in the Ghalon and taking care of Gannoir. There was no evidence for such a person.

Inspiration struck. "I'm going to cut my other foot," he told Dynny. "Our scabs have to look like they're the same age. Just in case anyone asks. I have to be able to show them a wound that looks like yours, with an oozing cut. Otherwise, we'll never make them believe your scab is my scab."

"Cut yesterday's scab off," Dynny suggested with an authority in his voice that Talag had never heard from his little friend before. "That will make it ooze more."

"How do you know that?" Talag asked, curious about Dynny's assuredness.

"I take care of people," Dynny told him proudly. "I learn slowly, but I learn. I know about wounds."

"Is it part of the Dynroc's job? Taking care of people who are hurt?" Talag asked.

Dynny nodded. "Take care of people. Make sure they get better." He patted the stone sarcophagus behind him. "I'm taking care of Mailu."

Talag glanced through the glass lid of the coffin. Mailu looked exactly the same. Beautiful. Injured. Pale. Dead.

He slid onto the floor and sat beside Dynny, pulling his pocketknife out. Wincing, he proceeded to slice the scab off his foot. Blood pooled on the floor. He wiped at it with the edge of his tunic and then pressed it on the wound to stop the bleeding.

Dynny smiled at him. "You're doing a good job. Save the people of Gannoir."

Talag sighed. His foot hurt.

Chapter 52: Tass

Tass felt the anger boil within her. What did Dwoyra want? Didn't she understand that Tass couldn't just bleed all day long? Didn't she understand that it hurt?

She probably didn't, a rational part of Tass's mind argued. Dwoyra is made of water. She doesn't have blood. She can't be wounded—not like someone with a solid body. Tass spent a moment reflecting on what kind of wounds a creature made of water could get, but couldn't think of anything that would be an equivalent injury.

The anger and the understanding struggled within her.

"Blood," Dwoyra still urged her.

"I can't," Tass said. "It wouldn't help. I don't have enough blood."

"Save Gannoir. Kill the darkness," Dwoyra pleaded.

"You don't understand. It hurts. It kills me. It's bad. Unjust. And it won't help. There are thousands of dark blotches. I don't have enough blood. It wouldn't make a difference."

"Fight. Fight the darkness." Dwoyra swirled around Tass faster and faster. Tass fought to maintain equilibrium. She didn't want Dwoyra to spin her, but she had no choice. She felt sick.

"Stop!" she cried in a strangled voice.

Dwoyra spun faster. "Blood!" Her cry was insistent, sorrowful, powerful.

"I can't!" Tass spat. Her words were lost in the whirlwind.

"Blood!" Dwoyra begged.

Tass curled into a ball, hoping to make her nausea subside. Anger, now, was the predominant thing she was feeling. The sense of understanding the watery creature was fading. Dwoyra was pushing her too hard. She was asking too much. Tass felt like she was going to vomit. "Stop," she said feebly.

Dwoyra stopped. Tass continued to spin for several minutes as the parts of the water that were not Dwoyra continued to churn around her. She was dizzy and sick. Was Dwoyra going to force her to bleed? If there was blood in the vomit, would it be enough to appease her water acquaintance? Tass's thoughts tumbled around her mind just as her body tumbled in the water. She didn't want to bleed. It was . . . unsustainable. She only had so much blood.

"For Gannoir . . ." Dwoyra begged. Tass could feel the water being's sorrow, like poison in the water around her.

"Okay," she finally conceded, more because she didn't want to be spun anymore than because she was willing to participate in Dwoyra's plan. "But you have to come and get it," she added with defiance. She didn't think Dwoyra would do it. How could water wield a knife?

Almost immediately she felt a stabbing pain in her shoulder, the shoulder that habitually hurt her the worst. She saw the water begin to glow a brilliant teal around her, contrasting with the orange light of the layer. She clapped a hand over her bleeding shoulder. "Enough!" she shouted. "Be content with that. I won't let you kill me!" Tass was unsure whether she had the power to stop Dwoyra. She had seen no weapon. Dwoyra must have pierced her skin with her own razor-sharp, watery fingers. Tass hadn't thought such a thing was possible. But it obviously was.

The glowing droplets of blood floated upward, toward the underside of the Orbokth.

"Aren't you going to make sure they obliterate some of the dark splotches?" Tass asked Dwoyra sarcastically.

She felt Dwoyra leave, following the blood. At least she would be satisfied for a while, Tass thought. She swam away, trying to put distance between herself and the part of the sea that was still sprinkled with her blood. Glancing back, she could see it, glowing yellow now, against the orange liquid of the seawater.

With a hand clapped against her wounded shoulder, she kicked her feet to swim. Despair settled over her. The Bec had refused her request. Opening a hole—a giant hole—in the Bec was not good for Gannoir. Therefore the Bec would never consent to it. There was no help there. And all Dwoyra wanted was blood. Dwoyra couldn't see beyond the immediate problem of quelling the tiny individual blotches of darkness. The holes in the Bec layer were a problem, Tass admitted. Someone needed to do something about them so that no more darkness came into Gannoir. But not now. Not until she had brought the skyboulder back. Not until she had brought Mailu home.

Bring Mailu home, the voices whispered around her.

Tass took a deep breath and turned to swim backstroke. Here was someone—or many someones—who were on her side. The voices wanted the same thing she wanted. They wanted to bring the skyboulder home. Did they have power like Dwoyra did?

"How?" she asked aloud in her gill-voice.

You, the voices answered smoothly. There was no accusation here, no demand. It was as though the voices knew she had finally decided to join them in their quest. They were on the same side. She could feel it.

"Tell me how," Tass requested.

She could almost feel the voices smiling.

Darkness . . . they hissed. Then they were silent, letting her think.

Darkness . . . How could the darkness be the answer? But of course, she realized, it was the darkness that could be her greatest ally. The darkness was seeping into Gannoir. Seeping into Gannoir through holes in the Bec layer. What if the darkness wasn't just physical blotches? What if the dark spots, like the Bec, had souls? What if the darkness was . . . rational? Thoughts filled Tass's mind more quickly than she could attend to them. If the darkness was rational, and it was coming into Gannoir, then it was coming into Gannoir because it wanted to come into Gannoir. Its will was to come into Gannoir. The darkness, then, would be on her side. It would be in favor of forging a larger gap in the Bec.

Something of conscience arrested her thoughts. The Bec was good. The Bec wanted to protect Gannoir. Presumably, then, the darkness was on the opposite side of the war from the Bec. Logically, then the darkness was evil and wanted not to protect Gannoir, but to destroy Gannoir. Shouldn't she side with Good? With Protection?

"Not good . . ." she muttered aloud.

Not good . . . not bad . . . the voices whispered.

Of course. That was it. The darkness didn't have to be bad in order to not be on the side of the Good. The darkness might be something else entirely. A neutral force. Rational, but neutral. Maybe she could use it to prise open the Bec, and then close it behind the skyboulder after it brought it back.

There were many holes in her plan, she realized. It wasn't even a plan thus far—just an alliance. She could talk to the darkness. Find out what power they had over the Bec. If she could get all the dark blotches to gather, to fight against the Bec, just temporarily, then she could make a hole large enough for the skyboulder to reenter. Just how she was going to snatch it out of the chaos and back into Gannoir was an unknown. But the voices would help her. The darkness would help her.

Together they would find a way.

Chapter 53: Xylo

Rahela sat uncomfortably on the expensive leather sofa at Ieska's apartment in Lucedth. Xylo and Ieska had decided that it would be better to talk to Rahela alone, without her husband Laso. If she had been a victim of Methiant Migas, she had perhaps never told Laso, which meant she would be unlikely to admit as much in front of him when confronted.

"Thank you for coming," Xylo said. "I know the past months have been excruciatingly hard on your family. Again, I'm so sorry for your loss. Igracio was ... was ... was everything," he finished lamely. He had wanted to say something about Igracio's tri-casted blood, about his heroic sacrifice, about the utter love he had shown in his attempt to save Tass, but nothing would have summed it up.

Rahela's eyes glittered. "Thank you. I appreciate your sympathy. And yours," she nodded at Ieska, whom Xylo had introduced as his fiancée and as an Esh-maor scientist.

"You're probably wondering why we asked you to come here alone," Ieska said softly. She paused.

Rahela nodded. "I'm assuming it has something to do with Igracio." She looked at Xylo and Ieska expectantly.

"We wanted to ask you about him," Xylo began awkwardly. "He was . . . unusual. His blood saved Gannoir. It was more powerful than the blood that had previously been submitted to the waters. Igracio's blood, and his blood alone, healed the Bilik. Something about him was different. We want to know why."

Rahela shook her head. "I don't have any answer for you. Igracio was just… Igracio. My son. My boy." A tear slipped down her face.

Ieska leaned toward the woman and took her hand. "I want to tell you a story," she began gently. She related the tale of her days in the lab, of the experiments that had been performed on a convict, of how those experiments had gone awry. "So instead of producing a tri-casted superman, he became almost uncasted. Nothing. And his personality shattered. He had a good side," she glanced up at Xylo, who nodded encouragingly, "but the darkness in him grew without bounds. He became . . . he became . . ."

Rahela's eyes had grown wide and frightened during the telling. As Ieska struggled to put her own nightmare to words, Rahela interceded. ". . . a rapist?" she whispered.

Ieska glanced at Xylo and then nodded. "I bore a daughter. The daughter of the convict. Unlike her father, she is not an uncasted nothing. She is tri-casted. A triad. Esh. Gulot. Mayim. All at once. She's different."

Rahela was sobbing now.

"It's your story too, isn't it?" Ieska asked gently.

Rahela nodded. "Laso knows. But we always hoped . . . we always thought . . . When Peodar was born he looked so much like Igracio. They could have been twins. We stopped worrying that

Igracio wasn't Laso's child. Clearly the boys were full-blooded brothers. Even when Igracio was re-casted Mayim, we didn't worry. It happens sometimes. Gulot parents can have Mayim children. They boys were so alike. I haven't worried about it at all. Not since it became clear that the boys were so alike. They had to have been full brothers . . ."

"I'm sorry." Ieska took the dark-haired woman into her arms and comforted her.

Rahela wiped her eyes. "It's too much. Too much sorrow. I'm glad, at least, that Igracio doesn't have to know. That he never knew what his father was."

"It's something," Ieska replied.

"Your daughter . . ." Rahela began. "Tell me about her."

Ieska complied, painting a picture of Sadi, with her finger and body tala, her glowing fingertips, her long black hair, and her happy demeanor.

"She knows?" Rahela asked.

"Yes," Ieska told her. "And there are others . . . other children of Mantais Nayro—that was his name before the experiments ruined him. They live together in a secluded space where no one can find them and exploit them for their powers."

"Powers?" Rahela pressed.

"Like your son," Ieska explained. "Their blood is special."

"We don't know all that the blood of the triad children can do, but we've seen the water at their enclave. It glows brighter than the sea around Lucedth. They're clearly special. And after knowing what was accomplished through Igracio's blood . . . well, there is much to be learned about these others, the children of Mantais Nayro."

"How many children are there?" Rahela asked. Xylo could tell she was already opening her heart to mother her son's siblings.

"We know of seven," Ieska told her. "Seven who live in hiding together. There may be more."

"At least one more," Xylo added. "Although we are not entirely sure of her identity."

Realization dawned on Rahela's face. "It's Tass, isn't it?" she asked. "I saw her fingers glowing the other day. An Esh trait. But she's Mayim. It's unusual. And it could happen, but . . ."

Xylo nodded. "We believe so. But you mustn't tell anyone. Not until we can tell Tass, before we can work to keep her safe."

"I won't," Rahela promised. "Oh, the poor child!"

"You may be asked to testify against Kleibald," Xylo explained. "We wanted to know about Igracio, but it doesn't make any difference to him at this point. But you . . . you can make a difference. You can bring justice."

"Against Kleibald?" Rahela looked confused.

"Because of the experiments. A man was ruined. And in turn, he brought destruction to others."

"Why not against this man, this Mantais Nayro?" Rahela asked.

"He's dead," Xylo told her. He explained about Mantais's confession, his remorse, and his suicide.

Rahela's eyes grew soft. "Thank you," she said. "Thank you for telling me. Somehow this has brought healing to a wound I didn't know was still bleeding inside me. He was sorry. He would have undone his actions if he could have. He was a victim too."

"So you'll testify?" Xylo asked.

"How can I? From what I understand, Kleibald left Gannoir. There's nothing that can be done."

"We're trying to bring him back," Xylo told her. "We want to prosecute him for his crimes."

Rahela nodded. "I'll talk to Laso. We'll decide together. And if there is anything I can do for these children, for Tass or the others, I would do it. For Igracio's sake. For my own sake. Please."

"Thank you," Ieska said, squeezing Rahela's hand. "We will consider you an ally and a friend."

Chapter 54: Talag

"We're running out of food! It's too late! We must go back," Gelu argued.

"The original plan still stands. Gannoir must be destroyed," Kleibald replied.

"I agreed to it when it made sense. When these spirits of yours were going to take us to a new world. Gannoir should have imploded when we left. It didn't. Now we're floating in the chaos waiting to die. We have to change the plan. We have to go home!"

"The voices have assured me that all is not lost. Once Gannoir is gone, they will give us that new world. It was a contract. We destroy Gannoir and they establish us on another world, somewhere we can begin again. Only this time, we would have full commerce with other worlds. And our offspring will be the core of the new civilization."

"My offspring, my son, will be Siann Dha. He will rule Gannoir. If we don't go back, we will die." Gelu's eyes softened at the thought of his son. He and his wife, Ceci, had no children. But with Mailu expecting his child, he would finally be a father. And with the spirits giving them a new world, his child, his son, would be the father of a people. The founder of a new civilization. "You really think there's still hope?"

"The spirits have assured me that it is not too late. We can still destroy Gannoir. With the power of the Dynroc to facilitate the connection between the chaos and the Ghalon, and whatever it is that Talag is going to give us, we will be able to do it."

"You've been watching Gannoir? We're in position?" Gelu asked.

Kleibald nodded. "I can see the scar through the scope. We're directly above it. Have been for days. The spirits can't physically manipulate the skyboulder, but we have a little power."

"What do you think it is that they want from the boy?"

"My grandson is the Dynroc," Kleibald reminded Gelu. "It could be anything, but I suspect it's some sort of corporeal waste. Skin. Blood. Hair. Even urine. Who knows? They didn't tell me that part."

Gelu frowned. "Do you think the boy is delaying on purpose? Is he reluctant to destroy Gannoir?"

"He has no idea of our plan. He believes Gannoir is in the process of implosion and that we're trying to save the people, bring them to another world."

"He's a fool."

"An idealist," Kleibald countered.

"Did you convince him that all the people of Gannoir were going to fit into the skyboulder?"

Kleibald laughed. "I told him they would be spirited to another world by the power of the Dynroc."

"And he believed you? Like I said, he is a fool."

"A useful fool, at least," Kleibald replied grimly.

Chapter 55: Tass

"Darkness?" Tass queried experimentally. She focused her eyes on a small dga covered with tiny blotches of blackness.

The dga waved its silvery limbs at her defensively. She reached for the creature, scooping it into her hand. It scratched and bit. Tass's hand began to bleed. She released the dga. She didn't want to obliterate the darkness. She needed a live ally, not a dead one. The dga swam away from her. Its metallic sheen was brighter, demonstrating that her blood had, in fact, freed it from its dark parasites. She sighed.

How was she supposed to talk to darkness?

Laughter rang in her ears, in her gills, making the inside of her head echo with their mirth. The voices were back. Maybe they could help her.

"Voices," she began, "I would like to talk to the darkness."

They laughed again. She wasn't sure why she thought of the voices as a plurality, but she did.

"Why are you laughing?"

You're talking to it, they told her.

"You're the darkness?" Tass tried to reconcile the muddy patches in the seawater around her and clinging to the dga with the silvery voices that effortlessly entered her mind.

"Of course."

The Bec had told her that the darkness was inside her. Was that what it had meant? That the darkness was talking inside her head? Relief washed over her. The darkness, then, wasn't part of her. It hadn't taken up residence in her soul. It was just a voice in her ears and gills.

"Can you help me bring the skyboulder back?" she asked.

We've been trying to get you to do that from the beginning.

"I don't know what to do. What do you need me for?"

Her gills whistled with the frustration of the voices . . . the darkness, she now had to label it. *You're mostly useless, you know,* it began, reminding Tass of the months of torment the voices had perpetrated on her. *But you have a body. You have a body, and we don't. We can communicate with bodily creatures, but we have no bodies of our own. For physical tasks, we need a physical being.*

"I don't understand."

The voices hissed angrily. *Worthless and lowly. You are all just dust and bile.*

Tass seethed and wondered if it were worthwhile to ally with the darkness. It clearly had no regard for her at all. It had spent months tormenting her, making her feel worthless, driving her to despair. She hated the voices with everything she was. But she needed them. With the Bec unwilling to help her, she needed the voices, these unbodied entities who could tell her how to bring her sister home, who could tell her how to find love.

She steeled herself for another attempt at communication. "You may think I'm worthless, but you need me, or you wouldn't be talking to me. What should I do?"

There was no answer. Tass began to worry that the voices, like Dwoyra, wanted her for her blood alone. She shivered in the cold water. Then she remembered that unlike Dwoyra, the voices were unbodied. There could be no watery knives here. They couldn't force her to bleed like Dwoyra could. And Dwoyra, she realized, hadn't forced her. Dwoyra had permission. Dwoyra is good, her conscience nagged her. And the voices . . . the voices . . .

Neutral, she reassured herself. The voices weren't evil just because they weren't on Dwoyra's side. And even if they were evil, that didn't mean she couldn't use them to get what she wanted. She would find out what she needed to know and then she would leave them be.

She thought of Igracio, who had given his life in his attempt to save hers. No matter how worthless the voices said she was, she owed it to Igracio to live and to live well. And to live well, she needed her sister. She needed Mailu. And Mailu was on the skyboulder.

"Is it my blood you want?" she asked the voices in her gill-voice. It was likely. It had been Igracio's blood that had facilitated the healing of the Bilik. Blood, then, would be the means by which it could be opened again. But she didn't want to die. She wouldn't. She would live without Mailu before she would let herself die. If she was dead, there was no point in bringing the skyboulder back.

But the blood negated the darkness. Light was life and light came from blood. Darkness couldn't exist where blood was abundant. It was a scientific fact.

The voices chattered at her incomprehensibly. She wondered what the reply would be.

Blood . . .

She waited expectantly.

Blood . . . The word filled her mind, oozing more thickly than actual blood, reaching to every corner of her being until there were not thoughts at all, just a bloody, pulsing whole.

Blood . . .

She forced her words through the morass in her brain and spat the words out. "Is it my blood you want? Is that the only thing any of you can think about?"

Bloodless, the voices told her. *All must be bloodless. All.*

Light is life and light comes from blood. It was the refrain of their world. To be bloodless meant to be dead . . . didn't it?

"I don't understand."

You will.

Chapter 56: Xylo

Torcalon made two trips that day, bringing his grandchildren across the sea to Rhosen Faide in his small boat. Of the children of Mantais Nayro, only Ninach had declined to come. Whether she was afraid or simply averse to the idea was not clear. She had remained firm, despite the appeals of her siblings.

Xylo and Ieska had not tried to be persuasive. They had presented the need simply and without emotional appeal. Gannoir had been invaded by darkness, and they didn't know how it was entering their world. Because the tri-casted blood was more powerful than the blood of an ordinary Siann Dha, and because they were able to withstand both heat and cold, Xylo believed their help could be useful in searching out any fissures in the Bec and in dispelling the darkness. He told them the story of Igracio's victorious, sacrificial death and let them understand the danger of the proposed mission.

Now they had all assembled at Torcalon's small home in Rhosen Faide so they could go together to Lucedth and then into Garradh Gannoir to begin the search. Finnan and Rhyder, Laetu's parents, and his sister, Camilly, had come as well, to look after the practical aspects of the journey. Pax and Laetu, were, after all, very young. Byid, Pax's younger brother, had begged to go with the others, but Bridima had felt it would be best if he stayed behind. All in all, the team consisted of the six willing triad offspring, Kari, Sadi, Unaleah, Gudall, Laetu, and Pax, as well as Ieska and Xylo, Rhyder and Finnan, and fifteen-year-old Camilly—eleven people in all— eleven people bent on saving the world. None of the six triads remembered life outside of their enclave at Cudth Deorth. Only Ninach, who had chosen not to come, had been old enough for memory at the time she was brought to the secret hideaway.

The flat, open spaces of the Rhosen clatries impressed them all. It was night when they left Torcalon's house, and just beginning to rain.

Unaleah shook her head. "I don't like it. It's so . . . exposed. In Cudth Deorth I feel safe. Out here, anything could happen."

"That's what I like," Camilly retorted cheerfully. "I want to know all about it. I want to know what it's like to live on the outside.

"Can you remember anything about your life before you came to Cudth Deorth?" Ieska asked her.

Camilly scrunched up her face as though trying to look inside her mind for her missing memories. "I remember a few things from when I was little, but it's mostly things that happened at home with my parents. I was only three when I came, you know."

"I was five when I came, and I don't remember much more than that," Unaleah said.

"What are you doing?" Xylo asked, looking at the two younger boys who had separated themselves from the group and were examining something on the ground several yards away.

Pax grinned. "There's no clatry in Cudth Deorth. Just the Orbokth and water."

"There are different animals on the clatry," Laetu added, poking his hand through one of the holes in the lattice-like clatry. He pulled out a mass of sea string and sea grass. A tiny ribbon snail clung to it, its long tentacles waving in dismay.

"There will be time for that later," Finnan admonished them. "Right now, we've got to get to the ferry."

With a sign, Pax and Laetu abandoned their scientific pursuits and rejoined the group, albeit with reluctance and a restless energy that gave Xylo hope that his plan would work. If the boys could swim down to the Bec layer, if they could endure the cold, then their natural curiosity would work in his favor—in all of their favor.

On the ferry, they got some odd looks from the locals, mostly due to the size of the group rather than to the presence of both body and finger tala on six members of their party. All the triad offspring had been instructed to keep their hands hidden in their pockets or in the folds of their robes as much as possible. They could pass for Esh. Camilly, however, waved her hands about freely. She was not the child of Mantais Nayro, and therefore was simply pure Mayim. The stares she got were on account of her long red hair. Mayim simply did not have long hair. It was inconvenient for swimming. All the Mayim had short hair. Whispers abounded.

"Should we tell her to hide her fingers too?" Finnan whispered to Ieska, casting a worried look at the people who were staring at her daughter.

Ieska shook her head. "It's a diversion. If they're looking at Camilly, then they're not looking at the others. Let them look."

Finnan still looked worried, but she didn't make Camilly stifle her exuberant personality or tuck up her fingers.

If the Rhosen clatries were a shock to the young people, Lucedth was an even greater one. With its towering metal skyscrapers and the crowds of hustling people in the streets, it made all the residents of Cudth Deorth uncomfortable. Xylo stopped at the first hotel they came to and secured rooms for them—one for Finnan and Rhyder and their children, Laetu and Camilly; another room for Ieska and the girls, Kari, Sadi, and Unaleah; and another for himself and the boys, Gudall and Pax. No one had slept on the ferryboat, and all were exhausted from their journey.

The next morning dawned dry and clear. The night's rain had stopped and the clear golden glow of firstlight illuminated the meager rooms. Ieska had been awake for a long time and had been sitting at a little table by the window writing in a notebook by the light of her faintly glowing fingers.

Sadi came up behind her and put her arms around her mother. "What are you writing?" she asked.

Ieska sighed. "I'm just trying to do some math. Trying to figure things out."

"What kind of math?"

"Blood math. Igracio's death closed the Bilik. His blood was powerful. There are six of you. Six triads like Igracio. Among you there should be six times the power."

Sadi snorted. "Only if we all die bloody deaths."

"I'm not going to let you die. That's what I'm working on. I know the blood-to-water ratios necessary for different levels of ymolenegth. I'm a scientist. And while we never ran tests on you and the others, we know your blood is stronger than the blood of the Siann Dha." She shook her head. "I wish, now, that we had done some scientific experimentation."

"Why didn't you?"

"There was no lab in Cudth Deorth. I did a little informal testing, but all it really told me was what I already knew—that triad blood is powerful. I didn't want to bring it back to the lab in either Nozoffi or Lucedth. It was too dangerous. I didn't want anyone to know about you and the others."

"Was my . . . father's . . . blood powerful?" Sadi asked.

"I've told you before—no. In trying to make a superman, we made a worm, morally and physically."

"His blood didn't make the water glow at all?"

"Only very faintly," Ieska replied. "More than someone's from the other side of the Orbokth, but nowhere near the brightness it created before we destroyed him."

"It's not your fault," Sadi reminded her mother.

"It is my fault," Ieska replied. "Mine and all the others who participated in the experiments. We knew what we were doing. The fact that we were ordered to do it makes no difference. What we were doing was wrong. It was presumptuous. It was arrogant. It interfered with the intentions of Tel-Maor."

Sadi stood up abruptly. "You believe in Tel-Maor?"

"I never did," Ieska said with a sigh. "But Xylo's been talking to me. He's been explaining his ideas about how the old mythologies could be literally true. He's very persuasive."

"You're in love," Sadi pointed out with a toss of her long dark hair. She grinned.

Ieska swatted at her daughter playfully. "Saoradi Thayl Nayro, I am enough of an intellectual to weigh another person's arguments rationally, in love or not."

Sadi stepped out of swatting distance. "You really think someone lives in the Ghalon? A super-powerful being who created the world and is now trapped—trapped—in the core of the world?"

"I don't know," Ieska said. "All my life I've been taught that such stories were due to the ignorance of the early ones. But now . . ."—she shook her head—"Xylo makes it seem like the myths could be true—or could be rooted in truth."

A knock at the door interrupted their conversation. When Ieska opened it, she saw Xylo and two strangers.

"You all awake?" Xylo asked.

Ieska glanced back at the sleeping forms of Unaleah and Kari. "Not quite," she told him.

"Come to my room then, you and Sadi. I have some people I want you to meet."

Chapter 57: Talag

Dynny looked at Talag with worried eyes. "Should I do it now?"

"I think we have to," Talag said. "We're all going to die if we can't get to a new world. And so are people on Gannoir."

"Okay." Dynny slipped off his shoe and began to pick at the scab on his foot. Talag did the same.

"We'll trade scabs," Talag said. "Just keep mine inside your shoe, like it just fell off your foot and landed in there. I'll take yours—the powerful one—to Grandfather."

"Because I'm the Dynroc," Dynny said, wincing as the crusted blood began to pull away from his skin. "I have to hurt a little bit so that no one will die."

"Yes." Talag had already peeled the little brown mess from his own foot and was examining it in the palm of his hand. It didn't look like anything special. Just dried, dead blood. He wondered if Dynny's would look different, if there was some way he would be able to discern the power the spirits seemed to think it had.

"Do it quickly," he advised, watching Dynny's hesitation.

Dynny looked up at him with pleading eyes.

"You can do it. It'll be over quickly. Then you'll never have to do it again."

Dynny took a deep breath and then ripped the scab off his foot. Blood oozed a dismal magenta out of numerous pinpricks where the scab had been. The skin around it was an angry red color, clashing with the magenta blood. He handed the scab to Talag.

It was no different from his own scab. Just crusted, dead blood. Dynny's scab still had wet blood covering its backside. Talag's was dry. Talag gently wiped Dynny's scab on the edge of his tunic and handed his own scab to Dynny.

"Put pressure on the wound," he advised as Dynny put his shoe back on and tucked Talag's scab inside.

Dynny shook his head. "I'm okay. It was like you said. It was bad for a minute but then it felt better. I'll make a new scab and I won't pull that one off."

"And I'll take your old scab to Grandfather," Talag said.

***

Kleibald stared at the proffered object in disgust. "What is it?"

"A scab," Talag told him, "from my foot. It's what the spirits told me to bring."

"You said it would be bodily waste," Gelu reminded his gray-haired crony.

Frowning in disgust, Kleibald took the tiny, crusted scab from Talag. He held it up to the light. "The spirits told you to bring this?"

"It is blood," Talag said. "Light is life and life is blood, right? My blood will bring life to the people of Gannoir. How soon do you think we can save them?" He thought of his few friends back home, his many acquaintances, his extended family. It had to work.

"Put it in the scope," Gelu suggested. "Maybe it will help us discern what is going on below us."

Kleibald pressed his lips together tightly. "It's worth a try."

"Don't you know what to do with it?" Talag asked. "The spirits didn't tell me that part."

"You should have asked them," Gelu snorted.

Kleibald turned toward the door to the food storage compartment. When he opened it, Talag could see that it was nearly empty. Kleibald stepped inside and opened a tiny metal door that Talag had never noticed before. A slim, round hole was behind the door, like someone had taken a drill to the rock. No light came through the hole, which was not to be wondered at since the chaos was not rumored to be well-lit. Kleibald put Dynny's scab on the tip of his finger and then pushed it into the hole. Then he pressed his eye close and peered through.

A ripple of laughter rung in Talag's ears and through his fire gills. The voices! He hadn't forgotten them, but their voices had been silent after he had determined to obey their command. He wondered anxiously why they were back, what else they wanted from him. To save the people of Gannoir he didn't mind bleeding again, but he didn't like making Dynny do it.

Kleibald pulled his head away from the hole.

"Well?" Gelu asked.

"Whatever the voices had in mind, it seems not to have anything to do with the scope," Kleibald said dryly.

"It makes no difference to the view?" Gelu asked.

"None whatsoever," Kleibald answered.

"Can I look?" Talag asked.

Kleibald shrugged. "Might as well. There's nothing to see." He stepped back and let his grandson approach the aperture of the scope.

Talag put his hands on the stony wall of the skyboulder and pressed his face close to the hole. At first, he could see nothing, but after some experimentation he found he could see a dim purple glow.

"Is it . . . Gannoir?" he ventured, looking over at his grandfather.

Kleibald nodded.

Talag couldn't tell whether the circle of pale light was the whole of Gannoir—a spherical body at an astronomical distance—or whether it was circular due to the size of the scope. He might instead be looking at a small section of Gannoir from very near. In the bottom left of the circle he could see the translucent brownish red smudge that was his—Dynny's—scab. The scab did nothing to increase his understanding of what he was seeing. It only served to obliterate the bottom sixth of the circle.

"We're close now," Kleibald told him. "We're right above the Bilik—the scar through which we left the world. If you look closely, you can see it."

Talag looked again. He squinted until he could see a faint line crossing his field of vision, a slight variance in the colors. He could imagine it he was seeing the Bec layer and the bright white scar that had only healed a few months earlier. "Is that how the spirits will bring them out?" he asked. "Will they come out of the Bilik?"

Gelu rubbed his forehead. "Fool . . ." he muttered.

"If we can figure out how to make this happen, I'm sure that will be the place," Kleibald replied smoothly.

Talag leaned back and looked up at Kleibald.

"You can go now," Kleibald said. "We'll let you know if there is anything else you can do to help."

"Okay." His dismissal was abrupt, and Talag felt that his grandfather was trying to get rid of him. The voices hissed in his ear, laughed, hummed, but did not speak any intelligible words.

Talag stepped out of the food storage room. "I'll ask the voices what they want you to do with the scab," he said earnestly. "Maybe they'll tell me."

"You do that," Kleibald said.

"Go now," Gelu added.

With a cold fear gripping his heart, Talag retreated.

Chapter 58: Tass

Despite her pleas, Tass was not able to get the dark voices to explain themselves. She was left to ponder the mysteries of their bloodless plans on her own. Frustrated, she decided to return to her nook in the underside of the Orbokth to rest. She propelled her body upward through the changing colors of the seawater until she came to the gentle greens nearer the surface. Her shoulders ached. Her fingers were glowing. She held her hands in front of her face, wondering what it was that made her fingers begin to glow. Was it because of Igracio? Was it because he, too, had been a Mayim with glowing fingers and he had given his life for her? Her fingers had been normal before everything that had happened. Maybe, though, they would have begun to glow as she grew older anyhow. Maybe it had nothing to do with Igracio, or with her brush with death.

She reached up toward the uneven ridges of the Orbokth and pulled herself into her sleeping hollow. Curling herself in a ball braced against the edges of her haven, she closed her outer eyelids and wondered what to try next.

No voices whispered through her gills. She wasn't sure if they had left her alone or if they were being purposefully silent. It didn't matter. She didn't have to do things their way—not if she could figure out a way of her own.

She ticked off her goals on a mental list as she pondered. Avoid Xylo. That was easily done. Xylo couldn't swim. All she had to do to avoid Xylo was stay in the sea. Of course there was Ceres. As his daughter-in-law, Ceres lived with Xylo. She was Xylo's emissary to the sea. Tass shook her head. She didn't have much to fear from Ceres. Ceres couldn't dive as quickly or as deeply as she could. She could outrun the young woman any day. Not only that, Tass knew she was smarter than Ceres. Ceres was sweet and caring, but she lacked intellect. Ceres was a typical Mayim. Slow, stupid, cheerful, obedient. Tass was none of those things.

And her fingers glowed.

Tass sighed and returned to her contemplation. Dwoyra would be harder to avoid. Dwoyra could not only swim quickly and deeply, she was also invisible. Avoiding Dwoyra would be nearly impossible. But Dwoyra, Tass knew, was good. Dwoyra would never hurt Tass without asking permission first. All Tass had to do was stay strong and refuse Dwoyra's requests.

Her thoughts turned next to the giant dga. Whoever had positioned the gleaming, metallic monster at the gate of the Bilik had created a formidable obstacle. She had tried to talk to it, but it hadn't responded. She wasn't sure if it was rational or not. Maybe it was no more than an enormous mechanical fish—a fish committed to guarding the Bilik. If it was a beast, however, someone had to be controlling it. Someone had given it orders to stand its ground, hovering over the scarred patch of ice. Tass wondered who had done it. Dwoyra? She exhaled heavily. No. Dwoyra would never team up with a creature encumbered with as much darkness as the dga. Who, then? She thought of those she knew. No one seemed likely to have stationed the beast. Even Kleibald and Gelu seemed like impossible choices. They couldn't access the water. The Bec? Tass dismissed the idea just as she'd dismissed the idea of Dwoyra's involvement. The Bec was unfailingly good. Light. Without darkness.

Maybe the darkness itself, having taking command of the dga's body, had manipulated it into its steadfast position. Could they do that? Tass didn't feel manipulated by the voices, just annoyed. But if the dga was irrational, she reflected, it was possible that the darkness had a more overwhelming influence.

She'd talk to the voices about it when she heard from them next. They were on her side. They wanted her to force the Bilik to open. They would know how much power she might be able to exert over the giant dga. She'd try to find them after she rested.

***

Tass pushed herself through the red layers of the sea down into the purple. She was freezing cold. She hadn't heard from the voices, but she thought they were with her. She felt it in her soul. Beyond her she could see the waving arms of the giant dga. The darkness clung to it, obliterating the reflections of the purple flames of the Bec and creating an eerie silhouette.

Tass felt her blood solidifying inside her veins.

"I can't," she said aloud in her gill-voice.

It was so cold it didn't hurt anymore. But she was in danger of forgetting everything she ever knew, even the reason she came. It wasn't going to work.

Tass turned around and kicked her feet below her, urging her body upward.

Laughter rang inside her head.

It hit her like a blow. Tass curled into a ball and let herself float toward the surface. As the chemical sea turned from red, to orange, to yellow, she felt her body begin to tingle with pain. She wondered how close to death she'd come, how close to death she still was. It hurt. Everything hurt.

The voices shattered inside her head. They felt as stinging, as miniscule, and as overwhelming as the pain.

"What am I supposed to do?" Tass shouted at them. Her voice came out in a tinny whistle.

You're an idiot, the voices informed her.

Strength began to flow through Tass's body. Her fingertips came to life again, but their dim glow was barely perceptible in the yellow seawater. "You need me," Tass reminded the voices. "You said so. I have a body and you don't. So instead of insulting me, help me!"

She's got it now, a silvery strand of darkness hissed. *We don't need her. We need her body . . .*

Sssss . . . the other voices added complacently.

Lend us your hands, the single strand requested. *Just for a time. Let your hands be our hands. Let your voice be our voice.*

"You're already inside my head," Tass said, suddenly frightened. "What do you mean?"

We don't need to be in your head. We need to be in your body. In your arms. In your legs.

Tass's heart beat more quickly. This was the sort of thing she had feared when the Bec told her the darkness was already inside her.

Possession. They wanted to own her. They wanted to edge her soul out of her body, to overcome her will with theirs.

"No!" Tass shouted, her voice growing stronger. "I'll do what you want, but you'll not do it through me. I am myself, and I have to stay that way."

The voices laughed, and Tass couldn't tell if they were angry with her.

You think she means it? one voice said.

They never do, another answered, his tone barely different from the previous speaker. The voices, which had been a sort of unified plurality, were now separating into their constituent parts.

"I do!" Tass informed them. "You want to use me. Well, I want to use you too. I want to bring my sister home. You want to open the Bilik. We want the same thing. We may as well work together."

I think she does mean it, a bloodless, pinched voice marveled.

If she reneges, we're not any worse off than we were before.

We lose time.

Time is nothing . . .

You agree to work with us? No turning back? The unity of the voices had returned.

Tass opened her outer eyelids and peered through the waters, trying to see the essence of the darkness that spoke inside her head. There was nothing. "I'll do it," she said, "as long as we have the same goals. Opening the Bilik," Tass said sternly.

Hold out your hands.

Tass held up her palms, facing outward. Her fingertips glowed with a faint white light, pale against the seawater. Then they became silhouetted against the illuminated seawater. Dark. Her fingers were dark. She brought her hands close to her face and examined them. The light of the ymolenegth did not light up her hands. They were more than unlit. They were more than dark. They were darkness itself.

"Get off of me!" Tass howled.

Laughter echoed, rippled through the water, through Tass.

You are withdrawing from our alliance? The voice was mocking her.

"You don't own my hands," Tass spat.

We're just on the outside, the voices informed her in unison. *Holding hands. Like friends. Allies.*

Tass narrowed her eyes and squinted at her darkened hands. She wiggled her fingers one at a time. Satisfied that she still had control of her motions, she relaxed. "When this is over, I want you off of my hands and out of my head," she said, scowling into the cheerful yellow water at an ally she could not see.

Not a problem, the voices chimed in a million cacophonous voices that were just a millisecond out of sync with each other, lending an echoing quality to their vibrations inside Tass's head. *Not a problem.*

Chapter 59: Xylo

Xylo watched Rahela as her eyes travelled over the group assembled before her. Her husband, Laso, stood behind her, steady and sure and silent, like a wall she could lean on if she needed to, but seemingly unwilling to interfere. He didn't look like either of his sons, Xylo reflected. Laso's blond hair was tightly curled and fuzzy. Although he was Gulot, his hair was close-cropped. He looked weary. Xylo wondered what he was thinking.

Igracio had looked like his mother. Rahela was slim. Her long, straight black hair hung down her back and her large, dark eyes reminded Xylo of Igracio not only in their appearance, but in the simple sincerity that shone out of them.

Xylo had already introduced the couple as Igracio's parents, come to meet the team that would finish Igracio's work of healing the remaining fissures in the Bilik. After everyone had been introduced, he brought up the factor that brought them together.

"As you know, these are Igracio's parents. And as I've told them, you six are the children of Mantais Nayro—Methiant Migas, and half-siblings to each other and to Igracio. He was, I believe, tri-casted just as you all are. I knew Rahela would want to meet you."

Rahela's eyes glimmered with tears, but she was smiling. "I see Igracio in all of you," she told them. "Your dark hair," she said, looking at Unaleah and Sadi. "Your big eyes." This was directed toward Kadi and Gudall. "Your innocent spirits," she added, smiling painfully at Laetu and Pax. "I lost my son, but I have found him again in you."

Laetu shifted his weight uncomfortably. "I'm sorry for your loss," he mumbled.

"Xylo told us the story . . . what happened," Kadi said with sympathy. "You must know your son was a hero. We're proud to call him our brother."

Rahela's tears were pouring down her face now. "Thank you. I'm so, so pleased to meet you all. I wish I'd known you sooner. I wish that Igracio . . ." Her face grew pinched.

Laso patted her shoulder comfortingly.

"Come with us," Sadi requested. "Come with us on the mission. It would help you. I know it would."

Rahela looked at Xylo. "The mission to complete Igracio's work? To heal the fissures in the Bec?"

Sadi nodded. "We could use another mother on this trip," she said, glancing at Ieska with an apology in her eyes. "There are six of us and only my mother and Finnan came to take care of us."

Rahela frowned. "I hadn't thought of it. Though I want to know you. I can't imagine you need more people to manage . . ." She looked at Xylo with an expression in her eyes that he couldn't read.

"We'd be glad to have you," Xylo said. "The caverns of the Dynroc are comfortable and extensive. Finding room for you is no burden."

Rahela turned to her husband. "Should I go?"

Laso's mouth tightened. "I don't see why not."

"Oh, but if you need me at home . . ." Rahela fretted.

Laso's face softened. "We always need you," he said in a low voice. "But go. Peodar and I will make do until you come back. Just . . . come back."

Rahela shook her head in disbelief. "Don't you know I love you and Peodar? I will always come back." She turned to Xylo and Ieska again. "I'll need to pack. How long do you think we'll be gone?"

Xylo took a deep breath and then exhaled. "There's no way to know. The mission may be a long one. Months. But nothing obligates you to stay that long. I can arrange for you to leave whenever it's convenient."

"Please come," Camilly intoned sweetly. "I'm not one of the special ones, but you seem like a nice lady and I'm sorry you lost your son. I really am. Maybe we can love you enough to help."

Rahela stretched out a hand to the cheery, red-haired girl. Camilly threw herself forward and hugged Igracio's mom. Rahela smoothed the girl's hair and a peace settled over her features. "Give me an hour to pack?" she requested.

***

"You were hoping she would volunteer," Ieska accused him.

Xylo and Ieska were walking through the streets of Lucedth on their way to meet with the elders. The day was still young and the sky only faintly misty. The metal skyscrapers reflected the pale orange hue of the sky, making them almost invisible.

"I was," Xylo admitted.

"Why?"

"Guilt, I suppose. She lost her son."

"You're trying to replace Igracio with his siblings?" Ieska looked doubtful.

Xylo sighed. "I know no one can replace Igracio, especially to his family. I just . . . I don't know . . . wanted her to feel like she was less alone. You know the children will help her in her grief over Igracio and in the anguish of learning that Laso wasn't his father."

Ieska reached for Xylo's hand. "I love you."

Xylo leaned toward her and kissed her forehead. "I love you too." He pulled away and opened the door to the building that housed the elders' council meeting rooms. They entered and made their way to the elevator.

***

"And so we've recruited a team of fit young people, together with some fitting chaperones, to help with the mission."

Arth frowned. "Are they Mayim? Esh? We could have taken the best of the best from the Calix or from the college . . ."

Xylo dared not glance at Ieska. He knew he couldn't betray the tri-casted children of Mantais Nayro. The council would one day learn about them, one day when the time was right. That time wasn't now. "They're Esh," he voiced decidedly. The triads had the finger tala of the Mayim as well as the extensive body tala of the Esh. It was the Esh-tala that would be harder to hide.

Arth shook his head. "But not from the college? They're Esh-qadar, then?"

"A mix of young men and young women," Xylo told him. "Strong. Healthy. Young."

Arth was clearly exasperated. "The skyboulder exited Gannoir by going down through the sea. It's hardly the Esh who should be the primary laborers in bringing them back. We need Mayim. Did you not recruit any on either of your visits to the Calix?"

So the council knew about his visits to the Calix. There were eyes and ears everywhere. He could only hope that they hadn't construed anything from his request to see Tass. After all, Tass had been part of the incidents of a few months back. It was only natural that he should visit her—as a friend, a mentor, a co-sufferer.

He turned his attention quickly back to Arth and his question. "No," he replied. "The Master left me feeling unsatisfied. I sought elsewhere."

"And you were without success," Arth surmised, narrowing his pale green eyes.

Xylo couldn't tell the man that the "Esh" he had recruited could swim. "Yes," he agreed.

Frigo motioned to be heard. He stood, looking dignified and earnest. "The Master of the Calix said he would be honored to provide a team dedicated to bringing the skyboulder back," he said when Arth had granted him leave to speak. "If you can wait a day or two, I can arrange for a small, talented group to be sent."

Xylo glanced at Ieska's worried face. "We're leaving for Garradh Gannoir today," he reported. "There is no time."

"We'll send them when they're ready," Arth answered. "Since the passageways between Luca and Garradh Gannoir have become well-traveled, such a thing is no trouble. You'll find housing and provision for them," he noted, looking at Xylo expectantly.

Xylo nodded. "Of course."

"We must bring this girl home, this Mailu Elisus Harreg, this triad. If Kleibald thought she had the power within her to save all

Gannoir from destruction, then we must get her back. And rescue Kleibald."

Inwardly, Xylo winced. The council was still operating under the delusion that Kleibald had been trying to change Gannoir for the better by attempting its inversion. They still thought he'd had a plan for saving them all.

"We'll be leaving for Garradh Gannoir within the hour," Xylo repeated. "I thank you sincerely for your cooperation and assistance in this matter."

Chapter 60: Talag

Talag lingered outside the metal door. He could still hear his grandfather and blue-haired Gelu talking on the other side. The scab—Dynny's scab—wasn't doing anything to the telescope. A sick knot of fear gripped Talag's stomach. If Dynny's scab was ineffective, did it mean that Dynny wasn't the Dynroc? His old fears that they had, in fact, transferred the title of Dynroc through their mock ceremony rose up and paralyzed him. He couldn't go back to Mailu's little chamber. Even if he didn't say anything to Dynny, even if he didn't try to explain, Dynny would ask. He would want to know if his pain had produced the desired result of advancing the cause of saving the people of Gannoir. Talag had lied to his friend once. He didn't want to do it again.

Behind the door the voices rose in argument. Talag couldn't help overhearing.

". . . not doing anything to the telescope . . ."

"It doesn't matter. The boy brought us his . . . scab . . . his bodily fluids. It's got to work. It must be the thing the voices were talking about."

Gelu spoke again. "How is some dried blood supposed to destroy Gannoir? It's just waste. Just offal."

"That's precisely what the spirits said was necessary," Kleibald replied smoothly. "We're working together with the spirits. Their goals are our goals. Destroy Gannoir. They have no reason to deceive us."

Talag's heart caught in his throat. Destroy Gannoir. His grandfather wanted to destroy Gannoir. He replayed the conversation in his mind, hoping he had heard wrong, that his grandfather really meant to say that Gannoir was naturally imploding and that his intent—and the intent of the spirits—was the save the people from imminent disaster. He strained his faculties, trying to twist the words so that they meant what he believed they ought to mean. It wasn't working. And, he reflected, deep down he'd known it all along. His skin felt like ice.

"Well, they're sure cutting it close," Gelu griped. "We're almost out of food. Are you sure that crusty little piece of meat isn't doing anything to the telescope? Giving us a view of how we can use our weapons to rip a hole in Gannoir?"

Talag held his breath, as though the sound of his breathing might obfuscate the words.

"It looks the same as it did before," Kleibald said sharply. "We're as close as we've been to Gannoir since we left. The spirits have caused us to draw near."

"Or gravity has," Gelu suggested.

"Or that," Kleibald agreed. "But the spirits didn't say we had to put the scab in the telescope. They just said to use it."

"Use it how?"

"Maybe the scab is the weapon," Kleibald said so softly that Talag could barely hear him.

"You're as big an idiot as your grandson," Gelu scoffed loudly. "It's just a little chunk of dried, dead blood. Lifeless blood. It couldn't even make ymolenegth if we tossed it into the water. We should go back to Gannoir."

There was a long pause. Talag wondered if the two leaders were talking too quietly to be heard.

"Lifeless . . . lightless . . ." Kleibald said softly. "That's it!" His voice grew louder. "Light is life. And blood makes light. And dead blood . . ."

Talag could picture the savvy grin that must be spreading over his grandfather's face. He'd seen that expression before but had never assigned a menacing intent to it in his mind.

"Dead blood makes darkness," Gelu acknowledged. "It might work."

"And not just any dead blood," Kleibald answered him. "The dead blood of the Dynroc. Blood that has no powers in itself, but which can link the forces together—the fire of the Ghalon, the powers of the wind and water . . . If anything can destroy Gannoir, it's death spreading through the fire, wind, and water simultaneously. Just as the living blood propelled us out of Gannoir, so the dead blood will bring a destruction just as powerfully."

"Do we shoot it at Gannoir?" Gelu guessed.

"Why not? We can always get more dead blood if we need it. The boy is my grandson, and he trusts me. As long as he thinks he's saving Gannoir, he'll be willing to give up every last drop of his blood."

Talag's face pinched him, and he felt like he was going to cry. It was true. If he thought his blood would save the people of Gannoir, he would give it. Knowing he didn't have to, that it would do no good, was no comfort to him. His grandfather was on the cusp of destroying the world. And Talag had given him the weapon with which to do it! He and Dynny had tricked Kleibald into accepting the blood of the true Dynroc. They'd accidentally participated in destruction. The only comfort was that if it didn't work, his grandfather would come after him, not after Dynny, for more blood. Dynny, at least, would be safe. Until the food and water ran out.

Talag had heard enough.

Chapter 61: Tass

"You want me to what?" Tass asked in shock.

Ride the dga. The giant dga, the voices repeated smoothly.

"First, the giant dga hasn't moved from the edge of the world since the Bilik closed. It's too cold for me there. I'll die. And second . . ." Tass objected.

We need bodies, the darkness reminded her.

Her fingers tingled, and Tass wasn't sure if it was her own emotion that was filling her hands with electricity behind the darkness that encased them or if it were the darkness itself that was manipulating her nerves. "I'll be a dead body if you make me ride the dga," she retorted darkly. "It's dangerous. If I don't die of the cold, then the dga will rip me to shreds."

Worthless . . . a singular voice chortled through her gills.

"I'm not worthless," Tass spat into the water.

Then ride the dga. Don't you want to bring your precious sister back?

"There has to be another way."

The dga is powerful. Powerful enough to weaken the Bec. And because of its metallic exoskeleton it's one of the few beings who can physically touch the Bec without instantaneously dying.

"And you want me to go with it. And freeze to death."

We've tried to manipulate the dga, the voices hissed in unison. *It's too stupid to understand. The most we can make it do is hover near the Bilik as though it had some sort of primal instinct to do so. We haven't been able to make it dig its way out of Gannoir. We can't manipulate its limbs. We have no bodies. And the creature has no mind. We can't come together at all. That's where you come in.*

"To manipulate its body? Or because I'm nearly as stupid as it is?" Tass complained.

You are nearly that dim, the voices laughed at her bitterly. *But it's your body we need. Push the arms of the dga. Make it understand what it's supposed to do. The skyboulder is just outside the world. If a hole were to open, it would get sucked in.*

Tass frowned. "That's not how it works." She remembered the things Igracio had taught her. "If a hole is made in the Bec, everything inside Gannoir will be sucked out. The chaos will draw it through. You've got it backwards."

An angry sizzle raced through Tass's gills, and she felt the darkness tighten its grip on her hands. She winced. "I'm trying to help," she reminded them. "We're allies. We both want the skyboulder to come home."

A single deep voice emerged from the controlled unison of the voices. *You don't need to understand the science. Just obey. Do what we tell you. Like you said, we're allies. We're on your side. And you're on ours.*

"I'll die," Tass protested.

It's the only way.

"I don't want to die."

You won't.

"You're lying."

You won't die. Your watery friend won't let you die. But by the time she comes to your rescue it will be too late for her to stop the work you're there to do. With your help, the dga will have sufficiently weakened the Bec. When the skyboulder slams into Gannoir, it will be able to break through.

Tass pondered this. Every time she'd approached the ice-fire of the Bec, Dwoyra had been there to pull her away. Would it be any different this time just because the darkness owned her fingers and whispered in his mind? She didn't think so. Dwoyra was Dwoyra. She wouldn't change just because Tass wasn't quite herself.

"Okay," she finally agreed. "I'll do it. For Mailu."

For yourself, the voices oozed.

"For myself. So I can have my sister," Tass agreed. "Now?"

We have hours to wait yet, the voices told her. *The skyboulder must be ready. It must be aligned and ready.*

"You can see the skyboulder?" Tass was surprised.

The darknesses have told us, the voices hissed agreeably.

"The little blotches of darkness . . . the ones that are seeping into the sea . . ."

From the outside, the voices confirmed. *Messengers . . .*

Tass shivered. All those tiny blotches of darkness, possessing the dga, manipulating them, perhaps, were continually crawling into Gannoir from the chaos outside. They could see the skyboulder. They could see her sister. They would know if she were still alive . . . if anyone was . . . Tass turned her mind aside to think of other things. She didn't want to know. Not now. Mailu was alive. She had to be.

Chapter 62: Xylo

There was a certain restfulness about being home, Xylo reflected. Already he had come to think of the caverns of the Dynroc as home. He wondered how that might change if—when—Dynny came back. He wasn't the Dynroc. Dynny was. Would the little man want him to stay? Xylo knew Dynny couldn't do the job alone. He would need an advisor, someone to be the mind behind the power he possessed.

He didn't want to return to Luca. He had come to love the forested land on the other side of the Orbokth. He hoped Ieska would come to love it as well.

He knocked at the ornate wooden door of the room he had given to Ieska and Rahela to share. "Are you ready?"

The door swung open. Ieska ran her hand over the smooth wood. "I'd heard about wood before, understood its biology and uses, but I never imagined it was so beautiful."

Xylo smiled. "There is much to discover in this land. Wait until you see the forest near the mine."

"I can't wait," Ieska smiled at him.

"Where's Rahela?"

"Coming," a voice called.

The group gathered outside, as no room inside the halls of the Dynroc was large enough for their company. The mist that filled the air was red with the light of the Ghalon, and it was comfortably warm—comfortable for the Esh, that is. Xylo knew that Ceres, with her yellow Mayim skin, wouldn't be able to bear it for long. That was why they had waited until late in the day to hold the meeting. The air was saturated and damp, albeit warm. The humidity would help Ceres' skin to stay hydrated despite the heat.

Xylo looked fondly at his son and his daughter-in-law. Case had an arm around his wife as they sat next to each other on a flat outcropping of rock. He was glad they had been thrown together by the elders, even though the mission had nearly claimed their lives. That was over now. Good things were yet to come. If, he thought wryly, they were able to protect Gannoir from the darkness. Nothing bad was happening yet, but it would. Xylo was sure of it. The blotches of darkness that Ceres was seeing in the water boded ill.

Once everyone was settled, Xylo introduced Ceres and Case and reminded his team about Kleibald and Gelu's plan to offer his son and Ceres as human sacrifices in their bid to invert Gannoir. Then Ceres began her tale.

"I'm glad to know you all," she said sincerely. "It will be a help to have a team to work with. I've been doing my best, but it's not enough." She looked at Xylo.

"Tell them about the darkness you're seeing."

She nodded and went on. "The sea has changed since I first came to Garradh Gannoir a few months ago. The darkness is increasing. I don't just mean that the ymolenegth is darker or isn't glowing. It's not just an absence of light. It's darkness itself, little blobs of darkness, seeping into the sea. Every time I swim, I see more of it."

"You think the darkness is coming from outside Gannoir?" Unaleah asked, her intelligent blue eyes filled with worry.

"I don't know what other explanation there could be," Ceres frowned. "There is more and more of it every day. Noticeably so."

"Could the darkness be replicating itself?" Gudall asked. "Maybe just a bit of darkness from the chaos seeped into Gannoir when the skyboulder burst out, and now it's reproducing."

"I don't know," Ceres replied. "That's what we have to figure out. We know the darkness isn't supposed to be there. Light is life. Darkness, then . . ."

"Is death!" Laetu interrupted. "We're here to conquer darkness and death."

Finnan put a hand on her son's shoulder. "Let's not get overly excited."

"Whether the darkness is self-replicating, or coming in from the chaos, it has to be stopped," Case told the group. "I'm Esh. There is nothing I can do about problems in the sea. But all of you can swim. You're the hope of Gannoir—you and others. Together we need to stop the darkness."

"Is there anything you can tell us about the dark blobs, as you call them? Anything that would help us know how they might be confined or defeated?" Sadi asked. As she cracked her knuckles her fingertips glowed more brightly.

Ceres took a deep breath and then exhaled slowly. "The only thing I've noticed is that the blotches are not usually free-floating.

They like to attach themselves to other organisms. They prefer dga, although I've seen other creatures hosting them as well."

"Dga?" Pax asked. He wrinkled his nose. "What are they? We don't have those in Cudth Deorth."

"You're lucky," Ceres told him. "They're small, creeping things with metallic exoskeletons and pincers. Nasty little things."

"Not just little," Xylo reminded her. "Tass said she'd seen giant dga, much larger than herself. It makes the idea of them even creepier."

"I'll fight them!" Laetu exclaimed. "I'm not scared of some shiny little monsters."

"And big monsters," Pax shuddered. "I don't mind fighting the little ones, but a giant one might be different."

"We're not planning to fight them," Xylo explained. "The dark blobs have attached themselves to the dga, but it may not be the fault of the dga. Instead of fighting the dga, we need to free them from the darkness."

"If we round up the dga, though," Sadi began, "then we'll isolate much of the darkness. Then we can determine if it's seeping in or if it's reproducing."

"Good idea," Gudall replied. "Do we have any idea how many dga are in the sea?"

"The sea is wide," Xylo said dryly. "Gathering every dga seems like an impossible task."

"Even if we gather a few, we can tell if they're reproducing," Ieska put in. "That would be a start."

"The other thing to look for," Xylo said, "is holes in the Bec layer. Places where the darkness could enter from the outside. This will be another dangerous element of the mission. The temperature near the Bec is necessarily cold. Beyond cold. Missions to the depths will need to be brief."

Rahela and Ieska exchanged worried looks. Pax and Laetu looked excited at the idea of danger. Kari was stone-faced. Unaleah leaned close to Gudall with an anxious expression.

Sadi grinned. "This will be an adventure," she said. "Ceres, have you been near to the Bec? How bad is the cold?"

"I've only seen the purple fire from a great distance," Ceres said. "By the red layer of the sea it's quite uncomfortable. Even your mind slows down."

"Do your fingertips grow dim?" Laetu wanted to know.

Ceres shook her head. "I'm Mayim. My fingertips never glow. Does the glow give off any heat?"

"No," Kari said shortly. "It doesn't."

"It would tell us how we're doing though," Laetu said. "If we got so cold our fingers stopped glowing, then we'd know things were really bad. We could swim back up."

"We're triad, though," Pax announced. "We should be able to swim wherever. Hot. Cold. Good. Evil. We're different. Better."

"I hope that's the case," Ceres said generously. "I can't do this myself."

"Gannoir needs your help," Xylo agreed.

The six triad young people looked at each other. They were already a team—they had been for their entire lives. Now they weren't just an isolated group of misfits. They were the hope of Gannoir. They had a purpose and reason.

Laetu grinned. "Let's do this!" He stood and held his glowing fingers up against a red sky. The others joined him.

"To victory over the darkness!" Gudall shouted.

The others echoed him.

Ieska looked at her daughter, beautiful in her youth and radiant with the glow of her new vision. "I know this is right," she murmured, "but I'm afraid."

Xylo put an arm around her. "I am too."

Chapter 63: Talag

Talag was crying by the time he got to the small chamber that housed Mailu and Dynny. His little friend looked at him with worried eyes.

"What's wrong?" Dynny asked. "Didn't it work? Do they need more blood?"

Talag only cried harder.

Dynny patted him on his shoulder and made soothing noises. "I can bleed more. It will be okay. We're going to save the people of Gannoir. We have to."

Talag shook his head. "We won't. We can't. Grand—Kleibald isn't trying to save Gannoir. He's trying to destroy it. I heard him." He slumped down on the floor and put his face in his hands.

"Destroy Gannoir?" Dynny's voice was trembly.

"And we gave him the scab. Your scab. We gave him the power of the Dynroc. So now he has the power to . . . to . . ."

Dynny's kind face wrinkled in consternation. "He has my power?"

"It was in your scab," Talag shuddered, still sobbing.

Dynny shook his head vigorously. "Light is life. And life is in blood. Life, not death."

"But that was dead blood," Talag pointed out. "Dead blood is death and darkness, right? Darkness and death for Gannoir."

"I shouldn't have given him my blood," Dynny mourned. "Should never have done it. I should have known better. Arros would have known better." His gnomish face crumpled in grief as he spoke the name of his mentor. "Arros would never have trusted Gelu."

"It's my fault," Talag cried. "I convinced you that my grandfather wasn't doing anything wrong. It's all my fault."

Dynny slid down to the floor and sat beside Talag. "Your grandfather is a bad man."

Talag snorted. "Yes, he is."

"Gelu is bad too."

"Yup."

"We have to stop them."

"We can't stop them. They have the scab. They have the power over the skyboulder. And they have some sort of weapon. They're going to shoot Gannoir with the scab. Blow it up."

"We can't let them," Dynny said stoutly.

"What choice do we have? We have no power and no time. Either they'll succeed and destroy Gannoir, or we'll all die of hunger and thirst. The food is almost gone."

"Then we have nothing to lose," Dynny pointed out with uncharacteristic acuteness.

Talag's sobs quieted. His breathing slowed to a more regular pace. "You're right," he said finally. "You're right. We have to try. We have nothing to lose."

"When all is lost it's like that," Dynny agreed.

"What can we do?" Talag asked, looking to Dynny for wisdom—the wisdom of the Dynroc.

"We have to get the scab back," Dynny said.

It was so simple. Get the scab back. Take away the power of the Dynroc and his grandfather could do nothing.

"All right," Talag agreed heartily. "Let's make a plan."

Talag and Dynny were still deep in conversation when Kleibald and Gelu burst into the room.

"There you are!" Kleibald exclaimed angrily. He yanked Talag to his feet and pushed Dynny rudely away. At Talag's frightened look, Kleibald attempted to put on a different face. "I'm sorry I was rude, boy," he said soothingly. "It's just that the situation is desperate. We need another scab. And we need it now. Before the food and water runs out. Before we all die. We have to . . . uh . . . rescue the others from Gannoir so that the spirits can take us to a new world. A . . . world of plenty where we won't have to worry about what we will eat and drink."

"What happened to the first scab?" Talag yelped, trying to wriggle out of his grandfather's grasp.

"It wasn't enough," Gelu told him. His blue-gray hair and somber expression underlined the gravity of the situation.

"What do you mean?" Talag asked. He knew what he had heard. They were planning on using the scab as a weapon.

"It's good blood," Kleibald told him. "We just need a little more. We need the power of the Dynroc. We must have it. All will be lost if we can't get the blood of the Dynroc."

"You can't have my blood!" Dynny cried.

Kleibald and Gelu turned toward the little old man in surprise.

"I'm the Dynroc and you can't have my blood!" Dynny repeated with bravado.

Kleibald looked from Dynny to Talag and back again.

"You turned over your title to my grandson," he said pointedly. "You're not the Dynroc."

A mix of emotions crossed Dynny's simple face.

"Don't . . ." Talag hissed, but it was too late.

"I am the Dynroc," Dynny insisted. "Talag and I were just pretending."

Talag groaned inwardly. Had Dynny forgotten that Kleibald and Gelu were trying to destroy Gannoir? If they took his blood, they would have the power to destroy the world.

Kleibald released Talag. Talag saw a look of satisfaction cross Dynny's face. Then he understood. Dynny was trying to protect him. Kleibald had come for blood—Talag's blood. Possibly a great quantity of Talag's blood. He felt emotion wash through his mind and heart. Dynny was trying to save him from dying at his grandfather's hands. How brave! How lovely! How . . . stupid.

"Don't!" Talag objected. "You'll give him the power to destroy Gannoir. Don't, Dynny! We're going to die anyhow. It doesn't matter who dies first. You can't do this!"

Kleibald's head whipped around to look at Talag. "What do you mean? Aren't you the Dynroc? Why would his blood have power?" Realization dawned as Kleibald saw what Talag was trying to hide from him. "He's still the Dynroc, isn't he? You've been deceiving me." His eyes narrowed. "That's why it didn't work." He turned to Gelu. "That's why it didn't work. We had Talag's scab instead of this imbecile's."

Kleibald snatched Dynny's arm and yanked the old man toward him. "It's your blood we need."

"No!" Talag shouted.

Gelu moved closer and grabbed Talag so that he couldn't intervene on Dynny's behalf.

"Wait!" Talag cried. "Wait! Dynny has a cut on his foot. You don't have to hurt him. Just get blood from the scab that's already there. Don't hurt him!"

Kleibald restrained Dynny while Gelu rushed to pull off the old man's footwear. Talag's scab fell out of Dynny's shoe onto the polished floor.

Kleibald saw it immediately. He looked from Dynny's blue-veined leg with its oozing wound to the dry scab in his hand. "Looks like we're in luck," he grinned smoothly.

Talag pretended to protest but the circumstances were better than he could have imagined. Not only would Kleibald and Gelu not make a fresh wound on his friend, the scab they were appropriating was his, not Dynny's. It had no power at all. He wasn't really the Dynroc. He made a feigned attempt to snatch at the scab and then let Gelu hold him back. Kleibald pocketed the scab.

"Stay here. Don't leave this chamber," Kleibald ordered. "You're worthless, both of you. All I want to do is save Gannoir and you're both fighting against me!" He strode through the door.

Gelu ran a hand over the smooth stone of Mailu's coffin. He cast a loving look at her pale, scarred, dead face. Talag saw the look he gave the dead girl and frowned. Gelu, then, still believed that Mailu could bear his child. After the two men left the chamber and the door had slid shut, Talag took a long look at the dead girl his friend was assigned to tend.

Then he gasped.

Mailu was just as lifeless as before, her welted skin showing the angry burns of the caustic seawater that had hastened her death. But her belly had grown noticeably. The folds of her garment fell off to the side, emphasizing her condition.

She was pregnant.

More pregnant than she had been days earlier.

"What?" Dynny asked.

Talag pointed wordlessly.

Dynny's face filled with hope as he looked at the young woman. "I'm a good caregiver," he said with a confident nod. "I'm taking good care of Mailu and the baby."

Gelu, then, had been right about one thing.

Chapter 64: Tass

Tass pushed the shimmering layers of water out of her path, propelling herself upward. She needed rest. She needed to think. She wanted to be alone, but with the dark blotches covering her hands, owning her hands, she knew it wasn't possible. Her mind was still her own, though. They didn't have that.

When she reached the underside of the Orbokth, she tucked herself into her sleeping nook and let her mind drift as far away as possible from the darkness in her hands. The voices weren't talking to her. There was relief in that. She tried to push away any thoughts that the voices might have suggested to her. She wanted to be alone in her mind. Alone with her thoughts. Her own thoughts.

Mailu. Her sister had loved her. The memories were dim, but Tass knew it was true. Her mother, Tass understood clearly, had never loved her, had never wanted her. Her sister had been Tass's one haven from the time she was an infant. Tass's scarred shoulders ached with the thought of her mother, Afa. Her soul was as damaged as her body. Maybe more.

Tass frowned. These weren't the thoughts she'd hoped to be pursuing. She was going to win. She was going to do great things. She wasn't trapped by her past. She wouldn't be a victim. She was the best swimmer at the Calix. Once she brought the skyboulder home, everyone would know who she was. And they would thank her. Satisfaction flowed through Tass at the thought of success, and she knew if the darkness hadn't been covering her hands her fingertips would be glowing brightly. She sighed and curled up to sleep.

***

Awareness came to Tass in a rush of fear.

Someone was watching her.

Slowly she moved her face to a position where she could see the sea beyond the curving crevice in which she had been sleeping. Her heart was racing as she peered into the turquoise waters.

An impossible sight—two Esh females—were treading water not far away, and they were looking at her, waiting for her to emerge. She could tell they were Esh by the lengthy body tala that connected their arms to their bodies like wings. Their long hair floated around their heads as well, a style that was rare, if not forbidden altogether, for the Mayim. Tass put her blob-darkened hand to her own cropped hair.

One of the Esh pointed at her and Tass knew she would have to emerge. It had to be a dream. Esh don't swim.

The young woman with long black hair beckoned to her.

"Who are you?" Tass shouted in her gill-voice from afar.

The two looked at each other in surprise. The yellow-haired girl, who looked much younger than her companion, gestured toward her mouth and then gave Tass a confused look that Tass understood immediately. They couldn't talk under the water.

Now both strangers were motioning for Tass to follow them. Tass wondered what was happening. Esh in the water? Mayim with long hair? People who could breathe in the seawater but couldn't talk? Curiosity won over reservations, and she moved toward them. They led her out from under the rock and onto its surface. It was midday, and the mist in the air was thick when Tass stuck her head out of the sea for the first time in days. The two long-haired girls climbed onto the shelf of solid ground and wrung out the dripping layers of their clothes.

"You're Tass!" the younger, blond girl exclaimed.

"Maybe," Tass admitted, not surprised that they knew her name. When Esh swam, anything was possible. "Who are you?"

"I'm Kari Coffya Ansidla," the blond girl replied with a smile. "I'm your . . ."

The dark-haired woman cut her off. "I'm Sadi. We were looking for you."

"Xylo thought you might have come here—to the waters around Garradh Gannoir," Kari told her.

Xylo! So that was it. Tass bristled. She was not about to join Xylo in his quest to close the gaps in the Bec layer. She had her own plans. She didn't want to be anyone's tool. With a glance at her blackened hands, she seethed resentfully. Not Xylo's tool, anyhow. The darkness wanted the same thing she wanted. Xylo didn't.

"He said you were the best swimmer in Luca," Sadi said, wringing the water out of her hair. "He thought you could help us."

"I already told him no," Tass replied.

"The darkness is going to overrun Gannoir," Sadi continued. "We have to learn more about it. And we need to find a way to swim to the edge of the world. You're our best hope."

Kari was tugging on Sadi's damp sleeve and giving her a pleading expression.

"Not now," Sadi hissed. "Not yet." Then, "Please. We need your help. Not for us. Not for Xylo. For Gannoir."

Tell them yes, the voices hissed in Tass's ears.

Now Tass was sure she was dreaming. The darkness wanted her to serve Xylo and his strange, half-casted minions? It didn't make any sense. She felt her fingers tingle and she wondered if it was because she was upset or if the darkness occupying her hands was doing something to encourage her to give in to its will.

Shaking her head as though she could shake the voices out of range, she scowled. "I already gave blood. If you know about me, you probably already know that." She smirked darkly and pointed to the angry white scars on her shoulders.

"We don't want your blood," Kari soothed.

That was a new one, Tass thought angrily. She continued to glare at the girls.

Kari and Sadi exchanged worried glances.

"We'd like you to work with us," Kari said softly. "We'd like to get to know you."

"Why?" Tass asked indifferently.

"Because you're our . . ."

Again, Sadi cut off the younger girl. "Not yet."

"When? We have to tell her. It might make a difference."

"Xylo said not to. Not until he can talk to her," Sadi replied.

"I'm your . . . what?" Tass asked.

Kari gave Sadi a pleading look.

Sadi sighed. "Fine."

"You're our sister!" Kari announced.

Tass stared at the girl. Now she knew this was a dream. "I have one sister," she retorted. "Her name is Mailu Elisus Harreg and she's been blown out of the world on the skyboulder. I'm going to get her back. I'm not interested in working for Xylo or for you, whoever you are. I don't care about holes in the Bec layer. I don't care about little blobs of darkness. I don't care about some mutant half-caste women who come and claim they are my sisters. I know what I have to do. And you can just tell Xylo that."

Tass turned and dove back into the sea. Anger rippled through her body with so much force that she couldn't feel the sea around her, only the buzz of her own blood heating every molecule of her being with ire. "Stupid long-haired, non-Esh, non-Mayim, stuttering, obnoxious fools!" she muttered as she dove. She pushed her body past her old hiding place and swum farther and deeper.

They weren't real.

They weren't real.

Esh didn't swim.

Mayim could talk underwater.

She had only one sister.

It was all a dream. She had to wake.

Tass kicked her legs violently, hoping to rouse herself from what felt like a nightmare. Sisters. Sisters she had never met. It wasn't possible. She'd only been four when she'd lost everything, but she remembered Mailu, and she remembered her mother. She would have remembered if she'd had two additional sisters. Even after everything that had happened, no one ever said anything about Afa having more children than just Tass and Mailu. Xylo would have told her. Or she would have remembered. Or she would have known somewhere inside herself that something—someone—was missing.

These long-haired, Esh-tala'd girls were strangers to her mind and to her soul.

As she pushed into the orange layer of the seawater, Tass reflected on how much more easily she was able to penetrate the icy depths of the sea than she'd been just a few months earlier. At the Calix, they were instructed never to go past the glowing yellow layers of the chemical sea. And few ever went that far. Somehow Tass had developed her endurance. She could do what others could not.

The further she went from the surface, the more unreal the strangers seemed. She'd been dreaming. Or hallucinating. But it was a good thing. She'd forgotten how persistent Xylo could be. Even if the strangers hadn't been real, they'd reminded her of truth. Xylo would be looking for her—Xylo and others. They'd be trying to heal the lesions in the Bec. If she was going to force one of the gaps to open wide enough to admit the skyboulder, it would have to be done soon, before Xylo and whomever he'd found to help him came down and stopped her.

Tass reached out her darkened fingers, grasping the seawater ahead of her and forced herself to swim lower, down into the frigid red layer. She would find the giant dga. She would befriend it somehow—or conquer it. It didn't matter which. Then she would use its strength to rip open the shell of Gannoir. With the darkness on her side, she couldn't lose. Could she?

Chapter 65: Xylo

"You left some significant details out of your instructions," Ieska pointed out dryly.

Xylo shook his head and took another bite of halas bread. "They know about the skyboulder. It was one of the first things I told them. I want Kleibald brought to justice. But for this initial foray, I just want information. I want to know about the darknesses. I want to know if they can see any way the darkness is seeping into Gannoir. I want to know if Tass is here. That's all."

Rahela frowned. "Is this about protecting Gannoir? Or about bringing the skyboulder back?"

"Can't it be both?" Xylo asked.

Ieska smiled gently. "I think it can. I've been doing some calculations, trying to mathematically assess our chances of bringing the skyboulder home while not exposing Gannoir to the danger of implosion. I think it can be done. But we're going to need the help of your invisible friends—the water and the wind that helped complete the gogyvehr. And we're going to need a way to bring fire under the sea."

"And blood?" Finnan's cheerful face grew worried. "You mentioned blood?"

"The triad children must not die," Rhyder's eyes narrowed.

Ieska shook her head. "They won't. In Lucedth, we all give blood on a regular basis. It will take a little more than what is extracted at a blood donation, but not much more. No one is going to die. But it's going to take blood to keep the darkness from overwhelming the sea."

Rahela bit her lip. Xylo noticed her distress and understood it. Her son was dead. He had given every drop of his blood to stop Kleibald from destroying Gannoir. And it had worked. He hoped that Ieska was right—that such a sacrifice wouldn't be asked of the six young triads who had come to work with him—seven if they could find Tass and convince her to join them.

"I can work on the fire thing," Rhyder volunteered. "I've done some metalworking, and I think there are ways to build a conduit that could safely carry fire through the water. Maybe the Laetu and Pax could help me." Rhyder's son, Laetu, and Pax, who was around the same age, often helped him with his projects.

"The Bec layer is cold," Xylo reminded him. "It would have to be not just able to keep the fire dry, but hot."

"Insulation?" Finnan suggested.

"Or speed," Ieska added. "If the fire traveled quickly, it wouldn't require as much insulation to keep the molecules from slowing down from a plasma state to a gas."

"I don't understand how this is going to work," Rahela said quietly. "Or why. Why bring Kleibald back? Why not leave him to die in the chaos?" Her eyes were full of pain.

"Justice . . ." Xylo began.

Ieska interrupted him and addressed Rahela. "I understand your concerns. It must feel like we're disrespecting Igracio's sacrifice by reopening the hole in the Bec." Her eyes were kind.

Xylo felt ashamed of himself for not understanding Rahela's perspective. He tried to explain. "There are others on the skyboulder. Innocent people as well as guilty ones. If it were just Kleibald and Gelu . . ." He shook his head. "But Dynny's up there. He's the Dynroc of Garradh Gannoir. It's a position that has a mythical significance. There are powers that go with the office of Dynroc. And"—Xylo knew he had to confess his other motives—"my ex-wife, my two children, and my two grandchildren are on the skyboulder."

Rahela gave him a grim look. "You're willing to take this risk because your family is on the skyboulder. You're willing to risk the lives of these six triad children. You're willing to risk letting more darkness inside Gannoir. You're willing to risk the implosion of the world. Your reasons are selfish."

Guilt washed over Xylo, but he didn't cave to it. "I admit some of my reasons are personal," he replied. "But even if my family weren't on the skyboulder, I would still want to seek justice for the evils Kleibald has done. I would still want to bring the Dynroc back. This is not just about me. It's about all of us." His expression was firm, but sorrowful.

Rahela's face crumpled. "Of course, you're right. I, of all people, should be more understanding. I know what it means to lose a son. And you're poised to lose two of your children and two grandchildren as well. It's not selfishness on your part. It's love."

Xylo felt worse. He had spent decades trying to put Ardanach, Gryff, and Aythylla out of his thoughts, out of his heart. Ardanach had betrayed him. His children had chosen their mother over him. The emotions he felt had far more to do with duty and retribution than they did with love. Was he obligated to confess even that to the others? Would it change anything if he did?

It would not, he decided. Let Rahela believe he longed for Gryff and Aythylla, his estranged children. He didn't even know the names of his grandchildren, although he could have requested that the elders provide that knowledge to him. He hadn't. Yet another sign that his motives were far from loving.

"Motives aside," Ieska jumped in, "we must stop the darkness from multiplying in our world. Light is life. Darkness is . . ." She shook her head sadly. "I think it is possible to bring the skyboulder back without destroying Gannoir or even destroying the sea. Once we find out how the darkness is getting in, then we can make a plan of attack."

"So the skyboulder is the priority?" Finnan asked.

"It's all a priority," Xylo said heavily. "And it all has to be done soon."

Ieska looked at Rhyder. "Let's go over some of my calculations after we eat. Then you can get started on the problem of how to get fire to the bottom of the sea."

"Rahela and I will keep everything rolling on the home-front," Finnan said, absently twisting her long red hair.

"And I'll try to find Gaoth," Xylo added. "We'll need the help of a rational wind to make this work."

Chapter 66: Talag

"What's wrong?" Dynny asked Talag, his wrinkled face knotted in concern.

"Everything's wrong," Talag retorted, sounding angrier than he'd planned. "We're going to die of starvation. My whole family is trying to destroy the world. And Kleibald knows you're the Dynroc now. The scab he took is mine. When it doesn't work, he's going to come after you. He's going to hurt you, Dynny."

Dynny frowned. "He's going to hurt me?"

"He's going to want more scabs," Talag pointed out.

"We have to stop him, remember?" Dynny said.

Talag nodded. "But how?"

"Tie him up?" Dynny suggested solemnly.

It was a stupid idea. They couldn't just tie up Kleibald. Gelu would untie him. Or his grandmother would. Or his father. Maybe he could convince them all that tying up their leaders was the right thing to do. He sighed. It would never work. He might be able to convince someone that he was right, but it was going to be impossible to convince everyone. "We can't," Talag replied bluntly.

"Why?"

"Someone would untie him. Then we'd be right back where we started. Unless . . ." Something occurred to Talag. "We're running out of food. Everyone knows it. If Kleibald and Gelu were found to be hoarding food, then we might be able to convince everyone to tie them up."

"They're hoarding food?" Dynny sounded shocked at this evil—much more appalled than he seemed about the men's plan to destroy the world.

"No . . . but we could make it look like they were."

"They're not hoarding food?"

"No. I mean, I don't know for sure, but I don't think so. We'd have to pretend, Dynny. Pretend so that we could get everyone on our side instead of on Kleibald's side. You don't want Kleibald to destroy Gannoir, do you?"

Dynny shook his head. "What should we do?"

"I'm not sure yet. But I will be soon," Talag promised.

By that evening they were ready. It had involved skipping two meals in a row, and Talag was famished. Ordinarily, skipping meals made him tired, but he was too agitated for exhaustion. That would come later, he knew. He and Dynny piled their provisions together.

"I don't think it's enough to make people mad," Talag frowned at the pile.

"Then we need to get more," Dynny replied logically.

"How? Someone's always guarding the food."

"Who's guarding it tonight?"

"Gelu, I think. They've not been trusting the food to anyone but themselves and Uncle Nadim," Talag responded. "How can we make Gelu leave the food so we can steal some?"

"We're not thieves," Dynny pointed out.

"Okay. Not steal, then. Borrow," Talag agreed. Then his face lit up. "I know. Gelu's main concern is Mailu and her baby. What if we tell him that something bad was about to happen to Mailu. He'd leave the food to go take care of her and the baby."

"Something bad's going to happen to Mailu?" Dynny turned toward the sarcophagus and peered anxiously into the dead girl's face.

Talag shook his head. "It's pretend again. Pretend something bad's going to happen to Mailu so Gelu will leave the food. Then we steal . . . I mean, borrow food so we can pretend that Kleibald has been stealing. Once everyone sees what he's done . . . what we've pretended he's done . . . we can tie him up. Then we can try to figure out how to get the skyboulder back home without destroying Gannoir."

"Because I'm the Dynroc," Dynny nodded. "The Dynroc has the power of home."

Talag wrinkled his nose. "What do you mean by that?"

Dynny shrugged. "Arros said so. The Dynroc has the power of home. The power of Gannoir."

"Do you know how to use the 'power of home'?" Talag asked.

Dynny shook his head sadly. "Arros didn't have time to teach me. And I don't learn so quickly either."

Talag sighed. "Let's just focus on getting Kleibald tied up now," he ordered. "We'll worry about getting back home after that."

Two hours later, Talag, Dynny, and Gelu were in the tiny control room of the skyboulder. Their plan had succeeded. Gelu had fallen for their ruse. They had successfully stowed food in Kleibald's packs. Then they had roused the others from their slumber. The outrage had been intense, leading Talag to conclude that, although he hadn't noticed it, tensions must have been rising between Kleibald and his willing captives for some days. He and Dynny had slipped away while the others were still wreaking their revenge on Kleibald. Even Gelu, when he returned from his vain mission to help a dead Mailu, turned on his ally. That was more than they had hoped for.

"We're close," Gelu told them. "At this point, I just want to get back to Gannoir. Kleibald betrayed me—betrayed us all. That much is certain."

Dynny frowned. He was still wary of accepting help from Gelu.

"How do we do it?" Talag asked.

"Kleibald weaponized the telescope," Gelu told them. "Once the blood—the dead blood—is locked into the missile launcher, we can lob it at the shell of Gannoir. It makes a hole, and we get sucked in."

Talag frowned. "Everyone knows that if there's a hole in Gannoir, the insides will get sucked out. It doesn't work the other way 'round."

"I'm just telling you what Kleibald said," Gelu glowered. "I want to go home as much as you do."

"Kleibald was trying to destroy Gannoir, not go back to it," Talag pointed out. "We should do the opposite of whatever he wanted to do."

Gelu shook his head impatiently. "It doesn't matter what his motives were. I'm done with that man. All I want now is to go home. And we can't do that without making a hole in the Bec—which we can now do because of the scab. We have the right one now." He glared at Dynny as though the failure of the previous scab had been his fault.

Talag and Dynny exchanged glances. They both knew that the scab Kleibald had taken was Talag's, not Dynny's, and wouldn't have any power.

"I'll have to bleed again," Dynny whispered.

"No, you won't," Talag hissed back at his friend. "We don't have time anyhow. We're too low on food and water."

"Just shoot the scab at Gannoir!" Gelu exploded. "Light is life, and blood makes light. This is dead blood. It makes death. It will make the opposite of light. Look." He gestured toward the telescope. "Look for yourselves and tell me what you see."

Talag pressed his eye up against the aperture. The circular vision glowed a bright purple beneath him. He could see the individual tongues of flame undulating in a primeval dance. Gannoir was shining with light. He turned aside to let Dynny look.

Gelu looked at them triumphantly. "See? Light. Gannoir is protected not by ice but by light. See what I mean? Once we shoot it with the scab, with darkness instead of light, there will be a hole. We can go through the hole to get back inside our world."

Talag supposed Gelu might be right. If the protection was light, and they removed part of that light, then Gannoir would be unprotected. But it wouldn't make any difference. Gannoir would implode just like Kleibald had planned. It wouldn't cause them to magically go back home. Unless somehow Dynny could figure out how to use the Dynroc's "power of home." But that also seemed impossible. At least, he reckoned, the scab in question was his own useless one and not Dynny's.

"All right," he agreed. "Let's do it. Let's shoot Gannoir with the scab."

Gelu smiled. Dynny looked horrified.

"Let's do this," Gelu said, rubbing his hands together in anticipation.

Chapter 67: Tass

The oversized dga writhed in the water. It was so large it was obscene, Tass reflected. It shouldn't be that large. No living creature should be that large. Blotches of darkness obliterated much of its sheen, dimming the painfully brilliant reflection of the purple fire. Tass felt her fingers tingle with anticipation . . . or dread.

The voices had explained what she was supposed to do, but not how she was supposed to do it. Take control of the dga. Direct its limbs to rip a hole in the Bec layer. The spirits would do the rest, whatever that was. Tass assumed it would have something to do with propelling the skyboulder toward the gap she and the dga were going to create.

She watched the dga for some time and at a distance. She was still in the red-orange layer of the sea, where the biting, acidic iciness felt like motivation instead of death. She had never been lower without either the lumalauae or a vauzigk to provide warmth to her. But the voices had seemed confident that she would be able to do what was required. She drew the acidic liquid through her gills and held her breath, feeling the substance warm inside her body. She could do it.

She would do it. She would overcome the dga. She would bring Mailu home. She was the best swimmer at the Calix. She had done things no other Mayim had ever done—ever done and lived, she mentally corrected herself, thinking of Igracio.

She couldn't call on Dwoyra for help. Not for this. She wondered why the rational water hadn't approached her yet, ready to keep Tass from death. Something about her overly protective friend's absence disturbed Tass. She wondered what the voices had done to keep Dwoyra occupied so that she wouldn't interrupt Tass at her task.

It wasn't important. What was important was for her to dive down to the giant dga and attempt to make contact. Steeling herself against the cold, Tass kicked her feet. She felt her body slow as she entered the red layer. She was too agitated to experience the sensation as "cold," but she did feel a frantic frustration as she tried to keep her speed steady. Glancing at her arms in front of her, Tass noticed that her normally yellow skin was a bluish pink. She was freezing to death.

"No!" she hollered in her gill-speech. She had to do this. She couldn't let freezing stop her. She kicked her legs toward the surface again, propelling herself downward, and saw the water turn magenta around her.

The dga rose up in front of her, and she marveled at its glory. Her body was in slow motion as she stretched toward it. Tass seemed to hover a body's length from the hideous creature. She had lost the power to push herself through the water. She tried to panic, but even her mind had slowed to a pitiful gelatinous solid. She was going to fail. She was going to die. Mailu would remain outside Gannoir. And everyone on the skyboulder would perish. She tried to care and found that she was too tired and too cold. She did not care.

Tass stopped trying to swim and at once felt her skin begin to sting. She was floating upward, through the magenta layer, then the red, then into the red orange. The chilly water there felt like fire to Tass's icy skin. Able to move again, she curled her body into a ball, trying to get warm. She tried to remember why she had wanted to attempt this impossible mission. Something . . . someone . . . Her arms were itching, and she scratched at them with her fingernails, noticing that her hands did not hurt. Unlike the rest of her body, they had been covered by the blobs of darkness. Somehow the darkness had acted like a shield against the frozen waters near the edge of the world.

So that was it, then. That was what she was going to have to do. The spirits had wanted it from the first, but she hadn't understood. She'd though they just wanted to possess her—to take over her body with complete disregard for her soul and her will. But that wasn't the reason. If she was going to go down to the barrier that separated Gannoir from nothingness, she needed to give herself over to the darkness. It was a matter of life and death.

Still, she rebelled against the idea. Tass had always been a loner. Whatever she could accomplish on her own, she accomplished. Whatever she needed someone else for . . .

She didn't need anyone else.

Igracio, she remembered. He had taught her to read. He had taught her the history of Gannoir. And the mythology. Without Igracio . . .

Stop it! she commanded herself. Igracio's gone.

Igracio, her mind persisted, would not have joined forces with the darkness. But, she argued with herself, it was a necessary darkness. Joining forces with it was the only way she could get what she wanted . . . what she needed. She needed her sister.

Tass looked at her blackened hands. She wiggled her fingers. The darkness hadn't hurt her. It had protected her. It would protect her when she manipulated the dga because manipulating the dga was what the voices wanted her to do. Uncoiling her body, Tass cried out to her one remaining ally. "Darkness! Voices! You asked to own me before, and I denied you access. I now give it to you. Use me to rescue Mailu. Use me to open the Bilik and bring the skyboulder home!"

A rush of what almost felt like glee coursed through Tass's body as the darkness took over. She felt no more pain, no more of the sharp, tangy sensation of the lower layers of the sea. She felt cozy and whole. She looked at her body to see whether the dark blobs had taken possession of all of her, and she saw . . . nothing. She should have seen something but there was nothing left. Nothing but darkness. Unlike the dga, which still had sections of shining silver glinting at anyone who happened to look, Tass was no longer visible at all. She was nothing. She was no one.

Nothing. You're nothing. Nothing but ours, the voices agreed with her.

"You can hear me thinking," Tass said aloud.

We're in you and on you and of you, the voices agreed. *The time is now.*

"The time is now," Tass echoed.

She felt a downward tug on her invisible body as the dga provided the motive power to her limbs. The seawater turned magenta and then purple around her. More quickly than she had thought possible, she found herself clinging to the back of the dga, her own darkness blending with the dark blotches that covered the formidable beast. Her arms reached out without her making them move and she grasped the forelegs of the creature. It was digging now. Digging at the purple fire that protected their world.

Digging.

Digging.

Mailu.

Chapter 68: Talag

"What are you doing?" Dynny had pulled Talag aside. Gelu was focused on shooting the weapon armed with the scab and it provided a moment where the two almost felt alone.

"Buying time," Talag retorted. "It's not going to do anything. It's not your scab, remember? You're the Dynroc. That's my scab. He's going to fire a couple drops of dried blood out into the chaos. While he's doing that, we can think about how to save Gannoir. Or at least save the people of Gannoir."

"You shouldn't trust Gelu like this," Dynny complained reproachfully.

"I'm not," Talag contradicted his friend. "But it does look like he wants the same thing we do. He wants to go home."

A ripple of laughter manipulated the air around Talag's ears. The voices were back. He wondered what they wanted. He laid a stilling hand on Dynny's shoulder so he could listen more intently.

. . . ours now . . . he heard a triumphant voice declare.

. . . thought it would be Kleibald . . .

. . . the boy . . .

. . . Tel-Maor stands no chance of holding his precious Gannoir together now . . .

Talag's blood ran cold. Had he erred after all? The voices seemed to be saying that Kleibald's plan, his evil plan to destroy Gannoir, was still in motion. All his efforts—and Dynny's—had moved the plan forward. It had been, after all, the voices' idea that they deliver a scab to his grandfather and Gelu. Talag felt like he couldn't breathe. His grandfather hadn't been in charge at all. The voices had been. And they still were. Only now they were using him instead of using his grandfather.

"Give it back!" he hollered, rushing toward Gelu.

Gelu pushed Talag away without taking his eye from the aperture of the telescopic weapon. "It's almost done, boy. Stand back!"

"Don't do it!" Talag cried. "You're going to destroy Gannoir!"

Gelu lifted his face from the crude hole that marked the presence of the telescope. "Of course, I am," he said lightly. "That was the plan all along."

"But . . . but . . ." Talag choked. "You said . . . you said . . ."

Dynny shook his head. "I told you we shouldn't have trusted him."

Gelu raised his eyebrows. His blue-gray hair looked sleek and . . . untrustworthy. "You thought Kleibald was manipulating me. Kleibald and his demons. You thought once you got rid of Kleibald with your obvious little lies, that I would turn on him and on his plans."

"But . . ."

"You were wrong," Gelu told him carelessly. "The spirits made promises to me. Promises far greater than the promises they made to Kleibald. Once Gannoir is destroyed and Tel-Maor has no physical haven, the spirits will give us a new world. And I'm to be the father of that world. When Mailu's child is born, my son and I will rule."

"But . . . all these people . . . the people on the skyboulder . . ."

"They'll be my servants, naturally," Gelu replied.

"And all the people of Gannoir . . . they'll die if Gannoir implodes . . ."

"Collateral damage," Gelu shrugged. "We don't need Gannoir."

"Give me back the scab," Talag demanded.

Gelu laughed. "It's too late. I've already shot the Dynroc's precious, dead, dark blood at Gannoir. There's nothing you can do to stop it now."

Talag gasped in horror.

Dynny tugged at his sleeve, and Talag glanced back at him gratefully. He'd forgotten that the scab was his own, not Dynny's. No matter what Gelu thought he'd done, he was mistaken. There was still time. There had to be a way they could still save Gannoir, if not their own lives.

But Gelu was still talking. "Just look if you don't believe me," Gelu said, gesturing toward the telescope. Just look and see what you've done to Gannoir."

Talag walked unsteadily forward and pressed his eye against the rocky aperture. The shimmering purple flame still burned a circle in his vision. But something had changed. In the center of the circle was a small darkness, rippling outward and creating a larger and larger area of dead fire.

"What's happening?" he whispered in shock.

"The hole. The dead blood of the Dynroc has created a fissure in the Bec. And it's growing," Gelu responded smugly.

Talag sank to his knees and put his face in his hands. "No . . . no . . ."

"It can't," Dynny replied staunchly. "It can't be happening because that was not my blood! It was Talag's!" he chortled.

Talag looked up at his friend miserably. "But Dynny . . . it is happening. It is."

Chapter 69: Xylo

"What have you found?" Ieska asked, looking at the clear flask Unaleah was carrying.

Unaleah frowned and peered at the object with concern in her blue eyes. "We couldn't bring back much," she reported. "Two tiny dga, each with a single spot of darkness."

"Well done," Ieska congratulated her.

"I wish it were more," Unaleah complained.

"Those dga are vicious little things," Gudall said with a relish. "Every time we tried to scoop them up, they lashed out at us." He held up a hand covered in scratches and dripping with blood. "I didn't mind bleeding," he said easily. "We could have captured any number of dga. But the problem was that it isn't dga we need. It was the dark blobs. The blood acts like antimatter to the dark blobs. Blood plus blob equals nothing." He grimaced and clenched his fists so that he wouldn't bleed.

"We were lucky we managed to trap two of them," Unaleah added. She held up a hand similarly scratched. "Hopefully this will be enough to tell if they're able to reproduce themselves."

"Where are the others?" Gudall asked. "I thought Xylo would be anxiously awaiting our reports."

"Xylo went to enlist the help of the rational wind," Ieska told him. "Finnan and Rahela went out to pick fruits and vegetables for dinner. A lot of edible things grow on the heights. Camilly and Ceres are fishing, also for dinner. And Rhyder is working on a device whereby fire can be taken down into the sea—with some help from Xylo's son, Case."

"So we're the first ones back?" Gudall asked.

Ieska nodded. "I'm expecting the others before long, though," she said. "Already, the dark side of the Ghalon is turning its face toward Garradh Gannoir. That was supposed to be the call to come home."

Kari and Sadi were the next to return. They brought the welcome news that Tass, although unwilling to help, was nearby.

"She didn't believe us when we told her we were her sisters," Kari lamented.

"You weren't supposed to tell her at all," Ieska chided them. "Xylo wanted to do it. Tass is sensitive."

"Grumpy is more like it," Sadi snorted.

"Be kind," Ieska admonished her dark-haired daughter.

Dinnertime came. Ceres and Camilly brought an assortment of fish from the shore far below the caves. Finnan and Rahela came with baskets full of fuuegn and rucloce berries.

"I know they're not the most nutritious food," Finnan apologized, "but since I'm not familiar with this area or its flora, it was the best I could do."

"We'll set out earlier tomorrow," Rahela promised.

Finnan and Ceres cooked the fish with the fungal Fuuegn, adding some sea salt for flavor while Gudall and Rahela sliced berries. Unaleah whipped the gwynant to top the halas bread that they found in the cupboards of the Dynroc's cave.

But Xylo, Pax, and Laetu still had not returned.

"There is more than a sliver of the dark side of the Ghalon showing above," Ieska worried. "I knew Xylo might be late, but I was expecting Pax and Laetu to come back."

"They probably dove deeper than they were supposed to," Sadi snorted. "Trying to be the heroes . . ."

"It was part of the mission to look for fissures in the Bec," Rahela said quietly.

"It was also part of the mission to come home on time," Case pointed out.

"Maybe they went farther than they thought," Unaleah suggested graciously. "It's easy to do in a strange place."

Xylo returned halfway through dinner.

"Is there any left for me?" he said, eyeing the half-empty bowl of rucloce berries hungrily.

"Sit down," Ieska said. "Have some food. Were you able to find the rational wind?"

"Gaoth met me on the heights," Xylo reported as he dished food onto his plate. "He understands the danger. He's going to find Dwoyra and coordinate a plan."

"What kind of a plan?" Case asked his father.

Xylo sighed. "It's complicated. Our hope is to heal the Bec layer. No darkness should be entering Gannoir. But bringing the skyboulder back requires us to make a large opening in the skin of our world. It will be difficult to prevent darkness from rushing in and water—and who knows what else along with it—from seeping out. That's where you all come in," he said, looking around the table at the triads. "It's your blood, your unique power . . ." He stopped. "Where are Pax and Laetu?"

"They haven't returned yet," Unaleah told him.

"We're starting to worry," Rhyder said grimly.

"I started a long time ago," Finnan added, shaking her head.

Camilly grinned. "They're probably goofing off. You know how they are. They found some creature they'd never seen or a cave they wanted to explore. They'll be back."

"They've done this before?" Rahela asked.

Camilly nodded. "I don't know why mom's so worried." She looked at Finnan and tossed her red head. "You know how they are."

Finnan pressed her lips together. "They should know better than that. We're in a strange place. They were told to come directly back here."

"They're boys," Gudall said with a grin. "And they're not helpless babies. They'll show up before the food is gone."

"They better hurry then," Xylo said, scooping another mound of sliced rucloce berries onto his plate. "Why'd you slice them? Half the fun of eating rucloce is that you don't know what you're going to get inside."

"It looked prettier that way," Rahela retorted with spirit. "Without slicing them all you have is a bowl of white orbs."

"I like seeing all the color," Ceres agreed. "And you still don't know what you're getting. The variety of flavors seems never-ending. Color alone doesn't give much away."

"How long did Gaoth think it would take him to find Dwoyra?" Case asked.

"I shouldn't think it would be long," Xylo answered. "It will depend more on how soon Rhyder can make the fire conduit." He looked over at the younger man.

"It's not going to be easy," Rhyder replied. "We have the materials, naturally occurring ores, and whatever the people of Garradh Gannoir can provide. But we'll need an accurate measurement of the depth of the sea. I need to know who long to make the pipes. And then there's the matter of propulsion . . ."

"So how long?" Xylo interrupted him.

"A month?" Rhyder guessed.

Xylo shook his head. "That's too long. Those on the skyboulder won't survive another month floating in the chaos. Their supplies must be limited."

Rahela shook her head. "What were they thinking? They had to know they couldn't live forever out there."

"They were thinking Gannoir was going to implode," Case answered. "Leaving was their best hope of staying alive."

"That's why Gelu dug the mine," Ceres added. "To make a hole in the Bec layer so that the insides of Gannoir would seep out and implode the world."

Rhyder's face brightened. "Would someone here have measurements from the mine works? That could shave some time off our estimate."

"I'm sure someone has," Xylo answered. "We'll go into Obumbro in the morning and find out."

"Will that cut enough time off?" Gudall asked. "Maybe if more of us were working on the project . . ."

"That would help too," Rhyder noted. "Everyone who can help should be helping."

"Me too?" Camilly asked.

"You too," Rhyder nodded at his daughter.

Finnan and Rahela stayed to clean up the remains of the meal while the others went with Rhyder and Case to begin work on the project, tired as they were. When the convenalations far above them glowed with the knowledge that the night was half-gone, Finnan and Rahela sought out the others.

"I don't like this," Finnan frowned. "Pax and Laetu are still gone. Even if they were dawdling, they should have been back by now."

"I agree with Finnan," Rahela added. "We need to do something. We have to find them."

"But where do we start looking?" Camilly asked. "They could be anywhere."

Gudall shrugged. "May as well start in the water. That's where they were supposed to be."

"That was the most dangerous of the tasks," Finnan complained. "And you gave it to the youngest of the children."

"Young bodies can withstand the temperature changes more easily," Ieska reassured her. "Studies have shown . . ."

"Those of us who can swim ought to go now," Unaleah interrupted her. "They could be in trouble."

"I can swim," Camilly volunteered. "It's about all I'm good for."

"Let's go, then," Gudall said. "Unaleah, Camilly, Kari, Sadi, and I will go to the mine and start searching the water."

"Don't forget us," Rhyder said, holding up a hand with the extensive finger tala of the Mayim and pointing to his wife. "We can swim."

"I'm happy to go," Finnan added.

"Me too," Ceres said. "That's eight of us in the water. We can split up into pairs."

"Ieska, Case, and I will climb into the heights," Xylo volunteered.

"That just leaves Rahela," Ieska noted. "Would you be willing to go into the city, into Obumbro, and start knocking on doors to see if anyone's seen them?"

Rahela nodded. "That's about the only thing a Gulot can do here. It seems odd to be the only Gulot. I was always in the majority at home in Luca."

Xylo watched as the eight swimmers and Rahela set out for the lower lands. He was not worried. Not yet. Pax and Laetu seemed like capable boys. He agreed that they had probably become distracted by an adventure all their own and had lost track of time. He wondered briefly how those deep in the sea could tell what time of day it was. The Ghalon would not be visible from the depths. Perhaps the rain that came at night clued them in. He didn't know.

He looked at Ieska and then at Case. "Ready to go?"

Chapter 70: Talag

Talag and Dynny leaned against the stony walls in what they now knew was the control room of the skyboulder. Gelu, satisfied that he had done what was necessary for his exalted future, had retreated to the small room that housed Mailu and her coffin, waiting to face the future with his very own Siann Dha and his tiny, growing son.

"I'm sorry," Talag said for the thousandth time. "I didn't mean for it to work out like this."

"I know," Dynny answered. But his voice was sad. Being the Dynroc was all he had, and Talag had inadvertently taken it from him. He wasn't sure who he was anymore.

Talag turned and peered through the telescope again. Either the dark hole in the Bec was growing larger or they were getting closer to Gannoir. Maybe both.

Either way it wasn't good. Their world was going to implode. They would never be able to go home. Would they die? Or would Gelu's plans work out? Would they all be deposited on a new world, ready to create a new civilization under Gelu's guidance?

He shook his head. He wasn't sure which was worse. That Gelu had been the more powerful of the two leaders on the skyboulder was a revelation to him. He wondered if he had ever understood anything about his grandfather at all. Kleibald was bad. But Gelu was worse. And the spirits, the dark spirits . . . they were the worst. They wanted to destroy not only Gannoir, but Tel-Maor himself. Through his ordeal, Talag had come to have a heartfelt belief in the supernatural creator of Gannoir. Just because he couldn't see him and couldn't feel him didn't mean he wasn't there. He'd talked to the spirits of the chaos. He could see them either, and during his previous life as a student, he'd been taught that the spirits were imaginary constructions of the ancients, meant to explain natural phenomena. If the spirits were real, then Tel-Maor must be as well.

He wondered what would happen if Gannoir imploded and Tel-Maor was released from his prison in the center of the world. It was odd . . . the creator being a prisoner in his own creation. He didn't understand why Tel-Maor, if he was powerful enough to make a world, would let himself be trapped by it. But it didn't matter anymore. Nothing did.

"I'm sorry," he said again.

"You're the Dynroc," Dynny said miserably. "And I'm not."

Talag wanted to cry, but he was too upset. Dynny was the closest friend he'd ever had. And he'd robbed him of everything he was. Some friend he was.

"I'm sorry," he muttered. "So sorry."

Chapter 71: Tass

Tass continued to ride the dga, exhilaration coursing through her body. She wasn't cold at all. She felt warm and alive. She couldn't see herself, but she could see the silhouette of her hands against the bright exoskeleton of the dga. Her arms moved without her permission, doing what was necessary to propel the dga to action. The dga hacked at the cold fire of the Bec with razor-sharp appendages.

Tass wondered idly what sort of thing the Bec was. Sharp claws couldn't cut fire. It had to be a solid. But it wasn't a solid either. It was something else completely.

The dga was making progress. What had begun as a pale seam, the scar from what remained of the Bilik, the hole that had only closed by means of Igracio's blood, was now marred by a small but growing patch of darkness.

She could feel the water around her urging her toward the tiny gap, pulling at her, tugging her downward. Somehow this would work. Once the hole was large enough, the skyboulder containing her sister would come barreling through the gap, back inside Gannoir. It would float to the surface. Someone would draw it to shore, and the people would come out. The progression of events was clear in her mind. It had to happen that way. The spirits—the voices—the darkness—would make sure of it.

As she surveyed the Bec, she could see other fissures, slits of darkness no longer than one of her hands. Every so often a bit of dark slime oozed into the water and floated away.

Indignation rose in her. Igracio had given his life to make the Bec whole. Yet here were gaps, fissures, injuries to the substance of the cold fire that guarded their world. She steeled herself against the injustice of it all. It didn't matter. Igracio was dead.

Deliberately, she tried to move her hands, to caress the dga, to reassure it that what it was doing was good and right. Her hands did not obey her command. She was fully under the power of the darkness.

"I'll not be afraid. I am not afraid," she said aloud in her gill-voice. "They're protecting me. They're enabling me to do what needs to be done. They're on my side."

Your side is the wrong side, a voice rang in her head.

She looked around to see who had spoken but she could see nothing.

Don't do this, the deep, agonized voice continued. *Don't let it all be for nothing. You are not on the side of Tel-Maor . . .*

"I know nothing of Tel-Maor," Tass interrupted. "He is nothing to me."

I serve Tel-Maor. I am a guardian of Gannoir.

Tass knew who it was now. She had talked with him once before. It was the spirit of the Bec, the rational cold fire. No wonder he was protesting. She and the dga were hacking at his body.

"You're a poor guardian," Tass shot back, marveling still at the new ease with which eloquence came in her gill speech. "There are holes all over. The darkness is seeping in."

Help me. Help Gannoir, the Bec pleaded.

Tass shook her head. "I want my sister back."

At the cost of the whole world?

Tass hesitated for a moment. Was it worth it to bring back Mailu, who was possibly deceased, if it caused Gannoir to collapse in on itself? Was life without Mailu so unbearable that she would risk everything and everyone to bring her back?

At her hesitation she felt a surge of heat course through her limbs. The darkness. Her ally was the darkness. And as long as she served the darkness, she served herself. If she switched alliances and decided to obey the Bec, the darkness would leave her. She would die of the cold. And Mailu would be forever trapped in a rock floating in the chaos outside Gannoir. There was no good to be had by siding with the Bec, no matter what it said.

As she turned her mind back to the darkness, she felt its warm caress filling her body. The darkness would take care of her. The Bec, she felt sure, would leave her to die.

"Carry on!" Tass ordered the dga. She felt the darkness spur her hands and feet to even greater speed in the dig.

Chapter 72: Water

A dripping company of eight stood on the shore of the mine. The rain was falling heavily from the dimly lit heights above them as the water returned to the sea after the day's evaporation.

Camilly was shivering. It wasn't cold, but she was afraid. So afraid.

"Something is really wrong down there," Sadi noted. Her black hair hung down, plastered to her back.

"The water shouldn't pull like that," Gudall agreed.

"I barely made it back up to the surface," Finnan said, putting her arm around her shaking daughter.

"Something sucking the water down," Ceres noted. "It's almost like it was when . . . when . . ."

"When everything happened?" Kari said softly.

Ceres nodded. "The water spun. It went up toward the Ghalon and down. Like a funnel that went from the Ghalon all the way to the bottom of the sea."

"There's no funnel now," Rhyder noted, looking at the smooth surface of the water.

"If Pax and Laetu are caught in that . . ." Unaleah worried.

"They can breathe in the water," Sadi said abruptly. "They may be down there, but they're fine. They're fine."

"I want to believe that," Finnan said.

"Don't you?" Camilly turned toward her mother.

"It gets cold if you go too low," Ceres noted. "Really cold."

"Cold enough to kill?" Gudall asked heavily.

Ceres nodded. "I think so. I never went that low. Tass did."

"And Tass was all right?" Sadi queried sharply.

"Yes. She had Dwoyra for a protector. She didn't say much about what it was like, but she did tell us that much," Ceres answered.

"We need to find the others," Finnan noted. "They need to know that something is happening. Otherwise, we may be too late."

Before they'd gone any distance at all, they met Xylo, Ieska, and Case hurrying toward them.

"Something's wrong!" Camilly announced, her teeth chattering with anxiety.

"We know," Xylo said. "We could tell from the heights. The water levels are low. Too low. Lower than I've ever seen them. And we've been watching for a while. Ever since we began to suspect that there were holes in the Bec."

Grim silence prevailed for some moments as everyone absorbed this new information.

"It's begun, then," Finnan noted. "The world is imploding."

"It looks like it," Ieska said gravely. "The water is seeping out to the chaos."

"Can we stop it?" Gudall asked.

"We're going to try," Ieska retorted angrily. "It's that or die."

"We'll have to put the plan into motion immediately," Xylo said. He looked at Rhyder. "Not a month from now. What do you have?"

Rhyder shook his head. "Just a few small sample containers I made for fire. No bigger than my fist and made of soft metal. It's impossible. We can't make something that's large enough and long enough in the time we have remaining."

"How much time do you think we have?" Sadi asked.

Kari squeezed the water out of her long blond hair. "We have all the time there is," she said bravely.

"That may not be very long," Sadi retorted dryly.

"She's got the right attitude, though," Case said. "We have to do what we can with the time and assets we have."

"But the Bec is full of holes," Ceres said with an imploring look at her husband. "What can we do?"

Case shook his head. "Plug the holes. Stop the water from escaping. Stop the darkness from getting in."

"And bring back the skyboulder," Xylo added. "If a hole exists that's big enough to cause the drop in sea levels that we've seen, then readmitting the skyboulder should be possible."

"If the skyboulder is close," Ieska hedged. "It may be thousands of miles away. Even if it's close to Gannoir, it might be on the other side of the world."

"It will take a miracle," Ceres said.

"Or some very careful planning," Ieska said.

"We can take the fire down as deep as we can," Gudall volunteered. "If Rhyder has some capsules, it shouldn't be a problem. He said they're only as big as his fist."

"It was the fire from the Ghalon combined with the power of Gaoth and Dwoyra that sealed the hole before," Case noted. "We need Gaoth and Dwoyra."

"And the fire and capsules," Rhyder added.

"And blood," Ieska said quietly. "It's going to take blood."

The four triads looked at her stoically. They knew whose blood she meant.

"No!" Camilly wailed. "They'll die!"

"They won't die," Ieska answered. "But they must bleed. And bleed a lot. It's the only way to obliterate the darkness. If we can stop the darkness from coming in, then we can stop the water from going out."

"You really think so?" Finnan asked.

Ieska nodded. "I've done the math. I've done the science. I understand the structure of Gannoir. It has to work."

"I'm willing," Gudall volunteered.

"Me too," Sadi announced with bravado.

Kari and Unaleah nodded their agreement.

"If my blood would help . . ." Ceres began.

Xylo stopped her. "It's the triad blood we need, not Mayim blood," he told her.

"Anything would help, though, right?" Ceres said.

"We're going to need your help elsewhere," Ieska replied. She took charge, something for which Xylo was grateful. The mission to bring back the skyboulder was his, but he wasn't qualified to speak to the science like his fiancée was.

"Rhyder and Case—go back to the workstation and bring the supplies down here for carrying the fire. The rest of you—get in the water. If you're already bleeding, bleed," she said, looking pointedly at the wounded hands of Gudall and Unaleah. But all of you, bleeding or not, get in there and find Dwoyra. We need her help."

"I'll try to find Gaoth," Xylo volunteered.

"And I'm going to go into the city, into Obumbro, to see if I can find Rahela. It doesn't matter if she's found anyone to help us. We should all be together when we launch this mission."

Xylo understood what Ieska had left unsaid. There was little hope of success. Death was imminent. Being together to face it was more important that fighting. He tried not to let the knowledge of their coming failure show in his face. There was still a chance—a slim chance—that they would save Gannoir. And an even slimmer chance that they would be able to bring the skyboulder back. His desire for justice would never come to pass now. He would never have the satisfaction of knowing that Kleibald had been punished for killing his little son, Dochym, or for trying to destroy the world, or for all the crimes that resulted from his efforts to create a three-in-one. Yet this disappointment paled next to the notion that they were all about to die—would die unless they could stop the seawater from seeping into the chaos and causing Gannoir to implode.

Chapter 73: Xylo

"How do we do this?" Kari asked.

"Split into teams," Sadi answered.

"Same teams as before?" Unaleah assumed, looking at Gudall.

Sadi shook her head. "We should at least split up you two since you're both so bloody. Spread it around, right?"

Camilly giggled. It wasn't funny but it was comical.

Sadi took charge. "Camilly, Finnan, and Ceres, you stay closer to the surface. You're not triad so you can't swim as far down. Spread out. If Dwoyra is anywhere above the yellow layer of the sea, you'll find her. Kari and Gudall, you search the red layer—lower if you can. Unaleah and I will take yellow and orange."

"What does she look like?" Camilly asked.

"Ceres?" Sadi directed the question.

Ceres shook her head. "I don't know, really. Tass explained it like she was part of the water, but doing things water doesn't do, like poking people or creating a barrier. And talking."

"Invisible then?" Gudall asked.

Ceres nodded. "That's what I understand."

"There must be a reason Gaoth was having difficulty finding her," Xylo interjected. "So look for anything unusual. That might give us a clue about where she is."

With a collective sigh, the four triads dove into the water of the mine. Camilly, Finnan, and Ceres took a moment to strategize before entering the water, splitting the shoreline into three sections to search.

"Don't forget to look on the underside of the Orbokth, too," Ceres instructed them. "She could be anywhere."

And then they disappeared into the shrinking sea.

"Are you coming with me?" Xylo asked Ieska.

She shook her head. "I'll stay here to coordinate efforts once the others come back. They may find Dwoyra before you get back with Rahela."

Xylo nodded and looked at the dimly lit city nestled against the cliffs of the Orbokth in the distance. "Good. And if things end before I return . . ." He squeezed her hand.

"I know," Ieska smiled. "I love you, too."

As they swam through the golden sea, Sadi reflected that she was glad Unaleah was with her. The older girl's bleeding hands dribbled hope into the water slowly but surely. The darkness was growing less. She couldn't talk under the water. Ceres had explained that it was a higher-level skill learned in one's final years at the Calix. Tass had been able to do it, she explained, but then, Tass was different. She herself had never been skilled at gill-speech. It took years to learn to do it properly.

Sadi wondered how they were going to find Dwoyra. Finding an invisible creature made of water seemed like an impossibility.

The downward tug of the sea was new to her. Sadi fought the pull of the water and pushed her body upward. Unaleah did the same, dribbling occasionally drops of blood as she did. Each droplet met a blob of darkness and together they became nothing.

We're going to win, Sadi told herself. *We have to.*

Gudall scratched at the wounds on his hands, trying to make them bleed more. It hurt, but he was willing to do what it took to help, even if it wasn't the task he was supposed to be doing. Kari swam beside him, her long blond hair stained red by the glow of the water around them. Fish and other sea creatures frantically swam upward, fighting the tug of the chaos yanking them down.

Gudall let the current draw him lower. Dwoyra could be anywhere, he reflected, but it was likely she was working to save Gannoir. She'd be near the edge of the world, then, he reflected—just where he and Kari were assigned to search.

The seawater changed from red to magenta, and Gudall felt his limbs grow stiff with the cold. No clothing he could imagine would insulate them against this. Most of the creatures around him now were dga, each sporting tiny blotches of darkness. He felt heartened as he saw his blood cleansing them, freeing them. Each shiny freed dga joyfully shot upward, as though it had been the darkness and not the vortex drawing them downward.

In the distance he could see something shining, glowing with flickering purple light. It was silhouetted against a darkness he had never before seen in the sea. Seawater glowed. This, whatever it was, didn't.

As he drew nearer, he could see how large the shining object was. It was a dga—a giant dga. The dark blobs covered it, making a peculiar shadow on its back in the shape of a person. It seemed to be digging at the darkness behind it. Frantically digging. He glanced over at Kari to see if she was seeing what he was seeing.

She looked back at him with frightened eyes.

Their battle was clear. The dga was digging at the purple fire, and it was succeeding. He now saw the darkness for what it was—a hole in the Bec. He wondered why he was not dead. The cold was intense. His mind and body were working so slowly he thought he could have been staring for any length of time—days, weeks, years—and not realized it.

He swam as near as he dared and flung his hands at the thing, spattering it with tiny droplets of blood. Pinpricks of purple light appeared wherever his blood hit the dark blotches. The person-like silhouette moved. He gasped, accidentally drawing the caustic seawater into his air-lungs. The blotch wasn't just shaped like a person—it was a person.

Grabbing Kari's hand, he shot toward the surface.

They hadn't found Dwoyra.

They'd found Tass.

Camilly swam around the edge of the mine, staying near to the surface. She'd taken the wedge nearest the town of Obumbro. Even by the dim light of the convenalations and through the falling rain, she could see the shimmering, whitewashed houses in the distance. Would Dwoyra be near the town? She wasn't sure. So far nothing seemed odd except the absence of the usual water creatures that filled the seas. But Ceres had warned her about that. The mine was devoid of life in the areas nearest the surface. It wasn't the sign they were seeking.

Camilly drew the sweet water into her gills. It was nearing firstlight, she realized. The concentration of the liquid sea was almost pure water, lacking the acidic taste it had most of the time. Only during the hours just before and just after the Ghalon turned its fiery side toward the land did the sea taste sweet.

Camilly tried to soak up awareness from all her extremities. Dwoyra could be anywhere, and she could be any size. She could choose to hide herself among the water, Ceres had told her. Sometimes she only pulled the molecules together enough to form a finger's width of touchable body. Camilly had to be aware and alert.

Wherever Dwoyra was, they all knew she would be working to fight the darkness, to save Gannoir. It was unlikely that she, a fifteen-year-old girl with no special talents, swimming along the surface of the water, would find the watery being.

Popping her head out of the water into the air and rain above it, she looked around. She had made her way halfway through the section of the mine assigned to her. She wondered how her mother and Ceres were faring. She ducked her head back under the water and kept swimming.

When she finished searching the shoreline, she began to swim back and forth across her portion of the lake, trying to cover every inch of the water. It occurred to her just how easily Dwoyra could avoid them if she wanted to. Even if Dwoyra had a solid body, she would be hard to find.

A tiny silver dga shot past Camilly, surprising her by its presence in the barren water. It wriggled its tiny, metallic legs and squirmed quickly away. Dga. Hadn't Xylo said something about dga? Or had it been Ceres? She couldn't remember.

Curious, Camilly followed it. She could justify leaving her search area because, after all, she'd been on a mission to find something unusual, and this—a dga above its depth and in a lifeless sea—was certainly unusual.

A glimmer in the distance caught her eye. The tiny dga was not alone. Many dga had gathered in a sea-mat of silver, shimmering in the turquoise ymolenegth. The phenomenon was ethereal and otherworldly. Even in Cudth Deorth, a haven of beauty, Camilly had never seen anything like it. As she drew near, she noticed that every few minutes one tiny dga would shoot out from the one of the sides of the net as though propelled by a force other than what was natural.

"Blood! Blood! Now! Hurry!"

The words whistled through her gills. Camilly wondered if she were hearing the words in the same way she heard words on land. Was this gill-speech? If so, who was the speaker?

She pushed herself closer to the formation of dga. Suddenly she felt her skin stinging. She looked down to see a stream of light oozing out of her arm. She was bleeding. A second later something struck her leg with a similar result. Brushing at her skin, she saw that her attacker was a miniscule dga. It had pricked her arm and then her leg, drawing blood.

"Was it you who called?" she thought at it.

Then she realized who it must have been. She swam for the surface and poked her head through the glassy ceiling. "Mom! Mom! Ceres!" she hollered. The rain had slowed to a gentle mist and the first sliver of daylight was shining on the roof of the world above her. "Mom! Mom!"

Another prick hit her in the foot, and then another and another. "Mom! Mom! Help!" She fought against her exquisitely tiny attackers. She wasn't triad. It wasn't her blood they wanted, she thought uselessly. "Mom!"

Chapter 74: Gathering

Case and Rhyder were standing on the shore with Ieska by the time Sadi and Unaleah returned.

Sadi shook her head. "We didn't see anything out of the ordinary in the yellow or orange layers of the sea. It was bitter cold down there. Strange creatures I hadn't seen before surrounded us. But no sign of Dwoyra or of Tass."

Unaleah rubbed her bleeding hands and sighed. "Are we the first ones back?"

Ieska nodded. "From the sea, anyhow." She gestured toward Case and Rhyder. They were standing beside a small sea-string net bag.

"The fire capsules?" Sadi asked.

Ieska nodded but looked worried.

Sadi and Unaleah climbed, dripping, toward the two men. Rhyder reached into the net bag and pulled out a lopsided metal orb. Its surface had the dull sheen of mother-of-pearl instead of the reflective surface of the dga.

"I thought you said they were the size of your fist," Sadi commented. She made a fist. "They're little."

"I was approximating," Rhyder told her defensively.

Sadi held out her hand. "Is there fire in it already? Can I hold it?"

"They're hot," Case warned her.

Sadi gestured impatiently and stretched out her fingers. "Give it here."

Rhyder pulled one of the lumps out of the bag and gingerly dropped it into Sadi's hand. She dropped it almost immediately. Fortunately, the shore was covered by vegetation and the capsule was undamaged.

"Told you it was hot," Case said.

"It'll cool off once it's in the water," Sadi noted.

"That's the problem," Rhyder answered. "While we were waiting for you to get back, we dropped one into the mine water, just to see what would happen." He reached down and picked up one of the capsules that was not in the bag with the others. He handed it to Sadi.

"It's cool," she marveled. "I figured the water would help."

"That's probably not a good thing," Unaleah said quietly. "Not if we're supposed to carry fire to the bottom of the sea."

Sadi groaned. "So what are we going to do?"

"I've been thinking about it and . . ."

Ieska was interrupted by shouting. "We found her! We found her!"

They all turned toward the mine water. Camilly, Ceres, and Finnan were climbing onto the shore. All were dripping with blood that ran down their arms and legs as they emerged from the water.

Case gasped. "Ceres! Are you all right?" He ran to his wife.

"I'm fine. It's not as bad as it looks. The dga . . ."

"But the important thing is that we found Dwoyra," Camilly interrupted them. "She's here in the water."

"How did you get her to come?" Ieska asked.

"Ceres could talk to her a little. Mom and I could hear her, but we couldn't talk back to her."

"She's been working with the dga," Ceres told the group. "Sending them out to draw blood from any creature they could find. You know, to fight the darkness. But she's here now, ready to work with us."

"She made them hurt you!" Case was indignant.

"For Gannoir," Ceres replied earnestly. "It's worth it. I know we didn't think it would be my blood, but it has to be someone's."

"Any sign of Laetu and Pax?" Finnan asked.

Ieska shook her head. "None. Xylo's not back either, nor are Kari and Gudall. We need Xylo to go find Gaoth," she fretted.

Case lifted his head and turned in several directions. "I think he's here already," he said. "I've met him, remember."

"Tell him to talk to Dwoyra," Ieska requested. "We have to make our plans slowly and carefully and everyone must be involved."

Camilly pointed toward the center of the lake. "I think I see Kari and Gudall," she said.

"Good," Ieska nodded. "As soon as they get here, we can work out our plan."

"What about my dad?" Case asked. "And Rahela?"

"They'll be along shortly, I'm sure," Ieska said. "But we can start without them. It's the triad—the four of you, plus Pax and Laetu, whose roles will be critical."

Gudall reached the shore before Kari. He looked upset.

"What's wrong?" Finnan asked.

He shook his head. "It's worse than we thought."

"What do you mean?" Ieska said, leaning forward.

"You spoke of tiny fissures in the Bec—little holes where the darkness was creeping in. Holes smaller than the palm of my hand. We might have been able to fix those eventually. We would have had time. Holes that size wouldn't cause Gannoir to implode. But what we saw . . ." He shook his head.

Kari climbed out of the water, shivering.

"Are you cold?" Finnan asked her.

Kari shook her head. "Just upset," she replied. "I don't see how anything we do can make any difference now."

A murmur rumbled through the group. Ieska motioned them to silence. "Tell us what you saw," she requested.

Gudall ran a hand through his damp black hair. "It sounds incredible . . . unbelievable, but you've got to believe me."

"Believe us," Kari chimed in.

"A giant dga is digging a hole in the Bec," Gudall informed the group gravely.

"And that's not all," Kari said. "It's not alone. There's a girl on its back. We think it's Tass. She's . . ." Kari winced.

"She's covered in darkness," Gudall reported. "The blobs that are riding the tiny dga like parasites have completely eclipsed her body. She's all darkness."

"She's directing the dga to dig?" Ieska asked sharply.

"It looked like it," Gudall told her. "The hole is already large."

Silence settled over them as they internally eulogized their world. They might have fixed tiny holes. They might have stopped

Tass and the dga from their fateful task. But there was no way to fix a gaping cleft in the fabric of their world.

Ieska's eyes grew hard. "No. No! She will not do this thing. I don't know why she wants to kill us all. There must be a way to stop her."

"But how?" Camilly asked, tears in her eyes. "The sea level is lower now than it was when we got to shore, and that was only a few minutes ago. What are we going to do?"

"I wish Xylo were here," Ieska muttered.

"Me too," Case said. "What we need is another miracle. Like the one that happened last time. I thought it was all over then, but it wasn't. With Dwoyra and Gaoth, and with the blood in the water, it worked. The gogyvehr was completed, and the Bilik was sealed shut. It can be done."

A wail rose from someone in the back of the group.

All heads turned to see who it was.

Rahela had returned with Xylo. It was she who had cried out.

"Oh," Camilly breathed softly. "Don't forget . . . it wasn't just Dwoyra and Gaoth and blood in the water. It was Igracio's life." Her eyes shone worshipfully as she spoke of the fallen hero.

Xylo put an arm around Rahela and looked at Ieska pleadingly. "No one must die this time. No one."

Rahela pushed his arm off. "My son died for Gannoir. Are you saying no one else ought to? Are you saying his sacrifice ought to have been for nothing? That Gannoir is going to die regardless?" She looked at the people in the group. "In this short time, you all have become precious to me. Like my own children. My son's blood siblings. He had an uncommon power in his blood, just like you all do. Your blood, your lives, may be the only hope for all Gannoir. For all of us. For all of them." She gestured toward the unsuspecting village of Obumbro. "And for all Luca. Igracio was willing. Are you?"

"Yes!" Camilly shouted, overcome with emotion.

"You're not triad," Unaleah pointed out. "And of course we'll do whatever is necessary. If we don't, we'll die anyhow, right?"

Slowly, Gudall, Kari, and Sadi nodded.

Rahela turned toward Ieska and Xylo, who were whispering together. "Tell us what needs to be done."

Chapter 75: Sadi

"Do you think this is going to work?" Sadi whispered to Gudall as they dogpaddled toward the middle of the lake.

"Stop talking," he ordered with a garbled dribble. "You'll let the capsule fall out of your mouth."

Sadi shut her mouth. She knew he was right. The only way to get the fire capsules to the bottom of the mine and out to the Bec without losing the fire, was to carry them in their mouths. And only the triads could bear it, being creatures not only of water and land, but of fire. The burning capsule didn't feel as hot in her mouth as it had felt in her hand. She didn't understand why, but she was grateful for that small mercy. She was going to her death. Potentially. One way or the other.

Xylo had notched the skin of the four triads on their feet, their upper arms, and their legs, letting the blood flow out in thin but steady trickles. It was necessary, he explained, to have triad blood to make whatever was supposed to happen, happen. Ducking her head under the water, Sadi could see the glowing trail that marked the path they had taken to get to the center. It was straight down from there. Down to Tass and the dga in an attempt to fill the water with blood and stop the darkness from conquering.

Ieska had been precise and direct. It wasn't the bleeding that would kill them, she explained. Even with only four triads, since Pax and Laetu were still missing, there would be enough blood. No one would need to be exsanguinated. No. The dangerous thing, the thing that would either kill them or not, would be the powerful electrical current shooting out of the Ghalon into the water. Gaoth would channel it from the heights toward the mine, and Dwoyra would direct it toward the gap in the Bec. At just the right moment, the triads would spit the capsules into the blood-soaked water, giving the electricity the extra boost it would need to seal the gash.

It wasn't that she didn't trust Ieska. Ieska was a scientist and a mathematician. She knew about such things. But Sadi wondered if it would all come together the way Ieska had designed. It seemed unlikely that everything and everyone would be in the right place at the right time. The electricity had to flow through all four of the triads, in order to work, Ieska had explained. Blood is light and light is life. And the darkness must be expelled. She wondered where that left Tass. Even if she, Gudall, Unaleah, and Kari survived, Tass might not. She was directly in front of the gap. Unless they could rescue their errant sister, there was little hope for her.

Sadi wanted to be derisive. This whole thing was Tass's fault. She didn't deserve to be rescued. So what if she was backward and angry because her parents had rejected her. Sadi's own mother, Ieska, has stood by her, but several of the other triads had been abandoned— Ninach, Gudall, and Pax. And they weren't busily trying to destroy the world. But it wasn't about Tass. It was about Gannoir and everyone living in it. If Tass could be rescued, they'd rescue her. And if not, then . . .

On the shore, the others waited and watched. Xylo and Ieska

had gone to the heights in case Esh were needed nearest the fire. Rahela had been instructed to remain on the shore, representing land—she was the only Gulot among them. The three Mayim stood with their feet in the water, ready to be used if they were needed. Case stood beside Rahela. He was Esh and had volunteered to go with Xylo and Ieska, but Xylo knew his son wanted to be with his wife, so he told him to stay with her as she stood in the edge of the water.

They were no longer alone. People from Obumbro, seeing the fantastic glow from the mine, had gathered around. Case had tried to shoo them away, but Rahela told him to let them stay.

"They're people like us. They should know what's going on, what's being done for them and for Gannoir," she explained.

Case didn't argue. He knew that Igracio was worshipped in Obumbro because of his sacrifice and because he was one of the Siann Dha. The people of Obumbro were growing more accustomed to having the Siann Dha in their midst, but they still treated them like celebrities. It made him uncomfortable.

Case watched the water began to slowly spin, imperceptibly at first, unless you were expecting that to happen. But soon it was obvious to everyone that the water was swirling around the circular mine basin. The crowd was talkative and loud. He could hear them talking about "the last time this happened" and heard several references to Igracio. When the wind began to whip at his cheeks, he felt turned to stone. There was danger, mortal danger, he knew.

Ieska stood beside Xylo. They had climbed the Orbokth behind Obumbro and were looking down on the scene below. They saw the water glowing with the blood of the triads.

"I wonder where Pax and Laetu can have gone," Ieska mused aloud.

Xylo's expression was grim. "Even irresponsible boys would have been back by now. Something's wrong."

"That's what I think too," Ieska confessed. She shook her head. "I'm sorry this isn't turning out the way you wanted."

"What do you mean?" Xylo asked.

"The skyboulder. We're not going to be able to bring the skyboulder back. It all happened too fast. If we'd had time to plan, to get precise quantities of blood and fire into the water to counteract the seepage that would have happened when a hole large enough to admit the vehicle was made, it could have worked. But now . . . by the time we can finish what's going on here it will be too late for anyone on the skyboulder. They'll be dead."

Xylo sighed. "It has to be enough. Instead of being brought to justice, Kleibald will end up dead because of the evil he caused."

"Your grandchildren and children as well," Ieska said gently. "I'm so sorry for this double blow. We did all we could."

"I know." Xylo's face was full of pain. He shook his head. "I wish I'd known I had grandchildren. I wish I'd been able to meet them."

"It's not your fault."

"I know."

The wind, Gaoth, swirled around them in a mini cyclone of motion.

"They're ready," Xylo said. "Things are going to happen quickly now. Whatever happens, I love you. I wanted to marry you. Remember that."

Ieska grinned at him. "Why do you think it's you who won't make it through this? Maybe you're the one who will have to remember me." Her eyes softened and grew teary. "I love you too."

They held hands as the wind and water started to whip all Garradh Gannoir their wake.

Chapter 76: Tass

The gaping black hole in front of her grew larger. Tass strained her eyes looking at it, looking through it, trying to see if the skyboulder was approaching.

All she saw was darkness.

Her arms moved with mechanical precision now, urging the giant dga forward. She didn't feel tired or cold or excited or . . . anything. She almost felt as though she were watching herself from a distance. The dark voices ruled her body. Her soul was huddled in a corner of the picture, watching and waiting until she could reclaim herself.

Mailu.

She tried to block out the light from the purple fire in order to concentrate on the darkness. Opening her outer eyelids didn't help. It only made her eyes sting.

Mailu.

The dark voices wanted this as much as she did. They were guiding the skyboulder home. She wondered how large the hole would have to be before her sister and the others floated through it into the sea. She pictured skyboulder bobbing on the surface as the grateful citizens of Garradh Gannoir pulled it to shore and helped those inside to exit. She would be a hero for bringing Gelu back, though she didn't think that was a good thing. And Mailu. They would bring Mailu's sarcophagus to shore. Her sister would open her eyes and look at Tass lovingly. Mailu couldn't be dead. Whoever had said that was wrong.

Tass felt her limbs slow down, and she wondered what was happening. The spirits hadn't bothered to talk to her since she had ceded use of her body to them. Why would they? They had what they wanted. And soon, so would she.

She gazed at the darkness and finally saw something there. A huge rock was hurtling toward Gannoir at a speed that was sure to do more than provide it with a gentle introduction to the sea under the mine. At that speed it was going to do damage.

Tass willed herself to swim away, to get to a safe place, but it was no use. She had no more use of her own arms and legs than she would have had over anyone else's. The skyboulder was going to slam into her, into the giant dga, into Gannoir, and they'd all be smashed to pieces.

And there was nothing she could do about it.

Chapter 77: Impact

"It's happening," Rahela said, looking up toward the hills where she thought Xylo and Ieska must be.

The wind and the water were swirling in unison. There was no longer a clear division between the air and the water. Her hair whipped around her head, keeping her from seeing clearly. Where were the others? She stumbled toward the mine, hoping to find the others so they could cling to each other. She'd never be able to stand otherwise.

Finally, she caught hold of Case. She didn't have to say anything. There wasn't anything to say. Crackles of electricity burst from the Ghalon and spun with the wind and water. She finally understood what it meant to be Siann Dha. The fire, the land, the sea . . . all becoming one, joined by an electrical circuit that could save Gannoir. She didn't know how it would work, only that it would. That it had to.

The six who were together at sea level clung to each other. Rahela, the Gulot, and Case, the Esh, stood on the shore. Ceres, Camilly, Rhyder, and Finnan were in the water. But they were one in spirit, wondering what would happen.

The ground began to shake. Case and Ceres exchanged a significant glance. It was just what had happened the last time. Cracks appeared in what had been the shoreline. The water and wind had joined together in a powerful death spiral. Looking down, Rahela could see the depths of the sea beneath the mine, the rainbow colors of the seawater glowing brightly in their layers.

Fire shot down from above and at the same time a violent earthquake slammed Gannoir. No one was left standing, even among the crowd that had hung back from the edge of the mine. It was long before the reverberations quieted. The wind and the sea returned to their spheres, and the bruised company crawled to their feet.

Under the water, the four triads tried to focus. Sadi desperately wanted to speak to the others, but with the capsule of fire in her mouth and the inability to speak underwater, she couldn't. The seawater around them grew colder as they progressed downward. Sinking was easy. The suction created by the hole in the Bec was horrifying. Sadi wondered if she would be sucked out of the world right along with the sea. She wished they'd had more time for instruction before they'd come. When, exactly, was she supposed to spit the fire out? How much was she supposed to bleed? How would she know if it was working?

They all felt the change in the motion of the water when the cyclone began. Sadi struggled to swim against the current, to keep moving toward Tass, the dga, and the Bec despite the water's powerful motion. The four had been holding hands throughout their dive, but now the force drove them apart. Sadi could still see where the others were—or had been—by the bright ymolenegth caused by their blood. She was alone. She—and each of the others—would have to decide on their own when the right moment to spit their projectile was.

She could see Tass now, that blackened form apparently gleefully riding the back of the giant dga. The dga continued to dig industriously. There were other holes in the Bec too, the fissures whose existence Xylo had posited. The ones they would have been able to fix, given time.

There was no time.

The water swirled around her more forcefully now. She lost track of the others and wondered if she would ever see them alive again. All seemed to be glowing, whether with blood-ymolenegth, or fire, or the light of the Ghalon she knew not. Suddenly she saw the dga rear back, throwing Tass from its back. Sadi darted forward. That was her sister. She would save her if she could. Fighting the current, Sadi slowly made her way toward the floating, blackened body of her younger half-sister.

A crash and a powerful blast of light shot through the sea. Sadi reeled as the water stopped moving. She felt nauseated. Unwittingly, she opened her mouth, and the fire capsule shot out. She saw it explode in a million pieces and settle on the Bec. Dizzily wondering if she'd just ruined everything, Sadi tried to get her bearings.

The water wasn't spinning anymore. The light had dimmed. She could barely see. She wondered if something was wrong with her eyes.

Tass.

She'd been going toward Tass, she remembered. Her arms and legs ached, and she wondered why everything suddenly hurt so badly. Looking down she saw an ambient glow surrounding her limbs, and she knew she was bleeding badly, seemingly from every pore. She wrapped her Esh-tala around her body and let herself float, trying to absorb what had happened.

What had happened?

She didn't know. She bumped into something, and by the light of the ymolenegth she decided it must be Tass. The girl's body was limp and covered entirely with blobs of darkness. Sadi opened her arms and enfolded the twelve-year-old girl and started pushing toward the surface.

Gudall, too, had accidentally expelled the fire capsule when the blow had hit the water. Vomiting blood, he didn't care if he lived or died. Where were the others? The spinning had stopped but he still felt sick. He could see the Bec now, the purple fire. The explosion of fire from the capsule had settled into the tiny cracks, sizzling there. He looked in the direction in which he thought he'd last seen the dga digging, but the enormous creature—and its rider—were gone.

Something was in its place, though. Something large and dark. Was it the hole? Was he even inside Gannoir still, or was he outside in the chaos floating in the seawater that had escaped? He wasn't sure.

Swimming toward the darkness, he put out his arms to see what would happen. He was cold. Very cold. One of his feet was bleeding badly. He looked down to see the bright ymolenegth obscuring his vision. Part of him was glad he couldn't see how badly he was hurt. The icy waters of the deep had slowed his heartbeat enough that he suspected he wouldn't bleed out. He kept swimming toward the darkness. It seemed larger than it had the last time he'd seen it.

He bumped into something rough that scraped his face. Was it ice? Mentally he rejected the idea. What, then? The Orbokth didn't extend so low, and yet it was like the rock of the Orbokth.

Then he knew.

Chapter 78: Talag

Talag groaned. Every inch of his body hurt. He tried to get up but found that he couldn't. Turning, he managed to peer through the telescope but found that it was full of water and debris. What had happened?

"Dynny?" he croaked. "Dynny?"

The old man moaned.

Talag dragged himself toward the sound. "Dynny?"

His gnomish friend didn't answer. Finally, he found the old man and wrapped his arms around him. "Don't die, Dynny. Don't die."

He didn't notice that the water was seeping into the skyboulder through the aperture of the telescope.

Chapter 79: Missing

Case, his arms still around his bride, looked up to see his father and Ieska gliding down from above, their tala outstretched and silhouetted against a fiery sky. He rubbed his wife's hand, willing her to come around.

"Is it over?" she murmured.

Case was too grateful to find her alive to answer.

Xylo and Ieska approached.

"Is it over?" Case managed to ask.

Xylo nodded. "I think so. For good or for ill, whatever was going to happen has happened."

"What happened?" Case wondered.

Shaking his head, his father answered, "We won't know for sure until we get a report back from the waters. The triads will be able to tell us if the gaping hole in the Bec was healed."

"If they're still alive," Ceres murmured. She was still lying down, unable to rise.

"Where are the others?" Xylo asked.

"You couldn't see them from above?" Case asked, sitting up and pushing himself to his feet. He looked around.

"The earthquake scattered everyone," Ieska told him. "From a distance we couldn't tell who was who. A great number of people disappeared into the forest when it hit."

"We might be the only survivors," Case realized.

Ieska scowled at him.

"Whatever happened, it wasn't the immediate destruction of Gannoir," Xylo noted with scanty optimism.

Case nodded. He ached all over, but he was alive.

Soon, a welcome sight greeted the trio. Finnan, Rhyder, and Camilly emerged from the water, seemingly none the worse.

"What happened to you?" Xylo asked.

"We were thrown into the water when the earthquake hit," Rhyder told them. "We were churned about for a bit, but once things settled down, we found each other and stayed there until we thought it was safe to make our way to shore."

"I'm glad to see you," Finnan said, directing her comment toward Ceres. "When we didn't see you in the water, we feared the worst."

"She'd have been better off in the water," Case lamented. "We were thrown onto the ground when it hit. We're pretty banged up." He cast a worried glance at his wife.

"Are you okay, Camilly?" Ieska asked.

Camilly nodded. "I just want to see everyone else. Where are they?" Her teeth were chattering, but not from cold.

"None of the triads have returned," Xylo told her. He shook his head, trying not to let the girl see he was as worried as she was.

"Rahela's missing too," Ieska noted.

"And Pax and Laetu," Camilly reminded them.

"If they were in the water when this happened, maybe they're okay," Case mused.

Xylo shrugged. "That remains to be seen. The water was hit just as hard as the land, maybe harder, depending on the depth. If what we were hoping for happened, and the gap in the Bec was healed, then the greatest destruction may have happened near the edge of the world."

"So, if they were down there . . . if any of them were near the edge . . ." Camilly fretted.

"They may still be alive," Ieska said. "Let's not lose hope."

The spectators began to emerge from the forest with various injuries, climbing laboriously over the devastated ground. No one was unscathed. And none of them understood what had happened. More people came as well, people who had been safe in their houses on the Orbokth at the time of the quake. Everyone knew that something monumental had occurred, and they all wanted to know what it was. Xylo, as acting Dynroc, was their source of authority and information. But he had few answers to give them, only speculating that a great danger had been averted. He fervently hoped it was true.

"I'm going to swim down," Finnan volunteered. "If they're hurt, they may need help to get back to the surface."

"Let's go," Rhyder agreed with his wife.

Ieska shook her head. "Give it a few minutes," he suggested. "A great fire shot from the Ghalon into the seawater. The chemical composition may have changed. It may be difficult to breathe in the new compounds until it diffuses."

Rhyder shook his head. "That makes it even more urgent that we go now. Our children are down there."

"I agree with Mom and Dad," Camilly said. "I'm going too."

"No, Camilly," Finnan objected. "I can't lose you too."

"Laetu will be okay," Camilly predicted. "And so will I. You'll need more help."

"Let her come," Rhyder decided firmly.

Ceres pushed herself up off the ground, groaning as she did so. "I'll come too."

"You can't," Case pointed out. "You can't even stand."

"I'm just bruised," Ceres contradicted him. "The others may be worse off. There are four of them. There are four of us. I have to try."

"You can argue about who's going for as long as you like," Finnan spat. "But I'm going." She dove into the placid blue liquid sea of the mine.

Ieska shook her head. "Foolhardy."

"Brave," Rhyder answered. He followed his wife.

Ceres dizzily made herself stand. "I can do this."

"You can do this," Camilly agreed, smiling wanly at her new friend. She took Ceres' hand. "Let's go."

The two made their way to the water, tiny Camilly with her long, damp red hair in sharp contrast to statuesque Ceres with her short-cropped dark hair.

Case watched his wife go with an anguished face. Xylo kept a hand on his son's shoulder lest he race into the sea after his bride. Xylo knew better than most that the seawater did nothing good to the skin of an Esh.

Chapter 80: Two

Xylo held up his hands to still the murmuring of the crowd. "My people," he began. They looked at him expectantly. "As you know, just a few months ago, the elements worked together with the Siann Dha to complete the gogyvehr, to seal the hole in the protective layer that surrounds our world."

It wasn't exactly accurate. He left out the part about Kleibald and Gelu's plans to destroy Gannoir.

"Today, you have witnessed the second round of these efforts. It was brought to my attention that there were fissures in the Bec. We are working to heal these fissures to ensure that life on Gannoir can go on for centuries just as it always has. Unfortunately, this has caused some disturbances in the Orbokth. Rest assured that we will do our best to remedy any damage that has been caused by our efforts."

"Is this going to be happening all the time?" someone called out of the crowd.

Not knowing the state of the Bec, Xylo had no way of knowing the answer to this. "We will try to give you adequate warning before any future quakes," he said vaguely. "And I apologize that this experiment startled you. Please return to your homes and go about your business."

The crowd began to drift away, much to Xylo's relief. He, Ieska, and Case stood on the shore, waiting for the others to return.

Unaleah was the first one found. Camilly and Ceres tugged her onto the shore. A trail of glowing ymolenegth trailed behind her from her bloody wounds.

"I'm going back down," Camilly said as soon as they were ashore. "Ceres, stay and take care of Unaleah."

Ceres sank down on the shore. Xylo nodded with approval, seeing that Camilly's command was not so much for Unaleah's sake as it was for Ceres'. Ceres, he suspected, was more seriously hurt than simple bruises could account for. Squeezing her long hair into a single column, Camilly dove back into the mine.

Ceres and Unaleah limped up onto the land. Unaleah was coughing and bloody. Case and Ieska helped them find a smooth boulder to sit on while Xylo rummaged in his knapsack for the healing balms he had brought with him from the Dynroc's caverns.

"I'm okay," Ceres insisted weakly. "Check Unaleah first."

"What was it like down there?" Xylo asked as he treated the deep gashes on her face and running down her side. Her Esh-tala looked like raw meat on one side of her body.

Unaleah coughed again. "Cold. Although I think the cold may have saved my life."

Ieska looked at the girl curiously.

Unaleah pushed her dripping black hair out of her face. "My body was starting to shut down," she remembered. "I could feel my blood running slower inside me. I was barely breathing. And it was hard to think." She winced as Xylo applied an herb paste to her wounds.

"What happened to the Bec?" Xylo asked. "Were you able to find the hole? How the water was seeping out so quickly?"

Unaleah spoke. "I didn't see anything. We were holding hands, Kari, Gudall, Sadi, and I. We were swimming toward the bottom of the mine, trying to get as near to the Bec as we could. We each had a fire capsule in our mouth. We'd come up with a few hand signals so we could all release the fire capsules at once. We were just waiting for the right time. We figured we'd know it when it happened."

"Were you able to release them all at once?" Xylo asked, wondering if that was what had caused the vehemence of the quake.

Unaleah frowned. "Something slammed into me. It was like nothing I've ever felt. We were holding hands and swimming downward and then suddenly we were . . . blown apart." She shook her head, shuddering. "I tried to keep the fire capsule in my mouth, but I couldn't. When it hit me . . ."

"When what hit you?" Ieska interrupted.

"I don't know. I don't know what happened. I felt the blow, like the sea itself had risen up against me, and then I was shooting toward the surface, separated from the others."

"Gaoth and Dwoyra," Case whispered.

"Was it the spinning of the vortex that split you apart?" Xylo asked.

"No," Unaleah frowned. "We were able to counter the spinning by holding onto each other and circling the epicenter of the vortex." She closed her eyes, remembering. "The water was spinning around us, but we were still. You told us what happened last time— how the fire shot down from the Ghalon onto the Bec. We were waiting for the vortex to clear the liquids of the sea from the Bec, to open an airish channel from the highest heights to the lowest depths. Once that happened, we would spit the fire capsules into the center. We were all bleeding just enough. The ymolenegth was spinning in the water. Light was surrounding us . . ." She coughed again.

"And then something hit you?" Xylo clarified.

Unaleah nodded.

"Do you think it was Dwoyra?" Ceres asked.

Xylo shook his head. "Dwoyra was causing the spin. It had to have been something—or someone—else."

"Maybe there's more than one watery being," Ieska guessed.

"It's possible," Xylo frowned.

"Maybe it was the electrical shock from the Ghalon that forced them apart," Ieska postulated. "It would have been the right time for it."

"Fire traveling down from the Ghalon . . . through the vortex, and hitting the Bec . . . it could be," Xylo mused.

"Wouldn't she have burns?" Ceres asked. She rested her head against a stray boulder and closed her eyes.

Case sat down next to his wife and smoothed her spiky hair. "She's got something there, Dad."

Xylo examined Unaleah. Her wounds were pink and oozing, but there was no indication that she had been burned. He looked worried.

"They're triad," Ieska reminded him. "Their ability to conduct electricity is far above the capacity of any of the rest of us. Electrocution might not result in burns for the triads."

Xylo nodded grimly. "Internal damage?"

"Possibly."

Ieska held Unaleah's hand. "You're going to be okay," she reassured the girl. But her eyes were full of grief and worry.

"Are the others okay?" Unaleah asked.

"You're the first one back," Xylo told her. "You didn't see any of your siblings after that blow that drove you apart?"

Unaleah shook her head. "I shot toward the surface when it hit me. That's how I got these," she said, pointing to the cuts on her face and side and her scraped tala. "I hit the Orbokth hard. It's rough. It cut me." She shook her head and began to cry. "If I got hurt this badly, what about the others? I need to know. I need them now."

Ieska brushed away her tears. "They'll be back. They'll be okay. They must be."

Xylo's heart wrenched within him. What had he done? He had brought these six young people out of their paradise and into Garradh Gannoir on a dangerous, possibly deadly mission. He loved Ieska, and yet he had asked her daughter to risk her life. His wrinkled face grew dark and thunderous. He would have appeared angry to anyone who didn't know him well.

"It's okay," Ieska said. "They all agreed to this mission. They knew what they were risking."

Xylo's expression was silent and still. He didn't respond.

"We had no choice, remember?" Ieska pressed.

Xylo bit his lip. "I know," he said heavily.

The thick golden mist in the air seemed to mirror the agony of the tiny group on the shore. They almost didn't see Rhyder and Finnan's heads break the surface. A second later, Gudall's face appeared. His eyes were glazed, and both sets of eyelids were shut. Unaleah put a hand over her mouth to stifle an agonized scream. Xylo watched them come ashore grimly.

"How badly is he hurt?" Ieska asked briskly.

"He's alive," Rhyder told her.

"Barely," Finnan added.

Ceres crawled toward the unconscious man and began to examine his injuries. He was in worse shape than Unaleah, whose wounds, though painful and ugly, seemed to be superficial. Gudall had obvious broken bones—foot, leg, rib. A trickle of blood ran from his mouth, and he gasped for air.

"Put him back in the water," Ceres ordered frantically.

The others looked at her in surprise.

"He can't breathe," Ceres insisted. "Look at him."

It was true. Gudall's skin was an unnatural color, and a gurgling noise interrupted every breath he took.

"If it's just his air-lungs that are damaged, then in the water he'll be able to breathe with his gills," Ceres explained quickly. "Hurry!"

Finnan and Rhyder eased the broken body of Gudall back into the water of the mine and shoved his head under. Instantly his labored breathing grew easier, and his normal color returned. Ceres sighed with relief. She entered the water and put pressure on Gudall's bleeding, broken foot. The bright glow of the ymolenegth surrounded the wounded leg with a disturbingly cheerful glow.

"Where did you find him?" Xylo asked.

"Nestled under the Orbokth," Rhyder told him. He pointed to Gudall's back. Bloody wounds showed through gaps in the young man's tunic. "If he experienced the same forceful blast that Unaleah did, then his story is probably a lot like hers. Hit the Orbokth hard and got hurt."

"Is he going to be okay?" Unaleah asked.

"Depends on his lungs," Ieska told her. "He's going to have to stay in the water for a time."

Finnan and Rhyder stood knee-deep in the water, keeping Gudall safe while Ceres ministered to his bleeding wounds.

Finnan scanned the shore anxiously. Xylo knew what she sought. Her son was still missing. And her daughter had not yet returned from the sea. Finnan's eyes grew more and more panicky as the minutes went by.

Rhyder scowled and glared, first at his increasingly hysterical wife and then at Xylo and Ieska.

Gudall did not wake.

They remained like that as the Ghalon turned its dark side toward them. The rains began, filling the chemical sea with its surface coating of water. Finnan's fear and Rhyder's anger faded into weariness as the hours passed. By the time half the night had passed, both were lying in the water, cradling Gudall to make sure his head remained submerged. Ceres had crept out of the water, and she and Case had fallen asleep beneath a tree in the muddy wash that had previously been a green, grassy field. The constant rain kept their faces clean, imbuing them with a look of peace and innocence that Xylo hoped permeated more than just their appearance. He sighed and looked up at the convenalations shining blearily above him in the rain.

"I see the box fish," Ieska said, pointing upward.

"It's my favorite convenalation," Xylo said.

"I know," she replied.

"Do you think the others will return?" he asked.

Ieska pressed her lips together tightly. "Two. Only two of the triads have returned, and both badly injured. Pax. Laetu. Kari. Sadi. My precious Sadi."

Xylo's heart ached. How he wished he had never tried to save the world. They would have all died, but they would have all died together, and none of it would have been his fault. "I'm sorry."

She shook her head. "You and I both know that we had no choice. The sea was being sucked into the chaos. The world would have ended and so would the lives of thousands and thousands of people. We all did what we had to do."

Xylo bobbed his head miserably. "I know."

"I wish we'd had time to do it right . . . to close the gaps scientifically, rationally, safely. But there wasn't time."

"We couldn't have brought the skyboulder back," Xylo guessed. "It was an impossibility from the start."

"Yes," Ieska admitted.

"But you pretended we could."

"There was always a chance. We would have done all we could."

"For me?"

"Yes," Ieska admitted. "But also for justice. Not only justice for Kleibald and Gelu, but justice for the others on the skyboulder. The innocents. The ones who weren't part of the evil plan to destroy the world."

"Thank you," Xylo said.

"I love you."

"I know. I love you too."

Chapter 81: Tass

Tass saw it all. Although the spirits controlled her limbs, her senses still sent messages to her brain. How eagerly she had watched the giant dga dismantle the sheath of her world.

Mailu. Mailu was out there somewhere. The spirits were on her side—they wanted to forge an opening in the Bec as badly as she did.

Still, she was itching to reclaim her body. Her soul felt cramped, all curled up in a corner of her body, waiting.

She had felt the rising excitement of the darkness upon her. They were close. They had to be close. Once they were through . . . once the hole was big enough . . .

When the blow came, Tass felt her body detach itself from the dga. The dark spirits tightened their grip on her. As if time were moving in slow-motion, Tass saw herself spinning through the water, saw the silhouette of her darkened extremities flailing against the power that she hadn't expected. She fought to breathe, but the seawater felt wrong somehow. It wasn't like any liquid she'd ever drawn into her gills.

When she opened her eyes, they stung, and she closed them again. Her arms and legs were moving, trying to swim against an impossible current. She knew from the glow of the ymolenegth around her that she was bleeding badly, but despite her desire to curl herself into a ball to protect herself, the dark spirits still had control of her. They were making everything worse.

No! She shouted to herself. *Not worse.* The darkness was on her side. They were doing what they had to do to bring Mailu back.

Mailu. Mailu.

Then her soul slid into a state of sleep within her frantically swimming body.

Chapter 82: Xylo

Firstlight came and with it came Camilly, her red head rising from the water a welcome sight, glowing under the orange light of day. Finnan heard her daughter come and cried out the anguish of her heart.

"I couldn't find any of them," Camilly said heavily. "I swam all night."

"You're safe! You're safe," Finnan wept. She embraced her daughter with one arm while still using the other to make sure Gudall stayed underwater.

"What's wrong with Gudall?" Camilly asked with a worried stare.

"Unconscious. Broken bones. Bleeding wounds," Rhyder told her shortly.

"And he's damaged his air lungs. That's why we're keeping him underwater. Breathing through his gills is his only option until he heals," Finnan added.

"Is there . . . breakfast?" Camilly asked hopefully.

Finnan almost laughed. It was such a normal, Camilly-like things for her to have said. Normalcy was something she had been missing for what felt like an eternity.

"I think you're in luck," Ieska said, picking herself off the ground and rising to stand. "Look."

Xylo also climbed to his feet and looked into the distance. A muddle of townspeople was rounding the mine bearing carts that looked heavy.

Camilly grinned. "That's what we need!"

Xylo quickly counted the people on the shore and noted that no others had arrived during the night. Finnan and Rhyder still stood guard over Gudall. An optimistic Camilly stood grinning in ankle-deep water. Ieska was by his side, Unaleah was resting a short distance away, and Case and Ceres were still asleep, huddled together peacefully.

He watched as the townspeople grew nearer. Quickly, he roused a wide-eyed Unaleah and helped her into the water. "We can't let them see your Esh-tala," he said. "They'll figure out you've been in the seawater. We can't let them know you're triad."

Unaleah slid toward Finnan and tapped her on the shoulder. Xylo saw her whisper something in the older woman's ear. Finnan nodded, and Unaleah took her place, supporting Gudall under the water so that her tala did not show. Finnan climbed out of the water and rested on a rock on the shore.

The people with the carts drew near. It was impossible for them to drag the wheeled carts over the quake-riven land, so they began to draw items out of the carts, carrying them toward the remnant on the shore.

"It is food!" Camilly exclaimed. "Oh, thank you!"

A young woman with long, light-brown hair returned Camilly's grin. "I don't care what anyone says. I'm glad the Siann Dha have come to Garradh Gannoir." She handed Camilly a plate of food.

Camilly's eyes grew wide. "Zigk-moak? Methyglyn? Not to mention halas bread, fish cakes, and salt oranges!"

"The best we had," the girl smiled back at her. "Mom and I know you're doing your best to help us."

"I'm Camilly."

"I'm Rio. And this is my mother, Mara."

An older woman who looked a lot like Rio nodded and handed a plate of food to Ieska.

"What did you mean when you said you didn't care what anyone said. What are they saying?" Xylo asked.

Rio bit her lip. "A lot of the people are upset about the earthquakes. They say you're destroying Garradh Gannoir, and it would have been better if you hadn't come. They've forgotten the prophecies. They've forgotten you're Siann Dha."

Xylo shook his head. "What do you mean by 'a lot of people'? How many can you have talked to?"

Rio looked at her mother.

"There was a gathering last night," Mara told them as a young man brought another plate of food. "The people are divided. The Siann Dha are devils, some said. Others still believe in you and your goodwill toward us. We believe. We knew you would be hungry, so we brought you food."

"Good food," Camilly exclaimed, chewing the hot, crunchy, glistening strips of zigk-moak.

Xylo was disturbed by the news of the townspeople's change of heart toward him and his people. He accepted the plate of food from the young man as others brought breakfast to Case, Ceres, Unaleah, Finnan, and Rhyder. "I'd like to be able to tell you more about what happened yesterday," he said, "but I don't have all the details myself."

At Mara's scandalized look, he amended his statement. "We're still waiting for four of our . . . emissaries . . . to return from the depths. Please assure the people that a more complete report will be forthcoming. We are on your side. And we are on the side of Gannoir."

Another young woman appeared bearing a large bowl full of rucloce berries, uncut and undiscovered. Her face was a riot of confusion.

"What's wrong?" Xylo asked.

The young woman handed the bowl of berries to Xylo and then ran a hand through her chin-length black hair. "There was a woman in the woods. She's dead . . . or dying."

"Siann Dha?" Xylo asked urgently.

"Does it matter?" the girl snapped.

"Forgive us," Ieska said quietly. "We are still missing many of our company."

The girl's expression softened. She took a deep breath. "I . . . I couldn't tell. I didn't see any tala."

Xylo and Ieska looked at each other. Then they set their food down.

"Can you lead us to her?" Ieska asked.

"Sure."

That was how they found Rahela. Her long black hair had been singed at the ends and now only reached her shoulders. Burns scored her body.

"Is she alive?" Xylo asked without hope.

"She's one of yours?" the black-haired girl asked.

Ieska nodded and bent toward Rahela. "She's Igracio's mother."

The girl's eyes grew worshipful. "Oh! That's awful!"

"She lives," Ieska noted shortly. "But she won't live long if we don't get medical care for her." She looked up at the girl. "What is your name?"

"Juli," the girl said.

"Juli, can you fetch a doctor? And medical workers? Quickly?" Ieska asked.

Juli nodded and her black hair bounced against her head.

"Hurry!" Xylo urged her.

Juli ran.

"Should we carry her over to the shore?" Xylo asked.

Ieska shook her head. "Better to wait. Juli will bring the doctor here."

Xylo nodded. "The burns . . . do you think?"

"She was with us on the shore," Ieska said thoughtfully. "She was the conduit. The Gulot element in the electrical circuit from the Ghalon down to the Bec."

Xylo shook his head. "Are you sure? The triads should have been able to accomplish it all on their own. They are all three castes, and not only that, they have an amazing power of conductivity. You said it yourself. Remember last time? All it took was Igracio. A triad."

"I don't think so," Ieska said gently.

Xylo thought. "You mean it wasn't just Igracio? It was me . . . and Afa and Tass too? Three castes plus the blood of the triad?"

"Yes," Ieska said. "I've been wondering if that was the case for a while."

"But this time no Esh was burned. No Esh is bleeding. I saw Case . . . and you and I were together . . ."

Ieska held up her hand and showed Xylo a circular burn on her palm.

He gaped at his beloved, wondering how he could not have known what she had endured while he was standing right next to her. "You? You . . . you . . . you didn't tell me."

"It was over quickly," she said. "I'm fine."

"Are you sure?"

Ieska nodded. "Maybe I have a little triad in me since I gave birth to one."

"Maybe," Xylo agreed, awed by the woman beside him. "You think Ceres was the Mayim who acted as the conduit?"

"She's badly hurt," Ieska noted. "It seems likely."

Juli returned with a doctor and medics bearing a stretcher of tough seaweed. Rahela's condition was pronounced grave, and they took her into the town to be treated. Xylo and Ieska arrived back at the shore just as Rio and Mara and the others were collecting the empty breakfast plates and leaving.

"Remember," Xylo said. "Tell your people that we are on your side. I will have more information for them later. Please."

"I will," Rio promised. "We believe you, right, Mom?"

Mara nodded. "Indeed. We want peace between our people and yours. And we believe the prophecies. The Siann Dha were always the heroes, never the villains."

Chapter 83: Talag

The shock of the cold water revived Talag, and he climbed shakily to his feet. Dynny, too, looked more alert. Talag slowly moved toward the rocky aperture to see if the debris had cleared.

He could see nothing. Darkness met his gaze, but no water was pouring from the telescope. It must be coming from somewhere else, he thought. The water glowed blue with ymolenegth, causing Talag to catch his breath. Blood. Blood of the Siann Dha. That was the only thing that could create such bright ymolenegth. He examined his own body, trying to discern if he was the source. He was bleeding and bruised, but not to the degree that would have accounted for the blinding light that surrounded him.

"Dynny!" he gasped. The water level was rising, and if they were on Gannoir, and the water was seawater, which he suspected was true, it was caustic. He had to get Dynny and himself out of the water as quickly as he could. He was immersed to his knees, but Dynny was still sitting on what had become the floor of the chamber. Talag slogged painfully over to his friend and lifted him out of the water.

The old man's skin was pink and irritated, but he wasn't bleeding much either.

"What's happening?" Dynny asked, his childlike face mournful and sad.

Talag shook his head. "I'm not sure, but I think we're home. I think we're at the bottom of the sea."

"Are we going to die?"

"Maybe," Talag said truthfully.

"We should help the others," Dynny said. "I'm supposed to take care of Mailu."

The others! Talag had been so rattled, so cold, so stunned, that he hadn't reached the place where he could evaluate their situation objectively. Forty people were onboard the skyboulder. If he and Dynny were wading in knee-deep water, what were the others doing? Were they dead? Drowning?

He glanced at the telescope wondering if that was the source of the water. If so, maybe theirs was the only chamber the water had infiltrated. He shouldn't open the door, though he badly wanted answers. The other chambers might be completely filled with caustic seawater. In that case, opening the metal door could be the last thing he ever did. And if the other chambers were dry, then opening the door would release the dangerous liquid and free it to harm the rest of the inhabitants. There was no appropriate action to take.

Talag explained his concerns to Dynny.

Dynny continued to look worried and agitated. He rubbed at his raw skin, and Talag fretted, knowing how much more slowly the old man's body healed than his own.

"Come here," he beckoned, hoisting Dynny onto the rough, rocky wall. What had once been a seat was now tilted and sideways, another factor that made Talag believe they had returned to Gannoir. The center of the skyboulder was no longer "down"—no longer the source of gravity. All of the water clung to what had once been an exterior wall, and Talag discerned that the chaos must lie in that direction.

Again, he peered through the telescope, but no light was apparent. It was all wrong. The sea glowed, even if no one was bleeding profusely. If they were immersed in the sea, then he should have been able to see light. He stuck his arm in the hole. It was a tight fit and he couldn't get it in past the elbow, largely due to his Esh-tala. He stretched his fingers as far as he could and felt them grow warm. He knew his fingertips must be glowing and he wished he could see what they illuminated.

Wincing as the rough stone of the aperture scraped at his tala, he shoved his arm in further. The tips of his fingers touched something hot—burning hot. He jerked his hand back in surprise and anguish. When he pulled his hand out of the telescope and looked at his fingers, they were blistered and oozing. He stared at them uncomprehendingly.

"What's wrong?" Dynny asked.

"Something really weird is going on," Talag replied.

Chapter 84: Xylo

Ieska saw her first. "Sadi!" she screamed in relief and joy as her daughter's head broke the surface of the water. The girl seemed to be struggling.

Xylo held his breath, wondering how badly Sadi was wounded. She was moving so slowly and laboriously that Xylo thought her condition must be quite grave.

Sadi turned her face toward them, her bright blue eyes shining and alert. Her black hair was twisted in a coil down her back. "Help me!" she called out.

Ieska ran to her daughter, ignoring the burning seawater. It was morning, so the top layer of the sea was plain rainwater, innocuous and healthy, but Xylo knew her feet and lower legs must be in agony. Sadi, now half out of the water, seemed to be tugging at something that was still immersed. Finnan and Rhyder left the care of Gudall to Ceres and rushed toward the girl.

"Go," Finnan shooed Ieska. "We've got this."

Ieska reached toward her daughter and clasped her hand as if to reassure herself that Sadi was truly alive.

"Get away!" Finnan ordered.

"Go, Mom," Sadi agreed. "Finnan and Rhyder can help me with her."

Her?

Ieska hobbled back to shore to stand beside Xylo. Her feet were blistered, he noticed, but not yet bleeding. He turned his attention toward the water, wondering whom Sadi had brought with her. Kari? he wondered. It seemed likely since, according to Unaleah, the two had been holding hands at the time of the quake. Whoever it was seemed to be a shadow, a dark form silhouetted against the merry glow of the ymolenegth. A glimpse of blond hair reassured him that it was, in fact, the missing girl. Was she dead? Xylo's heart wrenched within him.

Finnan and Rhyder lifted the limp form from the seawater and carried it gently toward the shore. Sadi followed, her stride confident and strong. Ieska embraced her daughter when she arrived on the land, tears running down her face. She examined her daughter's body, looking to see how badly she was hurt.

Sadi shook her off. "I'm okay," she said. "I'm scraped and bruised, but not badly. Worry about her." She gestured toward the dark form she had brought from the sea.

"She's burned," Rhyder guessed, looking at the blackened skin.

Finnan peered at the slight form of the girl. "Her hair . . . Poor Kari! Her hair was always so long and beautiful. But this"—she bent and ran a hand through the stubble on the girl's head—"Would electrocution have shorn her hair off to a fingertip's length all over her head?"

"Mom," Sadi shook her head. "It's not Kari."

"Then who?" Ieska frowned.

"Tass," Xylo breathed.

Rhyder rolled the girl onto her back and listened to her chest, trying to tell if Tass lived. Unlike the rest of her, Tass's face was not consumed with darkness, and they could see clearly now she was not Kari. Her eyes were closed, and her yellow skin was smooth and relaxed.

"She's alive," Rhyder proclaimed. "Her heart is beating. Her lungs are working, albeit minimally."

"Warm her up," Ieska instructed.

Finnan sat down on the shore and drew the girl onto her lap, cradling her like a baby. She laid her cheek against Tass's cold one. Xylo crouched beside them and rubbed Tass's blackened feet.

"Is she burned, do you think?" he asked Ieska.

Ieska examined Tass's skin and frowned. "Her condition is unlike any burns I've ever seen. But with electrocution . . ." She let her voice trail off. "I just don't know. I've never seen anything like this."

"Is she warming up?" Xylo said to Finnan.

Finnan shook her head. "She's ice cold. It's probably why she's still alive. Her body hasn't had time to react to the injuries with death."

"Should we be trying to warm her up?" Case asked.

"We can't keep her on ice forever," Ieska said briskly. "She'll die of the cold eventually, even if the wounds never catch up with her."

Sadi sat down beside the group that hovered around Tass. "I need to tell you what I saw down there. Besides finding Tass."

All eyes turned toward the dark-haired girl.

Sadi continued. "Something slammed into us," she reported. "We were holding hands and . . ."

"Unaleah told us about the blast," Ieska interrupted. "Did you see what caused it?"

"Not at first," Sadi reported. "I felt myself somersaulting through the water away from the others. I couldn't tell what happened to them." She looked toward Unaleah who was resting on the shore with a glazed, pained expression, and then at Gudall under the shallow water. "Are they okay? And where's Kari?"

"Unaleah's got internal injuries, we believe," Ieska told her. "Gudall's worse. Broken bones and his air-lungs were damaged. He'll have to stay in the water until he heals."

"And Kari?"

"Not back yet," Rhyder told her grimly.

"Keep telling us what happened to you," Xylo urged her.

Sadi took a deep breath and then coughed. "Sorry. The chemical composition of the water was barely breathable." She sighed and took another deep breath of the misty air. "Like I said, the blast separated us from each other. I lost the fire capsule when it happened. It was like getting punched in the gut. There was nothing I could do. It didn't hurt me, though. I went back to see if I could find the others. I had a rough idea of which direction was 'back.' I could see the purple flames in the distance as well as something else." She hesitated.

"What? What was it?" Case urged her on.

Sadi scrunched up her face. "There was a gap in the Bec. Not like the dark gap we'd seen before. It was so strange. It's going to sound crazy, but it looked like the Ghalon at night, only the convenalations running through it were blue instead of red. Because of the extreme cold, I couldn't get close enough to investigate, but I've never seen anything like it before. And all the little holes in the

Bec—the black blotches we'd seen before—were gone. The purple fire was solid all around except for the gap with the blue lines running through it."

"Something electrical, do you think?" Rhyder asked.

"With everything that's happened that sounds like a logical assumption," Ieska mused.

"Maybe Sadi saw the electricity knitting the Bec back together," Finnan suggested hopefully, still holding Tass tightly.

"Blue . . . blue, you say?" Xylo asked.

Sadi nodded.

"Flickering light? Or steady," Xylo pressed.

"Steady."

Xylo's face convulsed with untold and unsorted emotion.

"What is it?" Ieska asked, seeing his agitation.

"I think I know what it is," he whispered.

The others looked at him expectantly.

"We did it," he declared hoarsely. "We did it."

"What?" Rhyder almost shouted.

"The skyboulder. The skyboulder is plugging the hole in the Bec!" Xylo chortled. "That has to be it!"

"And the blue glow?" Case asked.

"Blood," Xylo said grimly. "There were many people onboard the skyboulder. Dozens. And if this is the sort of wounds that happened to those in the water," he gestured toward Unaleah, Gudall, and Tass, "Then it's not unreasonable to assume that those on the skyboulder have serious injuries. Bloody injuries."

"And the skyboulder was cracked during the impact . . ." Case breathed.

"Then the blood is seeping into the water and creating ymolenegth," Rhyder finished.

"We have to help them!" Sadi declared.

Xylo looked out at Ceres holding Gudall. "There's little hope that anyone survived," he told the others bluntly.

Ieska put a hand on his arm. "There may be a chance," she said.

All eyes turned toward her.

"I did some calculations when I was working on the plan to bring back the skyboulder," she said. "The extreme conditions at the brink of the world would result in a state of matter—a state of space-time, actually—where time actually moves more slowly than it does on the surface."

"What are you saying? That they may still be in the process of dying? Not actually dead?" Xylo said with wonder.

Ieska nodded. "Rescue will be a delicate operation. Once we bring them into the warmer waters even a few dozen body lengths from the Bec they will begin to die. If we can get them out quickly, if we can bring them medical care quickly . . ."

"And air," Case reminded her. "Many of them are Esh, Gulot, or uncasted people from Garradh Gannoir. They don't have gills."

"We can work on that," Rhyder said, leaping to his feet. "I still have a supply of fire-capsules. They can bring both warmth and air to the depths."

"How long do you think we have?" Xylo asked Ieska.

Ieska pondered. "It's hard to tell. It depends on how slowly time is running at the brink, and on how much water has already entered the skyboulder."

"You think some may have drowned already?" Case asked.

"Yes. Certainly, if the evidence of the cracks in the skyboulder is any indication. They are bleeding and their vehicle is not watertight," Ieska answered.

"How quickly . . ." Xylo began.

"As fast as we can," Rhyder answered. "I'll head for the lab. Case . . ."

But the young man was already on his feet to follow.

"I'm coming too," Sadi said.

"Me too," Finnan agreed. "That is, if Ceres can keep sitting with Gudall." She looked at the younger woman, who was herself so gravely wounded.

"I can," Ceres said gently. "Go."

Chapter 85: Rescue

Xylo had moved everyone except Ceres and Gudall back to the caves of the Dynroc. It was better that the triads remain hidden. Gudall, submerged, could easily hide his Esh-tala. Finnan had retreated there with them to oversee their care. The citizens of Garradh Gannoir continued to bring food, despite the division in their community. By the time the team of Mayim arrived from Luca, bent on helping Xylo retrieve the skyboulder, their task was clear.

The Master had sent fifteen of the Mayim to be part of the rescue, among them Tass's former rival Sarhi, the deep-diver Bizu Xarmam, and Meb Oneira, one of the teachers at the Calix. It was a coordinated effort, largely directed by Xylo and Dwoyra. With lumalauae and vauzigks to provide warmth, the Mayim had no trouble swimming down to the skyboulder. Rhyder's modified capsules would bring air to those who hadn't gills so that they were able to reach the surface, if not safely, at least alive.

Xylo stood on the shore with Ieska and Camilly, ready to receive those whom the Mayim brought to the surface, to assess their condition, or to shroud them for burial.

One by one, desolate students of the Calix came to the surface bearing the bodies of the dead. Those who had been in the two chambers of the skyboulder that had cracked, allowing for an exchange of blood and water, were dead.

"We're not going to find anyone alive," Bizu mourned, flexing his long fingers and rubbing them to dispel the cold. Fifteen bodies were laid out on the shoreline, wrapped in cloths of woven seaweed. Gaoth, the rational wind, swirled around the bodies, forcing his airish fingers to probe their lungs, trying to restore them to life. But it was too late.

The next trip brought happier news. Six Mayim who had been aboard the skyboulder were dragged into the air, five of them injured, but alive.

"It's because we can breathe under the water," Meb Oneira said. "They are bruised and battered from the impact, but they survived because they could breathe down there."

"And because of the cold," Rhyder added. He and Camilly were participating in the rescue with the other Mayim.

Meb Oneira nodded. "I would never have expected something so deadly to be so life-giving."

"How many more chambers can there by on the skyboulder?" Camilly wondered.

One of the Mayim rescuers shook her shorn head. "Who knows? We've only emptied two rooms."

"There are eight rooms . . . ten compartments . . ." one of the rescued Mayim boys reported weakly. "Go quickly. Please. There are others. Forty of us onboard."

"And we've only brought back twenty-one, dead and alive," Rhyder noted.

"Nineteen others," Camilly said. "Let's go!"

The doors were stuck shut, and the opening of the next chamber was a perilous business, as the violent force needed to shatter the stone of the skyboulder had to be tempered by the idea that there might be living people just on the other side of the wall. It was dangerous for rescuers and rescuees alike, as the rescuers had to leave the life-giving warmth of the embrace of the lumalauae and vauzigks in order to break through the rock. The Mayim took turns going down, working, and then surfacing to let others take their place. Hours passed and day turned into night as they worked tirelessly on behalf of the remaining nineteen people.

As they broke into the first chamber, the icy water flooded it, and they realized that it had not been underwater before that. Eight of the ten people in the room were alive at the time the cold water inundated the chamber. By the time they were brought out, only five lived—Xylo's son-in-law Nadim, and four citizens of Garradh Gannoir—Minnidair, Benet and his wife Glenna, and a woman named Estraya. All were badly injured and were taken to medical facilities in Garradh Gannoir. Kleibald, his wife Ardanach, and Xylo's son Gryf were among the dead.

"That's nine more we have to find," Camilly proclaimed.

"There was air in that last chamber," Ieska noted. "There's hope yet. With the slowing of time and the cold, we may find survivors yet."

The exhausted Mayim continued their work. They had split into three teams now, so that at any point in time, one team was hammering away at the skyboulder, another was waiting onshore for their turn, and a third was sleeping. Xylo and Ieska took no rest, nor did Finnan back at the Dynroc's caves, as she tended Unaleah and Tass.

Rhyder surfaced with a young man clasped in his arms, a metallic capsule pressed to his mouth so he could breathe. The boy, though his skin was blistered from the caustic seawater, seemed less injured than most of the others. The girl that Camilly brought a second later was the same. They were able to stand as soon as they were brought to shore, and they hugged each other desperately.

"How were they able to escape with so few injuries?" Xylo asked.

Camilly giggled. "They were in the bathroom. It was small and they didn't get banged up as much."

"Together?" Ieska asked, raising her eyebrows.

Xylo grinned, glad of any positive note in the grim rescue. "They seem to like each other," he noted, looking at the couple who were embracing on the shore.

"He's Esh," Camilly noted.

"She's Gulot. It's not unheard-of," Ieska chastised her.

Ceres looked over at them from her place in the water. "I don't think she's Gulot. She looks familiar. I've seen her here in Garradh Gannoir."

"She's one of . . . them?" Rhyder asked, aghast.

"It would be a first," Xylo noted, looking at Ieska with a twinkle in his eye.

"A Siann Dha involved with one of the uncasted? It's . . . it's . . ." Rhyder sputtered.

"Beautiful?" Ieska suggested.

"Come on, Dad," Camilly said. "We need to dive again. There are still seven in the skyboulder."

"Not you," Ieska said firmly. "It's your turn to rest. Let someone else go."

The rescue continued.

"We found the food storage room," an exhausted Mayim reported upon surfacing. "Three people were inside—one dead and two living. The others are bringing them."

Sarhi came to the surface with a young girl in her arms. She was followed quickly by an older Mayim boy dragging a woman. Both were badly injured, but alive.

Xylo watched the medics from Garradh Gannoir tote them away. His face was drawn and haggard.

"You recognize them?" Ieska asked.

He nodded. "I didn't know either of them before I saw them enter the skyboulder," he said. "But I would know them anywhere. The girl is my granddaughter. And the woman is her mother, my daughter-in-law." He felt as though he couldn't breathe, so great was his anguish.

"They're alive," Ieska pointed out.

"For how long?" Xylo asked, not daring to hope.

Bizu surfaced next bearing the body of Xylo's daughter, Aythylla. Xylo fell to his knees and put his face in his hands. Despite their estrangement, somewhere deep down, he had always hoped for . . . something. Not this. Both his son and his daughter, the children of his first marriage, were dead. Case and Ieska strove to comfort him.

He let them.

Chapter 86: Talag

Talag heard the pounding, the crashing, the rushing of water as the other compartments on the skyboulder were destroyed and flooded. Talag hardly dared hope that rescue was at hand. He didn't want to get his hopes up. More than likely, the pressure and temperature of the water at the edge of Gannoir was shattering the structure of the skyboulder. One by one the different chambers filled with water. His would be next. He and Dynny would drown like all the others before them. Trapped at the edge of the world beneath a frigid sea.

The pounding was nearer now. He could discern differences in the noises. Bang. Scrape. Pick. Slam. His heart leapt. Surely the sea would not make such a variety of noises. It would be one quick crack and the end would come.

A trickle of seawater dribbled down from what was now the top of the room. Talag held Dynny's hand and watched it. Already his legs were blistered and bloody. He'd managed to prop his body against one wall of the chamber, propping Dynny up so that the old man wasn't subjected to the chemical sea. But he could not hoist himself without dropping his friend, so he hadn't tried.

"Please," he pleaded to whomever might be able to hear his thoughts. "Please." He thought briefly of Tel-Maor, trapped in the Ghalon at the core of Gannoir. He was a spirit, wasn't he? The spirits of the chaos had been able to communicate with him while he was on the skyboulder. Wasn't it possible that Tel-Maor could hear him even where he was, presumably at the bottom of the sea?

There was no "presumably" about it, he knew. The water was rushing in forcefully now, filled with a variety of colors of ymolenegth. That meant a lot of blood. Blood in the water. Light is life, and light comes from blood. He wondered if Kleibald and Gelu had made it out alive. It was a foolish thought. No one could have survived both the crash and the seawater. They must be dead.

He pushed himself higher on the wall, getting as close to Dynny as he could.

"What's happening?" Dynny's frightened voice asked him.

"I don't know," he replied. "But whatever it is, it's happening now."

The wall with the telescope crumbled, and something silvery popped out of the aperture. Talag barely had time to notice it before something grabbed him. Another silvery object was thrust in his face. He fought against his attacker. He couldn't see, couldn't breathe. The water was all around him. He wriggled and tried to look around. The water burned his eyes. He saw the impossible. Long, snake-like fish swirled around him and around Dynny. A blubbery vauzigk snuffled at his collar. Comforting hands patted his arms and dragged him closer to the sea creatures.

This was rescue, not death.

Or at least not yet.

Talag gave himself over to the person he had thought was attacking him. It doesn't matter, he thought. It doesn't matter what they do. I can't hold my breath any longer. I can't. I'm going to breathe the seawater. I'll die. I'll die.

When he could stand it no longer, he opened his mouth and drew in a frantic breath. His rescuer shoved a silver orb against his face, and he felt not the acidic taste of death, but the breath of life. He shut his eyes and let himself go limp. He felt his rescuer dragging him through the water, felt it grow warmer and warmer as they ascended. He was beyond anxiety. Whatever was going to happen was going to happen, without his approval or permission. There was nothing he could do.

After what seemed like a long time, he felt someone pulling the orb away from his face, and he panicked. He flailed his arms, trying to bring it back. They had saved him, but now they were trying to kill him. He kicked frantically, opening his eyes to see where the silvery mechanism had gone.

"You're safe, boy! Stop kicking!" someone hollered.

Talag drew a ragged breath and found that it was true. He could breathe. Every inch of his skin felt raw and stinging, but he was alive. He was out of the sea. He had made it.

"Dynny?" he croaked. "Where's Dynny?"

"They took him to the medical facility," a woman told him. She stood in the water, but her red hair was long and un-Mayim-like.

"Is he going to be okay?" he managed to ask, looking up at her.

"They'll do what they can," she replied, leading the staggering boy out of the sea.

He collapsed on the shore, exhausted, spent, and aching. He heard someone say, "It's him! It's the boy!" and after that he remembered nothing.

When Talag came to his senses hours later, he had only a vague recollection of the journey over the fractured shoreline via stretcher and the trip to the medical facility. Now he lay on a cot. Bandages covered his body and he'd been given clean, dry clothing to wear.

He looked around. He was in a long room, obviously carved out of the rock of the Orbokth. The stone walls had been smoothed and painted white, and he could see other people occupying cots in rows extending as far as he could see. He tried to sit up, but the motion irritated his burned skin. He was terrified. Where was he? Where was everyone? Was he the only survivor?

Logic told him that some of the others must have survived. That must be the meaning of the rows and rows of cots. A man was sitting on a stool next to his cot, something he hadn't noticed initially. The man sat very still, and his face was devoid of emotion.

"Who are you?" he asked. His throat hurt.

A light leapt into the man's eyes. "My name is Xylo," he said. "Who are you?"

"Talag."

"Your full name," the man requested.

Talag wondered what kind of strange examination this was. Oughtn't he be allowed to rest? But he complied. "Talag Dineaweth Xalantaka," he told the elderly man.

The man nodded. "My full name is Adam Anuilon Xalantaka."

"That's like my name," Talag said. "Xalantaka."

"It should be," Xylo told him. "I'm your grandfather."

Talag was confused. He had two grandfathers, his mother's father, and his father's father. His mother's father, Grandfather Dineaweth, had died before he was born. His other grandfather was

Kleibald. Was this man Kleibald? Had he transformed himself somehow through his ordeal in the water and in the chaos? He looked at the old man fearfully. "Grandfather?"

"Gryf Tolmara Xalantaka was my son," Xylo replied.

Talag shook his head. "My father was the son of Kleibald the Reformer," he said.

"Kleibald married my wife after she left me," Xylo told him. "He raised my children, Gryf and Aythylla. I am your grandfather. I'm sorry we never met before this. I didn't know you existed."

"Kleibald isn't my grandfather?" Talag asked, confused. If this was true, he would be happy. He no longer wanted anything to do with Kleibald.

"He never was," Xylo said.

Talag tried to examine the man who said he was his grandfather, but his eyes were dry and scaly, and he was too tired to think. Only one thought occupied his overwhelmed mind. "The others . . ." he said. "Did they survive? Did anyone make it out of the skyboulder?"

"Eighteen people are still alive," Xylo told him.

"Eighteen," Talag echoed. "Eighteen out of forty." His heart wrenched. "Who? Please . . . who?"

"We don't know the names of most of the survivors. Or most of the dead, for that matter. But your sister lives. And your mother," Xylo told him.

"And my father?"

Xylo shook his head. "I'm sorry."

"What about my gr . . . what about Kleibald?"

"He also perished," Xylo said.

Talag opened his eyes. "I'm glad," he said.

Xylo looked at him questioningly.

"Grand . . . I mean, Kleibald was trying to destroy Gannoir. I'm glad he's dead. Did Gelu die too?" he asked, sure that if justice had seen fit to rid Gannoir of his non-grandfather, then surely Gelu must have perished also.

"He was the last one we rescued," Xylo told him. "Gelu lives."

Talag closed his eyes. "He was the one who planned this," he told his new grandfather. "I thought my gr . . . Kleibald . . . was the one, but it was Gelu all along."

Xylo's eyes widened in surprise. "Gelu? Gelu planned this?"

"Gelu and the spirits from the chaos. And Kleibald. But Gelu was in charge."

Xylo nodded thoughtfully. "Thank you. This will help us as we try to move forward." He got up to leave.

"Please," Talag rasped. "Please . . . Dynny . . . the little man . . . elderly . . . did he . . . is he . . ." He couldn't bring himself to ask the question.

"He lives," Xylo told him.

Talag felt his body relax. Dynny was alive!

It was everything.

Chapter 87: Last things

A week passed before Dynny and Talag were reunited. They were both still scabby and sore but breathing more easily and able to move about.

Xylo had watched his grandson carefully, wondering what sort of boy he was. His granddaughter, Donamys, he had already dismissed as being just like his ex-wife. She was spoiled and demanding, thinking only of herself. The main reason she and her mother had survived was because they had been in the process of stealing food in the storage room when the skyboulder crashed into the Bec. The tiny room was sealed tightly against the seawater, and it was such a small space that their injuries were few. The mother was weak and whiny, and Donamys, loud and demanding. Maybe one day they could get to know each other, but not now. However, Xylo had hopes for a relationship with Talag.

Once Dynny and Talag were released from the medical facility, Xylo approached them. "Dynny," he began, "I know you will want to come back and resume your duties as the Dynroc of Gannoir as soon as possible." He turned to Talag. "I was wondering if you would like to come too. You could become better acquainted not just with me, but with my son, Case, and his wife, and my fiancée."

Dynny shook his head sadly. "Not the Dynroc. I'm not the Dynroc."

"You are!" Xylo exclaimed. "Arros handed down the power of the Dynroc to you. Just because I've been the acting Dynroc in your absence doesn't mean that . . ."

Talag interrupted him. "He's right, grandfather. He's not the Dynroc anymore."

"What do you mean?

Talag explained what had happened on the skyboulder, how the power had switched from Dynny to himself. "I'd be glad to come back to the caves of the Dynroc," he finished. "I don't want to be the Dynroc, but it seems that I have no choice. And," he said, smiling at Xylo, "I do want to get to know the other side of my family."

***

By the end of the second week, most of the survivors of the crash had recovered enough to leave the medical facility.

Dynny and Talag had gone back to the caverns of the Dynroc with Xylo.

Ceres remained in Obumbro for several weeks longer, recovering from the electrocution that had permanently implanted the skyboulder in the Bec layer and closed the miniscule gaps through which the darkness had been entering Gannoir.

Rahela also remained hospitalized in a coma. Her husband and son had come to Obumbro to be with her.

Talag's mother, Milis, and his sister, Donamys, had gone back to Luca with his uncle Nadim. Xylo had a suspicion that Nadim would become the next Esh-maor, and he worried over it.

The five surviving Mayim occupants of the skyboulder also went back to Luca. Five were imprisoned on charges of conspiring to destroy the world—Gelu, a young man of Obumbro named Benet, Gelu's advisors, Lefty and Minnidair, and Lefty's wife, Estraya. Minnidair's husband had died in the catastrophe.

The other citizens of Garradh Gannoir—Benet's wife Glenna, and the unlikely couple, the Esh boy and the uncasted girl, were released to go home. The Esh boy had vowed to become a citizen of Garradh Gannoir and live his life among the uncasted. Already the girl's family worshipped him.

Tass was the most grievously injured. Her skin was still blackened, and she didn't wake.

"I'm taking her back to Cudth Deorth," Ieska decided. "She should be among family."

Xylo agreed. If anyone could bring Tass back to life, it was the four remaining triads. Kari, Pax, and Laetu had never returned. Xylo was hopeful that they were still out there somewhere, alive, but lost, but the others seemed to have lost hope. Even Finnan, he noted, seemed to find it too painful to keep hoping.

Mailu's stone and glass sarcophagus had floated to the surface six days after the rescue was completed. Her body was intact. The water had not penetrated the seal. And her belly was swollen with new life. Ieska took Mailu, coffin and all, to Cudth Deorth with the others.

As a people, they were broken.

But the world, the thing that mattered, was whole.

To be continued . . .

A Prelude to

Refraction

Book 3 of the Illumination of the Siann Dha

Darkness. Just darkness. She couldn't see. She couldn't hear. The only sensation Tass had was of the voices, the eternal, inexorable voices whispering, shouting, seductively uttering obscenities in her mind. The voices had consumed her. She was nothing and they were all. But somewhere, buried deep within all that she was, Tass was still herself. She was still Talassa Galan, best swimmer at the Calix, sister of Mailu, heroine of Garradh Gannoir. Somewhere. Somehow.

She waited, like a caterpillar in a cocoon, waiting for her rebirth. This couldn't be eternity. It couldn't. Trapped in a corner of her body, in a corner of her mind, she was a tiny grain of Tass, ready to come to life again.

Appendix A: Characters

Adam "Xylo" Xalantaka (A-dum (ZIE-low) zuh-LAN-tuh-kuh): elderly Esh who is now the acting Dynroc of Garradh Gannoir

Afa (Bracha) Elisus (AH-fuh ELL-ih-sus): Tass's mother, deceased

Amathys Warnder (A-muh-thiss WARN-dur): Student at the Calix

Ana Millton (ANN-uh MILL-ton): Student at the Calix

Aradamas Aonta (are-ODD-uh-mus ay-ON-tuh): one of Kleibald's henchmen

Ardanach (ARE-dan-ack): Kleibald's current wife; Xylo's ex-wife; mother of Gryf, Aythylla, and Dochym

Arros (AIR-ahs): The 58th Dynroc, deceased

Arth Mathan (ARTH mah-THAN): member of the elder council of Luca

Aythylla Tolmara Xalantaka (ay-THILL-uh toll-MAR-uh zuh-LAN-tuh-kuh): Daughter of Xylo and Ardanach

Benet (BEN-et): uncasted man from Garradh Gannoir

Bizu Xarmam (BIH-zoo ZAHR-mam): Student at the Calix

Bridima Iommy Metuenu (brih-DEE-muh EYE-oh-mee met-oo-AY-no): Mother of Unaleah and adoptive mother of Ninach; one of the matriarchs of the band of triads

Byid Aphanista Pendefeth (BEAD AH-fan-ee-stuh pen-DAY-feth): Pax's twelve-year-old brother

Caedi Aphanista (KAY-dee AH-fan-ee-stuh): Deceased mother of Pax and Byid

Camilly Louloudi Efteri (kuh-MILL-ee loo-LOO-dee eff-TARE-ee): Mayim daughter of Finnan and Rhyder

Caro Sapor "Case" Xalantaka (CAR-oh suh-PORE zuh-LAN-tuh-kuh): Xylo's son; Esh

Ceci Maraena Suergas (SEE-see muh-RAY-nuh SHARE-gus): Gelu's wife

Ceres Klee (SAY-rees CLAY): Mayim wife of Case

Chwerta Sapor (SHWEAR-tuh suh-PORE): Xylo's second wife; mother of Caro and Yasamina

Dallasha Budach (doll-AH-shuh BOO-dock): member of the elder council of Luca

Dano Eidales (DAN-oh eye-DAL-ess): Xylo's son-in-law; married to Yasamina

Dochym Tolmara Xalantaka (doe-KEEM toll-MAR-uh zuh-LAN-tuh-kuh): Died at age 4; Son of Xylo and Ardanach

Donamys Dineaweth Xalantaka (DOH-nuh-mis din-AY-uh-weth zuh-LAN-tuh-kuh): Talag's sister

Dwoyra (DOO-y-r-ra (roll the "r")): the rational water (pronunciation is approximate; hard to replicate with lungs instead of gills)

Dynny (DIN-ee): Mentally disabled elderly man who has been named the 59th Dynroc

Estraya Androkas (ess-TRAY-uh AND-roh-koss): Lefty's wife

Finnan Ruadhi Louloudi (FINN-ann roo-ODD-ee loo-LOO-dee): Mother of Laetu and Camilly and wife of Rhyder; Mayim

Frigo Nerhial (FREE-go ner-I-ull): member of the elder council of Luca

Gaoth (GAY-oth): the rational wind

Gelu Pagos (GAY-lue puh-GOHS): Leader of the people in Garradh Gannoir

Glenna Prasinus (GLEN-uh PRAH-sin-us): Benet's wife

Gryf Tolmara Xalantaka (GRIFF zuh-LAN-tuh-kuh): Son of Xylo and Ardanach; governor of the Nepell clatry

Gudall Metuenu-Nayro (GOO-doll met-oo-AY-no NAY-roh): Twenty-four-year-old triad, adopted son of Bridima

Hamell Barat (HA-mel bah-RAHT): Deceased cousin of the Barat family

Ieska Thayl (YES-kuh THALE): Esh-maor scientist in Luca, one of the matriarchs of the band of triads

Igracio Barat (i-GRAH-see-oh bah-RAHT): Gave his life for Gannoir some months earlier

Juli (JOO-lee): uncasted citizen of Garradh Gannoir

Kari Coffya Ansidla (CARE-ee coff-EE-uh ann-SEED-luh): Sixteen-year-old triad, daughter of Widman

Kleibald (CLAY-bald): the Esh-Maor; leader of Luca

Laetu Louloudi Efteri (LIE-too loo-LOO-dee eff-TARE-ee): Thirteen-year-old triad; son of Finnan and Rhyder

Laso Barat (la-SOH bah-RAHT): Igracio's father

Lefty Binsaid (LEF-tee BIN-suh-eed): Friend and advisor of Gelu

Mailu Elisus Harreg (my-LOU ELL-ih-sus hah-REG): Tass's sister

Mara (MAR-uh): uncasted citizen of Garradh Gannoir; Rio's mother

the Master: Runs the Calix, the school for the Mayim

Meb Oneira (MEB oh-NAY-ruh): Teacher at the Calix

Methiant Migas (Mantais Nayro) (METH-ee-unt MEE-gus/man-TIE-us NAY-roh): Petty criminal subject to nefarious experiments that resulted his destruction, soul and body

Milis Dineaweth (MILL-iss din-AY-uh-weth): Gryf's wife and Talag's mother

Minnidair (MIN-ih-dayr): uncasted woman of Garradh Gannoir

Nadim (nuh-DEEM): Aythylla's husband and next in line to be the Esh-Maor of Luca

Ninach Ansidla-Nayro (NIE-nock ann-SEED-luh NAY-roh): Nineteen-year-old triad; adopted daughter of Widman

Pax Aphanista Nayro (PAX AH-fan-ee-stuh NAY-roh): Fourteen-year-old triad; brother of Byid

Peodar Barat (PAY-oh-dahr bah-RAHT): Igracio's brother

Rahela Barat (ruh-HAY-luh bah-RAHT): Igracio's mother, now a member of the team trying to save their world once again

Rio (REE-oh): uncasted citizen of Garradh Gannoir

Rhyder Efteri (RIDE-er eff-TARE-ee): Father of Laetu and Camilly, husband of Finnan; Mayim

Saoradi "Sadi" Thayl Nayro (shore-AH-di "SAY-dee" THAYL NAY-roh): Ieska's daughter, one of the triads

Sarhi (SAHR-ee): Student at the Calix

Talag Dineaweth Xalantaka (tuh-LAG din-AY-uh-weth zuh-LAN-tuh-kuh): Son of Gryf and Milis, grandson of Xylo, step-grandson of Kleibald, and hopeful savior of those aboard the skyboulder

Talassa (Katurima) Galan (tuh-LA-suh (kah-TUR-i-muh) guh-LAWN): Twelve-year-old Mayim who doesn't want to be wanted just for her blood.

Tel-Maor (TELL may-OR): the god-like being who supposedly lives in the Ghalon

Torcalon Nayro (TOR-cuh-lawn NAY-roh): Father of Methiant Migas and ferryman for the triads

Tsakali Oeloor (tsuh-CALL-ee WEE-lore): member of the elder council of Luca

Unaleah Metuenu Dion (oo-nuh-LEE-uh met-oo-AY-no DEE-on): Twenty-five-year-old triad, daughter of Bridima

Widman Xunisso Ansidla (WID-man zoo-NEE-soh ann-SEED-luh): Kari's father

Yasamina Sapor Xalantaka (yeah-suh-MEE-nuh zuh-LAN-tuh-kuh): Daughter of Xylo and his second wife, Chwerta; married to Dano

Appendix B: Places

Calix (CA-licks): School for the Mayim

Cudth Deorth (KOODTH DAY-orth): the secret verdant valley where the triads live

Gannoir (gan-oh-EAR): Heavenly body upon which the story takes place

Garradh Gannoir (guh-RAD gan-oh-EAR): Open area within the body of Gannoir where Gelu is the leader and no one is casted

Lachar (luh-CAR): Training college for the Esh-maor

Luca (LOO-kuh): Open area within the body of Gannoir where the four main characters live

Lucedth (loo-SAIDTH): Capital city of Luca

Nepell (neh-PELL): Clatry over which Gryf Xalantaka is the governor

Nozoffi (no-zo-FEE): Clatry that holds the school for the Esh-maor

Obumbro (ah-BUM-bro): Main city in Garradh Gannoir

the Rhosen (ROW-zen): reddish clatries at the far side of Luca, mostly agricultural

Rhosen Faide (ROW-zen FIDE): the farthest clatry of the Rhosen

Zafir (zuh-FEER): Clatry on which the Calix is located

Appendix C: Glossary

Bec (BECK): Soulish layer of ice on the exterior of Gannoir

beakfish: small predatory fish

Bilik (BILL-ick): Hole in the bottom of the sea

bonefish: fish with a crusty, marbled exoskeleton

cincinny fish: yellow fish with long, curly fins

clatry (CLAT-ree): Lattice of super hard stone that floats atop the water in Luca; cities are built atop it

convenalation (CON-ven-ih-lay-shun): Constellation made by cracks in the dark side of the Orbokth through which red fire gleams

dga (JAW (but the "j" has a little "d" in it)): Insect-like fish with a hard, metallic exoskeleton

dulcimel (DULL-sih-mell): Berries that are made into wine; too sweet to ear without processing

Dynroc (DIN-rock): Spiritual leader of the people of Garradh Gannoir

Esh (ESH): People of the fire caste

Esh-maor (ESH may-OR): Leadership caste

Esh-Maor (ESH may-OR): The title for the leader of Luca

Esh-qadar (ESH kuh-DAR): Ordinary people of the fire caste; often soil miners

Feollyr (fay-oh-LEAR): rodenty creature only found in Cudth Deorth

fuuegn (FOO-ain): Sweet-tasting fungus grown in the midlands of the Orbokth

Ghalon (guh-LAWN): Ball of fire at the core of Gannoir

ghloam (GLOWM): The time when the light has just left the sky and night has begun

globus (GLOW-bus): Spherical mass of jelly-like tissue that puffs along by spewing liquid; covered in glowing dots of color; about 4 inches long

gogyvehr (GO-gih-vair): The catastrophe that turned Gannoir inside-out

Gulot (GOO-lot): People of the earth or land caste

gwynant (GOO-ee-nant): Whipped sea-tree oil; Usually spread on bread

halas bread (HALL-uss BRED): Plain biscuit-like bread made from pellig flour

iridis (EAR-ih-dis): Rainbow shimmer that lights the skin of the Esh

lumalaua (LOO-muh-low-uh ("low" as in "allow")): Sea creature shaped like an eel; feathered, with phosphorescent appendages; magenta at the head, fading to pink, orange, and then yellow at the tail;

Mayim (my-EEM): People of the lowly water caste

mellila shrimp (meh-LEE-luh): make honey

methyglyn (METH-ih-glin): Alcoholic beverage made from mellila

mhowis goat (MOW-iss GOAT): Thick-bodied goat-like mammal that lives in the heights of the Orbokth

Orbokth (OR-bawkth): The rocky borderlands at the edges of the sea

pellig (PELL-ig): Type of sea-tree. The bark is stripped, dried, and ground into flour

ribbon snails: Mollusks with tentacles

rucloce (roo-CLOWSH): Blue-foliaged plant that produces large, waxy white berries with a variety of flavors and colors at the center

salt orange: grows in the sea

sarxworms: aquatic worms that are a good source of protein

scolopendra (skah-low-PEN-druh): Like giant flying centipedes with membranous wings

sea bramble: aquatic tumbleweed

sea reeds: useful sea plant similar to bamboo but thinner

sea-string: Webbing made by sea spiders

seagrass: They make mats out of it

Siann Dha (shawn DAH): The "Old Ones"—people with fire in their blood

tala (TAH-luh): Webbing either between the fingers of the Mayim or between the limbs and body of the Esh

ugaz (OOH-gaz): Life-form with a mammalian body and a vegetable soul; has no head

vauzigk (VOW-zik): Blubbery sea creature similar to pinnipeds

vervol (VAIR-voll): flying creatures similar to salamanders

ymolenegth (im-MALL-in-eth ("th" like "the")): Blue glow in the sea; Blood keeps it glowing

yovod (yoh-VAHD): Big cat that roams the heights of the Orbokth

zigk-moak (ZIG moke): Delicacy made from the charred flesh of the vauzigk

Appendix D: Triad Family Tree

Unaleah Metuenu Dion, age 25
> Mother: Bridima Iommy Metuenu
> Acting father: Arx Dipheyn Dion (deceased; not named in book)

Gudall Metuenu-Nayro, age 24
> Mother: not named in book
> Adopted by: Bridima Iommy Metuenu

Saoradi "Sadi" Thayl Nayro, age 22
> Mother: Ieska Thayl

Ninach Ansidla-Nayro, age 19
> Mother: not named in the book
> Adopted by: Widman Xunisso Ansidla

Kari Coffya Ansidla, age 16
> Mother: Tueema Coffya (not named in the book)
> Adoptive father: Widman Xunisso Ansidla

Igracio Barat, deceased at age 15
> Mother: Rahela Barat
> Acting father: Laso Barat
> Half-Brother: Peodar Barat

Pax Aphanista Nayro, age 14
> Mother: Caedi Aphanista
> Adopted by: Finnan and Rhyder
> Half-Brother: Byid Aphanista Pendefeth

Laetu Louloudi Efteri, age 13
> Mother: Finnan Ruadhi Louloudi
> Adoptive father: Rhyder Efteri
> Half-Sister: Camilly Louloudi Efteri

Talassa "Tass" (Katurima) Galan Elisus, age 12
> Mother: Afa (Bracha) Elisus

About the Author and Illustrator

About the Author

Lisa Pelissier lives in Oregon where she is a homeschool mother of four and self-published author. She also works as a freelance wordsmith. Lisa has a B.A. from Biola University in Christian Education with dual emphases in music and elementary education. In her spare time Lisa enjoys making art, playing the piano, and singing. She has three kids still at home, six cats, two bearded dragons, and a sparse colony of giant hissing cockroaches.

About the Cover Illustrator

Helen Holmes is an aspiring artist and illustrator. At only sixteen, she has illustrated for seven books (including this one). She is homeschooled and a self-taught artist. She enjoys drawing, playing with her pug, Shredder, and making up her own stories as well.

www.SneakerBlossom.com